THE SLOW BURN
OF SILENCE

A Snowy Creek Novel

ALSO BY LORETH ANNE WHITE

LORETH ANNE WHITE

THE SLOW BURN OF SILENCE

A Snowy Creek Novel

Text copyright © 2014 Loreth Anne White
All rights reserved.

Published by Montlake Romance, Seattle

www.apub.com

ISBN-13: 9781477824450
ISBN-10: 1477824456

Cover design by Marc Cohen

Library of Congress Control Number: 2014903549

Printed in the United States of America

For Pavlo, my patron of the arts.

CHAPTER 1

April. Spring.

When does something begin and end? The ripples from a stone cast into a pond, do they start with the smoothness of the pebble that first attracts the eye, the impulse to feel it against your palm, to make it skip over water . . . do they end with the last tiny lap of a wave on the distant shore . . .

I look up from the manila folder in my hands. The lawyer—Guthrie—is watching me, a measured quality in his eyes I imagine he reserves for delivering news like this: earth-tilting, life-shattering news. Through the window behind his head, a froth of pale pink cherry blossoms frames a peek-a-boo view of the snow-capped Lions peaks against a bluebird sky. A fat bumblebee ticks rhythmically against the glass. I can hear the muted hum of traffic down Lonsdale. A car horn. A man calling out. A delivery truck beeping as it reverses. Life going on. Everything normal.

Yet not.

Seventy-two hours ago I was with Trey in Bali, our engagement promise to ourselves. The call came while we were lying naked and entwined under a soft white net draped from a bamboo ceiling. My sister and brother-in-law had died in a house fire. As their only living relative, I'd been appointed guardian of their eight-year-old daughter. Trey and I took the first flight home.

Now, sitting here in this lawyer's North Vancouver office, I can finally understand why I sometimes feel a quiet and inexplicable frisson of unease when I look directly into my niece's eyes.

It's because they're *his* eyes.

His blood that courses through her veins. His DNA. The same DNA used to convict him . . .

Every instinct in my body screams to reject this news, to toss the file back across the lawyer's lacquered wood desk. But this is Quinn we're talking about, my little dark-haired, mysterious niece. I was there the day Sophia and Peter brought her home, all wrinkles and snuffles and those adorable newborn stretches. A memory washes into my mind: I'm eighteen, and a tightly swaddled bundle is being placed into my arms. It's the first time I've ever been entrusted to hold such a tiny human being, and the responsibility feels suddenly overwhelming. Emotion burns into my eyes. I can recall the texture of the blanket, the sweet-sour smell of milk, the child's raven-black hair, soft as spun silk under my palm as I stroke her tiny head.

The smile on my sister's face that day is something I can never forget. And from that day forward, Quinn was ours. No thought of her birth parents. Just us. The future, a new, extended family.

Another memory swirls into the first—the texture of blue-black hair under my palm, the same color hair . . . a kiss that drowns me . . . the same deep, indigo-blue eyes fringed with impossibly thick lashes . . . My heart races.

"Why?" My voice is hoarse. The bumblebee *tick, tick, ticks* against the pane. Pressure rises in my chest.

Guthrie leans forward, a look of calculated compassion entering his eyes. His tone goes all soothing and placating, and resentment mushrooms sharp, sudden in me. I resent his patronizing demeanor. My anger is misplaced, I know this, yet it's there, taking hold of me, filling my chest, pushing up against my throat, hammering inside my head.

"You're Quinn's closest relative, Ms. Salonen. Your sister felt—"

"I mean why did they adopt *her*. Why—" I catch myself, panic rising, stark reality lacing through me. "Oh God, I'm so sorry. That came out wrong. I didn't mean that. I . . ." I take a deep, slow breath. "You're certain? There's . . . no possibility it could be a mistake?"

"No mistake. He is the birth father. The documentation is all there." Guthrie nods at the manila folder still clutched in my hands. "It was a direct placement. The birth mother agreed to the adoption before the parties contacted the agency that handled the paperwork. The birth father's paternal rights were waived in the adoption decision, in view of his conviction. It's not uncommon in a case like this."

"So he doesn't know? He has no idea where his baby went?"

"He was not told where the child was placed, no."

I try to swallow against the tightness closing my throat. My skin is hot. Dark memories thread into my mind like ink tendrils into water, swirling, curling, clouding the present, blurring plans for the future with Trey. We've all worked so hard to bury the past, the whole town has. But sometimes all one can do is plaster over the cracks with the concrete of industry, because underneath the fissures remain, waiting for some little tremor to open them up into black maws hungry to swallow you up again. Like now.

My attention is pulled back to the bee bashing its fuzzy head against the glass. Why is it even trying to get in when there are blossoms outside, freedom?

"Why didn't she tell me?" I whisper, staring at the bee.

But Guthrie remains silent. Because it's damn obvious why. I was eighteen and utterly, madly, wildly in love with Jebbediah Cullen when it happened. In one way or another, I think I'd loved Jeb since I was a child, first as a friend—the real soul mate kind— then it grew more complex. Sexual. Deeper. Jeb always had my back. He showed me a new way of looking at the world. In spite of our fight that sparked the terrible series of events that night, I had every intention of spending the rest of my life with him. The sexual assault, the murder—Jeb's shocking outburst of violence, the baby, the betrayal—it ripped my life apart, tore the soul right out of my body. I lost focus, drive; crashed, tanking my ski racing career, obliterating my dreams of a second Olympic gold. And they weren't just my dreams: they were the collective dreams of the Snowy Creek community. I was their Golden Girl, Rachel Salonen, raised right in their own valley, taught to ski on runs that my grandfather helped carve with his ax and chainsaw into the flanks of Bear Mountain before I was even born.

Then came that cold autumn night two girls went missing. Amy Findlay and Merilee Zukanov, my classmates. Amy was found brutally assaulted, pregnant with Jeb's child. Nine years later, Merilee is still missing.

And now Quinn is mine to care for, this living, breathing embodiment of Jeb's betrayal, of that night of violence. I am to take this dark-haired little girl with the haunting indigo eyes back home with me to Snowy Creek, where it all happened. This daughter of the renegade I once loved so much.

He's from the wrong side of the river, Rachel. A half breed. Raised by an Irish drunk and a native woman . . . you can do better, Rachel . . . he's going to hurt you, Rachel . . .

"Ms. Salonen?"

My gaze jerks back to the lawyer.

"Is there someone I can call?" Guthrie says quietly. "Someone who can perhaps be with you now? Maybe—"

"I'm fine." I sit up straight. "This is just so . . ." I fight the sudden bite of pain. "It's so damn Sophia, you know that." My heart hammers. "She's a bleeding heart, always has been, always trying to save the bloody world. She was Amy's victim's services counselor, did you know? That's how she and Amy met, when my sister still lived in Snowy Creek. The police called Sophia in after they found Amy wandering dazed and half-naked on the tracks. Amy's parents are staunch Catholics. They wouldn't hear of terminating the pregnancy, and Sophia and Peter . . ." My voice cracks. I pause a moment, struggling to gather myself, then I say more quietly, "They'd been trying for years to have a child. I can see it all now, how it must've happened. Sophia and Peter stepping in, offering to adopt, to give the baby—a little victim herself—and Amy a second chance."

My chest hurts. I miss Sophia already, like an open wound laid bare to salt and wind. Just knowing my sister will never again be at the other end of a phone line, ready with her calm, sage advice. A mentor. A mother figure to me. Always so balanced. Gone. My father also gone. And Quinn? Alone in the world now with just me. Panic clutches softly, sickeningly at my stomach. I'm twenty-seven years old. I'm not ready to be a mother—I don't know how.

"My sister had a heart too big for her own good," I whisper as I scrabble in my raffia beach tote for a Kleenex. The lawyer gets up, pours water into a glass, hands it to me.

"Thank you." I clasp the glass tightly; I don't want him to see that I'm shaking. I take a deep sip as my phone chimes in my bag. I ignore it. I know it's a text from Trey saying he's found parking and will be waiting for me downstairs in the plaza.

I think of him standing in the spring sun under the heavy magnolia trees, water sparkling off the Burrard Inlet behind him. How is he going to take this? He has no idea what I'm going to carry outside with me. I focus on setting the glass securely on the desk, then I blow my nose.

"Do I need to sign anything?" I say.

"Just these." Guthrie slides some papers toward me. "Your copies of the will, the adoption papers, the birth parents' medical information—it's all in the folder." He pauses. "I understand your niece is staying with a neighbor two houses down from your sister's place, and that she's seen a counselor."

I nod and blow my nose again. "We've been to see her already. We went there first." Images of the gutted, charred ruins slice back into my mind. Black skeletons of beams against blue sky. Yellow police tape fluttering in front of Sophia's rhododendrons. The blooms are a deep cerise, Sophia's favorite color, her spring garden coming to life while the gardener herself is gone.

The fire broke out after Quinn left for school. The neighbor across the street was the first to see smoke and call it in. Possible cause, the fire commissioner's office and police said, was a ruptured gas line. The blaze was furious and fast, fueled by the explosion of a propane storage tank. It was fully engaged by the time firefighters arrived on scene. Too hot to enter, they stood back, watching, controlling the spread of the burn while keeping the crowd of onlookers at bay. Everything inside the house was gone.

Sophia's body was found in her office adjoining the main house, where she was likely overcome by smoke. Peter was discovered crushed under a beam at Sophia's office door. Initial speculation was that Peter might have been trying to rescue his wife when the burning rafter came down on him.

They told me it could take weeks, months even, before a joint investigation by the Royal Canadian Mounted Police, the coroner's service, and the office of the fire commissioner could determine the exact cause of the blaze and deaths.

I finish signing the papers and get to my feet. And just like that, at age twenty-seven, I'm now legally responsible for an eight-year-old girl. Trey and I are going to drive home with her to Snowy Creek, a few hours north into the Coast Mountains. The weight of this is suddenly crushing. I need to figure out what room to put Quinn in. I'll have to buy her some clothes and other basic necessities before we head up. Plus a suitcase to put it all in. I'll need to enroll Quinn into Snowy Creek Elementary and arrange some kind of after-school care because the newspaper business my father left me four months ago is consuming all my time and energy, and it's going to go under if I can't secure some kind of financial backing.

My legs suddenly want to give out. I want to sit back down. But if I can't face this, how will Quinn? The child has lost her mother and father and everything she owns. She's going to be uprooted from the only life she's known. I need to be strong for my niece. For my sister. I need to protect this child no matter what life throws at me now.

I smooth down my creased capris. I'm still wearing the T-shirt Trey bought for me in Kuta among a bustling network of stalls, and I imagine I can even smell the lingering scent of coconut oil on my skin. Hooking the strap of my beach tote over my shoulder, I gather up the file, thank the lawyer, and make for the door, but I freeze suddenly as a thought strikes me square between the eyes.

Turning back to Guthrie, I say, "The University of British Columbia's Innocence Project is still fighting to have his conviction overturned."

"They've been working on it for five years now; who knows if anything will come of it."

"What if he gets out?"

"He will get out, Rachel, one way or the other. Whether his conviction is overturned or not, he'll be released once he's served his time."

I stare at him. "But he has no rights to Quinn. That's what you said."

"Correct."

"And he doesn't know about her. I just want to be certain he doesn't know that Quinn MacLean is his daughter."

"All Jebbediah Cullen knows is that Amy Findlay gave birth to his child and that the child was given up for adoption. He has no legal recourse to obtain any further information. And your sister has made clear in her will that she doesn't want her child to find out who her father is, either."

A chilling sense of foreboding ripples over my skin nevertheless.

Outside in the plaza the spring sunshine is too white, too bright. I shade my eyes as I search for Trey. It's the same place as when I entered the lawyer's building, yet it's as if a space-time continuum has shifted. Everything appears a little starker, off-kilter.

I catch sight of Trey sitting on a stone wall under magnolia boughs weighted with blooms. He's deeply sun-browned from our two weeks in Bali. He surges to his feet as soon as he sees me and comes forward with his strong, easy stride. He's bold, big, rugged. Like the mountains we come from. His hair is dark blond and streaked from sun and surf. As he approaches, I see concern enter his blue eyes.

He takes my hands in his. "You okay?"

Nausea rushes into my stomach. For a moment I can't speak.

"Come, sit down. Tell me what happened."

Guided by Trey's steady hand, I sink slowly onto a wooden bench. He's stalwart, a protector. He's been Snowy Creek's volunteer search-and-rescue manager for two years, and he's the kind of guy who never lets a teammate down. I stare at our hands as he laces his fingers through mine—his tanned skin against my pale tone, the shape of his muscled forearm, his body hair gold. The new diamond on my finger.

"I need to be a mother," I say quietly, looking at the ring.

"Hey." He cups my face, forcing me to look up into his glacial-blue eyes. "We expected this, Rach. It's going to be fine, we can do it." A smile creases his face and lights his eyes. "An instant family, how about that? It'll be good practice for when we have our own kids."

"It's not that simple," I say.

His features change as he reads something in my eyes, hears it in my voice. A cloud, a shadow, seems to pass over us. In the distance I hear sirens, a tug horn, the chug of an arriving sea ferry, gulls screeching in the wake of a fishing vessel.

"What do you mean?"

I clear my throat. "Sophia and Peter adopted Amy Findlay and Jeb Cullen's baby."

He's silent. Doesn't move. The cry of the seagulls grows frantic, and a ship's horn blows loudly. Voices reach us, people coming out of the offices for lunch, the plaza filling. A desperation claws down inside my chest.

He lurches suddenly to his feet, takes two fast strides away from me, then stands as still as a statue. He spins back. "What?"

I don't answer. I let him absorb the news.

"Fuck," he says.

My pulse starts to race. "No one knows and no one needs to. Sophia didn't want Quinn to find out, either, she said so in her will. She wanted Quinn insulated from this."

"And *him*?"

"He had nothing to do with the adoption. He doesn't know where his baby went."

He stares at me, something dark entering his face. That cold foreboding sinks deeper into my bones.

"Trey, please, come sit down. Just listen to me—"

"I don't get it. How could this happen? Oh . . . wait, that's why your sister moved away from Snowy Creek, isn't it? That's why Peter took a job down here, so they could take in and raise that monster's offspring, because Amy's family couldn't get the hell rid of it."

A spurt of defensive anger brings me sharply to my feet. "My sister helped a rape victim, Trey—a young woman torn between her family, her religion, and her rapist's baby. Quinn is *also* a victim here. She's an innocent kid who knows nothing about this and never needs to!"

"Jesus . . ." He paces under the magnolia flowers. The petals suddenly seem too fleshy, obscene, the fragrance too heady. I feel sick. He spins to face me, backlit by the sun. "We're talking about bringing the child of a convicted sex offender, a murderer, a felon, into our own home. Into our future, our lives."

"He was not charged with murder."

"And that makes it better? The only reason they didn't fry him for killing Merilee is because they couldn't find her damn body, that's why. She's still missing." He flings his hand out and points north. "Out there in the mountains somewhere. Her family is *still* without closure. And this . . . this bastard could be out within months if his conviction is overturned. On a goddamn technicality, because the defense counsel failed to present evidence that *could* have raised reasonable doubt. We all know he did it. And you want to bring his kid into our lives?"

"Listen to yourself," I say. "This is Quinn we're talking about. My niece. You know her. You've never had a problem with her before. It doesn't have to change now that—"

"How do you know it's his, anyway? Guthrie blabbed it out, just like that? 'Hey, Quinn is Jeb Cullen's kid'?"

I thrust the folder Guthrie gave me at him. "See for yourself."

He grabs it, flips it open, scans through the papers. Then he sits slowly on the bench, reads them again. He glances up. "This will was made five years ago," he says quietly.

"That's when Sophia last updated it. Guthrie said she'd made an appointment to come in next week and make changes. But . . . the fire happened."

"What kind of changes?"

"Guthrie didn't know. But whatever updates Sophia did intend to make, it doesn't change who Quinn's birth parents are. That's a fact."

"We need a DNA test."

I blink. "You don't believe what's in those papers?"

He glares at me. He's in denial. I can see. And he's hitting out at everything, including me, as he grapples with this.

"You can't be serious," I say. "What would you run test results against, anyway? The DNA profiles used in Jeb's trial? And how do you think we're going to access those records without pushing this into the open, without letting Jeb know he's her father?"

He rakes his hand over his hair. "She's going to find out one day. Quinn is going to go looking for her real parents, and she'll find out."

"Then we'll face that if and when it happens. She'll be older. She'll be better equipped to handle the truth at that point. But not now. Not so shortly after she's lost her parents. We need to honor Sophia's request. We have to keep this secret, for Quinn's sake."

He stares at me.

I sit next to him, place my hand on his thigh. "I'm having trouble processing it, too, but we'll get through this. It'll become easier in time."

He looks away from me. "You can't do it," he says softly, shaking his head. "You cannot take her back there, not to Snowy Creek."

"We," I whisper. "*We* are taking her home with us. Today. Why are you talking like I'm doing this alone?"

His gaze flicks back to meet mine. A strange look enters his eyes.

"Home?" he says, voice flat. And I feel my world tilt sickeningly as the ramifications of that single word hang between us. Home is where the crime happened. Home is the big house on the lake that my father left me after we lost him to cancer four months ago. Trey only moved in with me last month, before the trip. Our plan is to pool financial resources, fix up the place, rebuild the boathouse, and rent it out to offset the massive property taxes that come with owning lakefront acreage in a ski resort that has grown into a global tourist destination.

"Christ," he whispers. "The town will annihilate her if they find out."

"It's not for anyone in town to know."

"A secret," he says quietly. "We must keep that sexual pervert's kid a secret? We must live with the memory of what he did, in our house, our *home*?" He's quiet for a long while. A warm gust rattles the fat leaves and chases fallen cherry petals across the paving. A pigeon pecks at crumbs between the blossoms. I hear the horn of the ferry leaving the quay.

He snorts softly, watching the pigeon. "You know, I always thought you might actually still have a thing for him, that you couldn't let him go in spite of what he did."

I feel the blood drain from my face.

"I just had to say it. It's something that . . . it's always bothered me. This makes it all fresh. It brings back all the doubts."

"How *dare* you." I can barely manage to whisper the words.

He gets up, walks away, shoulders tight.

"Don't walk away from this, Trey! Don't walk away from *me*!"

He stops. Turns. Very slowly. His eyes glisten. The pain and confusion that I feel in my heart is echoed in the tightness of his features. He's fighting something deep within himself.

"How?" he says. "How can I take that child into our new, clean, beautiful life, into our future? I testified against him. So did you. We all helped put him away. This feels like we're bringing him back in some way."

I come to my feet and go to him. I touch his hand, struggling to mask the tremble in my voice. "It's not a decision I can turn away from, Trey. My niece has no one else in this world now but me." Emotion grows thick in my throat. "I'm going to look after her. But I love you, and . . ." Tears pool in my eyes. "And I don't want to lose you in the process."

He gathers me into his arms, holds me tight against his body. "I'm sorry," he whispers in my hair. He holds me like he always holds me, strong and sure. And he smells like he always does. Good. Masculine. For a moment I feel safe, and I'm seized by a desperate notion that perhaps it never happened. Perhaps I never spoke to the lawyer. Perhaps nothing has changed. Yet our world is not the same as it was moments ago. And there is no going back. Words come suddenly into my mind.

You can't exist in this world without leaving pieces of yourself, without affecting in some tiny way everyone, everything, you come into contact with . . .

Jeb told me that.

Sometimes the trail you leave is bold, destructive. It's flattened grass, moved rocks, easy to see. Other times the trace is barely there, invisible unless you know just how to look for it, and it can be like following ghosts . . .

He was showing me how to track a bobcat through moss when he said that. I was fifteen. The branches of the towering red cedars above us dappled the sunlight that fell to the forest floor. It was like being in a natural cathedral, the trees around us hundreds of years old, as old as Notre Dame. He kissed me that day, for the first time.

Pieces of you . . .

Quinn. My scars. My limp. Who I've become. All pieces of him, the past.

The trail left is bold and destructive, flattened grass . . .

I bury my face into the crook of Trey's neck, trying to blot out the memories. His skin is warm, slightly salty. The taste of him against my lips is familiar. Safe. He's my harbor.

"I'm so sorry, Rach," he whispers again into my hair. "I didn't mean it. It's . . . it's just a lot to absorb at once."

"I know," I murmur against his skin, my eyes closed.

"We can do this," he says. "We can and we will."

I nod. And I wish in my heart I believed him.

CHAPTER 2

Six months later. Early October. Autumn.

Jeb removed his helmet and walked toward the viewpoint barrier, legs stiff from his ride north into the mountains. At the edge of the lookout off Highway 99, he climbed up onto the concrete wall next to a sign reading "Do not feed the bears." He surveyed the colorful village nestled in the valley far below: a picturesque huddle of humanity cradled in a basin of densely forested slopes, scoured granite peaks soaring as far as the eye could see.

Snowy Creek.

Home.

After almost ten years he'd finally been exonerated by the courts, his conviction overturned. And just like that, at the decree of a judge, he was suddenly out, startled into freedom like a fish poured from a hatchery bucket into wide-open sea. One minute a convicted felon. Next a man at liberty to go where he pleased. No parole, no release orders. No restrictions at all. Innocent in the eyes of the legal system.

But not in the eyes of the people of that town.

While he might have left behind the max security of Kent Institution, there were still those who believed he'd done it, that his release was due to a technical error, a policing misstep. He still bore the cross of a violent sex offender. A felon. A murderer. He was not truly free. Yet.

Jeb's gaze rested a moment on the square clock tower rising from the village center, then swept across the colorful jumble of roofs and up the deceptively gentle flanks of Bear Mountain, into which ski runs had been carved. A line of gondola cars moved slowly between the village base and Crystal Peak, windows winking as they caught sunlight. The air was dry, cool. It was almost Thanksgiving here, north of the forty-ninth, and the resort was already prepping for the coming winter season, oiling the cogs and bullwheels of the ski machine that sustained the local economy. Next would come the giant equipment and clothing sales. Turkey sales, they were dubbed, and they would draw skiers up from Vancouver and from Washington State across the border in droves, cars clogging the highway from sea to sky. This land that his mother's ancestors used to hunt was now an internationally renowned destination resort controlled by the Banrock family, who'd developed Bear Mountain and much of the surrounding village real estate.

The Banrocks had turned the snow of these mountains into their own white gold.

Jeb's eye followed the line of gondola cars up to the Thunderbird Lodge, then took a leap thousands of feet higher to the crests of the ragged, glacier-capped peaks that sliced above the slumbering village into an achingly blue sky.

Those peaks gave measure to the vastness between earth and heavens. Their desolation and silent grandeur beckoned him, as did these great sighing forests. And as he stood here, a sense of peace finally descended over him. Of belonging. He could dissolve forever into this vast wilderness and barely ever need to cross the path of another human soul again. He'd be lying if he said he hadn't considered doing this after being imprisoned in a cell narrow enough to touch his fingertips to both walls. After getting just one hour of exercise per day for almost a decade, vanishing into that wilderness certainly held appeal. But what Jeb really wanted lay in the populated village down below. That town was his end game. Because someone in Snowy Creek knew where to find Merilee Zukanov's body. Someone had buried the secret deep, and Jeb was here to unearth it. No matter the cost to him or the establishment.

Because once he found that person—or persons—once he found Merilee's body, he could finally clear his name. His innocence would be proved. He'd be truly free, and he could finally meet his daughter. Only then would he allow himself into her life. That had been his promise to Sophia and Peter before they died, and theirs to him.

A dry wind ruffled his hair and Jeb lifted his face to it. Layered into the coolness were pockets of warmth. An Indian summer. He'd forgotten the taste of it. The feel of it. The sound of it. The way the breeze whispered in his ears with the voices of dead leaves, brittle grasses, crackling twigs, the soft swishing of drought-browned conifer tips. It was a dialogue that could only come after a killing frost. This valley was tinderbox dry, ripe for fire, whispering for it. Or for rain.

Jeb allowed his gaze to drift westward, where jewel-colored lakes were strung like beads along the twisting thread of the Green River. He followed the river course to where the valley funneled sharply between basalt cliffs. The cliffs where the old quarry was.

Where it had started nine years ago.

It had been autumn then, too, gold leaves clustered in the coniferous décolletage of the mountains where streams tumbled. Amy and Merilee had disappeared sometime after ten p.m. during a pit party at the old quarry. Amy was found a week later with no memory of what happened. Merilee was still out there somewhere.

Jeb inhaled deeply. The town was going to fight him. The outsider. The guy from the wrong side of the river. They were going to watch for him to make a slip so they could lock him back up where they believed he belonged. Or worse. They might try worse.

But Jeb was prepared. He was like the coho salmon teeming up these rivers now, fierce ruby-flanked warriors that had survived the killer whales and ghost nets of the wide Pacific waters until their bio-alarms had suddenly turned them toward the scent of fresh water and set them on a crash course for home. Those fish were hardwired to fight upstream, to bash themselves to ribbons over rocks and waterfalls just so they could return to the quiet mountain pools and eddies of their birth to mate, then die in a nutrient soup that would nourish their offspring in turn.

Like those fish, Jeb was hardwired for this place. This was his heritage. His home. He refused to let them take it from him again. He'd rather die here than end up back in that cell.

Traffic fell eerily silent on the highway behind him, and the dry wind soughed again through the trees, stirring branches as it moved like an invisible spirit through the forest. With the susurration came another thought, one he'd been struggling all day to hold at bay. But suddenly it was whispering, sparking, crackling like fire at the edges of his mind.

Rachel.

Jeb knew she had Quinn. He knew she still lived somewhere down in that valley. At some point, once he'd cleared his name, he was going to have to go through Rachel to access his child. His blood quickened as an image of her face in the courtroom flashed into his mind, the rawness of pain tearing at her features. If he was guilty of one thing, it was putting that pain into her face. For sleeping with Amy in the fiery aftermath of his and Rachel's last fight.

And God knew he'd paid. He'd paid every day for over nine years. Amy had also paid dearly. So had Quinn, and she still would, in so many more complicated ways.

Jeb drew air deep into his lungs. There was one road into this valley, one road out. It was time.

Pulling on his helmet, he returned to his black-and-chrome custom cruiser. He straddled his bike, booted back the kickstand, and fired the four-hundred-horsepower engine to vibrating life between his legs. He gunned back onto the highway with a throaty roar, giving his metal beast juice as he powered up the road, over-taking a red Volvo, g-forces gathering low and delicious in his gut. But as Jeb entered the resort boundaries, he slowed. This was Snowy Creek Police territory. He could not afford the slightest misstep.

He neared the first intersection. A forestry sign on the side of the road declared that wildfire danger was extreme, and open fires were currently banned. Jeb stopped at the red light, bike rumbling, his heart suddenly thumping and his mouth dry. Tufts of white fireweed seed wafted across the road, piling in soft drifts against the concrete road barriers and collecting against the brown cedar shake wall of the old Powder Hound Diner on the corner. The building had seen better days, but it was still standing. Kitty-corner across the intersection was the Husky gas station. It had been torn down and rebuilt in a rustic but high-end ski resort style. The red Volvo drew up alongside him. A woman in the passenger seat, maybe late twenties, turned to look at him. She met Jeb's eyes and he felt a sharp kick in his blood.

He hadn't been with a woman since Amy, since he'd been taken away in handcuffs at nineteen. He was twenty by the time his case went to trial. From there it was straight into max-security lockup. Now he was nearing thirty. He might look rough and ready—time had certainly taken its physical toll on him in prison. But there was a yawning gap in his life experience. And there was still only one woman he truly wanted.

One he'd betrayed. One who had helped put him in prison. One he could never have.

A young mother in yoga pants crossed the street in front of him, pushing a baby in a jogging stroller. A pit bull trotted at her heels, attached by a leash to her waist. Jeb wondered if they were heading down to the grassy beach along the shores of Whiskey Lake, if there was still a dog park there. His thoughts turned again to Rachel, and a day long ago.

"Jeb, do you think you'll ever leave this valley after school?" She'd been lying on her back on the sun-warmed dock, eyes closed, droplets of water shimmering like jewels on her lashes and goose-fleshed skin. Her nipples were hard under tiny yellow scraps of bikini fabric. He allowed his eyes to slowly travel the length of her body and he felt arousal. Pleasure. Heat. Life. Thrumming through his blood with each beat of his heart. He scooped up the wet tennis ball that had rolled against her waist and threw it into the lake for Trixie, Rachel's father's new border collie pup. The ball landed in the water with a plop.

"Why would I leave when you're here?" he whispered, bringing his mouth close to hers.

Rachel's eyes flared open at his sudden proximity. She stared up into his eyes, her own darkening with arousal. Then, suddenly erupting into laughter, she rolled onto her side, launched up, and raced to the end of the dock, where she dived into the clear water. Jeb got to his feet, watched the ripples fanning out from where she'd gone in as sleek as a fish. She surfaced a distance away and called out to him. "Race you to the far end!" She swam, kicking water splashes up into the sunlight. He'd watched her go, and something in him had known that day it wouldn't last.

He was pulled back to the present by a group of young snow-boarder dudes, baggy pants hanging low around their butts as they ran across the intersection with an awkward wide-kneed swagger, presumably to keep their pants on.

Jeb's skin felt hot.

It was all the same, yet all was new. As if he'd been put on pause while the rest of the world had gone on. Time, his youth, Rachel, robbed from him. A soft, dark anger swelled in his chest.

The lights turned green. He revved his bike aggressively and roared ahead of the Volvo, but quickly slowed back to the posted limit, tempering both anger and speed.

Violence, it turned out, came easily when you lived with anger swimming permanently inside you, when you were trapped in a cage with no other hope. But after a few early incidents in prison, Jeb had learned to accept his fate, to control his impulse to resort to physical aggression in the face of a threat. He'd turned his energy toward getting a degree instead. He'd begun to find reward in reaching small goals.

It was a simmering, hard-won control, and he was not about to lose it now that he was back. Patience, he told himself. The mind of a hunter. Be prepared to lie quietly in wait. Because there would be cracks, and cracks were where the light would get in.

Jeb aimed to first cut straight through town and head north into the Wolf River Valley, to his old home, the five acres of land his mother had left him. He'd check it out and set up shop. Tomorrow he had an interview scheduled with the editor of the *Snowy Creek Leader*. He was not here to hide. He was here to make his intentions known, to rattle cages, mess with minds. To shine a spotlight on people who might try to run him out of town. But as he neared the turnoff that led down to Snowy Creek Elementary, Jeb's chest constricted and he chanced a quick glance at his watch. If the school still followed the old schedule, it would almost be lunch break. And on a split, impulsive second, he took the left-hand turn off the highway and headed down the road to the elementary school, inexorably pulled by the possibility of seeing his daughter for the first time in his life.

He slowed to the posted school zone speed, his bike grumbling down the hill as he rode past the main entrance, aiming instead for the river, where he planned to double back into the neighboring subdivision and circle round to the rear of the school grounds, where the ball fields abutted a treed swamp. Where the kids used to go out and play at lunch when he had attended that same school.

He turned into the residential subdivision, rumbling slowly into a place of quiet, untroubled calm. A red scooter lay discarded at the edge of a lawn. A plastic truck and an expensive-looking bike lay in a driveway. People here trusted their neighbors. A baby kicked his chubby legs in a stroller on a porch. Two mothers talked over a fence while toddlers played on grass at their feet. Carved pumpkins, fat and orange, had already been placed in windows, harvest garlands on doors.

The mothers glanced up and stared at him as his bike growled past. A small terrier bolted from nowhere and yipped in his wake. The dog veered off as Jeb rounded the crescent. He parked off a cul-de-sac next to a small park with a brightly colored play structure. Leaving his helmet with his bike, he walked through the park toward a stand of alders that screened the park from the ball fields. Everywhere around him dry leaves and drought-burned pine needles whispered for rain. The first thing he saw when he came through the trees was the school building up on a rise, a red-and-white maple leaf flag snapping in the breeze.

And suddenly Jeb was thrust back in time.

He was nine years old, standing outside that same squat building, his hand tightly clutching his mother's. The fall wind was blowing cold, lifting the ends of her blue-black braid and ruffling her straight bangs.

As if it were yesterday, Jeb felt a surge in his chest, a mix of hot anticipation, anxiety. Fear of what lay ahead. It was to be his first year at the school, the first time he'd be missing the fall hunt with his dad. The first year his mother would not homeschool him through the winter.

She'd looked down at him that September morning, squeezed his hand in reassurance, and smiled, but her eyes were a liquid black over the sharp flare of her cheekbones, and they told another story. Jeb hadn't understood the look in his mother's eyes that day. Now he recognized it for what it was. Regret. She'd brought him to this public school to hide him, to protect him from something that had grown too dark and dangerous in their own home. She had wanted to keep him away from his father as much as possible that coming winter. It had been a terrible fishing season. Not many salmon had come up the coast. Which meant the long winter would be worse than usual.

And it had been. Far worse than the young Jeb could have dreamed.

Before the snows had melted that year, it was a nine-year-old Jeb who'd had to protect his mother.

A gust of wind swirled the memories away in a clatter of yellow leaves. Jeb sank down onto a wooden bench in front of the trees. A chopper thudded in the distance up high above Crystal Peak. Jeb checked his watch. Almost lunch break, but right now the school grounds were empty, the morning sun spooling gold beams through mist rising from the marsh at the north end of the fields.

He closed his eyes a moment, letting it wrap around him; the croak of a raven in a dead snag, the chatter of black-headed juncos pecking among dead leaves at his boots, the shriek of a lone osprey. The scents of fall. All things he'd missed for nine long years.

A bell buzzer sounded and a woman's voice came over a loudspeaker. His eyes snapped open. Up on the grassy rise, kids came out the doors like tumbling jelly beans in colorful jackets, scattering down the path, rolling out into the fields with the leaves. Their voices carried on the cool, dry air. His pulse quickened. He leaned forward, elbows on his thighs, eyes narrowing as he sifted through the kids' shapes. Would she come down to these fields, like he used to?

Would he recognize her?

For years he'd waited for this moment, just to see her. In living, breathing color. To maybe hear her voice, her laugh. Look into her eyes.

Just watch. Do not go near or engage her in any way. Not yet. Not until you are free. She must not know who you are . . . this is your promise to Sophia and Peter. To yourself. To your child . . .

He caught sight of a slight, dark-haired girl coming determinedly down the grass knoll. She wore a baggy sweater of brightly knitted rainbows, and her hair was a mass of wild curls, the color of a raven's feathers gleaming in the sunlight. Curls as wild and untamable as the surrounding BC wilderness. Like his father's hair. She walked with shoulders hunched slightly forward, forging ahead as if blocking out the world around her. She carried a book and a brown lunch bag.

Jeb quickly fumbled in his pocket and removed a wallet-sized photo album. He flipped it open to the most recent picture that Sophia had brought him in prison. But he didn't look at the photo. He was transfixed by the black-haired girl as she climbed up a stand of bleachers and sat on the middle bench. She put the brown bag beside her, removed and unwrapped a sandwich, took a bite.

Her knees were knobby under her jeans, legs thin, almost too long for her body. A little colt. She chewed as she watched the Steller's jays beginning to cluster around her, squawking and bombing in attempts to attract food. She broke off a piece of bread, tossed it out onto the grass. The electric-blue birds dived and cackled as they squabbled for a share. But his eyes were riveted only on the child.

In his bones, in every molecule of his body, he believed it was her.

Quinn. His daughter.

His blood in her veins.

Her DNA used to convict him . . .

A dull roar began in Jeb's brain—the sound of past and present, and future colliding. He closed his fist tightly around the photo album, as if holding control over his own fierce urge to go to her, speak to her.

There will come a time, a pastor once told him in prison, when you believe everything is finished. But that will only be the beginning.

That little girl was the beginning.

She was the reason for everything he was going to do now.

CHAPTER 3

As Jeb watched the child on the bleachers, an image of Quinn's birth mother curled like smoke through his mind, and he was thrust instantly back into the courtroom—Amy in the witness stand, her head bent forward, a fall of red-gold hair hiding her profile. She'd looked so thin, so pale, in spite of the fact she'd been about to give birth. Jeb felt a visceral stab at the memory. He'd learned from his lawyers that their infant would likely be surrendered in a private adoption, that his paternal rights in the decision would be waived if he was found guilty. While DNA from the fetus proved it was his, he hadn't even been told the sex of the baby as he'd sat there in the prisoner's box.

The scents of the courtroom filled his nostrils. He could feel the thickness of the tension in the room as the lead prosecutor had opened her case against him.

". . . On the night Amy Findlay and Merilee Zukanov disappeared, Jebbediah Cullen, the accused, was sexually frustrated and enraged," she told the jury. "Why was he so fired up? Because the evening before the party at the gravel pit, his then girlfriend, Rachel Salonen, had terminated their relationship during a heated argument over sex." The prosecutor paused, meeting the eyes of each and every juror. "Sex," she repeated, letting the word hang in silence for several beats. "The only reason Jebbediah Cullen even went to the gravel pit that night, by his own admission, was to confront Rachel Salonen. Witnesses will testify he arrived angry, and when he saw Rachel Salonen kissing Trey Somerland, his rage intensified."

She spun round and pointed at him in the prisoner's box. The jury's eyes snapped in his direction.

"That man," she said, "the accused, has had a history of violent behavior since he was a child. Rachel Salonen will testify to this. We will also bring forward witnesses who saw Jebbediah Cullen verbally threatening both Salonen and Somerland at the gravel pit that night. We will present irrefutable evidence that will place both Amy Findlay and Merilee Zukanov in Jebbediah Cullen's vehicle as he drove away from the gravel pit around ten p.m. We have witnesses who saw Findlay and Zukanov in Cullen's vehicle as he crossed the Green River rail bridge and turned north onto Highway 99." She paused. Her voice lowered.

"And seven days later Amy Findlay was found twenty miles north of that gravel pit, wandering half-naked, beaten, and dazed along the railway tracks with no memory of what happened. There were rope marks around her neck that match the climbing ropes found in Jebbediah Cullen's car. Medical testimony will show that Amy Findlay had been brutally sexually assaulted, that she was pregnant with Cullen's child. An empty blister pack of flunitraze-pam—also known as Rohypnol, or the date rape drug—was found in Cullen's vehicle, which medical experts will show can explain Findlay's loss of memory. That drug pack was in the pocket of a hoodie covered in Merilee Zukanov's blood. Merilee Zukanov who is still, to this day, missing. Zukanov's hair and one of the earrings she was wearing the night she disappeared were also found in Cullen's vehicle. As was a roll of duct tape. That man"—she pointed at Jeb again—"came prepared. He *planned* an assault. He's a man with a history of extreme violence from a very young age, a man who was physically frustrated by the sexual rejection of his girlfriend. A man, we will show, who possesses the distinct psychological markers of a sociopath."

Jeb inhaled deeply as he tried to stop the vivid images assailing him from the past, but they came anyway.

". . . Amy Findlay, is the man who sexually assaulted you in this room?"

"Objection!" his defense counsel yelled, lurching to his feet. "The witness has already stated she has zero recollection of the assault—"

"Withdrawn. I'll rephrase. Ms. Findlay, is the father of the baby you are carrying in this room, a baby that medical evidence has shown was conceived at the time of your disappearance?"

The room fell silent. The atmosphere grew heavy. Jeb could smell sweat. He could feel his mother's eyes on him. Rachel's eyes on him. The journalists' eyes on him.

Amy's head remained bowed. She nodded.

"Could the witness please answer out loud into the microphone?"

Slowly, Amy lifted her face. Her red-rimmed, watery-blue eyes met his. Jeb's chest clutched. *Tell them, Amy. Goddammit, please, tell them . . . please remember!*

She stared at him for several long beats. Sweat slicked down his spine.

"Yes." Her voice was thin. "That's him."

Noise rustled through the courtroom. A reporter left his seat, scurrying out the back door. Jeb heard soft sobbing. He didn't know it if was his mother. Or Rachel. He couldn't look.

"Please note, the witness has identified the accused, Jebbediah Cullen."

Even now, a sick, cold oiliness swam through his stomach, and as if it were yesterday, he felt the physical punch of the word. *Guilty.*

It beat against his brain.

Guilty.

On the count of sexual assault causing bodily harm . . .

Guilty.

On the count of forcible confinement . . .

Guilty.

Sweat dampened his torso and a cold, quiet determination calcified around his heart.

Two women had lost their lives. While Amy might have physically survived the assault, she'd buckled mentally. For nine long years she'd struggled in her own kind of prison. Then she'd finally cracked. She'd committed suicide in Snowy Creek the night before Peter and Sophia died in the house fire in Vancouver. Jeb didn't like the coincidence, the timing. He had his own suspicions about Amy's death, and about the house fire. He was here to find the answers.

He was here for retribution. To reclaim what was his. And he was going to start by probing into the lives of the four guys who had lied about him in court: Levi Banrock, Clint Rudiger, Harvey Zink, and Luke LeFleur.

Another courtroom memory snaked into his mind. Levi Banrock in the witness stand, the prosecutor questioning him.

"And who did you see inside the car with Jebbediah Cullen?"

Levi refused to look at Jeb in the prisoner's box. "I saw Merilee Zukanov and Amy Findlay in his car."

"You're certain it was them?"

Levi cleared his throat, nodded his head. "Yes. They drove right past us where we were sitting under some trees. Amy wound down the window, called out to us, waved."

Jeb's entire body went tight. It was a lie. Wasn't it?

He couldn't recall seeing Luke or anyone in the trees that night. He didn't remember Amy waving or calling out. But maybe she had. He'd had too much to drink. His memory of precise details was fuzzy, riddled with gaps. He'd been so steamed about Rachel he hadn't been focused.

"What did you see next?" the lawyer said.

Again, Levi cleared his throat. "I saw the car waiting at the tracks for a train to cross. Once the train passed, Jeb drove across the rail bridge and turned north onto the highway."

"With Merilee Zukanov and Amy Findlay still in his car?"

"Yes."

Nausea rushed into Jeb's throat. His eyes burned. His hands shook. It was a lie. A goddamn lie. He had *not* turned north. The girls had gotten out of his car at the rail crossing. He'd turned south. Gone home. Alone. Of that he was absolutely certain.

The lawyer called Clint Rudiger to the stand next. And one after the other, the four guys told the same story. They told the court Jeb had turned north onto the highway with those two girls in his car. And Jeb had been sunk.

He drew air deep down into his lungs, clearing the memory from his brain.

One or all of them had been protecting themselves or someone else—someone who knew where to find Merilee Zukanov's body.

And those men had not only perjured themselves to convict him. They had stolen his child from him.

Because of them, he'd never hugged his baby in his arms.

He'd missed her first smile, first tooth, first steps—every goddamn birthday. He didn't even know for certain it was her on those bleachers, although he felt it in his bones.

He'd not been able to hold his mother's hand, comfort her as she'd died. She'd passed on believing in his guilt. Believing he'd turned into something worse than his father.

And Rachel? She was lost to him forever.

He wondered if it was Rachel who'd wrapped that sandwich for Quinn, who'd packed her lunch this morning. Her hands. Her care. His child. Jeb breathed in deep, trying to control his pulse, the dizziness, the pinpricks of rage at the four who'd done all this.

It was not over. Not by a goddamn long shot. He could never reclaim those lost years. He could never dream of winning back Rachel. But that child hunched over her lunch bag in the field— she was the reason he needed justice. Not revenge, but legal restitution. The wrongs had to be set right. Someone had to pay. Closure must be found. He could not let her grow up to learn she might be the child of a rapist and killer.

As he watched, a small group of girls started down the rise. All blondes, all straight hair. Fashionable clothing. Little clones molding themselves to some cultural ideal, precariously balanced between childhood and adult awareness. They were older than the girl on the bleachers, and Jeb didn't like their body language, the way they were exchanging glances, a pack gathering courage from each other as they gravitated toward the girl.

Like a prison yard, he thought, his muscles tensing as he watched for the telltale tipping point, that edge from where things would go bad. If the targeted victim allowed it.

But the girl on the bleachers sensed them coming and glanced up slightly. She didn't engage eye contact. Instead she stuffed her half-eaten sandwich back into the brown bag, closed her book, got up, and made her way at an even pace down the bleachers. She began to cross the grass, heading away from the blondes toward a gravel pathway that snaked up into a wooded knoll on the far side of the ball field.

The cadre of blondes followed.

His heart beat faster. On instinct Jeb surged up from the bench and moved quickly along the dirt track that ran along the outside edge of the field next to the swamp. He was acutely aware of legal jurisdiction: the Snowy Creek Resort Municipality owned and maintained these ball fields. The school district paid for the use of them. He was within his rights to be on them, yet he adhered to the path off the side.

The dark-haired girl disappeared into the woods. The clutch of blondes halted under a large oak among a puddle of red-gold leaves, talking among themselves, casting backward glances toward the school building where yard monitors watched the younger children. One of the blondes lit a cigarette, passed it to another. Jeb judged them to be about ten, maybe eleven years old.

He went quickly up the path into the woods, looking for the child he believed was his daughter. The path opened out onto a sidewalk. She was on the sidewalk, checking left, then right. She crossed the street and headed for a small convenience store at the end of the road.

Jeb scanned the area. Cars were parked in driveways and along the curb. The old ski-style chalets looked empty. No one was outside. It was still shoulder season, the resort quiet during the week.

He followed her. Compelled. Part of him knowing he shouldn't do this. Yet he was physically incapable of breaking sight of his own daughter now that he'd finally seen her, as if in losing her around a corner now, he'd lose her forever. Another part of him wanted to be certain it was her.

She was walking fast. He absorbed her totally, the shape of her thin body, her gait, how she carried her head, the tightness in her shoulders. Was she afraid of those girls? Grieving for Sophia and Peter, the only mother and father she'd ever known? Missing her old school, her friends, her home?

Stumbling on paving that had been cracked by frost heave, she dropped her lunch bag. The book she'd been clutching fell open to the ground.

Lightning fast, on pure gut instinct, Jeb moved in, scooping up the bag and the open book. Heart racing, he caught the name written inside the cover—*Quinn MacLean.*

It was her.

He glanced over his shoulder again to ensure no one was watching. "Hey," he said, fighting to keep his voice light, normal. "You dropped something." He handed both bag and book to her.

She looked up at him, mouth tight, her features guarded.

He smiled into her eyes, his heart thumping. They were his eyes. And his father's. The same deep, indigo-blue Irish eyes. She had faint freckles over her nose. Jeb felt he might implode.

"Thanks," she muttered, taking the book and bag. Something inside him stilled in awe at the sound of his own child's voice. His eyes filled. Burned.

She turned, resumed walking, a little faster now.

Desperate to hear another word or two, he caught up to her.

"*Schooled*, huh?" he said, mentioning the title of the book as he matched her pace.

She clutched the book tighter to her chest, walking faster.

"My favorite character is Rain."

She stalled, glanced up, looking at him anew. "You've read it?

Jeb smiled slightly. "I've had a lot of time to read a lot of books. Some good, some terrible. I liked that one, though."

She frowned as she regarded him, her gaze going to the tattoo on his neck. "You read books for eight-year-olds?"

He swallowed. He'd read every single one of the books Sophia had told him Quinn was reading. He'd pinned her school art on his cell walls, even a medal he'd managed to persuade Sophia to leave with him. He knew his daughter's favorite color, what she liked to eat, what her favorite TV shows were.

He grinned. "Like I said, I had a lot of time."

Something relaxed in her, a light entering her eyes—ever so subtly—as curiosity began to edge out caution. His heart lifted.

"We had to read it for class last year," she said.

"And you're rereading it?"

She nodded. "Why do you like Rain?" she said.

"Because she marched to the beat of her own drum."

She eyed him, one brow lowering more than the other. "I like Cap."

"Why him?"

She chewed her lip. "Because he had no mother and father and he had to move away from his home. He was different and they all laughed at him. But he was a hero. He changed everyone at the school. He saved the bus driver. They all started to like him."

Jeb's stomach contracted. "Yeah," he said, gently. "Cap's a hero. He was all alone against the whole bunch and he never gave in."

Quinn's eyes shone suddenly with emotion, and Jeb noticed a slight quiver in her lip.

"Hey." He started to walk. She fell in step. "I didn't mean to upset you. About the book or anything."

She shook her head of dark curls. "It's nothing."

"You heading home for lunch?"

"I stay too far up the valley to go home for lunch."

"Really? Like way up toward the Wolf River?"

"No, on Green Lake."

His heart kicked. The Salonens' old place.

"Your parents must like it out there on the lakefront," he said. "It's pretty. I knew some people who lived there once."

"My parents are dead."

The flat, emotionless delivery hit him like a plank. He stalled.

"I'm staying with my aunt," she said. "Just for a while."

"And then?"

She gave a shrug and crossed a patch of emerald-green grass outside the small log-style convenience store. Three stairs led up to a narrow porch that ran the length of the building. A basket of purple and white flowers hung from the eaves, and a husky cross stretched out in a puddle of autumn sun outside the door.

She clumped up the wooden stairs in her little Blundstones. The husky raised its head, fixing them with one milky-blue eye, one brown, before dropping his head back to the deck with a soft doggie sigh. It struck Jeb hard and sudden. These small things—the color of grass, the sigh of a dog in sunlight, flowers—so many things a man could miss and forget the pleasure of in prison. At one point he'd believed that he would never again experience something as simple and true as a dog's contented sigh.

Quinn pushed through the door of the small store. A bell chimed over her head. Jeb followed. The dude behind the counter barely glanced in their direction. He was busy texting on his phone. Jeb noticed a closed-circuit security camera. Instinctively he turned his face away.

While he picked up a copy of the *Snowy Creek Leader*, Quinn found the candy she was looking for, including a stick of black licorice. She set her stash up on the counter, where the dude rang it in and bagged it. While Quinn was fiddling in her pocket for money, Jeb placed cash on the counter. The dude met his eyes, held a fraction, but no more than that. No flicker of recognition—why would there be? This kid would have been maybe ten years old when Merilee and Amy were taken. If he was even in town.

"Thanks, mate," the guy said, offering Jeb change. Australian accent. He was likely in the resort for a season or two. No fear of recognition at all. Jeb had to remind himself he was not here to hide. He was here to rattle cages, play with people's heads.

Quinn stared up at Jeb, surprise in her face.

"Hey," he said with a shrug as he tucked his paper under his arm. "I had some spare change."

She held his gaze, debating whether to accept this gift from a stranger. Then she smiled, a little shyly, and grabbed the bag of candy off the counter. "Thank you."

Jeb pushed open the door, letting her out.

She skipped down the stairs, seemingly over her indecision about him. Perhaps it was a rebelliousness he knew all too well, to befriend a stranger with long hair, a leather jacket, a tattoo.

Perhaps it was just a need for affection, friendship, in the face of her loss and displacement.

She started back toward the school, biting into her stick of licorice.

Jeb hesitated. He should back off now. There was still time. But after all these years, to finally see his own child, to hear her voice—it was a drug more potent than he could imagine, a thirst more voracious than he could quench. She glanced over her shoulder and threw him another shy smile. His heart nearly cracked. He started after her.

Just to the field, he told himself. Just to make sure those girls had gone. Just until he'd seen her go safely back into that squat school building.

Just one more . . . like his father with his drink . . .

"I bet your aunt and uncle are pleased to have you staying with them," he said. "Even if it's just for a while."

"My aunt isn't married." She took another bite of licorice. "She was going to get married but her boyfriend dumped her after I came to live with them."

His heart tumbled over itself. *Rachel's single?* "What was her boyfriend's name?"

She darted a look at him, suspicion flickering briefly through her dark-blue eyes. Yet something compelled her to speak. A quiet connection had been forged. Them against the world. "Trey. He doesn't like me. He left because of me."

Pow. Emotions punched through him. Trey Somerland. Trey in the witness box. Trey kissing Rachel by the gravel pit bonfire. Trey touching Rachel . . . his hand up her sweater.

Rachel and Trey, the reason for his anger that night. The reason it all started to go to hell.

His voice came out thick. "That's not why he left your aunt, surely."

THE SLOW BURN OF SILENCE

She gave a dismissive shrug, biting more of her licorice as she started down the shadowed path into the woods.

"So you and your aunt live alone, then, on Green Lake?"

"Uh-huh."

"Anyone else staying on the property? In . . . a boathouse maybe?"

"Nah. Just an old dog that used to belong to my grandfather before he died."

Seppo Salonen was dead? Emotion washed through Jeb. That must be why Rachel was in his house on the lake. Alone with Quinn. His blood raced, giving him a headiness he couldn't— didn't want to—articulate. Suddenly he wanted the impossible.

He wanted Rachel.

Fuck, he wanted it all now, his desires coalescing into an iron ball of need, muddying the purity of his focus. He wanted to win it all back.

They'd reached the end of the wooded path and come out onto the field. She stopped, looked up. "Thank you," she said, openly, having made some decision in her mind about him. "For the candy and . . . stuff."

"Our secret, 'kay?"

She studied him for a fraction, then nodded before turning and skipping across the grass toward the school. He watched her go on her skinny legs, hair shining in the sun.

"Anytime," he whispered to himself. "Anytime, Quinn."

He heard the school buzzer and he stood there in shadow, newspaper under his arm. His world utterly changed. This was what he'd come for.

Yet caution whispered in the rustle of the breeze through the dry pines. One wrong step, one spark, and it could all go up in a blaze. He could lose it all, forever.

He must not return to this school.

He must not interact with her again until it was over.

But as Jeb traversed the bottom edge of the field, making for his bike, he caught sight of the clutch of blondes coming out from behind the trunk of the large oak. Stubbing out a cigarette with bent heads and a whispered exchange, they began to cross over the field as a tight group, making a beeline for Quinn.

Quinn saw them coming and moved faster. She was smaller. Younger.

Jeb froze, watching as the group crested the grassy rise and crossed onto school property. The clutch of girls closed in, gathering tightly around Quinn, forcing her to stop.

Shock rippled through Jeb as one of the girls grabbed the bag of candy from Quinn's fist. Another snatched away the licorice stick, waving it in front of Quinn's face, laughing as Quinn lunged to claim it back.

One of the girls stuck out her boot and tripped Quinn. She sprawled down hard on the gravel, her book flying, pages blowing in the wind.

Rage flared, sharp and instant. Almost blinding, an electrical charge kicking down familiar neural channels, overriding the logic center of his brain. Jeb moved like lightning over the ball fields. Neck muscles wire tight. Vision narrowing. Up the rise. Onto school property.

One of the girls pointed and jeered at Quinn as she struggled onto her knees. Whatever the girl said froze his daughter. She held dead still for a heartbeat, as if trying to digest the words while staring at the blonde.

"No!" Quinn screamed at the bullies. "*It's not true!*"

The girls laughed. Jeb recognized the switch in his child the moment before she balled her fists. Quinn lurched to her feet, lowered her head, and barreled straight into the blonde's stomach, smacking the kid so hard she lifted off the ground and reeled backward, coming down hard into the dirt, hair flying.

Quinn spun round like a little wildcat, ready for a charge at the others, but they turned and fled toward the school, screaming for a teacher. Quinn turned the full brunt of her rage back onto the fallen girl, raising her leg to kick her in the stomach. Jeb reached them just in time. He grabbed Quinn by her shoulders, jerking her back off her feet. The blonde, bleeding from her nose, scrabbled onto her hands and knees and crawled over the gravel before managing to stagger up into a wild run for the school building.

Jeb set Quinn on her feet, spun her round to face him. He crouched down to her level, gripping her skinny shoulders tight. She was shaking in his hands. Her complexion was sheet white, tears tracking stains down her cheeks. But her eyes crackled with ferocity and she gritted her jaw.

"Quinn—" he said quickly, quietly, watching over her shoulders as two female teachers burst out of the school doors and started running toward them. She seemed unfocused.

Jeb shook her. "Quinn, look at me, listen to me."

Her pupils contracted slightly. She was breathing hard.

"I understand, I really do, that need to hit back sometimes. But whatever they said to you, whatever names they called you, violence is *not* the answer. Never. You have to trust me on this. I've been there. I know. No matter what they say, violence does not work. It comes back to bite you."

Slowly her eyes refocused fully and she met his gaze. Tears pooled afresh. He ached to snatch her away right there—leave. Just him and her. Protect her . . . but Jeb hadn't even been able to protect himself, shouldn't even be associating himself with her. Fuck it to hell, he'd broken his first goal. He'd interacted with his child. And on school property.

"Hey! You!" one of the teachers yelled. They were getting near, rushing over the gravel pathway, skirts and hair blowing in the wind.

"Go," he said urgently to her. "Just remember, be smart. Be better than them. Get them another way. Like Cap in that Korman book. And Quinn, just know this"—he couldn't help it, didn't even register before the words were out already—"I'll always have your back. Got that? Always."

And with that he left her standing there. He moved fast, down the hill, past the bench where he'd sat earlier, slipping into the grove of trees. He stopped in the shadows, where he belonged, and glanced back.

The teachers had reached Quinn. One dropped to a crouch in front of her, talking to her. The other came to stand at edge of the knoll and stared in his direction, shading her eyes as her gaze searched the shadows.

He stood stock-still. But inside his gut he was shaking.

For the first time in his life he'd goddamn touched his own daughter, his own flesh and blood. He'd held her slight but strong little trembling shoulders in his own powerful hands, seen the flutter of her heart in the pulse of her neck. Heard the sound of her voice. Seen her smile.

Witnessed her grit and determination.

A raw, overriding need filled his chest so tightly and fully it hurt—a need to take charge, to claim her. Protect her. His child had no one else right now. No one who could so fully understand her.

The teacher put her arm around Quinn, escorting her back to the school, bent over, talking.

How this was going to unfold now terrified him. In his move to keep his child safe, to protect her, to stop her from harming others in self-defense, he'd just drawn her into a dangerous orbit, and that teacher on the edge of the knoll was just going to be the beginning of his troubles.

CHAPTER 4

"Our rose among the thorns," Levi Banrock says as he curls his arm around my waist, edging me closer to his tall and athletic frame. I smile for the camera, and the big photographer from the *Sun* fires off several shots. I'm positioned between Levi on my right and the mayor and local First Nations chief on my left.

"If you could all gather in just a bit tighter," the photographer says. "I'd like to include the mural of Rachel behind you." He's referring to a giant stylized painting of me on the paneling between the soaring windows of Thunderbird Lodge. Through the windows is a breathtaking view of the ski runs that sweep all the way down to the village nestled in the valley far below.

In the painting I'm wearing a racing suit and helmet, and I'm blasting through the giant slalom course that won me gold at the Torino Olympics. Before I crashed in my next event. Before the end of it all.

I was lucky to survive, wheeled home in a chair after several surgeries in Europe, bravely trying to smile with the gold medal from my first event draped around my neck as a cadre of photographers waited to greet me at Vancouver International. Their nineteen-year-old fallen hero. It took two years to learn to walk again. This is my legacy in this town, the gold medal and the dashed hopes. I crashed because of Jeb. Shortly before my second event, a reporter had asked about his sentence and the role I'd played in sending him to prison. My pain at Jeb's betrayal, my own guilt, had surged afresh, cutting deep. I lost focus in the starting gate.

I startle back to the present and blink as the flash goes off. I'm jumpy—I heard on the news three days ago that Jeb is now free. I've been on tenterhooks since. All I want is to get this ribbon cutting over with. I want to be with Quinn. I know he doesn't know about her, but deep down I've got a bad feeling I can't seem to shake. I'm here for work, though. I'm trying to juggle it all—being a single mother, saving the newspaper from tanking, digging myself out of the financial hole that the taxes on my property have put me in.

It's my fame as a local celebrity athlete, plus my position as publisher of the *Snowy Creek Leader*, that has garnered me this invitation to the ribbon cutting and maiden voyage of the sparkling new Summit-to-Summit Gondola that reaches across the chasm between Bear Mountain and Mount Barren on the other side. Among the dignitaries present are the local member of parliament and the minister for tourism. My own staff photographer, Hallie Sherman, is busy shooting groups posing in front of a red ribbon strung across the glass doors that lead to the gondola terminal. On either side of the ribbon stands a Snowy Creek PD officer dressed in formal gear complete with wide-brimmed Stetsons, jodhpurs, high brown leather boots with spurs, and sidearms in holsters on Sam Browne belts. Their dress is a nod to the Canadian Mounties. Another way Snowy Creek works to attract tourism.

Jonah, one of my staff reporters, is chatting with a woman with a tumble of honey-blonde curls. As she turns her head, a sinister chill of foreboding spears through me. It's the resident psychic, Piper Smith, and I wonder why she's been invited.

Piper first arrived in Snowy Creek five years ago to film a docudrama on the "Missing Girls" for CBC's *True Crime* show. She returned to Snowy Creek later, to marry Merilee's much-older half brother, whom she met while filming. I've always felt uncomfortable around her. Perhaps it's the way she seemed to see right inside me when she tried to question me about Jeb all those years ago. The opening shot of the docudrama flashes into my mind—a reenactment of Amy walking barefoot and beaten down the railway tracks as snowflakes start to fall. Her hair is matted with blood, her face ghost-white, her eyes haunted black holes. Her clothes are ripped and covered with mud. I think of Jeb out of prison now, what he did to her. A shiver chases over my arms. I rub them as I watch Piper.

"He won't come back here," a voice says near my ear.

I jump. "Jesus, Levi, you startled me."

He's also staring at Piper. "I can't help thinking of that opening scene whenever I see her."

I swallow. "I know." I hesitate. "What makes you so certain he won't come back?"

He moistens his lips, still fixated on Piper in the crowd. "He'd be a fool; he'd have to have a death wish. What could he possibly want here?"

"But you're thinking it, otherwise you wouldn't be saying this."

Levi turns, holds my gaze for several beats. I don't like the edginess in his eyes. He, Trey, and I, along with three other classmates, all testified against Jeb. Together, we formed the core testimony that helped put him away.

"What if he wants revenge?" I say.

"He wouldn't dare risk it. If Jeb Cullen sets one foot back in this community, he'll be drawn and quartered, and he has to know it."

I suck in a chestful of air and nod.

"Hey, it'll be fine," Levi says brightly as he takes my arm. His trademark smile lights his green eyes. "Come, it's time for the speeches, and then we can get this circus wrapped up." Yet he pauses. "Just know that we're all here for you, Rach. You can call any one of us. Anytime."

"Well, that's reassuring. On one hand you say he won't come back, but on the other you think he'll come after me?"

"It's not going to happen." He hooks his arm around my shoulders, giving me a reassuring squeeze as he guides me toward the podium. I watch as Levi and his twin brother, Rand, climb up onto the small makeshift stage and position themselves next to their father at the podium. Hal "the Rock" Banrock takes the mike and thanks everyone for coming. He launches into a speech about the Herculean challenges that faced the Summit-to-Summit construction team and how the result will now draw tourists from around the globe, both summer and winter, boosting both the local and provincial economies. Through the floor-to-ceiling glass behind the Rock, the flags of many nations flap in a mounting high-alpine wind.

He better hurry with his speeches or this wind will grow too fierce for a gondola crossing. I check my watch. I'm beyond edgy now, thoughts of Jeb consuming me with an unspecified anxiety. Levi has just made it worse.

I glance at the flags again, trying to distract myself, and my gaze is pulled upward to the forbidding granite formation that is Crystal Peak. White geologic streaks cut across Crystal's somber face and sparkle in the sun. In this slant of light, the cables and metal ladders of the *via ferrata* are clearly visible. I think of my grandfather, Jaako, a Finnish immigrant and old-school mountaineer who told me tales of how *via ferrata* were built in the Dolomite region of Italy to aid the movement of troops through the Alps during the First World War. It was his idea to have a *via ferrata* system on Crystal. Rock jumped on it.

When Jaako first arrived in this valley, he teamed up with the Rock, a strapping mountaineer himself fresh out of Australia. Together they began to carve the first ski runs into the flanks of Bear Mountain. Each day they hiked up, and using bare hands, ax, and chainsaw, they forged a winter playground out of wilderness.

The Rock went on to monetize their efforts, securing government tenure for the land and founding Bear Mountain Ski Enterprises along with the Snowy Creek Real Estate Development Corp., which now specializes in resort real estate around the world. If one had to name a king of Snowy Creek, without a doubt it would be Rock Banrock. He's outlived three wives and most of his peers, and his offspring now populate, and pretty much run, this town.

My granddad, on the other hand, launched the *Snowy Creek Leader*. Where Rock made a financial killing, Jaako eked by monetarily, concerned more with esoteric pursuits—philosophy, literature, ecology. The truth. Jaako passed the newspaper down to my father, Seppo. And at age twenty-seven it became mine. And by God I've been learning the ropes fast. The company was about to tank after my dad's lengthy battle with cancer. But Hal Banrock stepped in, buying up a 49 percent share of the business. Now it's my job to find a way to keep the paper afloat in the digital era that is killing print. Along with Quinn's arrival, this past year has been a trial by fire. I have a sinking feeling today that it isn't over, by far.

Levi takes the mike from his father and my attention is drawn back to the Banrock brothers. Levi and Rand are almost carbon copies of each other, younger echoes of the Rock himself. Like their father, they stand around six two. Both have startling green eyes and thick shocks of sandy-brown hair. Levi is manager of mountain operations. Married with a toddler. Rand was recently appointed CEO of the Snowy Creek Real Estate Development Corp. He's single, a daredevil, bit of a playboy. I suspect Rand would prefer Levi's job, but that's how their father dealt the cards.

I check my watch again. One forty-five p.m. Claustrophobia tightens around my throat.

Speeches given, the ribbon is cut. Applause ensues, and the kids from the local choir burst out in song. My phone vibrates in my pocket. I check the number—it's the office. I let the call go to voice mail. They can manage without me for a few hours. A music duo with dreadlocks and guitars takes over from the choir and begins to belt out a local brand of mountain funk folk. Servers weave through the crowd with refreshment trays. Cameras click and flashes pop again. I'm in the first group to pass through the doors to board the gondola.

A cameraman follows.

The cabin fills to capacity, mostly journalists for this first car. There is room for twelve on bench seats around the windows, six standing. Levi elects to stand. The door closes and a bell clangs. The giant bullwheel cranks around and the cabin starts to move.

I feel a soft dip in my stomach as we launch out of the terminal and swing over the cliff into air. Immediately we're slammed by a gust of wind. Glances are exchanged.

"How much wind can it take?" says one of the CBC people.

"It's the most wind tolerant of our lifts," Levi says with an easy smile. "This gondola is designed to operate in gusts up to eighty kilometers per hour. But if the wind speed does hit max, there's an automatic shutoff, which can be overridden if need be."

Silence descends on the occupants as the sheer scope of the surrounding terrain takes hold of us. Suspended only by cable and towers, we move with a quiet electronic hum. In the center of the car is a glass bottom through which we can see the distant tips of towering Douglas fir, pine, the ski runs. Deer. As we cross the plunging chasm of the Khyber Creek drainage, the churning green-white waters of Bridal Falls come into view. From up here the water looks like lace spilling over shining black granite. My chest tightens as I recall the summer that Jeb and I hiked up to those falls. We found the ice cave hidden behind the water and crawled in.

"It really does give one a different perspective," the reporter from the *Sun* says in a hushed tone.

Levi nods. "These views alone will draw visitors. In summer the gondola will form a bridge to a hiking loop. In winter skiers will be able to access new downhill terrain on Mount Barren." He points as a red gondola cabin slowly approaches along the cables from the other side.

"Twenty cabins in total, one departing every sixty seconds. Total ride time between the Bear and Barren terminals is about fifteen minutes. The distance traveled across the chasm is 4.4 kilometers, or 2.73 miles."

"Strung between the shoulders of giants," says a woman from the radio station as she stares at the endless peaks in the distance.

The empty cabin passes us as we near a massive steel tower.

Thousands of feet below in the valley are the colorful roofs of the village. Khyber Creek is a mercurial ribbon as it snakes down to our town. From the village, a dirt road switchbacks up the flanks of Mount Barren. Higher up Barren's slopes, yellow machines hulk like mechanical dinosaurs, motionless in the forest. Levi points them out.

"We've been cutting new trail systems into the south flanks of Barren, but we had to suspend all operations due to the extreme fire hazard and drought. A small spark from one of the machines could be disastrous. We hope to get back on track as soon as the weather switches."

A bear and her two cubs lumber slowly below, heading down the drainage toward the populated valley. The drought has left a low berry crop in the high alpine, and this will mean greater potential for human-bear conflicts in town this fall as the bruins become desperate to reach hibernation weight. I make a mental note to ensure this is on the *Leader* story list for next week, along with reminders of the extreme, simmering fire hazard.

"That ski run down there"—Levi points—"is Rachel's Gold." He casts a glance in my direction and grins. "Named after our own hometown celebrity, Rachel Salonen, here, after she brought home the gold for Canada."

Everyone turns to look at me. I feel hot. I smile and nod. My phone vibrates in my pocket again, and an inexplicable charge crackles through me.

"Do you think the drought will mean a late opening for the mountain, then?" one of the CBC reporters asks.

"We're confident the weather will turn within the next week and that when the precipitation comes, it'll be in the form of snow at higher elevations," says Levi. "The longer-range forecast is also calling for a big series of storm fronts." He gives the trademark Banrock smile.

"What about lightning?" one reporter asks, looking up at the top of another giant tower as we hum quietly past.

"We have conductors, but in the event of a storm cell moving in, we would manually shut down."

A helicopter thuds down valley. Eyes watch and Levi preempts the next question. "There's no worry about aircraft hitting the cables, either. We're equipped with a state-of-the-art obstacle collision avoidance system which uses radar to alert any aircraft in the area to the presence of the gondolas. Strobe lights and loud noises over all radio frequencies will also alert pilots who come too close."

"And what happens if there *is* a shutdown, a catastrophic failure, people trapped in the cars?"

Levi laughs heartily. "You journalists. Here I am wanting to tell you about the increase in tourism, the boost for the economy, the fact we're one of the first gondolas in the world to run between two mountains, and you're all about catastrophe."

A ripple of amusement passes between the occupants.

Almost as if on cue, a heavy gust of wind buffets our car. There's a gasp and some nervous laughter. My phone buzzes, this time indicating a text message.

I slip my hand into my jacket pocket. It's from Brandy, Quinn's sitter. My pulse quickens. Brandy knows I'm going to be tied up with this opening today. I glance up. We're nearing the far terminal. It's two thirty p.m., the time Brandy should be picking Quinn up from school. Turning my back to the group, I open the text message.

Please call, need to talk.

I type back, *On gondola with press. Will call as soon as we dock.* I hit "Send."

A response blips back almost immediately:

Quinn's been in incident at school. She's fine but principal needs to talk, won't let her leave until you come.

Tension builds in my stomach. Our gondola cabin enters the terminal building, the giant red bullwheel turning smoothly, teeth locking over to a new track. The cabin bumps gently against its berth, slowing to a crawl as the doors slide mechanically open. I push to the front and hurry ahead of the crowd. I find an alcove, duck in. Quickly I dial Brandy.

"Brandy, what's going on?" I hold my hand over my exposed ear to shut out the noise of the machines, the voices of the journalists disembarking.

"Quinn got into a fight with four girls at lunch, but she's okay, physically. They tried to call you at work, then your cell. Then they called me, but I was in a ropes course all morning. They need to speak to you, Rachel. They want to keep Quinn until you get here yourself." There's a pause. "I think they called the cops."

"What on earth for?"

"Something about a guy lurking around the school property."

Panic licks. I think of Jeb—of his release.

"Where are you now?"

"Outside the school." She hesitates. "Quinn didn't even want to see me. They have her in the nurse's room."

LORETH ANNE WHITE

"I'll be down as soon as I can," I say. "Will you let them know I'm on my way?"

Brandy agrees, and I kill the call. I'm already running through the logistics of getting down the mountain as fast as I can. There are no chairlifts operational on the Mount Barren side this early in the season. The ride back to Thunderbird Lodge via the gondola will take fifteen minutes. From the lodge it's still another thirty minutes in another lift down to the village.

I catch up with Levi, who's talking to the group outside the terminal. Drawing him aside, I say, "My niece has had some trouble at school. I have to get down right away."

"We'll be firing up the Summit-to-Summit again in another twenty minutes or so, after the tour—"

"I need to go stat."

"Rachel, I can't—" He pauses, suddenly seeing the seriousness in my eyes, then says, "What kind of trouble? Is Quinn okay?"

"Physically, yes, but . . ." My gaze suddenly lights on an all-terrain vehicle parked next to a construction shed. I can get down via the dirt road from this side. It'll be shorter. "Can I borrow that four-wheeler?"

He frowns. I can see him mentally calculating risk, the insurance ramifications of a nonemployee having an accident on a company vehicle. His gaze dips quickly over my body, taking in my short skirt, tights, knee-high boots. A small appreciative smile curves at the corners of his mouth. "In that gear?"

"Levi, you *know* I can handle an ATV. I need to get down."

He hesitates, then says, "I'll have one of my guys drive you. Come." He takes my arm and escorts me over to a metal-sided outbuilding. Inside he finds a spare helmet, hands it to me as he asks a young mountain employee named Garth to chauffeur me down.

"We don't have spare goggles," he says as I yank the helmet down over my thick hair.

"It's fine." I mount the backseat, skirt riding high up my thighs.

55

"You going to be okay in that gear, Rach? I can look for some coveralls or something?"

"I'm fine. Thanks, Levi. I owe you." I tap the driver on his shoulder and he fires the engine. We bomb down the dirt switchback toward the village, glacial silt billowing in a gray cloud behind us. I squint into the dust, the wind forcing tears down my cheeks. And suddenly I miss Trey. I feel the hole in my heart. I miss being part of a team, having someone to call, to lean on. Even after six months of living with Quinn, I still have no idea how to handle her. It was her surly presence, the constant reminder of Jeb, that strained our relationship to the brink until Trey suggested we take a break. A break that became permanent.

Bastard, you didn't have the balls to stick it out and help me through this . . .

But I know, deep down, that I'd also made it impossible for Trey to stay. Quinn changed everything. Clearly she wasn't done yet.

———

Yellow buses pulled into the school parking lot, exhaust fumes puffing white clouds into the air as they waited for their loads. Temperatures were dropping fast, the sun already dipping behind the peaks. Jeb parked his bike behind a row of mountain ash red with berries. From here he could watch the school entrance without being seen. He cut the engine but kept his helmet on.

He should leave, head out to the Wolf River Valley, check out his old home and set up before nightfall, but he was incapable, knowing Quinn was still in that building, possibly in trouble. She'd drawn blood. There would be consequences, possibly even police.

Seeing his child snap like that had left a quivering, uneasy feeling inside him. Was her violent temper shaped by blood or by circumstance? How differently might he himself have turned out under different circumstances? With these thoughts came something new—a paternal guilt, the weight of responsibility. He knew what it was to be an outsider in this very school. He felt he was to blame for Quinn's circumstance now. And it sharpened his determination to prove his innocence, because he could not allow his daughter to think for one moment she was the product of violence, of rape, the child of a murderer. To be ostracized and bullied for it. He knew all too well that once a kid began to assume a label, it could become impossible to shake.

The buzzer sounded and the double doors bashed open, kids spilling out with screeches and laughter and yells and backpacks and hair flying in the wind. Cars and parents came, went. The school buses filled and left.

An old beater of a blue Ford truck drew into the parking lot, a young woman with striking red hair behind the wheel, someone Jeb didn't recognize. She waited in her truck, engine running. The grounds grew quiet, cars left. No sign of Quinn. The woman finally cut her engine, got out of her truck, and made for the entrance. Her flame-red hair hung almost to her waist. She wore jeans, a down vest, hiking boots. She entered the school.

Another twenty minutes passed before the redhead exited. She stood for a moment outside, looking a little lost. Then she moved into a protected corner and called someone on her cell phone. She gave a visible sigh of frustration when she got no answer. She texted instead, then paced, checking her watch, glancing at the school doors. She stopped suddenly and answered her phone.

Turning her back, she bent her head, talking. After she killed the call, she raked her hand through her thick mane of hair and cast another glance at the doors. She then left in her old truck.

Another hour ticked by. It grew colder, the light turning a soft lilac. Daylight would be four minutes shorter each day now as the earth tilted farther away from the sun.

Teachers started to leave, the parking lot growing emptier.

As the light dimmed even further, wind gusted harder, fed by mountain downdrafts as chillier alpine air sank to the valley. Leaves clattered across the paving. A police cruiser pulled into the grounds and drew up out front. A uniformed cop climbed out, female. She slammed her vehicle door closed, adjusted her gun belt, went into the school.

So, they'd called the police. Most likely because of him. His jaw tightened.

Jeb had broken his resolve to not engage his daughter. It had taken only the spark of those blonde bullies to ignite him, and now he'd brought trouble for her. The last thing he needed was for any link to be drawn between Quinn and himself. Not until he'd proved his innocence.

Not until he'd found out why those four guys had lied for each other and perjured themselves in court.

Not until he'd learned the truth.

A few more minutes ticked by as darkness seemed to crawl out from cool crevices. Jeb was grateful for his gloves, his helmet. A flock of geese flew high in a *V*. Honking. Lonely travelers crying as they departed for warmer climes.

Suddenly the school doors opened again. A woman with blonde hair came out with two of the blonde girls in tow. One of the girls was holding a wad of tissue to her nose. The other was crying. Moments later they were followed by a balding man and a slender brunette, each holding onto a blonde child of their own. The man and the woman talked with heads bent together, then they ushered their charges toward an Escalade and a pumpkin-yellow Hummer, respectively.

The Hummer and Escalade left.

Two minutes later the female cop exited the school. She paused as the doors swung slowly shut behind her. Jeb's pulse quickened and he eased back on his seat as the cop briefly scanned the parking

LORETH ANNE WHITE

lot before walking over the grass toward the hill that sloped down to the ball fields and bleachers.

She stopped at the edge of the hill where the teacher had stared after him, and she peered toward the trees where he'd been standing earlier. Briskly, she turned and strode back to her cruiser. Jeb had no doubt she was going to drive round there, take a look, canvass people in the neighborhood, asking about a tall dark stranger in a leather jacket, a man who'd come onto school property, touched the girls.

Tension whispered through him. The clock had started ticking. *Game on.* He hadn't intended it to start this way, or so soon.

The cop drove off the property, turned right, and headed down to the subdivision that led round the back of the ball fields. Silence descended, apart from the halyard and hooks chinking against the metal flagpole, the intermittent snap of the flag. Jeb glanced at his watch. Almost four p.m., getting dark. But Quinn was still in there.

The sound of an approaching engine suddenly reached him. A gray Dodge Ram wheeled sharply into the parking lot, tires squeaking as the driver pulled up onto the curb right outside the school entrance in the no-parking zone.

The driver's door swung open and long, boot-clad legs extended, followed by stockinged thighs, short skirt. The woman's chestnut-brown hair lifted in a wild tangle as the wind caught it. Electricity shot through Jeb.

Rachel.

He froze, heart hammering as he watched her reach into the back of the truck cab. She grabbed a down jacket. Yanking it over her sweater, she kicked the truck door closed behind her and hurried toward the school as she stuffed her keys into her jacket pocket. She had a slight limp. The crash, he thought. It had left her permanently, slightly, disabled. He tried to swallow, pulse racing. Mouth dry as bone.

59

Pushing through the doors with both hands, Rachel disappeared into the school.

He'd read about her accident in the papers. She'd been coming into the finish when she hit a rise at a bad angle, hurtling off balance into the air. She'd landed on hard-packed ice, spinning down the slope in a wild kaleidoscope of skis and poles. The edge of one ski had caught the orange race fencing, torquing one leg away from the rest of her body. She had come to a stop, blood running dark red against the white snow, the world watching in horrified silence as she lay unmoving, paramedics racing to reach her and bring a helicopter in.

A rush of high-voltage adrenaline charged through Jeb as he stared at the doors that had swallowed her. His reaction was so powerful, so visceral, it made him shake. This was the woman he dreamed about nightly. The woman who'd been his closest friend. The only woman he'd ever loved, still loved. And could now never have. Yet she was caring for his child. She was going inside there to do battle for Quinn. The irony struck hard.

There was no way in hell he could leave the parking lot now. He had to see Rachel come out, with Quinn. He had to see them both again.

CHAPTER 5

I march Quinn briskly back to the truck as I stuff the piece of paper with the girls' parents' names and phone numbers into my pocket. It's not even five p.m. and already darkness has fallen, temperatures hovering around freezing. The school parking lot lights have come on, a dull orange. Leaves scatter and swirl at our feet.

Quinn keeps her head cast down, shoulders hunched, mouth set in a tight line. I sat with the principal and the school counselor for almost an hour, trying to get Quinn to explain why she laid into those girls, but she refuses to speak. My heart is hammering.

I open the passenger door for her, but Quinn stands obstinately glaring at her boots, clutching her backpack so tightly against her stomach you'd swear her world depends on it.

"Quinn, c'mon. Please, get in. It's cold."

My niece refuses to budge.

An osprey swoops somewhere in the darkness overhead, wings *whop whopping* as it hunts something under the orange lights. I go still, and a chill suddenly crawls down my spine. I feel as if I'm being watched. With my hand holding the door open for Quinn, I peer into the surrounding darkness. It moves with shadows and rustles in the wind, but I can't see anything. Just a few cars, a van, no one around. Probably a bear, I think. But the uneasiness lingers.

Quinn suddenly looks up at me, as if sensing my fear.

"Quinn," I say more gently. "Please?"

The child climbs in and I slam the door, going round to the driver's side. I get in, start the engine. My hands are trembling. It's not from cold. I'm fraught with worry, anxiety, over Quinn. Guilt. She's tried me these past six months and I'm not winning. I don't know how to do this. Especially now.

Thank God there was no more physical damage than a bloodied nose. The school nurse attended to that. I'll have to call the parents tonight and apologize. So far there's been no word about charges, although the police were called in. I'm worried about how this will play out. But what's really eating me is the news that a man with black hair came onto the school property and broke up the fight. One of the girls claimed the man also followed Quinn into the woods before the fight.

Levi's words snake through my mind as I turn up the heater.

He'd be a fool; he'd have to have a death wish. What could he possibly want here?

I inhale deeply. Jeb doesn't know about his child. He *can't* know. How could he? The only other person who knows is Trey, and he's vowed to keep it that way.

As I wait for the truck to warm, I try again. "Why won't you tell me the reason you hit Missy?"

Silence.

Frustration bites. I concentrate on keeping my voice level. "It would really help to know what upset you like that, because then we can deal with it—"

"They're bitches," she snaps suddenly.

I count to twenty, then say, calmly, "So they said something that provoked you, something that made you mad?"

Quinn glowers in sullen silence at some arbitrary spot on the glove compartment.

"Look," I soften my voice, "I really do want to help you. Please tell me what went down on that field, because if those girls said something hurtful, that's bullying, and we can't just pretend it never happened. It'll only fester."

My niece turns her face abruptly away and stares out the window. Her knuckles are white and tight over the backpack on her lap.

I suck in a deep breath. *Take it easy. She's had a rough time. One wrong move now could send everything backward . . .*

"Okay, maybe we can talk about it over dinner. Let's get some takeout. What would you like?"

She remains mute. The heel of her Blundstone begins to kick at the base of the seat.

"Pizza?"

Silence.

"Fried chicken?"

"Not hungry."

I decide to let this ride, just a little. Maybe Quinn will be more receptive later tonight. Or tomorrow. It's the start of Thanksgiving break—there'll be no school for a week. Perhaps I could take time off work to just be with Quinn, do something special. A trip maybe. Conflict tightens in me. It's a tricky time to be away from the paper with all the potential advertising contracts in the works, with the winter season and big turkey sales ramping up. Banrock is also going to be breathing down my neck now that he owns almost half my company.

That deeper, darker fear snakes through me again—*a dark-haired stranger on school grounds. Jeb out of prison . . .*

"That man who stopped the fight," I say. "Have you seen him before? Or was today the first time?"

She keeps her head turned away. The kicking grows louder, more rhythmic.

Tension knifes deeper. "The teachers described him as having black hair and wearing a black leather jacket. They said he was crouched down, talking to you, but as soon as they approached, he hurried away and disappeared into the trees."

The kicking of her Blundstone boot intensifies. The sound hammers inside my skull.

"Missy and Abigail told Mrs. Davenport he followed you to the store earlier, and that you returned with a bag of candy. Is that true? What did he say to you?" I hate the pitch entering my voice.

The interior of the truck cab is warming. I wait a few more moments mostly because I don't know what the hell to do. The more I think about it, the more I worry it could be Jeb.

"Did you talk to him on the way to the store?"

Silence.

"Tell me, Quinn!"

She spins round, her eyes flashing. "They're bitches! They're all *liars*! He hasn't been following me—he was just walking past the school when it happened. He's not a bad man!"

Perspiration prickles over my brow. I take a deep, slow breath. "Did he buy you the candy, then? Did he ask you questions?"

"So what if he did? No one does anything nice for me. He's a nice man."

"Did he ask where you live?"

Silence, heavy and dark, boils back up around her like an invisible cloud.

I reach forward and ram the truck into gear, reminding myself she's lost her parents in a horrific fire. She's been uprooted and forced to live with a young aunt she doesn't even know that well. New town, new school. New friends. Ripped out of her life. Floundering.

We both are.

And suddenly I feel so alone, so unequipped. None of my peers have kids this age. Trey is gone. I have the big house, a business I don't fully understand yet. I miss Sophia and Peter. I miss my dad. The overall sense of loss is deep, a chasm in my heart. What have I done to bring this all down at once?

Triage, I think. Quinn *has* to come first right now. Above my business. Above my financial worries. My niece is teetering on the edge of a dangerous place, and my number one goal must be to keep her safe. If it means taking a holiday, even leaving Snowy Creek for a few weeks with Quinn, I'll take out a loan to do it.

I drive through the parking lot and up toward the exit. But as my headlights pan across a white van, I catch a gleam of chrome behind it. A bike. Something about it makes me glance up into my rearview mirror as I approach the parking lot exit. Wind gusts and shadows move, but I can't see anything from this angle. I turn left onto the road. For a moment it looked as though there was a man in a helmet on the bike. Perhaps it was a trick of light.

As I approach the intersection on the highway, the lights turn red. I bring the truck to a stop. While I wait, I try once more with Quinn. "I really wish you'd tell my why you hit those girls."

"I told you!" she yells. Her ferocity startles me. "They're bitches. Liars . . ." Tears, fat, start to roll fast and furious down her pale cheeks and she starts to shake violently.

The lights turn green. Instead of turning north on the highway, I quickly drive through the intersection and pull up onto a curb under the branches of an old oak. I reach out, wrap my arms around Quinn, draw her shaking little body against mine. And I just hold her tight. My chest aches with Quinn's pain. My head hurts. I stroke her hair. Soft under my palm. I remember her as a day-old baby in my arms.

Another memory flashes through me, of being in Jeb's arms. Wrapped in his protective care. Pain twists through my stomach. Ever since that day in Guthrie's office six months ago, Jeb and Quinn have become intertwined in my mind. I can't separate one from the other yet.

How could I have been so wrong about him? How on earth am I going to do this? I swallow against the tightness in my throat. I need help. I need to take her back to see the therapist.

"They're liars," she sobs softly into my jacket. "They're horrible, horrible liars. I hate them all." Her slender body judders as another wave of sobs wracks her body. "It's just not true."

"What's not true, Quinnie?" I whisper, stroking her hair. "You mean what they said about the man following you?"

"They said I was a bastard," she mumbles into my jacket. "They said I was adopted."

A dull roar begins to sound in my head. "They said . . . *what*?"

"They said Mom and Dad weren't my real parents."

My heart begins to jackhammer.

"It's not true," Quinn says. Then, sensing the sudden stiffness in my body, she turns her face slowly up to me, tears shining on her cheeks, her lip quivering. "I am *not* adopted."

I swallow. Panic crashes through me. Sophia wanted Quinn's paternity kept secret, but I wish with all my heart they'd at least told her she'd been adopted. Quinn's features change as she watches my face, feels my mushrooming tension.

"I . . . I'm not . . . am I?"

Oh, God, Sophia, wherever you are, please, give me a sign, help me . . . what do I say now? Why did you leave telling Quinnie about her adoption to me?

Trust.

I need Quinn's trust. Break that now, and I could lose my niece forever. But is this the time to tell the truth? Won't it hurt more now than later? I have to say *something*—those girls have cracked this open, and I won't be able to get this genie fully back in the bottle.

"Rachel?" Quinn's voice quavers now, thin, pleading.

Time stretches. The roar in my head grows louder. Whatever I say now will shape things to come, perhaps forever, between Quinn and me.

"*Am I?*" Quinn's voice is now shrill, laced with desperation.

Inhaling deeply, I say, "Quinnie, your mother and father loved you more than anything in this world. They *were* your parents in every way, but you're special because you have other parents as well, birth parents." Oh, God, this is coming out wrong.

"I . . . I don't understand." A glittering wildness enters her eyes. But there's no turning back. I take her cold little hands in mine.

"Your mother and father tried for a very long time to have biological children of their own, for years and years. They were desperate to have a baby, a family. But when the doctors said it wasn't possible, they decided to adopt. And then, out of the blue, you came along. You entered Sophia and Peter's lives and you were ready for them to take care of you. They brought you home when you were just a day old, a tiny newborn right out of hospital." My voice catches on a surge of emotion. I lean forward, move a strand of hair from her eyes.

"I was there the day they brought you home. I saw the smiles on their faces; it was the happiest day of their lives. You were theirs—ours—to love forever." My eyes burn as I try to hold it together. "They wanted a baby, Quinnie, and you found them."

She's grown dead still. I'm not even sure she's breathing. Worry cuts through me. I cup the side of her face. "They *were* your mom and dad, Quinn. I *am* your family."

A shudder runs through her body. Her face goes white, her mouth tighter. Her fists are balled. I don't know how to do this; there is no manual. I physically ache with need for my sister to be here, to help, to whisper some assurance in my ear. "They were going to tell you when you were a little older," I offer, but my voice is faltering now. "They just didn't get a chance."

She springs backward suddenly, shoving me away, and she swings her backpack at my face. The buckle smacks across my eye. "You're lying too! It's all lies! You're a bitch, too!" she shrieks. She pops open her seat belt and lunges for the door handle.

"Quinn! Wait!" I grab her arm, fear galloping through me. She glowers at my hand on her arm, eyes fierce. I can feel her limbs trembling. She's fighting herself. Fighting this knowledge, hitting back at it, trying to make it go away. The fabric of her psyche, her belief in who she is, her very foundations are shattering around her.

I swallow and loosen my grip slightly, fearful that if Quinn gets out of this truck now, she'll bolt blindly into the dark. The surrounding wilderness is a dangerous and cold place to get lost, especially at night. I've volunteered enough hours with Rescue One to know this firsthand. I *know* how many never come home.

"I love you," I whisper. "I love you very, very much. I loved your mother with all my heart, too. And Peter. We *are* family. Quinnie MacLean, that's you. We *belong*—" My voice chokes. "I hate what happened to your parents as much as you do. It's a terrible, terrible thing. But you and me, we're all that's left. We need to be here for each other. I'm scared as hell, too. Terrified, really, because I don't know how to be a good guardian. But I am here for you—I'll *always* be here. I promise you that. And one other thing I promise is that I'll try my best, my hardest. But I need your help."

The rawness in my voice reaches something inside Quinn. Her eyes lift slowly.

"I don't know how to do this either," I say. "But we're going to try, together, okay? Because if you beat me up along with the rest of the world and run away, where are you going to go on your own? If Mrs. Davenport kicks you out of school for violence, what are we going to do then? Where will we go then?"

A siren wails down the highway, winding away into the mountains.

"It sucks," I whisper. "I know that. But we'll deal with it. Baby steps. Each day we'll just aim to get through. Then one day, maybe it'll all be a little bit easier. Like a sunny break after a terrible storm."

There's a long silence.

A single headlight flares suddenly in my rearview mirror, momentarily blinding me. I turn and look out the back window. A bike has pulled off the road about a hundred yards back. The headlight is cut.

I think of the bike at the school. Disquiet whispers through me.

"I want to go home," she says, her voice soft, small. "I want my mom."

"I know." I gather her into my arms again and an indescribable sensation washes through me as I hold her against my breast. A ferocity. A feeling that I will do anything for this child now. Anything. I will keep her safe. I will make her happy. "We'll find a way," I whisper against her hair. "Together we'll put those girls in their place, okay? But we're going to do it in a smart way. We can't physically beat away all the bad things. Violence is not the answer."

"That's what he said."

Ice shoots through me. I pull back.

"Who?"

Her gaze holds mine.

"You mean . . . that man?"

Silence.

Fury, fear, chases through me. I turn in my seat and glare at the bike in the dark shadows.

"He's not a bad man."

"How do you know?" Urgency nips my voice.

Something flickers in Quinn's eyes, and in that instant, without a quiver of a doubt, I know it's Jeb. He's here. He followed and spoke to Quinn. He's on that bike out there. It was him waiting outside the school.

"Did he ask you where you live?" My words are clipped.

Silence.

"Did he?"

"Yes!" she spat. Her only tool is anger, and she's grabbing it back, wielding it again. "He asked if you were married. I told him your stupid boyfriend dumped you."

I can't breathe. "Does he have a motorbike?"

"No. I don't know."

"Does he have a tattoo, on his neck? A fish?"

Quinn turns her head sharply away.

I lurch forward, put the truck in gear, hit the gas, and squeal back into the road. Wrenching the wheel hard, I pull a U-turn across the boulevard, almost clipping a parked sedan on the opposite side. My tires squeal. My hands are tight on the wheel as I drive too fast, my heart thudding overtime, perspiration breaking out on my lip.

"Put your seat belt on," I snap as I remember she took it off.

"What are you doing? Where are we going?"

"Police station."

She swings round in her seat to face me. "No! You can't, please—he's *not* a bad man."

"And how do you know that? Because he bought you candy? Because he smiled nicely at you? There are some very bad people in this world who know just how to get at little girls." My voice is shaking. "You might *think* he's safe. Men like him can make you feel they're your friend. They can make you feel comfortable, happy. But they're dangerous. They're predators. You have to understand this. Terrible, terrible things can happen."

"He's *not* dangerous," she sobbed. "He's read my favorite book. He helped me when those girls took my candy."

I wheel sharply into the public safety building parking lot, tires bouncing as I hit the edge of the curb. I come to a stop, sit for a while, engine running, watching in the rearview mirror, heart pounding, sweat prickling over my torso. But there's no bike. There's nothing in the street save for the odd car. Maybe I imagined a man on the bike in the school lot. Maybe I imagined we were being followed.

I'm seeing Jeb in every damned shadow because I'm paranoid now that he's out. I drag my hands over my hair. My imagination is becoming my worst enemy.

The police station is attached to the fire hall at the back. Beside it is the Rescue One base. The light is on in Adam LeFleur's office, a yellow glow spilling out into the cold night. He's working at his desk. His large form is comforting. It's going to be okay.

We're all here for you, you know that . . .

I can do this. I can handle this. If Jeb is back and looking for trouble, Adam will move heaven and earth to lock him back up, for good this time. I unbuckle my seat belt.

"Come," I say to Quinn as I open my door.

Quinn presses herself deeper into the car seat, clutching her backpack over her tummy again. "I'm not going in there with you."

"Quinn—"

"You can't make me. I'll bite you. I'll kick you—I'll scream." She refuses to look at me. Her mouth is set in a sullen pout.

I glance at the police station. Frustration swells inside me. Taking my phone from my pocket, I dial the station number. The call clicks directly to voice mail, which gives the detachment office hours. I curse to myself. Short of dialing 9-1-1, I'm not going to get through by phone.

I open my door. Standing next to my truck, I yell up to the lighted window where I can see Adam bent over his desk. "Adam! Can you hear me?"

No response. He can't hear a thing through the double glazing. I look around—no one in sight. All is quiet.

"Okay," I say, bending back into the truck. "You stay here. But I'm going to lock you in the truck."

She remains mute, chin stubbornly jutted forward.

"I'll be just inside that window over there," I say, pointing to Adam's office. "The police will be able to see you from there, okay?"

Nothing.

Quickly I shrug out of my down jacket. "Here, put this over you so you stay warm."

She doesn't take it so I leave my jacket on the driver's seat beside her. I set the child safety lock, close and lock the doors. My truck locking system is faulty—if I activate the child locks, even the passenger side door can't be opened from the inside. Quinn will not be able to open the doors for anyone. Locking her inside fills me with guilt, but I'm desperate; I don't know what else to do. I can't wrestle her into the police station, and I can't risk her bolting into the night.

I hurry along the path, telling myself I'll just be a minute, and the cops are right here.

CHAPTER 6

Quinn hugged her backpack tight over her tummy. She desperately wanted to *not* believe Rachel. She wanted to hate Rachel. Make her go away. Make all the horrible things of the past six months disappear. She wanted her mom and dad back. She felt like a sock was stuck in her throat and those stupid tears were coming again.

She kicked her boot heel against the base of the truck seat, trying to stop the tears. But still they burned the backs of her eyes. She drew Rachel's jacket over her, up to her nose. It was fluffy and warm and smelled softly of her aunt's perfume. There was blood on it from when Quinn had bashed her above the eyes with the backpack. She banged her boot harder as she turned to watch her aunt run lightly along the path and up the concrete steps to the police station entrance.

Above the building a Canadian flag waved in the wind. White police cruisers and SUVs with red and blue stripes down the sides were parked in the lot in neatly angled rows. Beyond the building, high up above the waving flag, the dark shape of Bear Mountain rose up like a dark blot against the sky. Quinn could see warm yellow lights glowing from the Thunderbird Lodge restaurant and the gondola station near the top. Far above even the peaks, northern lights waved like greenish and yellow curtains, making the glaciers glow ghostly white.

As she waited, the truck windows began to fog up. Quinn pulled her aunt's jacket tighter. The street was empty and dark, leaves blowing along the paving.

They were all liars. She was not going to believe them. She just was not.

Quinn balled her fist and rubbed a little hole into the mist on her window. That's when she saw it, a black bike gleaming, the rider with a dark helmet and jacket, watching her from across the street, his exhaust puffing white smoke.

Her heart jumped. *It was him.* She was sure of it.

Excitement rippled through her. She rubbed the hole bigger and leaned forward, peering through it.

The man. Her shadow.

She wasn't afraid of him.

She liked him—he made her feel special, as if she had a guardian angel. Maybe her mother had sent him down from heaven to protect her, like in that book she'd read where angels were dark and handsome with tattoos and they watched over girls like her who'd been left all alone in the world.

Stupid Missy Sedgefield and Abigail Winters and the others spouting their bitch mouths off about seeing him following her through the woods, snitching about him buying her candy. The bike faded into soft focus as Quinn's breath caused mist to re-form over the window. She quickly balled her hand and scrubbed another circle into the mist. He was still there.

Our secret, 'kay . . .

Quinn felt bad for getting into the fight now. It had forced him out of the shadows to help her, and they'd all seen him. Now her aunt was tattling in the police station. Rachel was going to scare him away. Missy had told Principal Davenport about his black hair and black leather jacket. But they hadn't seen the tattoo that curved down the side of his neck. Quinn was pretty sure about that. By the time the man had crouched down to speak to her, the girls were running toward the school. It was a coho salmon tattoo. She knew because her dad had been a fisheries expert and he'd had carvings and Indian drawings of coho. He'd told her that the jaws and teeth of the male fish grew hooked and aggressive like that when they turned up into the rivers to spawn.

The girls had told Principal Davenport he was scary.

But he wasn't. His eyes were the deepest blue and he had the best smile ever. And now Rachel and the police might scare him away. Quinn rubbed another hole into the mist. He was still there, watching. She felt a warm little clutch in her heart. It was her job to keep his secret. A friend. A secret friend.

Our secret, 'kay . . .

———

A young female officer with a mop of dark, loose curls opens a door beside the reception counter fronted with bulletproof glass. Her name tag says Constable Pirello. Her gaze flicks over me but her expression is inscrutable. Typical cop.

"Come this way." She leads me into a bull pen of sorts with metal desks behind dividers. The walls and carpets are in tones of soft gray. There is only one other police officer at his desk at this time. The other desks sit empty.

"Would you like to take a seat; can I get you some water? Can you tell me what happened?" She's looking at my face.

My hand goes to my brow and my fingers come away sticky with blood from where Quinn hit me. With shock I realize I must look like a mugging victim. I'm covered head to toe in gray glacial dust, my hair is a snarled mess, and my face is bleeding.

"It's nothing," I say, looking at the blood on my hand. "I came down the mountain on the back of an ATV in a hurry to get to the school. My niece was having some . . . trouble."

Her left brow rises slightly and the woman appraises me with big violet eyes.

"I was at the gondola launch," I explain. "I must've bumped my head. I'm fine, really. I'd like to speak to Adam."

"You mean Deputy Chief Constable LeFleur?"

She has a French accent, I realize.

"We're old friends. I know he's here, I saw him in the window."

Something flickers through her gaze. She pulls out a chair next to the closest desk. "Please, wait here."

I remain standing as Officer Pirello strides down the hall. She manages to pull off the heavy gun belt and bulletproof vest look, her swagger somehow sexy, overly confident. I dislike her on the spot.

Adam comes down the hall with her. Pirello talks quietly to him as they walk. He looks up and starts slightly at the sight of me.

"Rach." He comes forward quickly. "What's going on? What happened?"

"ATV ride. Bumped my head. Adam, can we have a word in private?"

He hesitates, glances at Pirello. "Is this is about the elementary school incident, with your niece?"

I inhale deeply. "Partly . . . yes."

"This is Constable Annie Pirello," Adam says. "She recently joined us from Montreal. She's the one who took the call from the school. I think it's best she hears anything you might have to say."

Pirello regards me again with those big violet eyes and expressionless features. Self-conscious and suddenly irritated, I clear my throat and glance toward his office at the end of the hall. A part of my mind has started to backpedal.

"Fine," I say. "I was wondering if . . . any of the parents are pressing charges, or anything? I don't know what usually happens with something like this."

"No charges at this point," Pirello offers. She has a cute little gap between her front teeth, which also manages to make her look oddly sexy. For some reason this just galls me further.

I use my sleeve to dab at the blood on my brow. "Did the girls say why the fight happened?"

"None of them wanted to talk." Pirello's eyes hold mine, as if she's waiting for something else to drop, for me to tip my hand, give her further information. My palms grow damp.

"I understand there was a man who came onto the school grounds and broke up the fight," I say crisply.

Pirello nods, not giving anything away herself.

"The girls apparently told the principal that this man was watching my niece during lunch hour, down on the ball fields. Did Mrs. Davenport tell you that?"

"She did."

Irritation spikes. "And she also told you that he followed her to the Alpine Market, where he bought her candy?"

"That's correct."

"So what exactly happened?" I demand of Pirello. "Did you find out who he is? What he wants?"

"We have a general description from the girls and two of the teachers, but your niece would not confirm their version of events. If she has something to add, perhaps she would like to—"

"I want to know from *you* who he is," I snap. "Is he . . . known to police? Dangerous?" My gaze flicks to Adam, who is watching me strangely.

"We don't know who he is, ma'am," says Pirello. "He might have simply been a Good Samaritan who stepped in when he saw a schoolyard brawl."

"Then why didn't he stay when the teachers came out?"

"We don't know yet, Rachel," Adam interjects. "We've canvassed the neighborhood and spoken to the store clerk at the Alpine Market. All we've gleaned at this point is that he's about six two, black hair on the long side. Darkish complexion. And he was wearing a leather jacket and riding a bike."

A bike.

Pirello asks again, "Did Quinn MacLean mention anything else?"

A strange sort of defensiveness swells in me at the sound of my niece's surname on the cop's lips, my sister's married name. With it comes a sharp stab of fear that this Constable Pirello is going to go digging and find that Quinn is the birth child of a dangerous felon.

I don't want the cops—or anyone in town—to draw any kind of link between Jeb and Quinn. Suddenly I feel trapped. This is all happening too fast and I haven't had time to think it through. I reach for the edge of the desk, feeling dizzy, exhausted.

Adam touches my arm. "Rachel, are sure you're all right? Can I get you anything?"

I raise my palm. "I'm fine. And no, Quinn won't tell me anything. She's been through a lot lately with the death of her parents, and we're trying to work through it all. I . . . I was just worried. About potential charges and all. And who that man is. I should go. Quinn is waiting in the truck for me."

Pirello and Adam exchange a quick glance.

"If she does mention anything—" Pirello starts saying.

"I'll call. Thanks." I head for the door, completely unsure about what I'm doing, but gut instinct shuts me up. If Quinn finds out through someone in town that her father is some murderer and rapist, it will utterly crush her right now.

Adam catches up to me. He cups my elbow and leans across me to open the door leading out of the reception area.

"Don't worry," he says quietly, near my ear. "We'll keep an eye out for this guy. I'll put a police presence at the school after the Thanksgiving break." He hesitates, then meets my eyes. His face is close. "You're certain there's nothing else you want to tell me?"

Oh, now you want to talk, out of earshot of Pirello.

I hold his gaze. "No."

Something silent surges between us—the mutual knowledge that Jeb is out of prison. We're both thinking about it.

"I just got spooked today, Adam, that's all. I should've been there for Quinn when the school first called." I give a soft snort. "I'm still learning how to be a mother to an eight-year-old girl who doesn't want me in her life."

"You should both come round for dinner. I'll speak to Lily and have her call you. She's so great with kids. We'd love to see you and Quinn again."

"Yeah." I force a smile. "You and Lily have done well—two gorgeous boys. A real family. She's a lucky woman." I'm unable to keep the slight bitterness out of my voice. It's not that I resent what Adam has. It's that I wasn't able to manage this dream with Trey.

Something shimmers through his eyes. I start to leave, but he says suddenly, "You're worried it's him, aren't you? That's why you came."

I glance over his shoulder. Annie Pirello is watching us. Shrewd, probing eyes. Intense woman.

I look away, to the glass doors leading out of the police station, toward my truck in the lot. Quinn's little shadow is still there behind fogged glass.

"What if he does come back?" I say softly. "Can we stop him from being here?"

"Cullen's conviction was overturned. He's as free as the next guy, to go wherever he pleases. Law enforcement has no control over his movements. But there is also no reason for him to come back here."

"What about that land his mother left him, on the Wolf River?"

"It's derelict. There's nothing there for him. He'd be insane to even try to make something work here. He's not welcome in Snowy Creek, Rachel, and he knows it. What he did to those girls—people here will crucify him if he returns. There's still so much residual anger—hell knows what might happen if he sets foot in this town. I'm not sure I could control it."

"What if it's revenge he wants? For us testifying? You know, like that felon who comes after his lawyer in *Cape Fear*?"

Adam hesitates. "You're thinking he might go after your niece to get at you, is that what this is about? You think he'll come after our children, just to mess with our heads?"

I bite my lip. Deep down, even now, in spite of what I've been led to believe about Jeb, in spite of all the evidence presented in court, in spite of my own fears, in spite of today, I can't fully accept he's capable. When it comes to Jeb, I can't think clearly. Trey said there was something wrong with me, that I was sick in my head when it came to him. Maybe he's right.

Adam's features darken. "Look, if Cullen dares set one fucking foot in this town, we'll be on him like flies on shit. One slip—and he *will* make one, mark my word—we nail him. He goes back into Kent, for good this time. I'm not letting my mother's efforts go down the toilet here. She had a good arrest. This was not her team's mistake."

I hold his eyes and feel a sense of mistrust, a suspicion blossoming in Adam. He's not sure how to read me right now and it's making him edgy.

"Thanks, Adam." I go through the reception door and push open the glass doors to outside. Cold wind smacks into me.

"If you do see him, tell me," he calls after me.

"You think I wouldn't?"

He meets my gaze. Again, I feel his mistrust. I exit the building, doors swinging shut behind me. As I run down the stairs and hurry back toward the truck, I sense Adam watching me through the doors. I feel he's itching for it to have been Jeb, for me to have brought him something solid. He's dying to nail him, put him back, burning at the injustice of a felon his own mother put away being released on technicalities. If Jeb is indeed back in town, I can trust Adam will hunt him down. They don't need me. Or Quinn.

Whatever unfolds now, my job is to protect Quinn by keeping her apart from it all. I'll look up flights, book us on a trip tomorrow, get out of town. I have air miles. I can call my friend Emily about her place on Maui. Hopefully by the end of the Thanksgiving break it will all have blown over.

I reach for my keys and am about to chirp the lock when a male voice yells out of the darkness.

"Rachel!"

I stall, heart jackhammering.

A tall figure emerges from a silver SUV parked outside the Rescue One base. I recognize his stride instantly. Trey. I curse to myself.

It's Wednesday; practice night. After training, the Rescue One group and some of the firefighters and cops usually repair to the Shady Lady Saloon for beers. There was a time I'd join them. Volunteering for Rescue One used to consume my spare hours. Until Quinn. Until I could no longer bear seeing Trey in a social environment after our breakup.

The rest of the Rescue One guys are coming out of the base behind his SUV. Laughter and friendly jeers carry into the night as they make for the village on foot.

Trey reaches me, his breath crystallizing in the cold. "I heard about Quinn and what happened at school."

My gaze goes to his silver SUV. The inside light has come on. There's a woman inside Trey's vehicle, a kid in the back. With a start, I recognize the unmistakable fall of the woman's white-blonde hair. Stacey Sedgefield. A single mom. Missy's mother.

It was Melissa "Missy" Sedgefield who Quinn had punched in the nose today. It's Stacey's phone number on a piece of paper in my pocket.

Trey sees where I am looking. He clears his throat. "Stacey told me what happened. Are you doing okay? If there's anything we—"

"We?"

His eyes glitter in the reflected light.

"You and Stacey?"

"Look, it's—"

"Jesus, Trey . . . it's been what, four months?" My hurt is sudden and profound and irrational. We were going to marry, spend a lifetime together, and already he's found someone else. "You can stomach *her* kid, but not my niece?"

"That's not fair. It's not like that. It's—"

I raise my palms. "I'm sorry, I can't talk now." I turn my back on him, chirp the truck lock.

"Rachel, I need to talk to you," he calls after me.

But I ignore him. I climb into my truck, slam the door, shaking from cold.

"What's happening?" Quinn says, wide-eyed. She's tucked under my jacket and this gives me an indescribable spurt of relief.

"What did the police say? What does Trey want?"

I put the key in the ignition and quickly start the engine. In my peripheral vision I see Trey approaching my door. I ram the truck into gear and hit the gas, leaving him standing in a red glow as my brake lights flare briefly before I turn into the road. I glance up into my rearview mirror. He stands on the curb, watching me go.

I force out a huge lungful of air. "I didn't tell the cops anything about that man. I just asked what happened, and if there'd be charges." I cast another glance up into my mirror. The street behind is empty. "That was Missy Sedgefield and her mother Stacey in Trey's SUV. It appears you punched the daughter of Trey's new girlfriend." I probably shouldn't mention this to Quinn, but I just need a bond right now. I need her to know we're a team against the world, that we can confide in each other.

Quinn studies me for several long beats. "Trey is going out with *Missy's mother*?"

I pull a wry mouth. Inside I hurt. I tighten my hands on the wheel.

"Missy Sedgefield is a cow," she says.

I smile in spite of myself. "Yeah, well, I never got on with her mother, either."

"You knew Stacey Sedgefield from school?"

I shoot her a glance. "Yep. And I confess, I also wanted to punch her a few times back then."

Quinn stares at me in silence, and I can feel the whisperings of a bond. Spider thread and gossamer thin. But it's there. I want to ask again what Missy said to her, but I'm nervous about breaking this new connection. I want to build on it a bit first.

I crank up the heat and turn north on the highway. Quinn settles back into her seat, a strange and uneasy truce between us now. It's been a rough day. I shoot another glance into the rearview mirror, but see nothing strange. I allow myself to breathe.

———

Jeb watched Rachel go. Adam LeFleur was also watching her from his office window. And Jeb had seen Trey Somerland approach her truck.

He swore softly to himself. He wanted to know what she'd told the cops. He needed to ensure that she kept the secret of Quinn's paternity until he was cleared. He was worried it might already be out of the bag now.

Engine a low growl, he pulled slowly back into the street. But he didn't follow Rachel. He knew where she lived, thanks to Quinn. He'd go round later, when all was quiet and Quinn was asleep.

He'd forced his own damn hand by going to that school today. How Rachel was now going to react at the sight of him on her doorstep was anyone's guess.

Nerves, anticipation, remorse, things he couldn't define skittered through him.

CHAPTER 7

As we enter the more isolated northern reaches of Snowy Creek where there are no streetlights, the forest pushes in thick and dark on all sides. Aurora borealis undulates over the sky, giving the glaciers a ghostly glow. I steal yet another glance up into my rearview mirror, making sure the road is clear.

No one in sight.

I turn off the highway onto the densely treed peninsula that juts out into the lake where we live. There are only three properties on this peninsula. Mine and the houses of two absentee neighbors who are here only during the winter months. A familiar depression sinks over me as I take my old truck down my rutted driveway. Twigs scrape against the doors, reminding me of the pruning I haven't done, of all the other things I still need to fix. Jobs that Trey and I had planned to tackle as a team. Rebuild. Landscape. Renovate the boathouse on the water so we could rent it out for extra income. As we approach the house, I notice the bulb in the porch light has blown. The place is in blackness.

I curse softly as my headlights illuminate the wooden gate to the small courtyard off my kitchen where I store recycling. The gate hangs on its hinges, banging in the wind. A mess of scattered tins roll on the concrete in front of the kitchen door.

I'd thoroughly washed those tins before putting them into my recycling container outside. But the bears are growing desperate as they scavenge for anything they can to help them reach hibernation weight. I need to clear this mess up. My first priority, however, is getting some warm food into Quinn before running her a bath. Keeping her routine as best as I can. Finding a way to talk further about what happened today.

I reach into my glove compartment for my headlamp.

"Wait here a second while I check that the bear's gone," I say as I get out of the vehicle. But Quinn doesn't listen. She clambers out of the truck, slams the door, and stomps over to the front entrance, clutching both my jacket and her backpack. I take hope from the fact she's still holding on to something of mine. She punches in the key code and lets herself in, banging the door closed behind her.

I stand in the dark, alone. Inhaling deeply, I scan the yard with my flashlight. At the same time I kick cans and make as much noise as I can to ensure the bear stays away. When I'm certain it's gone, I gather up the tins and bag them. But hair prickles softly up the back of my neck as I detect a sound under the rush of wind. I freeze. Listening intently. But I don't hear it again. Yet, once again, I sense something watching me from the darkness. Fear, visceral, curls into me.

Quickly, I grab the last tin and go inside with the garbage bag, locking the door behind me. I lean my back against the door for a moment, closing my eyes, gathering myself. My heart is racing.

It was probably the bear. I'm just being paranoid. But as I remove my dust-caked boots and pad on stockinged feet into the kitchen, that sense of unease, foreboding, lingers.

Trixie thumps her tail when she sees me, but the old girl doesn't get up from her basket the way she used to. She's comfy where she is. She trusts the food will come. There's no sign of Quinn in the kitchen. Nor in the open-plan living area on the other side of the counter.

"Quinn?" I flick on more lights and turn up the heat. As light floods the downstairs area, Quinn is nowhere in sight.

"Quinnie?" I call as I climb the stairs. I try her bedroom door. Locked. My heart sinks. I rap softly on the door. "Quinn, are you coming for some supper?"

"Not hungry," comes the muffled voice from inside. She's been crying.

"You need to eat something—"

"I said I'm not hungry. Go away."

I close my eyes. "Quinn, we should talk."

Silence.

I stand there, lost. This is exactly the kind of dilemma I would have called my sister with. We might not have spent much time together these past few years, but whenever I needed help, Sophia was there for me at the other end of the phone, and then some. The punch of loss is so acute it takes my breath away. My mother died when I was eight, Quinn's age. So I understand, perhaps, a tiny bit of Quinn's pain. Sophia, eleven years older than me, stepped into a mothering role. I wish Quinn would allow me to do the same for her. I fight back tears. I'm tired, that's all. I'll feel stronger about it all in the morning. I'll have a better plan. We'll go on that trip.

I take a scalding hot shower and wash the dirt and the day from my hair, but I still can't seem to shake the chill in my bones. I apply disinfectant cream and a plaster to the small cut on my brow, and dry my hair. Dressed in soft sweats and a down vest, I head downstairs in my socks. Once Trixie has been fed, I make for the fireplace.

Getting down onto my knees, I ball up old newspaper and stack kindling, then logs. I light the fire, and as I watch the flames crackle and whisper to life, I think of the logs that Trey and I chopped and stacked in the spring before going to Bali. I wonder how it all went so wrong so fast. Quinn's arrival was a catalyst, for sure, but there were deeper issues at play. His words sift into my mind.

You know, I always thought you might actually still have a thing for him, that you couldn't let him go . . .

I get up and pace the living room, wishing I'd bought blinds for the floor-to-ceiling windows that look down over the dark garden to the boathouse and lake beyond. The moon is rising. Whitecaps on the black surface are ghostly in the lunar light. Tonight the leaves from my birch are all gone, branches poking up into the sky like the gnarled fingers of an old man.

I rub my arms and I think of soup. But I'm not hungry, either. Instead I pour whiskey from a bottle of oak-aged scotch that Trey left behind. I take my drink and my laptop to my grandfather's old armchair by the fire.

As I sip the scotch, I search Google for newspaper articles and commentaries on Jeb's trial and recent release. Clicking on a *Vancouver Sun* feature from three days ago, I read again an overview of the original court case and the Innocence Project's fight to overturn his conviction. According to the article, the UBC Innocence Project lawyers argued that Jeb's own defense counsel in the initial trial had been aware of, but not presented, evidence that there was DNA from another male on the bloodied hoodie found in the back of Jeb's car. The hoodie that contained the empty date-rape drug pack. The hoodie had also been logged into evidence later than the rest of the contents found in Jeb's car. Police claimed this was technical error, and that the presence of other DNA did not clear Jeb. But based on this the judge threw out Jeb's conviction, saying that had this evidence been presented by the defense counsel in the initial trial, it would have raised reasonable doubt.

The judge did not rule, however, that Jeb was innocent.

The result, claimed one newspaper columnist, was a violent man being set free. Another columnist argued that the police, the prosecutors, and the defense lawyers had all developed tunnel vision in an "overzealous" attempt to secure a conviction for a man they all believed was guilty of a heinous crime in a small community. In doing so, they'd shot themselves in the foot because a guilty man now walked free because of it.

Jeb himself refused any interviews.

I click on a photo and Jeb's face fills my screen. Simmering, dark, sensual. A young Jeb. The way I knew and loved him. His father's smiling Irish eyes, wickedly sensual at times, and at others, so full of deep mystery. One look from those eyes used to melt my stomach, give my skin tingles. I sip my drink and feel warmth spread through my chest—even now his eyes still do it for me, just in this photo. God, what am I going to do with myself? How am I going to rid myself of these twisted, conflicted memories? These feelings? It's not easy to describe the depth of what I once felt for Jeb. I don't think many people can understand what we had.

When he first came to Snowy Creek Elementary, I was fascinated with him. He seemed apart from everyone else, mysterious. Special. He appealed to something in my imagination. He disappeared later that year, when his father died, but he returned to school the following spring. We became friends, kicking a ball on the bottom fields during lunch. Gradually he began to show me my own world through new eyes. It was the first time, I think, that I realized there were people in this world, like the First Nations community in the valley over, who thought and lived in a different way. It became an adventure, exciting. I started to meet him outside school, and while my girlfriends were hanging out in the village and shopping and going to movies, he and I went on adventures in the woods. He set the tomboy in me free. We played. We discovered. He allowed me to remain a kid inside my heart far longer than my peers. And slowly we grew into our respective sexuality. It was a thrilling sensation, to touch him, have him touch me. Jeb quite simply became part of me. Of who I was.

And then he told me his deepest, darkest secret. He told me why he had disappeared that first winter.

It was the ultimate confession. The ultimate bond of trust. And I betrayed that trust. In the trial. I used his deepest, most personal secret to help send him away. Guilt whispers through me.

I click on another photo, this one taken outside the courthouse near the start of the first trial just over eight years ago. In this image the angle of the sun accentuates Jeb's dusky skin, the flare of his cheekbones. His long black hair gleams. I can see his tattoo—the angry, masculine mouth of a coho swimming up his neck. Jeb told me once that the coho salmon possessed three traits he valued most: courage, tenacity, and a ferocity of purpose at the end game.

I wonder, now, about his own end game.

Gently, I brush the screen with my fingertips, touching his face. Familiar feelings of hurt and affection mushroom inside me. With them come the anger, hatred, and bitterness of betrayal, and it all swims like an oily cocktail in my gut. This man raped and left my schoolmate for dead. Quinn's mother, Amy. Another schoolmate is still missing, presumed murdered. The judge has not said he was innocent of this. There is still no one else the police are looking at for the crime. That's because the cops still believe he did it. It's because there's no one else they even suspect. Everything still points to Jeb.

I curse and swallow the rest of the whiskey before sloshing another two fingers of the amber liquid into my glass.

Here's to you, Trey. Here's to you, Jeb . . . here's to some seriously messed-up past.

I take another swig and scroll quickly through several more newspaper articles, stopping suddenly as a photo snares my attention. I click on it and the enlarged image floods my screen.

It's a group sitting at a picnic table outside the courthouse during the hearings to have Jeb's conviction overturned. They're having lunch. A sunny day. At the table are legal counsel for the Innocence Project, an older Asian woman—the retired tech from the police lab who testified in Jeb's favor about the DNA—plus a blonde woman I recognize instantly as Piper Smith. It was Piper's true crime docudrama that brought to light the errors in the police evidence log and the existence of additional DNA on the hoodie. Piper was the first to get the lab tech to talk. But it's another face in the group that has my heart beating suddenly.

Sophia's face.

My sister is sharing lunch and laughing with this group. This does not look like an adversarial relationship. My pulse quickens. I carefully set my whiskey glass on the side table and check the date the story was filed. Seven months ago. A month before she died.

Sophia attended those hearings to free Jeb? How could she be so apparently intimate with this group fighting for the overturning of his conviction? Surely it would have been the opposite, especially given Sophia's knowledge that Jeb was her own daughter's birth father. Wouldn't Sophia and Peter have been fighting their damnedest to see he *stayed* behind bars?

Frowning, I scroll farther. I find another photo of Sophia and one of the Innocence Project lawyers conversing on a bench outside the courtroom during a recess. There's an intimacy in the way their heads are bent close.

I sit back, a strange sensation settling into me.

What were you doing at those hearings, Sophia? Why didn't you talk to me . . . ?

Guthrie's words curl through my mind. He said Sophia made an appointment to come in and update her will. But she died just before she could do it.

What changes, Sophia? Were they to do with Quinn?

The wind moans in the rock formations across the water, an eerie sound like howling wolves that always gives me a shiver. I reach for my glass and take another sip of Trey's very fine, very expensive, cask-aged scotch, and exhaustion falls like a blanket over me. I shut down my laptop. Tomorrow I'll look up flights, book something, call in to work. I'll ask Cass, my editor, and Marjorie, my sales manager, to jointly manage their respective sides of the business for a week. I'll explain that I have an emergency and need to get out of town. If they lose the prospective advertising accounts in the process, I'll deal with the fallout later.

It's going to be fine.

By the time Quinn and I return, Jeb might have left town, or Adam might have taken him in. I rest my head back against my granddad's chair, letting the comfortable old arms enfold me, enjoying a few more moments of the warm fire and the sound of crackling logs, before heading up to bed.

———

Something starts me awake.

My eyes flare open. I listen, hands tense on the armrests.

I must have fallen asleep in the armchair. My head feels thick from the scotch. The fire has died to pulsing embers, and cold seeps in from corners of the room. Outside, the wind has increased, shifted direction, and is now wailing like banshees through the rocks on the other side of the lake. Was that the sound that woke me?

I don't think so.

Tiny fingers of fear touch my skin. Quickly, I gather the fleece blanket from the back of the chair around my shoulders and pad up the stairs. I listen at Quinn's door. All quiet. Just the howling of wind in the rocks.

Yet the chill deepens through me.

I try the door. It opens. Quinn is sleeping in a puddle of silver moonlight, her dark hair tangled over her white pillow. Tiptoeing in, I draw the duvet up gently around my niece's shoulders. I stand for a moment, watching the rhythmic rise and fall of her chest, listening to her soft breaths. My chest squeezes. She's stubborn, like her father, erecting walls of anger around her sensitivity for her own protection. The thought startles me, and I wonder if it will cease one day, or if I will forever be reminded of Jeb, of the past, when I look at Quinn.

Bending down, I place a soft kiss on her hair. Her scent reminds me of kittens. Hay. Sunshine. This child *is* different from her dad. I *will* forget. It'll all fade, eventually. I just need to give it time.

The fact Quinn is sleeping peacefully, that she's unlocked the door, brings a measure of peace to me. One day, one baby step at a time . . .

But as I exit the bedroom, gently drawing the door closed behind me, a clatter sounds outside in the yard. Trixie begins to yip downstairs. Adrenaline sparks through my body.

I rush down to the kitchen window, peer out into the night. All I can see are the swishing skirts of conifers, dark shadows interplaying with the silver moonlight over grass. I watch for a while, trying to discern other movements, hoping to see the hulking black shape of a lumbering bruin. Because then I'll feel safe. I'll know it was nothing to worry about. I go to the other window, from where I can see the boathouse. Waves are lapping against the dock, which is rocking and swaying against its moorings. An old canoe is tethered to a rack on the wall of the boathouse, and a piece of rope is whipping against the siding in the wind. A flying pine cone suddenly smashes against the windowpane, right near my face. I gasp and jump back, my heart slamming into my throat. Then I give a soft laugh.

That's all it is. The wind hurling things around—branches, cones. Something must have landed on the metal roofing.

I glance at the clock. Ten p.m. Still time for a decent night's sleep. But as I head for the stairs, a gentle rapping sounds at the door. I freeze. It's not cones or branches, or wind.

It's him.

He's come.

I know it—instinctively. Fear grips my throat. For a moment I'm unable to move, to breathe.

Again, the rapping sounds, a little louder, more insistent. Trixie whines and starts barking loudly. I shoot a glance up to Quinn's door on the upstairs landing, and panic slices through me. I can't let Quinn wake, or find out he's here. Fighting fear, I rush toward the front door and flick on the outside light. Then I remember the bulb has blown. I peer through the peephole. My heart stalls.

Jeb.

In the silvery moonlight, all shadow and darkness.

I begin to shake deep down inside my belly.

He bangs just a little louder. "Rachel!" he calls. "I need to talk."

Trixie barks wildly.

I'm frozen with terror, indecision. And something else, darker, trickier, a primal kind of mouth-drying thrill I can't even begin to articulate. Oh God. I drag my hand over my hair. I should call the cops. Adam will put him away for trespassing or something.

Except he's not trespassing. He's a free man knocking on a door.

Images from the news stories race through my mind. Sophia's face in the pictures. Her smile, her intimacy with the Innocence Project lawyers—what am I missing?

"Rachel! Please. It's important."

I swallow, grab my cell phone off the table, slip it into my sweater pocket. Holding Trixie by the collar, I unlock the front door, opening it just a small crack.

But Trixie escapes my grasp and barrels through the crack, slamming the door open wide as she jumps up on Jeb with soft whines and body wiggles. I stare, dumbfounded. The dog remembers him. The old girl is acting like a pup again. Goose bumps chase down my arms.

Jeb's gaze locks with mine as he reaches down to ruffle the dog's fur, and my mind crumples in on itself, time warping, overlapping. Stretching.

He stands there like a ghost conjured out of my memory. Dark, tall, devastatingly, dangerously good-looking. Dressed in black jeans, black biker boots, a white T-shirt under his leather jacket. And he's petting my dog as if it's a decade ago. After all these years. Out of prison, here at my door. A dull roar starts in my brain. My knees turn to water. I reach for the doorjamb.

"Jeb," I whisper, my voice coming out hoarse.

He steps forward and I brace myself, yet I'm unable to back away. I'm trapped, a mouse in the serpent's gaze. His features catch the light from the hallway behind me. His jaw is tight and shadowed and strong, his features a little too gaunt, his raven-black hair a little too long. Wild. Everything about him is untamed. The brackets around his mouth have deepened. He seems taller somehow. The years in prison have done nothing to diminish his quietly crackling presence. In fact, it's more powerful, a kinetic energy I can feel on my skin. It raises my hairs with its electricity, as if drawing me toward him on a cellular level.

It's been eight years since I last laid eyes on him in that courtroom. Nine since I've been near him. Spoken to him. Touched him. Kissed him.

"I think she remembers me," he says, giving Trixie another ruffle. The dog settles at his boots with a happy whimper. Memories swirl. Trixie as a pup, following Jeb and me over the grass. Swimming in the river. Jeb showing me how to teach Trixie to track through a dewy field early one morning. The three of us lying on a rug under soft sunshine, watching summer snow floating against an achingly blue sky. An endless sky. Like our dreams had been. Our future.

The horrifying opening image from Piper's docudrama suddenly swallows the memories: Amy dazed and beaten and half-naked on the railway tracks.

I shake myself back to reality, slide my hand into my pocket, curl my hand tightly around my phone. "What do you want?" I say. "Why did you follow my niece at school? Is it revenge that you've come back for—to punish us all?"

Something flares hard and sharp through his features. He regards me, gaze unwavering, intense, his carotid pulsing fast and steady beneath his tattoo, making it seem alive in the tricks of moonlight and shadow. I've made him angry, and it makes me scared. I've been shown what he is capable of.

The wind howls again, and it rushes through the pine forest branches around us with the sound of an ocean.

"The last thing I want is to hurt you, Rachel." His voice is deep, thick. I detect hurt.

I swallow. "Then what are you here for?" What does one say, how does one bridge the years of silence, the accusations, the bitterness, the goddamn hurt? The unspeakable loss, the hollowness, the betrayal, the rage? It all hangs like a sudden gaping black maw of a wound, nerve endings exposed to the wind.

"Is Quinn asleep?" he says quietly.

My mind scrambles in on itself. "What?"

"I want to know if she's sleeping." He looks over my shoulder into my house. "Where is she?"

I lunge forward and grab Trixie's collar. I drag her away from him, into the hall. I shut her inside and I stand in front of the closed door in my socks, the paving ice-cold under my feet. I take my phone out my pocket, hit nine, then one. My thumb is poised over the keypad. "You've got exactly one minute to tell me what you want, then get the hell out of here before I call the cops."

He raises his palms. "Take it easy." His eyes flick between the phone, me, and the door. "I just want to talk to you, okay? About Quinn, but I don't want her to know I'm here."

Confusion rattles through me.

He has the markers of a sociopath . . . he's a smooth and accomplished liar . . .

He comes closer. Too close. I step back but my body butts up against the hardness of the door. I've trapped myself. I'm all alone out here. I don't know what he wants. My thumb goes for the last one of a 9-1-1 emergency call.

But before I can press down, he jerks forward and snatches my wrist in a grip so tight my fingers go numb and I drop the phone. It clatters to the cold paving at my feet. I stare at the phone on the ground, heart beating like a drum. Slowly I raise my eyes.

His fingers are a vise around my wrist. His skin burns mine. His eyes laser me. His face, his lips, are close. So close. His scent so damn familiar. A muscle memory of desire, savage and raw, slices through my fear. I start to shake.

"And you'll tell the cops what?" he says quietly, eyes still burning into me. "That I came to see my daughter?"

My stomach turns to water. I stare at him, speechless, brain spinning.

"I know, Rachel. I know she's mine."

"How?" I manage to croak out. "How can you know?"

"Sophia," he says quietly, releasing my arm. He picks up my phone, hands it back to me. "Your sister was helping me. She was the one who first approached the Innocence Project. She and Peter helped pay for the lawyers."

My knees give out and I slump back against the door.

A pinecone bombs onto the metal roof of the carport as another sharp gust rushes through the conifers, shadows moving, dizzying. Swirling me down into some dark and confusing place.

"Sophia *told* you?" I whisper. "When? Why?"

He watches me in silence for several beats. "I'm sorry. I thought you might have known she was working with me. She's believed in my innocence for at least five years now. I thought . . ." He pauses. "I thought she might have told you."

I feel sick. I can't think. "So that's why you've come? For Quinn?"

He glances away, as if deciding what to tell me.

"No," he says, finally. And I feel it's a lie. I feel like he means to say, "Not yet." Nausea rides up into my throat.

"But it's why I had to speak to you tonight. I made a mistake going by the school today. I hadn't intended to involve Quinn, or you. Not yet."

Yet.

"But then there was the fight. I saw you go to the cops. I need to know what you've told them, because I need this kept secret." He's quiet for another beat. "For Quinn," he says. "For my daughter. And it's my promise to Sophia and Peter."

I slide my back down the length of the door and sit on the cold step, seized by a sensation that perhaps he doesn't exist. Maybe I've dreamed this up, it isn't happening. Maybe I'm still asleep in the armchair by the fire.

Jeb crouches slowly down in front of me. He places his hand on my knee, ever so gently. It's warm. Solid.

"God," he whispers. "You look so good." His eyes sparkle with moisture in the moonlight. "It's been so long." His features are hungry, devouring me. His body gaunt. Strong. He's still as wild as these mountains and forests. And the things in them.

Everything that drew me to Jeb in the first place, that feral magnetism, something unchained. His poetry, his deep passion for these mountains, this land. His courage, tenacity, the way he always moved to the beat of his own drum. It draws me now—my heart, my body, at war with my mind. My vision blurs and I'm overcome with a desire to lean into him, be held by him, have him make all the years and tragedy just go away.

But then I think of Quinn. Sophia.

"I . . . I don't understand."

"I'm innocent, Rachel. I've come home to prove it. And when I do, I want access to my daughter. I want to tell her the truth."

CHAPTER 8

Rachel's complexion looked ashen in the moonlight, pain, fear, brightening her eyes. But Jeb saw something else too, dark and shimmering, as he crouched in front of her. He could also feel it, an electricity crackling between them, something that told him it hadn't died. An atavistic part of Rachel still gravitated to his pull, and he to hers. It excited something deep and secret and carnal in him. And it worried him. He'd come to tell her why he was back and what he needed for Quinn's sake, then he planned to step away from them. Something told him this was going to be far more complicated.

"I don't believe you. How can I believe Sophia was helping you? How can you be innocent when Amy gave birth to your child . . . Amy was brutally raped . . ." Wind blew strands of dark hair across her face. Jeb fought the urge to move the strands away, to tuck them behind her ear. To ask her about the small bandage above her eye.

"Rachel," he said softly. "It was consensual with Amy. It happened before she was taken and hurt. I never denied that I slept with her."

His words seemed to crash into her like a physical punch. She blinked sharply, pain tearing afresh over her beautiful face.

"I was set up by those four guys. Luke, Levi, Clint, Zink—for some reason they all lied about me driving north. But I didn't lie in court. Not once. And the last thing in my life I wanted was to cause you pain. If there's one thing I'm guilty of, it's that. And I am so, so sorry."

She drew her knees in close, hugged them tightly to her chest. She was shivering and her eyes were big, dark holes. Her lips . . . he wanted to feel those lips against his. He ached for her suddenly with every molecule of his being. Being so close again, touching her . . . he thought he'd plumbed the depths of all kinds of new emotions when he had first seen and touched Quinn. His daughter. But this was different. Raw. All-consuming. Overriding. He was almost afraid of the ferocity of his desire and love for this woman. Jeb knew that what he felt for Rachel was something he'd probably built out of all proportion during the long, lonely years in prison. He hadn't had the occasion to even meet anyone new, someone who might displace his obsession. All he'd had was the memory of what they had once shared, and he'd dwelled on this. It had become a psychological coping tool.

But this was reality now. This was the present. She'd lived a whole life in those nine years. He had to get—and keep—things in perspective. He had to deliver his message, then stay well clear of both Rachel and Quinn until he'd proved his innocence.

"It was a stupid mistake," he said. "A hotheaded, hormonal, teenage, knee-jerk reaction to our fight, after you said it was all over between us. I didn't believe you meant it. I thought you'd sober up, get over it. Then I saw you the next night in Trey's arms at the bonfire, him kissing you, his hand up your sweater." He watched her.

She swallowed.

"Do you remember," he said quietly, "what our fight was about?"

She glanced up at the stars, as if the night sky might yield answers, offer escape, as if gravity might somehow stem the emotion he could see glittering in her eyes. Those deep-brown eyes so full of hurt he'd put there.

"You wanted to make love. Have sex for the first time. I . . ." Emotion grabbed him. "God, I loved you so much. You were so drunk. I was desperate to have you, but I wanted us to wait. I wanted it to be special, because . . . because you were everything to me. I wanted you in my life forever." He swallowed against the thickness building in his throat. "I had plans to marry you, Rach. I wanted us to have a family, a proper one. I wanted a chance to be a good father. "

Like my own father never was . . .

"You were leaving for Europe to train for the Olympics, and I was so afraid you'd be gone to me forever if we didn't sort things out before you left. I came to find you at the gravel pit that night. I knew what drugs would be there. I knew what every guy there wanted. I came to take you home, to keep you safe . . . and there you were, on a blanket with Trey Somerland. Do you remember what he said to me that night?"

She met his gaze, her pulse fluttering at her neck.

"Trey called me a halfbreed and you laughed. You broke me in two that night."

She cast her eyes down. Wind ruffled her long hair. "I was drunk," she said softly.

"I know. That's why I came to take you home."

A shudder wracked her body. "The prosecutors said you went on a rampage because of me, that you also started getting wasted." She said the words so quietly he could barely hear. Jeb leaned closer, touched her knee again. She didn't pull away, didn't flinch. He could detect her scent. Fresh soap. Shampoo. Alcohol. His gut tightened.

She looked up, right into his eyes. "They said you turned violent because of the drinking, because you weren't used to it, and that you took Amy and Merilee to hurt them because you really wanted to hurt me. I saw them get into your car, Jeb. I *saw* you leave the pit with them."

"I'd already had consensual sex with Amy by then," he said, very quietly. "I was taking her home. She was out of it. We both were at that point. Merilee wanted a ride, too. But they both got out of my car at the Green River rail crossing. They'd seen some people across the clearing, and the girls ran over to them. I didn't see who they ran over to meet. I only discovered in court that it was Levi, Clint, Luke, and Zink. That's the first time I heard those four guys claim they all saw me going north on the highway with the girls.

"There isn't a day that goes by where I don't run through my memories of that night, Rachel, trying to see faces, trying to see exactly where those guys were sitting under those trees. But my brain was spinning at the time. I was fired up, drunk . . . I have gaps. But I *do* know I was being eaten up by what I'd just done with Amy. I was so consumed with self-recrimination I didn't even look back to see where the girls went after they got out of my car. I just drove straight home. I did *not* turn north with them in my car. Those four guys who said I did—Levi, Clint, Zink, Luke—they perjured themselves in court. I want to know why they lied for each other. Did one of them do it? All of them? Or are they protecting someone else? Whatever it is, I'm going to find out."

Her eyes narrowed as she searched his face, looking for a way to measure the truth of his words. Deciding how much to trust him. She was warring within herself. She opened her mouth.

But before she could speak, Jeb raised two fingers, almost touching her lips.

"I know," he whispered. "The evidence all told another story. I'm not going to try and convince you right here, tonight, after all these years, that the prosecution's story was a lie. That I was set up." He paused. "I'm going to *show* you. I'm going to show all of them. *That's* the reason I'm back. To prove my innocence, to find out who did this. To find Merilee's body. And to see that justice—real justice—is finally done. It's not revenge I want, but restitution. I have a right to that. To my daughter. To my home."

He watched her face, the myriad of emotions chasing through her features. Believing him now would mean tipping everything else onto its head, ripping apart beliefs she'd held for almost a decade.

"If you didn't do it . . ." Her words faded.

"I know; it's hard to swallow. If you believe in my innocence, you must believe someone else attacked Amy and Merilee and left them to die. Maybe even a person you consider a friend. It means there's been a conspiracy of silence for almost a decade to protect that guilty party. It means someone in this town knows where Merilee's body is, someone who could give closure to the Zukanov family, someone who was prepared to let an innocent man rot in max security for something he didn't do."

Rachel's gaze jerked suddenly up toward the second-story windows of her house, and Jeb detected a stiffening in her posture.

"Yes," he said, reading her thought process. "Once I've done this, I do want access to my daughter."

"Jeb—"

"It was Sophia's and Peter's promise to me, and mine to them. That when I proved my innocence without a doubt, they'd welcome me into their lives. They'd grant me access to Quinn. It was why Sophia started working with me after she began to believe I might be innocent, after she'd met Piper Smith. That docudrama, it all started there, five years ago, things coming out. Sophia knew she'd have to tell Quinn one day about her adoption, and that Quinn would ask about her birth parents. Or perhaps even go searching herself. Sophia didn't want Quinn for one moment to believe she'd been conceived in violence, that the blood of a killer and brutal rapist ran through her veins. Once this was over, Sophia planned to let Quinn know I was her birth father, and we'd all work through it together."

She just stared.

Jeb reached down and picked up the fleece blanket she'd dropped at her feet. Moving carefully, he draped it around her shoulders, bringing his face close to hers as he did. Again he detected the scent of alcohol. He wondered how often she drank. Alone? He thought of his father, of things gone wrong. And his sense of purpose fused into a hard, burning coal in his gut. He was going to put this right.

"Amy would have been a part of it, too," he said. "If she'd wanted, and been ready." He hesitated, not wanting to say too much yet about Amy's death.

"You're asking me to believe that Amy and you and Sophia and Peter were going to have one big, happy open adoption? Amy, who believed you raped her and killed her best friend?"

"Amy *knew* there was something locked in her memory. It was starting to come out. She was beginning to fear she might have helped put an innocent man away. It started to happen after Piper interviewed her, after the *True Crime* documentary . . ." He hesitated again, worried about saying too much, too quickly. "Sophia began to believe that Amy did actually form memories that night, that she was lucid despite the drugs, but that she'd blocked them in a form of posttraumatic retrograde amnesia. Sophia was trying a new hypnosis technique to help Amy access those memories. She even tried the technique with me."

Something tightened in Rachel; he could see it—walls going up. She clutched the blanket tightly across her chest, anger seeping into her features.

"Everyone was part of this? Except me? *I'm* kept out of this? Yet I'm the one left with Quinn?" She glared at him. "Why should I believe you? There's just your word. Everyone else is gone now. Sophia, Peter, Amy . . . they're all dead." Bitterness spiked her words. "Not one of them can verify a damn thing you're saying!"

Urgency bit through Jeb. The last thing he wanted was for her to shut down. Quickly, he took the wallet-sized photo album from his pocket. He opened the cover, held it toward the light spilling out from the kitchen window.

"Here, see," he said quietly.

Rachel bent over, her hair brushing his hand as she did. One by one Jeb slowly turned the pages of a young life: Quinn as a newborn baby; Sophia holding her; Quinn's first birthday, face awash with chocolate cake; Quinn without her front teeth; Quinn the day she turned seven.

Rachel's hand went to her mouth as her shoulders sagged. She gave a single sharp inhalation. "Sophia . . . brought you these, in prison?"

He nodded.

"She never told me," she repeated. "She never breathed a goddamn word."

"She didn't want to cause you pain. She was fighting to free a man you helped put in jail. A man you felt betrayed you in the worst possible way. She didn't want to butt heads with you over this and have you thinking she was betraying you, too. She wanted to be sure first."

"Fuck Sophia!" she said suddenly, scrabbling to her feet against the door. "Damn her to hell! She couldn't tell me all this . . . all this stuff. Yet she made me guardian in her will, letting me find out the truth in the most shocking way possible—through adoption papers—that you're the father. I was good enough for *that*? But not to be a part of all the rest?"

He grasped her by the shoulders, and she went stock-still.

"She didn't expect to die, Rachel, before she could finish what she and Peter started."

"Get your hands off me," she hissed. "Just back away. Get the hell off my property." She was vibrating, fire crackling through her veins. Distance, she needed space to try and absorb this. He was messing with her head.

"Listen to me—"

"You think you can just walk in here, tell me there's been some conspiracy for the last nine years? That group of guys you say perjured themselves—they're upstanding members of this community. Clint is the fire chief now. Levi is manager of Bear Mountain operations. Zink owns the Shady Lady Saloon. And while Luke might be gone, Adam is now second-in-command of the SCPD. They're fathers, husbands, brothers. *Good* people. Those guys *are* Snowy Creek."

He drew in a long, slow breath. "It's easier, isn't it, to place the blame on the 'other,' the outsider. To attack the loner." He paused. "Like those girls attacked Quinn today."

She glowered at him, but he saw something shifting through her eyes.

"Sometimes," he said, "in a small town like this, a community knows that a contract to forget can be as powerful as a promise to remember. Sometimes the secrets are lying right there, in plain sight, but everyone chooses to turn away, pretend it never happened, because then they won't have to question their own lives, their own children, their own husbands and brothers. They won't have to look across the dining room table and see a monster looking back." He paused. "History becomes something agreed upon by mutual consent, and the guilt is anesthetized by silence."

She glanced away.

"Look, I've had a very long time to think about this. And I'm not asking you for anything other than to keep Quinn out of it all, to keep the secret of her identity until I can finish this." He hesitated, then said. "What did you tell Adam, the cops?"

She remained silent.

"You told them I'm back?"

Her eyes flared to his. "No. I didn't."

"Why?"

She swallowed. "I . . . I don't know why. I should have."

She hadn't exposed him.

That smoldering coal in his belly ignited sharp and sudden, starting a hot burn of dangerous hope, of desire. A burn Jeb knew he wasn't going to be able to extinguish now.

"I saw Trey approach you," he said quietly. "Outside the police station. What did he want?"

"The whole town knows you're out of prison, Jeb. It's been in the news. They thought you wouldn't dare return. But after today, the incident at the school . . . I think Adam believes you're already here, in Snowy Creek. So does Trey."

"I forced my own hand. It was my mistake. I plan to keep away now, but it's why I had to come tonight, to let you know not to be afraid. And to make sure no one knows I'm her birth father. As long as no one knows that Quinn is connected to me, nothing can touch her."

Wind gusted, cold. Straight off the glacial lake.

"They'll annihilate you. They'll skin you alive. This whole community is your enemy. Do you even know what you're up against?"

"I've had almost a decade to think about what I'm up against." He paused. "I have nothing else but this. I have a right to come home. To prove I belong. I have a right to find out why those guys lied for each other, who they are protecting."

She stared at him, the gravity of the situation sinking in.

"I'm taking Quinn away tomorrow," she said. "Away from town for the Thanksgiving break."

"Good. This is good. I don't want either of you involved in this."

"You can't hide for long."

"I don't plan to hide. I plan to rattle cages. I plan to shake something loose."

A light went on upstairs, flooding out into the dark. Her gaze shot up to the lighted window. Panic whipped through her eyes. "You better go, now. Please."

He took something from his pocket. "Here." He pressed a piece of paper into her hand. "My cell number."

"I don't want it."

"We want the same things, Rachel. We want to keep Quinn safe." He leaned forward, and so fast she didn't have time to blink, he brushed his lips softly over the side of her cheek. Her hand went to her cheek and their eyes held, just a moment.

Then he spun round and made for his bike.

———

I watch him go, long, powerful strides, boots crunching over my gravel driveway as he makes his way to where his bike gleams in black shadow. He's caught a thread in my heart and he's pulling it away with him, unraveling the fabric of my life, undoing my mind, spooling out the years between past and present.

He straddles his bike.

"How?" I yell after him into the wind. "How in the hell do you think you're going to do this on your own?" He reaches for the ignition.

"Publicity," he calls back. "Under a bright media spotlight so they all know why I'm back. I want everyone to start watching everyone else's reactions. I want them second guessing each other. That's where the cracks will happen. That's where the light will get in. I'm going to the paper—I have an interview with the *Leader* editor tomorrow. I set it up yesterday."

I'm momentarily stunned.

He kicks the stand back on his bike, fires his engine to a throaty growl.

"You can't—I won't let you do this. I *am* the paper!"

But the rumble of his engine and the rush of wind through pines drowns my words. He pulls out from under the trees and grumbles up the driveway. I hear the sound of his engine change as he reaches the highway and accelerates. He's going north. He's going home to Wolf River.

I run to the edge of the path in my socks and stare after him into the dark. Wind whips my hair and the blanket around me. Time stretches and I start to shudder—a deep, muscular seizure that has nothing to do with cold and everything to do with being moved from one world to another.

A band of yellow light suddenly knifes through the dark behind me.

"Rachel?"

I whirl round. *Quinn.* Standing in the doorway in her pajamas, backlit by the light in the hall. Trixie comes running out from behind her, sniffing the ground where Jeb stood.

"Is something wrong, Rachel?"

I hurry back to the house. "Oh, honey, no, everything's fine. Come, let's go back to bed." I call Trixie in, close and lock the door. The warmth inside doesn't even begin to touch the cold in me.

Quinn doesn't move. She's staring at me. Quickly I wipe my face. I must look a wreck. I'm still shaking. I can't hide this from her.

"Was it him?" she says. "Was he here?"

"Who, Quinn?"

"The man."

I crouch down, anxiety lacing through me. "No one was here."

"Don't lie to me! I heard voices. I heard his bike. Trixie woke me."

"Come, let's go back up to bed." I place my arm around her. She balks.

"What did he say?" she demands. "Why did he come? Did you chase him away?" Accusation glints in her eyes.

"Listen, you like him, I can see that. But why do you like him so much? He's a stranger. You don't even know him."

"My mother sent him."

"What?"

"From heaven, to protect me."

My jaw drops. "What makes you say that?"

Her eyes shine, and her lips start to wobble. "Because there are angels in heaven who come down when . . . when . . ." She sputters and tears fill her eyes.

Reciprocal emotion burns into my own eyes, the weight of it all pressing down heavily. "Oh, Quinnie, come here." I gather the small body of my niece into my arms and hold tight. I wrap the fleece blanket around both of us, a protective cloak, bonding us together. I put my face into her hair and drink in her scent, and I let my own tears fall. She senses my need. Her little arms wrap around my neck, tentatively at first. Then she squeezes so tight it steals my breath. We stay like that for several moments, blanket around us, cocooned against the world. The way I want to keep it. I will fight for this kid. And I am so worried now that Jeb will have more right to her than I.

"Aunt Rachel?" She mumbles into my neck.

Aunt, she called me *aunt*.

Quickly, I swipe the tears off my face with the hem of the blanket, and I sit back.

"You okay, Aunt Rachel?"

I nod fast, hug her close again. So tight. A feeling of love blossoming hot and soft through my chest. A powerful energy, an urge to protect. Is this what it feels to be a mother? This terrifyingly vulnerable yet powerful thing, this overriding desire to shelter and safeguard your child?

Irony strikes home harder than ever. Not my child. Jeb's child. Quinn and I are finally bonding and he's come to ask me to keep her safe. Keep their secret. Because then he wants to take her away.

And all I've been worrying about was him discovering the truth. My whole world has suddenly been tilted on its head.

"You want some of that soup now?" I manage to say. "Because I sure could use something warm."

Quinn nods.

She sits on a stool at the kitchen counter while I warm soup. We eat together. We're closer than we've been in six months. And now Jeb is threatening to tear it all apart.

———

Later that night I'm sitting in bed listening to the howl of the wind, wondering where Jeb is, what he's doing right now. Wondering how much I can believe him. The courts have cleared him, that much is fact. Does this negate the waiving of his paternal rights? Is it retroactive to the adoption decision? And if he wants to be in Quinn's life, where does it leave me? Do I have any legal recourse? Does he first need to go to court to assert his rights? My emotions, my feelings, my questions, scramble about in my chest and refuse to settle.

It feels like a lifetime ago that I was up on the mountain for the ribbon cutting this morning. Before the incident at school.

As long as no one knows I'm her father . . . nothing can touch her . . .

My thoughts turn to Trey outside the police detachment. Missy Sedgefield in the back of his vehicle. Stacey in the passenger seat.

Rachel . . . I heard about the incident at school . . . I need to talk to you . . .

Panic licks suddenly through me. Missy was the one Quinn punched. It had to have been Missy who told Quinn she was adopted. How did Missy know?

Trey? You didn't!

I lunge for the phone on my bedside table. My clock reads almost midnight. I don't care. I dial Trey's cell. A woman's voice, sleepy, answers.

Shock, hurt, anger. It ripples through me all over again, and for a moment I can't speak. Four months. I guess that's all it takes to scrub away a promise of marriage, plans for a lifetime of commitment together. I manage to clear my throat. "I'm looking for Trey."

"Who is this?" The voice sounds crisper suddenly.

"Is Trey there?"

A pause. "Hang on."

I hear shuffling. Bedding?

"Hello." His voice is thick, sleepy.

My heart begins to *whump*. I want to ask him why. How he could do this. What does he see in Stacey Sedgefield? Was I worth nothing to him?

"It's Rachel."

A pause. "Jesus." Another shuffle. He's getting out of bed?

"Do you know what time it is?" he whispers sharply. I imagine him moving down the passage. In my mind's eye I see his house, him going to his study, closing the door behind him. Then he says, "Are you okay? It was him at the school today, wasn't it? Missy described him to me. He was following Quinn. Did you tell Adam that he's returned?"

Tightness clamps around my chest.

"It wasn't him," I lie. "That's not why I'm calling. How does Missy know that Quinn is adopted? Did you tell her? Did you tell Stacey that Jeb was Quinn's father?"

"Jesus," he whispers. "I would never do that. We have a deal, a promise."

"Yes," I say quietly. "We also had a promise to get married. Now you have another woman sharing your bed, answering your personal cell phone. Has she moved in that fully already? How do I know what you've told *her*?"

Silence.

I curse silently for even letting the words out. I feel as if I'm on some kind of roller coaster, plunging down, down, down, g-forces building low in my stomach. And there's no way out but to go through it. I look out over the moonlit lake. "So, how did Missy and the other girls know she was adopted?"

"Everyone knows that much. It was never a secret that your sister and Peter adopted a baby. When you brought Quinn to Snowy Creek . . ." He hesitates. "Stacy and I were talking, about . . . you know, us, Quinn coming into our lives. Us breaking up. Missy must have overheard the adoption part."

"You told Stacey it was Quinn who broke us up?"

Several more beats of silence. When he speaks again, Trey sounds tired. Very tired. Sad. "Stacey asks, every now and then, why we broke up. She can't let it drop. She thinks I'm not over you."

I swallow.

"I explained to her that Quinn's arrival was just a catalyst. It was a lot of things that added up. You're the one who made it about Quinn." He heaves out a heavy sigh. "You want to know what I didn't tell Stacey? That it was you who couldn't follow through with the engagement. That you were using Quinn subconsciously as an excuse, a buffer, because you never got over Jeb, over his betrayal. And with Quinn in our house it was suddenly like Jeb's ghost living with us full time, haunting us in our own home."

My hand tightens on the phone, and I squeeze my eyes shut. It takes several beats before I can speak again with a level voice.

"What were you going to tell me outside the police station?"

"That I thought Jeb might be back in town. Like I said, Missy described the man who broke up the fight, and she told me that same man was following Quinn earlier. I wanted to tell you to be careful. If it is him, if he's back, we don't know what he wants. He might try to get at our kids, hitting us where it hurts most."

I think back to the night at the gravel pit. Trey was with me the whole time. He wasn't one of the four guys who allegedly perjured themselves about Jeb going north. He saw only what I saw—Merilee and Amy in Jeb's car, leaving the pit. He told the court the same things I did. I want—I *need*—to trust Trey.

"Whatever happens, Trey, please, you can never tell anyone who her biological father is. Even if Jeb is back, even if the shit hits the fan, Quinn cannot be a part of it. I can't let her get hurt. I owe it to her. I owe it to my sister's memory. You can't let an innocent child get screwed up for life because of what might happen now. Do you understand?"

"Of course I understand. I . . . I never wanted it to go wrong between us, you know." He pauses. "I tried. I really tried to make it work."

I suck in a deep breath, and I can't answer, because I know it's true.

"I'm going away with Quinn," I say. "For the Thanksgiving break. I'm leaving tomorrow if I can get a flight. I just . . . I wanted to hear that you hadn't—wouldn't—tell anyone, that we weren't going to come back to some hurtful revelation from schoolkids. Or worse."

"Look, I'm sorry about the incident with Missy today. God, I can't tell you how sorry I am. And if that was Jeb watching Quinn . . . it's good you're leaving for a while. And, Rachel." He pauses. "If he does come anywhere near you, call 9-1-1. We've got your back. All of us."

All of us.

Jeb's words circle through my mind.

Sometimes in a small town like this, a community knows that a contract to forget can be as powerful as a promise to remember. Sometimes the secrets are lying right there, in plain sight, but everyone chooses to turn away from them, pretend it never happened, because then they won't have to question their own lives, their own children, their own husbands and brothers . . .

"Thanks." I hang up. Nausea is slick and cold in my stomach. Jeb has succeeded. He's sown doubt in my mind. He's started rattling my cage.

———

Annie Pirello sat alone in her squad car, parked in deep shadow across the street from the Salonen house. Deputy Chief Constable LeFleur had assigned her to watch the house. LeFleur believed the man who'd come onto school property and followed Salonen's niece today was a violent sexual offender who'd been recently released from prison. A man who once used to date Salonen. LeFleur believed the man might try to approach Salonen or her niece again.

It looked as though the deputy chief was right; a man in leather, on a bike, had arrived at the Salonen house shortly after ten p.m.

Annie had called it in, but she'd been told to hold her position, just watch, wait for a possible 9-1-1 dispatch. But no emergency call had come. She'd gotten out of the car and crept closer. Through the trees she'd glimpsed Salonen and the dark-haired man talking, arguing. Touching. Talking some more.

There was unfinished business between those two. Something very intimate. He'd brought news that appeared to have shocked Salonen badly.

When he left, heading north on his bike, Annie had called it in again, but she'd been ordered not to follow. No laws had been broken. They had nothing on him. Yet.

The lights upstairs in the Salonen house went out around midnight; she could just glimpse the upstairs windows through the trees from the road. Annie reached forward, fired the ignition. Her headlights came on.

She drove back to the station to clock out for the end of her shift.

CHAPTER 9

As Jeb pulled onto the old property, ectoplasmic fingers of soft, green northern light reached across the sky, grasping, withdrawing, curling, taunting, in a silent music of the cosmos. In the trees it was dark, deserted, the cabins hulking shadows along the silvery river.

Jeb parked his bike in a grove near his mother's old log house. He removed his helmet and sucked the chill air down deep into his lungs. He could scent loam, pine resin, forest detritus, things you didn't smell behind concrete walls and barbed wire. This was now his land, left to him by his mother when she had died six years ago, five acres among towering cedars along the Wolf River. The homestead was isolated, surrounded by nothing but wilderness for miles. Endless forest and rivers and soaring mountains and plunging valleys stretched west—all the way to the Tilqua Ice Cap and beyond. To the east lay Snowy Creek. Ski town. Tourists. This was a place in the middle. Like Jeb himself, never belonging fully to the reserve over in the next valley, nor in the ski resort.

He'd been happiest, and saddest, here.

The house was set back near the logging road for ease of access. Farther down toward the river stood an old barn where they'd kept chickens. In summer he and his mother had planted a vegetable garden near the barn, fenced off from deer. Bears had been a problem, the occasional grizzly coming down from the high alpine and breaking into the chicken coop. Sometimes a cougar or coyotes would also try. Along the river were eight small cabins that Jeb had helped build for the river-rafting business his mother had started before he was incarcerated. Jeb had helped guide the first trips.

He got off his bike and dug a flashlight out of his pannier. Slowly he walked over to the old house, thoughts turning to his mother and the dreams she'd had for this place, for him.

One of his most profound regrets—and he had many—was that she'd died not knowing it was all a lie. She'd died thinking her son was a rapist and murderer.

Jeb ran his beam over the walls of the house. Shadows leered and shivered, then darted back into the safety of blackness as he moved. Clapboard had been ripped from windows, the glass long gone. The front door listed on its hinges. Water stains ran like dark tears beneath the vacant window holes. A sad, crying house.

Graffiti tags had been sprayed over the sides, aggressive angular strokes that jumped and sparred with shadows as he moved his flashlight. A failed enterprise, lying rotting in the bush—that was what his old homestead looked like. A sense of violation, grief, overwhelmed him, and remorse tasted bitter on his tongue.

Jeb clumped up the front stairs and traversed the collapsing porch, his boots heavy on old wood. He creaked open the listing door. Shadows leaped and shimmered inside. The dank smell of mold filled his nostrils. He panned his light across the floor, cobwebs lifting softly in the wake of his movements. Old newspapers, magazines, beer cans littered the floor. A circle of charred wood and ash scarred the center of what had been their living room; someone had built a fire on top of the carpet and hacked a hole into the roof for a chimney. An old mattress huddled in a far corner.

The taste in his mouth turned foul, and the rage he'd worked so hard in prison to control started to fester again, itching, scraping, clawing at him to get out, to wash over him with its familiar hot burn. Jeb closed his eyes and controlled his breathing. He drew Quinn, and Rachel, to mind. Anger could have no more place in his life. Not if he wanted to win them back. Breathing steadily again, he slowly entered the room. Small claws skittered over wood, a critter disappearing behind the mattress.

As Jeb entered the kitchen, a fetid smell slammed into him. He gagged, putting his sleeve over his mouth as he panned his beam over the kitchen floor. Dead raccoon. Used condoms. Spirit bottles. Broken bong pipe. He could almost hear the mocking laughter of teens. Heavy breathing. Humping. Images filled his mind, flickering like flames in the bonfire at the old gravel pit. The sex. The nightmare that had started that night. Nausea washed through his belly.

He stepped back outside and breathed clean air in deep. But his heart was hammering. He was fighting the rage that was trying to calcify around his heart. He would not be forced away by this. He would not be run out of town. He had a right to be here, to rebuild his home.

He wanted to think forward. Of Quinn. Freedom. Not this.

Not the way his mother had died here, believing in his guilt, shamed by the community on the fringes of which she'd lived all her life.

He couldn't change that past. That tragedy. But he had a future to fight for. And he had to fight smart.

He moved down to the row of cabins along the water where rafting guests and fishers used to stay. More graffiti. More vandalism. The river chuckled and whispered. He turned his back on the buildings and stared out over the water.

The northern lights reflected eerily over the dark, swirling surface, catching ripples and eddies, the odd little splash. On the opposite bank black spruce speared into the ghostly green sky.

A sense of peace finally washed through him again as he listened to the water. No matter the desecration, this was where he belonged, this land, this valley, and these mountains. This forest where he never felt lost or alone. And down here by the water he could sense the spirit of his mother. Not in the defiled, derelict buildings decomposing into the forest.

Jeb could almost see her face in the patterns of light on the river—the flare of her high cheekbones, her almond-shaped eyes, her coppery-brown skin. Grace and strength. Beauty and wisdom. A passionate love of her heritage.

Things that Jeb's father had whittled down.

Jeb's first memories were of the Wolf River and salmon. His mother hanging orange-pink strips of flayed flesh over wooden racks to dry in the brief warm winds of a Pacific Northwest summer, her dark hair hanging in a fat braid down the center of her strong back, swatting at clouds of mosquitoes, her wolf dog watching, waiting for her to toss him a scrap.

Another memory washed through his mind, his father returning at the helm of the *Jolly Roger*, his dancing eyes the color of wild irises, his cheeks ruddy and wind-burned as he dragged in his wake a flotilla of shrieking and wheeling gulls. The briny smells of the harbor where they'd traveled down to meet him. The excitement, the industry along the docks. The noise of his boyhood when the boats came in. The worry in his mother's eyes as they had met those boats.

Then would come the autumn hunts, just him and his dad weighed down with packs, trekking out from the trailhead into the endless wilderness in search of caribou. Moose. Whitetail deer. The crack of gunfire in a misty dawn. Blood, warm, slippery and viscous on his hands, steam rising from hot entrails as he learned to gut and to sever limbs, field dress and pack out his kill before the conservation officers got to them—because his father had never played by the book.

Those autumn kills had meant survival through the winter when blankets of snow lay quiet and heavy, before the salmon teemed up the coast again and his father could take the *Jolly Roger* back out into the ocean.

And when winter grew deep and dark, his father would start to drink again. The low Pacific Northwest clouds and the long, dark days would sink his Irish-Canadian father into a deep depression. He'd self-medicate. It would make his moods worse, and the violence would start, a cycle as predictable as the run of the salmon. The flight of the Canada geese. The return of the hummingbirds. The coming of the snows.

After his dad's death, as Jeb grew older, he'd helped his mother start the river-running business. In the fall he'd pick mushrooms; he made a small fortune in chanterelles each season. He'd do some trapping during winters, between school. And later he started guiding fly fishers to the best trout streams, secret places only he knew. Places he'd taken Rachel.

Yet another memory washed through him—his arms wrapped around Rachel as he showed her how to hold the light bamboo rod, how to cast the fly so that it flicked lightly on the surface of the water just at the edge of a deep, shadowed pool. She laughed, and he saw wonder in her big brown eyes as she cradled her first rainbow in her hand, keeping it underwater as she unhooked it and gently freed it from the cup of her hands.

She'd had tears in her eyes when she'd let it go. She'd told Jeb it was like holding, controlling, the pulse of life itself in her palms. It was a connection he'd given her and it warmed his heart.

He inhaled deeply, drawing his mind back to the present as he made his way back to his bike and untied his bedroll. His plan was to sleep for a few hours, recharge. He'd do some work around here in the morning, then tomorrow afternoon was the interview he'd arranged. He brought his gear down to the river's edge and unrolled his mat under the gentle, nurturing boughs of a hemlock.

Jeb climbed into his down sleeping bag, and lay on his back, one arm hooked beneath his head as he listened to the water and watched the ghostly play of aurora across the sky. As he lay there, he wondered if he could ever win Rachel back. Was it even possible?

The idea had lodged like a barbed hook, muddying his purity of focus. He'd have to be careful. His desire to see his daughter, his impulse to follow his heart, had already cost him today.

He closed his eyes, drifting into a light sleep.

———

Jeb jerked awake.

He lay dead still, trying to discern what it was that had disturbed the rhythm of his sleep. Was it that the aurora had stopped playing across the sky? That the pattern of the river had changed? The wind had increased, a steady rushing sound like an ocean on a distant shore. A sharp westerly.

But there was something else. A cold sensation of malintent snaking through the trees, fingering toward him—he couldn't explain it. Yet the sixth sense of a hunter told him something bad was out there, coming.

Cautiously he extricated himself from his sleeping bag and moved into a crouch on the dry bed of needles, listening intently as he peered with naked eyes into the blackness. The moon had sunk behind the peaks and the stars had moved across the sky. It was much darker than when he'd arrived. Jeb waited for the soft crunch of dead leaves that would signal a big cat's careful approach, or the familiar cracking and breaking of brush that foretold the presence of a large ursine beast. He inhaled gently, mouth slightly open, testing the wind. He used to be able to almost taste the fetid scent of a bear or the horsiness of a moose.

That was when he heard it. Engines approaching. Very distant, layered under the swish and rush of wind through forest. The engines grew louder. More than one vehicle coming. Tension whipped through him.

There was no other development along this road. Only this place. Beyond it was mountain, then another valley, which was Indian land.

Could it be kids returning for another night of drunken vandalism?

From his blind under the heavy hemlock boughs, Jeb watched as headlights swung into the property. A truck and an SUV came bumping down the rutted track, stopping near the log house.

The truck was dark blue, maybe even black. Four doors, long box. He could make out a *D* on the plate, but nothing more. The SUV was pale. Silver? Hard to tell in darkness.

Doors opened and three men got out. The interior lights lit them up briefly, showing black clothing, dark ski masks pulled low and tight over their heads. They left engines running and head-lights on bright. Moving like ninja silhouettes across the glare of the headlights, they made for the house. One carried a flashlight and a tire iron. The other two lugged gasoline cans. Every muscle in his body went wire-tight.

With fast and choreographed intent, they glugged gasoline around the house, splashing it across the porch, the steps.

Jeb drew back into the shadows, rage mushrooming inside him—they hadn't even checked if anyone was inside.

One of the men threw a match. The whoosh and crackle was instant. Flames, orange against black, licked quickly up the walls and ate into the old rafters, bright sparks and burning chunks shooting up into the night.

Two of the men lit the ends of sticks. Carrying their fiery torches, they ran down to the old wooden cabins on the river, lighting one after the other. Fire rushed and roared, flame light dancing like molten copper over the river surface as the fruits of Jeb's mother's hard labor burned.

He was unprepared for the power of pure hatred that burned through his blood. Those men *knew* he was back. They'd come to send a message with gasoline and a tire iron. Or worse. And with the drought, they risked burning the whole goddamn forest.

He'd expected the establishment to turn on him. Vilify him. Try to run him out of town. But not so soon, not being preempted like this. Was this what his mistake today had cost? Had Rachel betrayed him?

He fought the urge to break cover, go after them, smash them down, rip the masks from their faces. But he was unarmed. Outnumbered. And he refused to do it this way, to be tempted back into violence by faceless cowards who crept in under the shadow of darkness and masks.

Patience, Jebbediah . . . Out of the blackness and roar and smoke he heard his father's voice. The sober dad on an early winter hunt. Before he'd started drinking heavily again.

. . . Patient as that bear up on the ridge, see it? Watching us, scenting us with its open mouth? There, now it's gone. That's the dangerous bear, Jebbediah. He's the one who is going to come quiet from behind. He's going to track us for days, stalk us, not charge up front . . . be that bear, Jeb. That's how you get your kill . . .

Slowly Jeb crept out from under the hemlock. Keeping in shadow, he sifted through the darkness toward a stand of cotton-woods at the far end of the property. But his bike was across the clearing, on the other side of the vehicles and the blazing cabin. He stayed hidden, waiting for his chance.

Fire swelled to a loud roar, licking up surrounding trees. He could feel heat on his face. Flaming debris shot higher and was driven farther by the fierce dry winds into new trees, where boughs exploded into fresh flames, the blaze crackling into the forest with mocking, greedy glee. Those masked men had given life to a hot monster that was feeding off wind and a season of drought. And it was eating hungrily up the forested flanks of the mountain toward the Indian reserve on the other side.

A cold, sick sensation dropped through Jeb's stomach. They had to know the forest was a simmering tinderbox. Signs warning of the extreme fire hazard were posted everywhere through town. They could see which way the wind was blowing—away from Snowy Creek. Toward Indian land.

Someone yelled down by the water. "Sleeping bag—he's here!"

They'd found his gear, knew he was here. They were actively looking for him now, a new electricity driving their movements. Pressure built in Jeb's chest. He had to get to his bike. Sound the alarm before the fire got over that hill and took a small, scattered rural community by surprise.

He made a dash for it, running in a low crouch around the back of the burning house. Heat blasted his face. He was almost there. But as he neared his bike, an explosion ripped through the house behind him. It drew the men's attention, and the new burst of flames illuminated Jeb with hot orange light. He heard voices yelling. "Over there!"

They raced toward him.

He straddled his bike. No time for the helmet. He fired the ignition.

But before he could move, the tire iron slammed down hard across the backs of his shoulders. Wind punched out of him, the impact lurched him off his bike, which skidded out beneath him and smashed into trees.

Another blow came down for his head. But Jeb rolled to the side as the tire iron thudded into the ground, the point just catching and splitting skin open across his temple. Blood leaked into his eyes, his ear. Jeb sprang into a warrior crouch and reached for a log. No words were spoken as they came for him again. He swung the log up, cracking one of the men across the cheekbone. The man grunted in pain. But the move cost Jeb, and he took a punch in the gut from another assailant. As he stumbled backward, a blow was landed to his head. His vision went red, then black, then spiraled with pinpricks of light. He staggered sideways, taking another violent blow to the stomach.

Winded, he slumped to the ground. He lay there, unable to move, to breathe, the world around him swimming into a slow, hot, syrupy molasses tinged with the acrid scent of fire. One of the men kicked him in the ribs. Steel-toed boot. Pain sliced through his body. Another moved in for a kick. Jeb rolled onto his side, curled into a ball. Through his own blood he saw the tire iron rising high. The eyes of the man holding it glinted in the slit of his mask.

But before his assailant could bring it down for a kill stroke, another *whump* of hot air, rushing heat, and flying shrapnel knocked them all sideways. Someone screamed. There was more yelling. Jeb heard words, disjointed, swimming in his head.

"Old propane tank . . . behind those trees . . . exploded. Fire reaching trucks . . . whole place is going to blow . . ."

Jeb rolled onto his stomach and tried to drag himself toward his crashed bike, inch by inch. Heat was all around him. Blood coppery in his mouth. His world a nauseating, spinning kaleidoscope of fire and smoke. Couldn't make it . . .

He rolled sideways, tumbling down into a creek bed of soggy mud, wet leaves.

He heard engines. Vehicles leaving. The roar of fire grew loud.

And his world went black.

———

I wake to the sound of sirens and lie there listening as the wails thread up the valley, growing louder and louder. They're coming my way.

In a small town like this, the sound of sirens is different from a big city. It's personal. Close. The chance you know the person hurt, in need of help, is high, and you always wonder if it might be someone you love. Especially if your loved ones are out on that treacherous highway in winter. But Quinn is safely tucked in her bed.

My bedside clock glows green: 2:02 a.m.

It's around this time the village bars disgorge their patrons. Likely a drunk driving accident. I reach over to my bedside table, grope for my scanner, turn it on. I've gotten into the habit of keeping a scanner close by ever since I took over the newspaper.

Voices crackle over the radio waves. "Fire dispatch . . . Ladder Thirty-Three responding . . . Code Three . . . Ladder Forty-Five . . ."

I sit bolt upright, adrenaline slamming through me.

Fire.

It's happened. The worst of fears, given the dryness in this valley. It could turn into an interface blaze where wildfire meets urban development. The whole ski resort could blow. Quickly I get up, grab my robe, go to the window. Over the lake I see nothing but clear night sky, the jagged line of dark peaks and the ghostly glow of the glaciers. From the direction of the flag down by the dock, the wind is westerly. Brisk.

Another voice crackles over the scanner. "Westside Road. Banks of Wolf River. Lot R-one-one-four . . . the old river lodge . . ."

I freeze as I register the address.

Jeb.

Spinning round, I grab my cell phone and the scanner, and run quickly to the other side of the house, taking the stairs up to the attic two at a time. Out of the attic window facing west, the sky over the mountains glows a soft, dull orange. Horror fills me. The wail of sirens turns piercing as fire engines pass on the highway above my house, then began to twist along the valley to the north. The same direction Jeb went.

Quickly I dial the number Jeb gave me. I pace as it rings. It goes to voice mail. I try again. Same.

I dial my reporter on call.

"Blake, it's Rachel." I speak fast. "Big fire up the Wolf River Valley. Can you get there with a camera, or call Hallie?" I hang up before he can even answer. My hands are shaking now, sweat beading as I punch in the phone number for Brandy, my sitter.

After Trey left I developed a network of sitters I can call on, even at crazy hours, because of my search-and-rescue volunteer work and the after-hours business that comes with running a newspaper. The SAR work eventually gave way—I couldn't keep it all up. But there are still newspaper production days, the schmoozing. Brandy answers on the second ring.

"Brandy, I've got a callout," I lie. I haven't been paged yet. But Levi, Clint, Zink, and Adam, Luke's brother, are all affiliated with Rescue One, and Jeb has planted just enough doubt in my heart for me not to trust anyone right now. The timing of this fire, the location, is ominous. I need to get there before the others. "Can you get here stat?"

"Is it fire?"

"Yes."

I hear a muffled sound, a whisper. I close my eyes. Shit, Brandy is with someone.

"Look, I'm sorry—"

"I'll be there in five," she says.

I rush downstairs and fling open my closet door. As a certified SAR volunteer for Rescue One, I always have a full bag of gear ready. Winter, summer, and anything in between. This town has many volunteers like me, all with very full lives, sacrificing their time, sometimes at considerable financial cost, with no other reward than to rescue others. A unique team that helps knit together the fabric of this mountain community.

A team managed by Trey.

A team I've been feeling increasingly alienated from.

As I change, I hear more sirens and the staccato chop of a helicopter.

"Quinn!" I knock on her door, then open it. "Quinn, honey, wake up, listen to me. I've got a callout. Fire on the west side. Brandy is on her way over. Don't leave the house, okay? Stick with Brandy. If anything happens, if the wind switches, you listen to her. Do as she says. Okay, honey?"

"Fire?" She sits bolt upright, her eyes instantly wide and full of terror.

It hits me like a brick between the eyes. Her mother and father died in a fire. Her house went up in flames. I crouch down, move a fall of curls from my niece's brow. "It'll be fine," I say. "It's out in the wilds. Far away."

Quinn's hand clutches at my arm. "Aunt Rachel . . . you can't get hurt. You can't go. You can't."

I am all Quinn has left.

Conflict torques through me. I temper my voice, keeping it calm, comforting. "It's okay, Quinnie. I promise I won't let anything happen. I'm just going to see if I can help. I'm not going anywhere near the flames, all right?"

She just stares at me, her hand tight on my arm. The sound of the chopper grows loud overhead, rattling the windows as it moves toward the wildfire.

"I'll wait until Brandy gets here, okay?" I pat the comforter, inviting Trixie to jump up on the bed. Quinn's shoulders relax and she smiles at the sight of Trixie. This is a treat.

"Trixie will stay with you, keep you comfy."

Quinn lies back on her pillow and I pace in her room, urgency mounting in me. As soon as I hear Brandy's truck coming down the driveway, I say a quick good-bye to Quinn and rush down the stairs. I run for my truck as Brandy is climbing out of hers.

"I'll stay until you get back, no worries!" she calls after me.

"Keep the radio on," I yell at her, opening my door, tossing my gear in. "Just in case the wind switches!"

By the time my Rescue One pager beeps on my belt, I'm already speeding north on the highway. I'm supposed to call in if I can attend. I don't respond. I'm afraid to trust anyone. I expected the town to crucify Jeb. But this? Jesus. Could it be possible? Could someone have set fire to his property knowing the drought conditions—someone on the Rescue One team, even? The fact Jeb is not answering his cell has my heart thumping.

I think of Adam's words.

Hell knows what might happen if he sets foot back in this town. I'm not sure I could control it . . .

My heart feels sick as I realize just how deep into the fabric of this town, into my own life, the events of that night still cut.

Wind scatters twigs and debris across the highway. My fists tighten on the wheel as I negotiate a sharp bend, tires squealing. I reach for the truck radio, tune it to the local news station, listening for the weather report. If the wind switches, we risk a serious interface fire. The ski resort would be doomed. Millions in second homes, condos, investments, the mountain infrastructure could go up in flames. Tourists and residents would need to be evacuated. There's only one road in and out of Snowy Creek. It's a logistical nightmare.

I smell smoke as I wheel onto the unpaved logging road into the Wolf River Valley, my truck jouncing over ruts. About five miles in, the forest is dense on either side of the road, the trees high. Smoke smells strong and the sky is bright orange. The west side of the mountain is already fully engulfed. Up ahead I can see the pulsing lights of fire trucks, emergency vehicles. Orange cones line the dirt road. A police barricade.

An officer steps into my headlights, holding up his hand. I draw to a stop and lower my window. The cop is young, new—I don't know him.

"Rescue One," I say, showing him my provincial emergency membership card. "The rest of the SAR crew is on the way to set up a command base."

He checks my card, goes round to the front of my vehicle, checks my plate.

"Fire line is about one klick up ahead," he says, handing my card back. "Started at that old river rafting lodge. Burned clear through there already."

Jeb's place.

Sweat breaks out over my body as I take my truck farther down the potholed logging road and enter the burned area. Trees stand black and smoking. I don't go as far as the flashing lights of the fire trucks and ambulances parked farther up the logging road; I pull off at the top of Jeb's driveway and get out of my truck. No one is here—they have no reason to be. The fire has already blown through here, and this place has been deserted for years. The fire crews are all up at the fire line, fighting the active blaze.

Clicking on my headlamp, I walk onto what was once the Cullens' river rafting camp and am stunned. It's a blackened, scarred mess of smoldering embers and ash. The aftermath of a war. It definitely looks as though the fire started here, given the wind direction. It must have eaten quickly through this place. Wind whips hair across my face, and I hold it back as I cut through the clearing, crunching over burned grass, thankful for my protective boots. The scent burns the back of my throat. The area still feels hot. I tie a bandana over my nose and mouth, then move toward the smoldering house where Jeb and his mother once lived. Fear at what I might find coils low in my gut.

Near what was once the porch I see what looks like a melted gas container. A raw kind of rage, a deep sense of violation surges through me as I walk around the smoking ruins of the house and see another can. This one has escaped the fire and lies a distance away. Crouching down, I pick it up, sniff. I cough, my eyes watering as fresh gasoline fumes burn down my nasal passages. I upend the can and drops trickle out. I glance around. There are vehicle tracks. They look fresh.

Jesus, whoever did this had to have been aware they'd start a massive wildfire. I get to my feet.

"Jeb?" I call.

I move round the side of the ruins, see his bike lying on its side under a blackened tree. His helmet, damaged by fire, lies nearby. Adrenaline explodes through me. I race toward the bike. It's smashed, gas tank exploded. Turning in a fast circle, I suddenly see something pale in a ditch. Skin—human flesh. Dark hair. I can make out part of his jacket. My mouth goes bone-dry.

Part of me wants to run away, to not see what's in that ditch. But my feet move, a roar sounding in my ears. As I get closer, I see his jeans. Boots. Him. His body. He's not burned. The fire has leaped over this wet and deep creek bed. But his face and hair are dark with blood. He's motionless.

"Dear God," I whisper as I drop to my haunches in the ditch beside him. I reach out, touch his neck. *He's alive.* He has a pulse. He's breathing. My heart explodes into a rapid-fire staccato beat.

"Jeb! Jeb, can you hear me?"

A soft moan comes from his chest as he moves his head. Then slowly his eyes open. He stares up at me, blinking into the glare of my headlamp. He has an open gash on his head. His pupils contract uniformly against the light. A good sign.

"Rachel?" he croaks.

My heart clutches, relief overwhelming. "Where do you hurt? What happened?"

"Ribs." He gives an unearthly groan as he tries to roll over.

"Wait, don't move. Can you feel your extremities, wiggle your toes, fingers?"

He concentrates, moving both arms and legs.

"Any back pain?"

His mouth twists. "Pain all over."

I glance up toward the EMT lights pulsing red through the trees. My first instinct is to call for help. I reach for the radio on my belt.

"No." His hand clamps down on my arm.

"I need to get you to the clinic."

"They . . . they tried to kill me."

"Who?"

"Three men. Ski masks. Torched the place . . . I . . . just help me up. Please . . ." He tries to sit, but gasps in pain and sinks back down into the wet loam.

Worry burns through me. "I need to get you medical attention—"

"How did you get here?" he says.

"Truck."

"Alone?"

"Yes."

"Where is it, your truck?" he asks.

"Just back there. Near the top of your driveway."

"Get me to your truck." He gives another unearthly groan as he pushes himself into a sitting position.

"Jeb—"

"Please, just help me to your truck." He gets onto all fours then leans on my arm as he struggles, hunched over, onto his feet. Blood leaks afresh from his head wound. His complexion is deathly in this light. I hear people yelling in the distance as another stand of ancient trees whooshes up in flame. They're moving the fire line. Sustained-action wildfire crews are arriving. Helicopters and air tankers are hovering somewhere above the smoke.

"They came prepared." He coughs. "Gasoline. They knew I was here. They laid into me, tire iron, boots. But they fled when the old propane tank blew. If it hadn't blown, I'd be dead."

Ice slicks down my spine. Who knew he was back? And so fast? Adam, Trey? The old gang? Who else?

I shoot another glance at the shadows moving between the trees up near the road. Trey and the others will be here any moment, if not already, setting up a command base, ensuring no one is left unaccounted for in the forest. Clint, as fire chief, will also be somewhere close. Adam, too, most likely.

"Wait here," I say. "Do not move. I'll bring the truck closer."

I run, legs pounding, breath rasping, smoke burning my lungs. I fling open my door and hop in, starting the engine before the door is even closed. I drive over the burned clearing.

He's trying to lift his bike. I fling open the door, rush over to him, leaving the engine running.

"Don't be an idiot, Jeb." I try to take his arm.

"Need to get the bike in the truck."

"Forget it. You're not thinking straight. You've had a concussion. We can't get that bike into the truck without a ramp anyway. Besides, it's wrecked." I take his arm, drape it over my shoulders, accepting the brunt of his body weight as we stumble back to my truck. Another spurt of worry gushes through me. The wound on his temple needs stitches, but my fear is internal brain injury, possible hematoma. Things could get worse. Fast.

"Get inside," I order, helping him up into the passenger seat. I open my first-aid kit and find a wad of padded cotton.

"Here, press this against your wound. You need to stop that bleeding. Hold it tight."

I go round the driver's side, climb in, and put the truck in gear. More sirens are approaching. The chopper is hovering lower, louder. I accelerate back onto the logging road and bomb down it as fast as I dare. As I near the police cordon, a vehicle approaches from the opposite direction. Silver SUV. Rescue One plate. Trey.

Shit.

"Get down," I whisper harshly. "Now."

He does. Head on my lap. I feel his blood soaking into my jeans on my thigh.

Trey stares at me as he drives by, then hits his brakes. I glimpse Harvey Zink in the seat beside him. But I keep going, my focus dead ahead. I wave at the cop as I drive around the cones. As soon as I'm clear of the cordon, I floor the gas, fishtailing on loose sand and gravel as we blast back down to the highway. My heart is beating in my throat, my torso damp with sweat.

Both Trey and Zink have seen me out here. So has that rookie cop. What will it mean?

Jeb lifts his head off my lap.

"Stay down," I say, stealing a glance at him.

He smiles up at me, a crooked smile twisted with pain. My heart gives an odd kick.

"Like Bonnie and Clyde," he says. "Like old times."

I feel a smile of response against my will. That old spark. It's back. It never left.

"Damn you, Jebbediah Cullen," I whisper, fists clenching the wheel. "Goddamn you."

His smile turns into a grin, then a grimace as we jolt over a ditch and bounce onto the paved highway.

CHAPTER 10

Quinn watched out the front window, her hands pressing tightly down on the sill. Brandy was in the kitchen, making hot chocolate. The television was on and reporters were talking about the fire and what would happen to Snowy Creek if the wind shifted. Brandy had put the radio on, too, and was listening to the weather forecast.

She had long, thick hair that reminded Quinn of flames, but Brandy didn't know anything about fire. She was a ski patroller and an ice climber. She threw avalanche bombs in the winter. Which is why she did other jobs during summer, like babysitting and working at the kids' mountain bike camp as a group leader. She said she loved kids and was going to have a whole bunch of her own one day.

The sirens screamed up on the highway and a helicopter crossed in front of the burnt-orange sky above the peaks. Scary feelings scrambled about in Quinn's chest and wouldn't rest no matter how many deep breaths she took.

"Where is she?" Her voice came out funny.

Brandy came to her side and set a mug of chocolate on the sill, small white marshmallows melting on top.

"Rachel is going to be fine, sweetie. She's just helping to make sure they get all the people out of that area."

"What area is it?"

"It's up the Wolf River Valley."

Her lip quivered. She didn't want anything to happen to Rachel. All she had was Rachel. She should never have said those bad things to her aunt. This was her fault.

"Will the fire come this way, like they're saying on TV?"

"No. Not unless the wind changes, and that's not going to happen according to the meteorologists. By the time the wind does eventually switch they'll have the fire under control." She smoothed down Quinn's hair. "Hey, it's going to be okay. You really should get some sleep, you know. It's still a long way to morning."

"What's on the other side of those mountains?" Quinn said, staring at the orange glow.

"Well, there is a First Nations reserve. But they'll have enough time to evacuate if they need to."

"But it'll be all burned? Their houses?"

"I hope not."

Quinn looked at Brandy. She had eyes the color of honey. "My mother and father burned in a fire," she said. "My house burned."

"I know," Brandy said softly. "I'm so sorry."

"Do you have a mother?"

"We all have mothers, one way or another."

"But do you have a live one?"

Brandy hesitated and her brow creased. A funny look entered her eyes. "In some ways, but in others it's as if she's already gone. She doesn't remember things anymore. She's got Alzheimer's. She's in a home in Vancouver."

"She doesn't remember you?"

"No. Not even who she is, really. It's a different kind of death."

Quinn studied Brandy for a while. "My mother sent me an angel."

"Did she?" Brandy took a sip of her herb tea.

Quinn nodded. "To watch over me. In case something happens to Rachel. I . . . I don't want anything to happen." Tears, those stupid tears suddenly wanted to come again, and it made her face feel hot and angry.

Brandy put her arm around her. She smelled like vanilla and nice things. Like mothers smell. And it made Quinn's eyes burn hotter.

"Rachel's going to be fine."

Quinn pulled away and stomped into the kitchen. She didn't want to like anybody else, because they could die, too. But she froze as she heard a car engine. Her heart started pounding and she ran back to the window. Headlights were peeping through the trees. *Rachel!*

Quinn exploded in a flurry and raced for the front door. She flung the door open to the night. Wind rushed at her, making her hair fly back as she dashed outside. Trixie followed, nails skittering over the wood floor.

"Quinn!" Brandy called as she came after them. "Wait up. You haven't got any shoes on!"

The truck door opened and Rachel stepped out. Quinn stopped in her tracks. Her aunt's face was white and streaked with soot. She looked wrong.

Brandy's hand was suddenly on Quinn's shoulder, restraining her. Quinn's eyes flared up to Brandy's face. Her sitter was looking at Rachel as if something was wrong, too.

But Rachel marched right up to them both and dropped to her haunches in front of Quinn. "Hey, kiddo, made it back. What are you guys still doing up?"

Quinn flung her arms around her aunt and squeezed. She felt herself shaking, so she held even tighter. "You smell like smoke," she muttered into Rachel's neck.

"Everything's fine, Quinn." Rachel leaned back. "It's all fine. Don't worry." She smiled and pushed hair back off Quinn's brow. But there was a strange tightness in her aunt's face. And although Rachel was smiling, her eyes weren't.

Rachel glanced up. "Brandy, can you stay a while longer? I need to get the gear from my truck down into the boathouse where I can clean it."

Brandy's gaze flicked to the truck. Quinn followed her eyes. She thought she saw a movement inside the truck, a shadow. There was another person in there. Silence hung for a few beats. And the swish of trees and distant thudding of choppers, faint sirens, seemed louder.

"Sure," Brandy said. "Come on, Quinn. We'll go inside."

"No. I want to stay with Rachel."

"Quinnie, you need to get back into your bed, okay? I'm right here, in the boathouse. Brandy will stay until you fall asleep."

"Is that blood?" Quinn said, examining her palm that had touched Rachel's thigh.

Rachel swallowed. "It's all fine. I helped carry someone who was bleeding a little. Now go on inside."

Quinn felt her insides go tight. She glared at Rachel. It wasn't fine. She could tell. Something was wrong and they weren't telling her. There was blood on Rachel's thigh, and someone in her truck.

"Go, please."

Quinn cast her eyes down and followed Brandy back into the house. But as soon as she was inside, she rushed over to the big windows that looked down over the garden toward the lake. She saw Rachel driving her truck farther down the garden pathway and over the grass toward the boathouse. Quinn had never seen Rachel take her truck down there before. She parked it close to the boathouse, behind a hedgerow.

"Quinn, it's bedtime, come."

She pressed her hands firmly against the glass, ignoring Brandy. She could just make out the shadow of Rachel helping someone out of the truck. A man. He was bent over and leaning on her. Trixie was following them.

The angel?

Quinn's heart beat faster.

Brandy crouched down beside her. "It's time for bed . . ." But then Brandy saw what Quinn was looking at and she fell silent, watching, too.

Quinn suddenly grasped Brandy's hand—she didn't want anyone else to see him. "I want to go to bed. Now."

Brandy craned forward, narrowing her eyes, trying to see down into the dark who was with Rachel.

"It's nobody," Quinn said, tugging at her hand. "She's got nobody."

Brandy looked at her, a frown forming on her brow. She had that funny look in her eyes again.

"Can you read to me in bed? Please. I want to go now."

Her sitter hesitated. "Sure." Casting a backward glance to the window, she led Quinn upstairs.

———

Jeb leaned heavily on Rachel as she helped him into the boathouse. The interior was cold, dark. The door banged shut behind them in the wind. He groaned as she led him over to the bed and eased him down.

She put her first-aid kit on the table and dragged the table up to the bed. Her movements were tense as she lit the old kerosene lantern. With a soft whoosh, flickering flame threw gold light onto the walls, highlighting the old snowshoes, fly fishing rods, a carved wooden fish. An old black woodstove still squatted on tiles in the corner, logs stacked neatly beside it. And past shimmered into present.

Jeb flashed suddenly to being eighteen again, he and Rachel making out here, on the rug in front of the burning stove. Trixie had been curled in her basket by the fire, snow falling thick and silent outside. It was into this boathouse they'd run for drinks from the fridge during the hot summer months, days of bathing suits and diving from the dock into the glacial water, lying in the sun, canoeing across the lake to explore the ghost squatter settlement in the woods on the opposite side of the lake.

Trixie went to lie on the woven rag mat in front the stove even though it wasn't lit—some old memories died hard. Some were wired right into the neural pathways of one's brain. They were a part of you, in the way a tree grew around a piece of metal, which then became part of the trunk, a part you couldn't extract without killing the tree.

"Still no power down here?" he said as wind whistled in under the door.

Her gaze ticked to his. Worry darted through her eyes. Quickly she opened her kit, snapped on a pair of latex gloves.

"No. My father kept meaning to wire the place, but—" Her voice caught. She pulled up a chair and sat in front of him, drawing the lantern closer across the table.

"My dad liked the romance of kerosene lanterns, candles, the fire in the pit on the beach." She removed several packets of sealed antiseptic wipes. "We were going to renovate, after his death. But . . ." Her voice faded as she focused on tearing open a pouch.

"We?"

"Hmm." She removed the wipe.

"You mean you and Trey?" he insisted.

Her dark eyes flashed up. She met his gaze for a moment, but Jeb was forced to blink against the glare from her headlamp. She returned to her task at hand. Outside, far across the lake, Jeb heard the wind howling like lost wolves. Goose bumps whispered over his skin.

"Let me see this." She lifted the wadded and bloody compression pad he was still pressing to his head. She began to wipe away blood with disinfectant. It stung. Jeb focused on her mouth.

"How long has your father been gone, Rachel?"

"Ten months now. Cancer."

"That's a lot of loss in a short space of time. First your father, then Sophia and Peter. Then Trey leaves?"

"Yeah, I'm a regular pariah." She fell silent as she cleaned farther along his wound.

"Your father left you this place?"

"And the newspaper."

Surprise rippled through him. "The *Snowy Creek Leader*?"

"Hold still, Jeb."

He thought of the woman, the editor he'd called yesterday. Cass Rousseau.

"So *you* run the paper?"

"I'm the publisher."

"Cass Rousseau is your employee?"

Her jaw tensed. "I said hold still, dammit. I need to see if you've got any debris in here."

"I never saw it," he said, wincing again as she seemed to move more briskly. "You taking after your dad, your grandfather." He tried to smile. "You're following in their footsteps, becoming the social crusader."

Abruptly she set the cloth down on the table and ripped open a pack of butterfly sutures, her mouth a flat, tight line. "The newspaper business is not some crusade. It's just business, pure and simple. Social crusading was Sophia's job, not mine." She held the edges of his gash together, applied a suture, then another. "Sophia was the one always going on about social justice and equality. She was the astute, philosophical one, like my dad and granddad. Me, they say I was more like my mother. I was the athlete. The coddled baby of the family. The one who used to live in the moment." A bitterness laced her words, and Jeb heard self-disdain.

"Used to live? You're talking past tense."

Her gaze ticked back to his. She held his eyes a moment, then looked away again, a fall of dark hair hiding her face. Compassion washed through him. She seemed so alone.

Rachel finished applying the adhesive sutures in silence. The shutters rattled in the wind. Choppers continued to pass overhead and sirens could be heard in the distance.

"You should get that stitched if you don't want a scar. But it's not terribly deep," she said. "You're lucky."

"Yeah, you got that all right. I'm the lucky one."

She breathed in deep, clicked off her headlamp, and removed it before peeling off her latex gloves. "You said it was a tire iron that did this?"

"Just caught the sharp tip."

"That's luck in my book. You'd be dead otherwise. Skull could have been crushed. There's still a chance of internal swelling and a mild concussion."

Silence hung. The wind moaned and fingered under the door. Cobwebs in the corner lifted softly. She studied his face, his eyes, and Jeb sensed she was trying to see beyond physical injury. She was still unsure about him.

"Where else do you hurt?" she said.

He gave a wry smile.

"Okay, where does it hurt most? Talk me through it."

"Ribs. Breathing. Everywhere."

"Jacket off."

He tried, winced. She helped him. Her hair fell across his cheek and he caught the scent of smoke from the fire. Her hands were warm, soft. Rachel was made up of memories, of all the things that had been good in his life, before life as he knew it had been stolen from him.

She draped his leather jacket over the back of a chair. "Now let's get your T-shirt off so I can see the rest of you."

Jeb tried to lift his arms, a soft groan escaping him, pain sparking across his chest as Rachel helped him pull the shirt over his head.

"Oh, Jesus," she whispered as she caught sight of the red welts, the bruising developing. "Can you lie down?"

She helped him onto his back. When he caught her eyes again, he saw they were dark with worry. Rachel placed her hands gently on his ribs, palpated. He watched her face, the seriousness in her features. This cabin was cold without his shirt. Wind whistling and flagpole chinking outside. Water slapping against the dock. He shivered.

"I'll get the fire going and get some warmth into here in a sec," she said, speaking faster.

"Do you remember when we used to sneak in here, Rach?" he whispered.

She cleared her throat. "You might have some broken ribs." She sat back. "I need to get you to the clinic. You should get proper stitches on that gash, X-rays, and your ribs taped up."

"You do it. Tape me up."

"Jeb—"

"Do it," he said quietly. "Please."

"I have basic wilderness first aid. You should get X-rays—"

"I've dealt with worse in prison. I'm going to be okay."

"They beat you, in prison?"

He said nothing.

She looked sick. Abruptly she started unrolling a piece of medical tape. "How did this happen?" Her outrage was sharp, sudden.

"I went home, saw the place had been trashed, so I set up my bedroll down by the water, under a hemlock, thinking I'd start clearing things out in the morning. I was sleeping down by the river when they came."

"*Who* came?"

"I don't know. There were three of them in two vehicles; one truck, dark blue or black, long box. And a light-colored SUV. Maybe silver."

"Can you lift your arm up, extend it over your head?"

He did. She felt along his rib cage. He closed his eyes, wincing as she pinpointed the pain.

"There?"

He nodded.

She ripped off a piece of tape, peeled off part of the backing, and began to stick it in a vertical line alongside the point of pain. "Did you catch the vehicle plates?"

"No." He winced again as she plastered the strip of tape down the side of his torso. "Just the letter *D* on the truck plate."

"And you're sure they were men, not kids out for some kind of joyride?"

He snorted. "Damn sure."

She peeled the backing off another strip of tape, laying this piece down parallel to the first, on either side of the key area of pain.

"They were dressed completely in black with ski masks. This was premeditated—they came expressly to trash the place, and they came for me. Somehow, they already knew I was back."

Her hands stilled for a moment as she noticed something. "That's a nasty scar," she said quietly, nodding toward the puckered line just above his left nipple.

"It's old history."

She held his eyes.

"Prison. I don't want to talk about it."

Rachel's mouth tightened as she peeled the backing from a third strip of tape, which she stuck across the other strips, stretching it tightly around half his torso.

"I saw the gasoline cans," she said.

"Do those vehicles sound familiar to you?"

She looked away, breathed in deep. "They're standard ski resort issue. A dime a dozen." She got up, went to the freestanding wardrobe, an antique piece of furniture her father had bought over a decade ago in Oregon. She opened the door, took out a T-shirt and a flannel lumberjack shirt. She brought them to him and helped him ease first into the T-shirt, then the soft flannel.

"My dad's," she said wryly. "I never could get rid of his gear down here. Or the stuff in his office. They'll fit." Her fingers touched his neck as she eased his arm into the fleece shirt, and she stilled near his tattoo. Her eyes glistened. "I'm so sorry, Jeb."

He met her gaze. But she lurched suddenly to her feet, took several paces away. She dragged her hands over her hair. "I knew they'd be out to get you, Jeb, but I can't believe someone would do *this*—risk a massive wildfire, endangering a whole community on the other side of the valley."

He said nothing.

She swore softly. "We should go to the police."

"The police—you serious?"

She stared at him, realization dawning in her eyes.

"You told me Adam believed I was back," he said.

"Oh, Jesus, you don't think Adam . . . he's—"

"He *is* the police, Rachel. It was his brother who claimed I turned north when I know for a fact I turned south and went home that night. His mother was chief constable at the time of the investigation. It was her team of investigators that took me down. Luke's gone now, but it still leaves Adam with something to hide."

She paled as the gravity of his words sank in. "So you think it was one of those three guys, or even Adam, tonight?"

"They lied for a reason. They framed me to protect themselves, or someone else."

"What about vigilantes, Jeb? There are so many people here who hate you with such violent passion. They blame you for Merilee's mother dying of a broken heart. They say it was you who ultimately caused Amy's suicide. What if it was enraged townsfolk? What about Merilee's father? Or her brothers? If they know you're here—"

"But would they *all* know so quickly?"

Rachel stared at him, a flicker of guilt in her eyes. "You think this is because I went to Adam."

"I didn't say that."

She stomped over to the stove and dropped to a crouch. She yanked open the stove door and started balling up newspaper, which was stacked in a copper pot on the side. She rammed the balls into the stove, then cracked pieces of kindling over her knee. She laid the kindling over the paper. She lit the fire, watched while it caught, added some logs, then closed and latched the stove door. Orange fire flickered warm and comforting behind the glass window. She went over to the boathouse door and wedged a rolled-up towel into the gap between the door and the flooring.

"It'll warm up soon," she said, dusting her hands on her jeans. "You want to lie there, or sit here on the sofa where it'll be warmer?"

He got to his feet, wincing as he moved, and he slowly lowered himself onto the sofa by the fire.

The warmth from the stove was almost instant, the atmosphere cozy. Outside, the wind howl seemed a little more distant. Trixie came over to snuffle his hand before going to curl back in front of the flames.

Rachel went to the fridge, got out two bottles of water. She handed one to him. "You want anything to eat?"

He shook his head, opened the bottle, drank deeply.

"You still don't drink alcohol?" she said.

"No. You?"

She lowered herself into a chair to his side, and he could tell she was thinking back to the gravel pit. "Sometimes."

"Like earlier tonight?"

She met his gaze. "Yeah. Like earlier tonight. Like when I heard from Quinn that a dark-haired man with a fish tattoo down the side of his neck followed her at school."

"You were scared."

"Damn right, I was." She leaned forward, arms resting on her knees. "For almost a decade I've been led to believe you did this thing. It all pointed to you and no one else. When Quinn described you, of course I was afraid."

"And now?"

She watched him in silence, warring with something inside herself. As wan and exhausted and soot-streaked as she was, she'd never looked more beautiful to him, bathed as she was in the coppery glow of flame light.

"You were attacked," she said quietly. "Left for dead, your place torched. That much looks to be fact. This forces me to ask why. It plants doubt in my mind about those guys who testified about you driving north. And it makes me wonder how news of your return could have traveled so fast. The only way that could happen is if those guys called each other. That forces me to wonder about Adam." She inhaled deeply.

"You're asking me to believe that upstanding members of this community, my friends, could have been responsible for a brutal sexual assault and murder. That these fathers, sons, brothers, husbands, have been harboring a heinous secret for all these years and now they want to stop you from exposing them? How do you think that makes me feel, Jeb? It makes me feel . . ." Her voice caught, and her eyes glittered in the firelight.

"If it's the truth, it makes me responsible, too. It makes me feel that I should have believed in you, stood up for, fought for you. That I should have trusted my heart and my instincts all those years ago." She paused, struggling. "I'm sorry," she whispered. "I am so sorry that we fought that night. That I said things I didn't mean. I'm sorry about being with Trey."

"You slept with him, didn't you? You lost your virginity that night?"

Pain, remorse, twisted over her face, and it tugged at his heart.

"Hey," he said quietly. "You were eighteen. We were all young. We made mistakes."

"How can you be so goddamn generous, Jeb!" she snapped. "*We* locked you away. *We* stole years of your life."

"You know what matters now? That you believe me."

She surged to her feet, went to the window, stared out at the lake, arms folded tightly over her chest. "I don't know that I do," she said. "Everything you've told me makes sense, but so did everything they said back then." She was silent for a long while, just the crackle of flames and wind outside, the slap of water against the dock. The distant thudding of helicopters fighting the wildfire.

"My grandfather used to talk about the banality of evil," she said, staring out the window. "It was a phrase first used by a woman named Hannah Arendt, a German-American political theorist. She used it in her 1960s thesis, where she postulated that all great evils in history, the Holocaust in particular, were not executed by fanatics or sociopaths, but by ordinary people who accepted the premise of their government or state. She argued that they participated in evil things with the view that their actions were normal." She paused, then turned to face him.

"I believed in the authorities back then—the cops, the lawyers, the parents, elders in this community. I trusted them. And in so doing I accepted their premise that you were guilty. I went along with them. And it makes me sick to the stomach that I—we—might have been so wrong." She came over to him, seating herself on the coffee table in front of him. So close he could touch.

"You're right about one thing," she said quietly. "We do want the same things. I want to keep Quinn safe. And now I also want the truth. I want proof. However it comes. Someone tried to kill you tonight. Someone is responsible for arson. And I want to know

THE SLOW BURN OF SILENCE

who and why. But I'm not going to fall into the same trap this time. I'm not believing *anything* until I can prove it to my own satisfaction." Her gaze lasered into his. "I'm going to help you, Jeb. But I'm going to do it for me. For Quinn. For Sophia and Peter. For the Zukanov family."

"No," he said. "You're going to stand back. I don't want you involved."

She gave a snort. "I *am* involved. Look at me now, here, with you." She took a drink from her water bottle. "You said you've already set up an interview with Cass Rousseau?"

"Yesterday."

She moistened her lips, screwed the cap back on the bottle. "Cass never mentioned it. What time? Where?"

"Shady Lady Saloon. Happy hour. When everyone's coming down from the bike park, thirsty. In full view of tourists, locals. I plan to tell her why I'm back. And I'll name those four men to start. Shine a media spotlight on them."

"It could be libelous if we run something like that."

"Not if it's handled right. It's a fact that those four testified. Clint, Levi, Zink, and Luke. It's public record what they said. It's a fact my conviction has been overturned, that the judge felt I didn't get a fair trial. It's a fact I didn't drive north—because I know I didn't. Which means those who said I did lied. I'm going to say that. I'm going to make it known that someone in this town is covering up the truth, keeping Merilee's family from closure. If there's an innocent one or two among them, they might weaken under the public scrutiny, turn on each other to save themselves. That's my goal—rattle their cages until something shakes loose."

"I have veto power, you know."

He regarded her. "And people would then wonder why you, too, want to silence me. You who also testified against me, who told the court something I'd confided to no one in my life but you."

Her eyes flashed. Her pulse pounded in the pale column of her neck. "Jeb, I—"

He raised his hand. "I get it. Banality of evil and all. You believed them. You felt obligated to tell them what I'd done, that I had a history of violence, that my mother covered it up."

"They pushed me."

Silence, the past, hung heavy and solid between them.

She blew out a heavy breath and pushed a lock of hair off her brow, exposing the small plaster above her eyebrow.

"How'd you get that cut?" he said, nodding toward the small Band-Aid.

She hesitated. "Quinn hit me."

"Why?"

"It's nothing."

"Rachel—"

"I said it's nothing."

Tension crackled between them; his urge to know more about his child was fierce. That she was having trouble with Quinn was important to him. He cared. But he could see that now was not the time to push. He had to pick his battles. And his first mission was to go after those guys who had lied in court.

"Tell me about them," he said slowly. "Those four. I read in the papers that Luke was killed in the Congo. Anything new there?"

She shook her head. "He was on a demining mission when the area was attacked by rebels. There were no survivors. Both Adam and his mom took it hard. His mom quit the SCPD not long after. She's now suffering from a form of dementia. Adam meanwhile quit the Mounties and moved back here with his family to take the second-in-command position when it came available."

"Who does Adam answer to?"

"Chief Constable Rob Mackin. He's a straight shooter, I think. I like him."

"And Mackin in turn answers to the police board."

She heaved out a frustrated breath. "Okay, I see where you're going with this. Yeah, civilian police board. And on the board, along with the mayor, is Hal Banrock, Levi's father."

"Levi, who also lied," he said.

She didn't reply.

"You mentioned Adam moved back here with his family; he's married?"

"To Lily Gallagher. You remember Lily from school?"

"Yeah. Quiet, pretty girl."

"She worked in retail for a while but is a stay-home mom now. They have two boys, eight and five: Tyler and Mikey. They seem to have an idyllic marriage."

"What about Levi?"

"Big name in the ski business now, runs the ski hill. He's also married, a small baby."

"And Clint is now fire chief?"

"A fairly recent promotion. He married his pregnant girlfriend, Beppie, and joined the military right about when you went to prison. But after a peacekeeping deployment in Sierra Leone, he quit the army and came back to Snowy Creek, where he joined the fire department. They have three daughters and live on a small ranch in Pemberton now."

She rubbed the knee of her jeans, got up, paced, then stopped to stare out the window over the lake. Jeb allowed his gaze to slowly traverse the length of her legs in her slim-fitting jeans, the tight shape of her ass. Low in his belly, desire stirred in spite of his pain, in spite of this situation. He wanted her. Desperately. A slow, smoldering fire of desire had been building insidiously in his gut from the moment he'd laid eyes on her again, outside the school. A fire that had never died, but had been fanned hotly back to life.

She glanced over her shoulder at him, gold light catching her profile. His chest hurt. His mouth was dry. He took another swig of ice water, finishing the bottle.

"Tell me about Trey," he said.

Her shoulders stiffened visibly. "He wasn't one of the four. He saw the same things I did, you leaving the pit with Merilee and Amy in your car."

"Trey is a friend of the three remaining guys. They all go back. They stick together now."

"He isn't the only one tight with those guys." She sounded defensive.

"What happened between the two of you, Rachel?"

"That's got nothing to do with this." Her words were suddenly clipped, brooking no further discussion. She either trusted Trey fully, or she still felt something for the guy.

"What about Harvey Zink?"

She inhaled deeply and turned back to face the window. "Zink . . . he's a bit of a mess, really. Owns the Shady Lady Saloon, does very good business. He was married and had a kid but is divorced now. His ex has custody and still lives in town. He goes on big drinking binges every now and then. No steady relationship but there always seems to be a string of young women."

"Zink, who dealt drugs at school. Who had access to Rohypnol, the date rape drug."

She spun to face him. "The empty Rohypnol blister pack, Merilee's blood in your car, how *did* that happen?"

"I plan to find out."

"You mean, it could have been planted?"

He said nothing.

She came, sat down beside him. The old sofa creaked. She looked at her hands, her thumb worrying her empty ring finger. Slowly, almost inexorably, he reached out, covered her hand with his. "I didn't do it, Rach."

She didn't move.

"Look at me."

She did. Her face was so close, her eyes a liquid chocolate brown, skin so smooth. Acting without thought, he cupped the side of her jaw, and her lids fluttered, lowered. His blood sank hot, fast to his groin. She leaned almost imperceptibly forward, and Jeb brought his mouth closer to hers. He could feel her breath on his lips. His heart began to slam so hard he thought it might bust out of his broken rib cage.

He brushed his lips softly over hers, tentative, a question. Her body trembled. And he pressed his mouth down hard over hers, shades of scarlet and black, swirling, whirling through his brain as her mouth opened under his, sweet, warm, inviting him in, her body sinking bonelessly against his, her hand sliding up the back of his neck, cupping it, drawing him into her.

She angled her head, a soft moan coming from her throat as her tongue slipped into his mouth, tangling, slicking with his, mounting in pace, tension, aggression. He could feel her pulse hammering in unison with his, faster, harder. He felt he might have died and was finally, after all these years, after that tiny cell, the barbed wire and fencing . . . he was finally coming home. And God knew nothing was going to stop him or send him back now.

Pain roared through his torso, his ribs, but he didn't care. Logic, the sound of the moaning wind, the chinking flagpole, the distant, thudding choppers, the crackling fire, the sleeping dog—it all slipped away, fading into just this one pure sensation of Rachel in his arms, something he'd never truly dreamed possible again.

Jeb slid his hand into her shirt and found her breast. Tears of exquisite pleasure burned behind his lids as he felt the firm, soft swell, the tightly aroused nipple. Liquid fire arrowed into his groin, and he grew so hard he felt he might explode. His penis, his body, the cut on his head, his ribs, ached with each pound of his heart.

This was more than arousal, than sex. This was everything. This was love, reawakening, rekindling, starting a fire so fierce and poignant in his heart and belly, Jeb knew he would stop at nothing now. This was being alive. And nothing could match being held in the warm, enveloping arms, feeling the care and affection and desire of another human being after nine long years of being so isolated and cold and alone.

He felt her hand moving gently down his waist, sliding between his thighs. She cupped his groin. And Jeb was sunk.

CHAPTER 11

He is hard and lean in my arms, a warrior broken but not diminished. His muscles are tight with pain, yet he doesn't seem to care as he slides his hand down my back and cups my buttocks. His other hand threads through my hair, fisting, pulling hard enough to make my eyes water as he kisses me deeper.

My hand is between his legs. The sensation of his erection bulging stiff under my palm is dizzying. Heat floods to my groin. My nipples tingle in response. I'm being sucked down into a place where there is only sensation. I grapple for reality, for logic, for air, a part of me knowing this is wrong. We're not ready. It could all still go so terribly bad. Yet it's something I've ached for on some level since our relationship turned from friendship into something more, and since the night of our fight. I wanted him that night and he turned me down, and the whole world went to hell.

I feel his tears, wet against my face. I taste the salt of them sliding between our lips. His emotion, his need for me, cracks my heart open wide. He's consuming me all over again—past, present, future, spiraling into one dangerous vortex of dark, simmering, sexual power. I'm breathless, sinking, drowning, into this dark man. This renegade I think I've always loved.

And suddenly I'm desperate for all of him. Naked against my bare skin. I want to wrap my bare thighs around him, feel him hard inside me. I can't breathe. I fumble with his zipper . . . a ringing sounds in my ears. No, a tune. Ringtone. I slow the kiss, heart slamming as I try to surface. It's my phone, ringing in my pocket. Reality slams back with a punch.

I pull back, breathing hard. His eyes are inky pools, his features etched with desire; something untamed has been released in him.

"I . . . I need to get this." I spin away from him, scrabbling in my pocket for my cell as though it's a lifeline. I shouldn't have done this. I don't even want to think about what it means now.

I answer. "Hello." My voice comes out thick, husky.

There's a beat of silence.

"Where in the hell are you?"

Trey. Electricity sparks through my body. My gaze shoots to Jeb. He's watching me with a feral intensity that unnerves me.

"Just a second," I say into the phone. I turn to Jeb, "I'm going to take this outside."

He says nothing.

I step out into the icy wind coming off the lake. I move out of the puddle of light coming from the boathouse window and stand in the shadows of a tree where Jeb can't see me. "What do you want?" I wrap my arm over my stomach against the cold. My jacket is inside the boathouse.

"You didn't answer the callout."

"I wasn't able to attend."

"I saw you out there, you *know* I saw you. What in hell is going on? Is he with you?" His voice is clipped. I hear another wailing siren in the distance. The western sky glows dull orange. Caution whispers through me.

"What do you mean?"

"I mean Cullen, goddammit. He was *there*, at the old Wolf River lodge. They've impounded his bike. He set fire to the place; the entire mountain is burning now. He's back for revenge, he's trying to burn the whole resort down, that's what they're saying."

My heart kicks. "Who is saying?"

"The cops. Adam has a forensics ident crew and arson team out there right now, combing the place."

"They think *he's* responsible for arson?"

"They found gas cans and matches."

My mouth turns dry. I'm seized by a sense of history repeating. If they take Jeb in for questioning again, it could be like last time. He might never come out.

"Did you bring him out, Rachel? Is he with you now?"

"Listen to me," I say quietly, debating just how much to tell Trey. "Jeb went home to his land. He was asleep when three masked men arrived. He saw them setting fire to his place. He was attacked, beaten badly, left for dead. The *only* reason those men didn't kill him was because they fled when the old propane tank exploded."

There were several beats of silence.

"So he is with you."

"Why did you call, Trey? To find out if he's here? Because that's none of your damn business."

When he speaks again, his voice is cold, hard. "The cop manning the roadblock saw you out there tonight. Zink saw you. I saw you. They're going to come knocking on your door in the morning. They're going to look at you as an accessory to arson. Don't be a fool about this."

Shock slakes through me. I think about the way I picked up that gas can, the possibility I've left prints. Fear is suddenly raw in me. I've seen what the cops and courts did to Jeb all those years ago. And if what Jeb claims really is true, I can't trust they won't try to do the same to me—to both of us. In order to hide the dark, terrible secret buried in this town. Whoever did rape Amy and kill Merilee might have much more at stake now—kids, wives, important positions in the community. The collateral damage of exposure would be far-reaching.

"Did you hear me, Trey? Jeb was *attacked* by three men. They started the fire. Who were those men? That's the question you should be asking."

"He got to you."

I swear softly.

"Rachel." His voice changes. "I . . . I'm worried about you."

Wind whips hair across my face. Waves splash and the old dock creaks against the push of the lake.

"Are you, really? Or are you worried about protecting someone else? Are you worried Jeb's going to find out who really raped Amy and killed Merilee?"

"Don't do this. Don't put yourself on the wrong side of the fence here. That man is a smooth-talking, sociopathic, self-serving liar. You never did get that, did you? You still feel something for him. You're playing with fire, Rachel. You're going to get burned."

Fury whips through me. I kill the call, clutching the phone tight in my fist. And I stand there, trying to get my bearings, shivering in the cold. A fresh wave of icy fear washes through me as a thought strikes me. Trey is the only one who knows the secret of Quinn's paternity. And he's making me the enemy. My ex-fiancé and I might just land on the opposite sides of a battle line being drawn right through the heart of Snowy Creek. Will Trey use the information against me now, against us?

I hold my blowing hair off my face and curse. I—we—have no choice but to trust that whatever Trey feels about Jeb, he won't hurt an innocent kid, no matter what comes now.

That man is a smooth-talking, sociopathic, self-serving liar. You never did get that, did you . . .

I think about everything Jeb has said. I think about the past. I think about what Trey is saying. Doubt shimmers inside me. What do I do? My grandfather Jaako's words of Finnish wisdom flash suddenly through my mind, as if he's out here in the wind somewhere, over the lake, giving me the answer.

There are two ways to be fooled, kultaseni, *my little gold. One is to believe what isn't true; the other is to refuse to believe what is true.*

He was quoting Søren Kierkegaard when he said that, a Danish philosopher, theologian, poet, and social critic from the 1800s. An existentialist, like Jaako was. I still have his old leather-bound books on my library shelves.

People see what they want to see, or what they are told to see, and once that picture starts to fill your mind, logic starts bending things to fit. My job is to tell the truth, kultaseni. *That is my belief with this newspaper of mine . . . that's why I started it.*

Heat, emotion, a mess of feelings swamps through me. I've been entrusted with this legacy, my grandfather's vision, my father's business—the newspaper. My sister has also entrusted me with her child. My sister who believed in Jeb, who was fighting to clear him, for his child's sake. My sister who died before she could finish her fight.

I look up at the sky. I feel them all. Here. My family. Looking down, watching me now. I rub my arms. I need to find the truth. I need to do what my grandfather and father would have done. I need to stand by my sister. *There are two ways to be fooled, kultaseni . . .*

I will not be fooled.

I pocket my phone and return to the warm glow of the boathouse. I open the door, holding it firmly as the wind tries to snatch it from my hand. As I draw it closed behind me, I see Jeb wincing as he struggles into his leather jacket.

"Where are you going?"

Those liquid obsidian eyes meet mine. His long hair is matted in places with blood, his skin a dusky soft brown. Heat spreads low through my belly again. He's the most beautiful, striking man I've ever known. But I will not be fooled. Not by my own libido. I'm going to get the truth. I might not like the truth, but it's the only way to set this all straight.

"I'm going to find a motel," he says.

"Motel—what are you talking about?"

"I don't want you part of this. I can't put you in danger."

"I *am* part of it."

He makes for the door.

I block him. "Wait. You have no transport, you have no—"

"I can get a cab, rent a room. I have funds untouched since I was incarcerated. My mother never spent a thing she earned from the river company. My land still has value. Every penny I ever earned, I've saved." His gaze pins mine. "I was saving so I'd be in a good place to marry you."

My stomach bottoms out. I press my palm against my abdomen.

"And I have my bike—"

"The police have impounded it."

He stills. A darkness fills his face.

"They want you for arson," I say.

"What?"

"They say you did it; set fire to the west side. They found the gas cans, matches."

"Who was that on the phone?"

"It doesn't matter who—"

"Who?" he barks.

A flicker of fear sparks through me. I take a step back, glare at him. Memories snake round my brain. I think of what he did to his father.

Jeb sees my response and something changes in his eyes immediately as he tempers his flare of passion. But the moment niggles, an uneasy little reminder. A tiny whisper of doubt.

You're playing with fire, Rachel . . . you're going to get burned . . .

"It was Trey, wasn't it?" he says more calmly. "What did he say?"

I swallow. "He says the police have an arson and forensic identification team out there, and they're looking at you for burning the place up."

His eyes narrow and a muscle pulses along his jaw.

"You can't let them take you in, Jeb, not even for questioning. You need to stay here."

He comes up to me, stands close, places his hands on my shoulders. His voice is gruff. "What else did Trey say?"

"That they're going to look at me as an accessory. That they saw me out there tonight." I curse. "I touched that gas can. My fingerprints are on it."

"See? *This* is why I need to go."

"No, this is why you have to stay. Here, in this boathouse. They can't touch you on my property, not without sufficient evidence and a solid warrant. They have no right." I pause. "You were pre-empted, Jeb. You can no longer do this alone. You need my help. You need *me*."

"Why are you doing this?"

"To give you a chance. So you can tell your story to the media before they take you in. So you can start rattling those cages and shaking something free. So that those three men who attacked you can't hide behind masks of anonymity. Someone, something, will slip. Someone will notice, or remember some detail. And I'm going to make damn sure it's *all* over the media, starting with Internet, social media, television." My voice is shaking. I try and modulate it. "So, you need to stay here, in the boathouse, at least until the interview is over tomorrow evening."

A wry smile twists his sculpted lips. "I love you, you know that?"

Cold drops like a stone through my stomach. Moth wings of panic flutter in my chest. Suddenly I need distance, fast.

"And while you're here," I say coolly, ignoring his comment, "you'll stay away from Quinn. That's understood, right? As long as no one connects you with her, no one has any reason to bother her."

He holds my gaze for a long moment. The wings of panic beat harder. But he doesn't push it. Instead, he says, "I thought you were going away with her. For the Thanksgiving break."

"First the interview tomorrow. I'll see what happens after that. Meanwhile I've got Brandy, Quinn's sitter, booked full-time for the break. The original plan was for Brandy to take Quinn with her to bike camp every day. Brandy is one of the camp guides. We'll proceed as planned tomorrow. And you'll stay inside this boathouse until the interview—I don't want Brandy or Quinn seeing you. You can use my father's SUV to get to the Shady Lady. I'll bring you the keys." I hesitate. "Jeb, will you promise me one thing?"

He watches me, a wariness entering his eyes.

"Don't lie to me. Not even by omission. Promise you'll be totally open with me about everything, even if you think I'll find it hard to swallow." It's a gauntlet of sorts that I'm casting down at his feet. I want desperately to be able to trust him. Fully. I want him to *show* me he's telling me the whole truth.

But he remains silent. There is something in his eyes, something I can't put a finger on that leaves me uneasy. Tension shimmers between us. Dark, viscous. Sexual. Dangerous in its power to consume.

"I won't lie to you, Rachel," he says quietly. "I never have." He steps forward, takes my arm, draws me close, and he whispers over my mouth, his breath like warm feathers, "Trust me, please." His lips meet mine, but I jerk away, heart slamming. I turn and make quickly for the door.

"Get some sleep," I say crisply, my hand on the knob. I'm unable to meet his eyes again. "I'll bring breakfast, supplies for the fridge in the morning."

I exit and run up the lawn to my house without looking back. Dawn is not far behind those peaks. I fear we don't have much time.

———

Jeb stood at the window and watched Rachel running up the garden, her hair blowing in the wind. Her limp was a little more marked. She had to be tired. His chest hurt and it had little to do with damaged ribs.

He had not anticipated her owning the newspaper. He'd had no intention of involving her in this way. Now they were looking at her as an accessory to arson. She was being positioned with the enemy against her own hometown.

Remorse twisted through him, along with something darker, trickier. A crackling anticipation that sparked with unease. *Don't lie to me . . . Not even by omission . . .*

He hadn't told her his suspicions about Sophia's and Peter's deaths. Nor his concerns over Amy's suicide, the timing of it all. It would've been too much for her, on top of everything else today.

Promise you'll be totally open with me about everything, even if you think I'll find it hard to swallow.

He inhaled deeply, watching her disappear round the side of the house. The boathouse windows rattled in another blast of wind, and flying debris ticked against the panes.

Besides, they were only that, dark suspicions. Nothing proved. Yet. He was not hiding anything.

———

Lily LeFleur wasn't cut out to be a cop's wife. She worried. All the time. She knew what could go wrong, and it ran away with her imagination. She listened to the distant sirens as she paced her living room, tapping her wrist with her fingertips in an effort to stay calm. The night sky in the northwest glowed a dull orange. The west wind was strong, branches scratching against her windows, cones bombing on the roof. She had the radio on softly, set to the local station. The boys were asleep, or she hoped they were. They were safe on this south end of the valley. Adam must be tired. He'd been on shift since early this morning, hadn't even come home for supper. This was unusual.

When Adam had worked undercover in Edmonton, he was gone for long stretches, weeks sometimes. When he came back, his mind was filled with rough stuff he couldn't talk about. The other RCMP wives had said she needed to let him decompress, that she should stand back, allow him to watch mindless television, do whatever it was he needed until he came round to being in a good place again.

But Lily was not good at standing back.

She hated being alone, and when he returned after a job, *she* needed to talk, to be held, to physically comfort. It ate at her not to know what he was thinking, feeling. They used to fight about it. He'd get angry, say she was overly needy.

It was why they'd moved back to Snowy Creek. He'd quit the Mounties and taken a top job with the local force. A more administrative job. Lily liked that. This ski town was low on crime, or at least it was a different kind of crime; things were occasionally stolen out of cars left unlocked in the skiers' day lot. There were drugs, kids getting into trouble, drunk drivers . . . but essentially a safe village in which to raise their sons. To keep her husband home. Alive.

Lily passed the cabinet. Then again. She checked her watch. Three a.m. Adam could be out all night helping with that fire. She went to get laundry, needing to busy her hands, fight the urge to go to the cabinet.

She sorted through his stuff, separating light and dark. Something made her do it, put his black T-shirt to her nose.

Perfume. She could detect perfume. She went stone still. She sniffed again, burying her nose deep, a sick, dark feeling bleeding through her chest, pushing up into her throat. Carefully, she laid his shirt out flat on the washer, going over it inch by inch as if it might yield some forensic clue.

She picked out a lone, long hair, held it up to the laundry light. Coppery gold.

Lily didn't recall leaving the laundry and opening the cabinet, didn't even think about it until she was on her third glass of vodka and feeling sick with the taste of it yet unable to get enough to make the hurt and anger, the humiliation and rage, the desperation, fear, and loneliness go away.

When Adam came home she was in bed. She heard him come in. Her bedside clock glowed 4:12 a.m.

She lay dead quiet, room spinning softly, edges of her mind blurred. He showered in the bathroom as she lay there listening to the water. Which was worse? That he was in danger on the job or fucking some slut? Maybe he'd been sleeping with other women when he was allegedly working undercover in Edmonton, too. Maybe that was why he hadn't ever warmed to her immediately when he came home. Tears burned in her eyes.

He came out of the bathroom in the dark. The bed shifted as he got in. Lily wondered if he'd been washing off fire smoke or the scent of the woman he was screwing.

He reached under the covers, touched her with his fingertips. "Lily?" he whispered.

She squeezed her eyes tight, didn't move a muscle. Didn't want him to smell the drink on her breath.

"Night," he whispered. The bed moved as he turned away from her, rolling over onto his side.

———

Annie Pirello clicked open another article. They hadn't called her to help with the fire, at least not yet. She'd already done a double shift today. But she couldn't sleep either, so she was sitting at her kitchen table researching anything she could find on Jebbediah Cullen. Coming from Montreal, his story was new to her.

She sat back, sipped her tea, listening to the faint sound of choppers up valley, the sirens, the police chatter on her radio as she read the piece on her laptop screen. It detailed the crime nine years ago. Annie noted that it was Chief Constable Sheila Copeland LeFleur who had been the top cop in charge at the time. Adam LeFleur's mother. Luke LeFleur, her younger son, had been one of the key witnesses, along with Rachel Salonen, Clint Rudiger, Levi Banrock, Trey Somerland, and Harvey Zink. She set her mug down and clicked open another story.

Luke LeFleur, according to this article, was killed in action during a peacekeeping deployment five years ago. It was noted in the article that Luke's father, a Mountie working undercover in Alberta, had died a hero when he was shot by a member of the gang he'd infiltrated. Luke had been five years old at the time, Adam nine. Sheila had been left a single mother of two boys. They'd moved to Snowy Creek not long after the shooting when Sheila Copeland LeFleur accepted a job with the Snowy Creek PD. Annie rubbed her brow.

This town was like so many other small communities, close-knit, everything interlinked. While the resort community of Snowy Creek could see up to forty thousand visitors over a busy ski weekend, the full-time resident population was closer to ten thousand. Many were transient workers from other countries, and under the age of twenty-six, which left a smaller, more tightly knit core of true locals who probably closely guarded their own interests against a constant sea of seasonal change. Nine years ago, the population had been even smaller.

And now it looked as though Cullen was back.

Annie got up, went to the window, drew the blinds. She was also pretty sure there was still something between Cullen and Salonen, from what she'd seen through the trees tonight. She wondered what it was, because when Salonen had come into the station earlier tonight, she'd clearly been spooked by the idea of a dark-haired stranger.

Annie knew scared when she saw it.

What had changed between Salonen's visit to the station and Cullen's visit to her house?

CHAPTER 12

Beppie Rudiger was out before sunup. The grizzly had returned during the night and tried to get into her beehives. She was now rigging a higher voltage electrical wire around the grove where her hives were stacked. She'd promised the girls they'd have fireweed honey to sell at the farmer's market this fall, and so far it wasn't coming together.

The gray dawn sky was hazy from the distant wildfire, the air tinged with the scent of smoke. Clint would probably stay at the apartment in Snowy Creek until the worst of this was over. She spooled out the wire and came to a post. Reaching into her tool pouch, she muttered an oath. Her wire clippers were gone. She racked her brain, trying to think where she'd placed them. Or whether one of the girls had asked to borrow them. She glanced up toward the house on the far side of the field. Clint's taxidermy shed was closer. He had cutters in there.

She stomped in her gum boots up to the shed, which had been built under a giant cottonwood that would have to go because roots were pushing into the foundations.

Beppie found the key under the rock, let herself in.

The smell of pelts was thick. Mounted animal heads peered at her from the wall next to his giant walk-in freezer. The fake eyes seemed to follow her as she made her way to his work counter.

No wonder the girls got spooked coming in here. She didn't like it either, for reasons she couldn't quite explain. It wasn't that she didn't like hunting. She was a capable hunter herself. She could field dress an elk with the best of them. She found the clippers she needed in one of the drawers, then stilled as something near the back of the drawer caught her eye. A woman's ring. Clint collected things, animal heads, antlers—hunt trophies. He also kept unusual trinkets he found in the woods.

Beppie picked it up. It was silver with a hexagonal turquoise stone. She turned it between her fingers, something tugging at her that she couldn't place. Inside were the initials CL. Disquiet rustled deeper into her. She slipped the ring into her pocket and shut the drawer carefully so it wouldn't look like she'd disturbed anything. Clint hated anyone coming in here.

But as she turned, she bumped over a glass jar of eyeballs. They scattered across the countertop, rolling to the edge and pinging to the floor.

Beppie dropped to her knees, quickly gathering up the eyes. One of the bigger ones rolled between two sloped floorboards and disappeared under the counter. She reached under, stretching her arm into the several inches of space between counter and floor. Her hand came in contact with what felt like a flat metal chest. She moved her fingers along the smooth surface until she found a handle. She dragged it out to see if the eyeball had rolled behind it. It was an old tool chest. Padlocked. About the size of a briefcase. Dust was thick under the counter, but the surface of this chest was devoid of it, as if it had been recently wiped clean, or used, or only recently shoved down under there.

Curiosity whispered through her. Somewhere outside, a helicopter thudded up high. She tried the padlock. Definitely locked. Getting up, she went to the board on the wall above the bench where her husband hung all his keys on hooks.

Not one of them fit the padlock.

Beppie heard a voice calling in the wind. She looked up, heard it again. Susie. Her eldest daughter, calling for her. Hurriedly Beppie shoved the chest back under, positioning it carefully, sweat beading. Clint really hated anyone coming in here; she shouldn't have. She put everything back in position, including the keys, and went out with the cutters.

"Mooom!" came the voice from behind the row of trees leading up the house.

"Down here, Susie!" she called, dusting off her pants. "Almost done with the fencing. You got breakfast ready?"

Susie popped round the trees and grinned, her thick blonde curls tussling in the smoke-laden wind. "Yup," she said, nodding her head brightly. "Oatmeal and the blueberries I picked near the river." She was seven years old, her front teeth were only just missing, and her nose and cheeks were freckled. Beppie's heart squeezed with affection.

"I'll finish here and be right up."

———

Jeb lay dead still.

There was someone inside the boathouse. He was being watched. He could feel it, and it raised the fine hairs on his body. The sense of presence must have woken him. He kept his eyes closed, waited, every muscle in his body primed, ready to roll, spring.

Seconds ticked past. He could hear that the wind had abated a little. He could sense the dull light of a Pacific Northwest dawn outside.

Slowly he opened an eye. Shock slammed through him. But he controlled himself, controlled his breath. Opening his eyes fully, he met her stare.

"Hey," he said quietly.

Quinn's features were grave as she regarded him. She didn't move, didn't say a word. Her hair was a wild, wind-blown mass of soot-black curls, her nose and cheeks pink from the outside cold.

It was warm in the boathouse, though, embers still glowing behind the glass in the old stove. The light outside the windows was flat, gray. Waves chuckled against the dock and slapped along the shore. He heard a train in the distance, a screeching rumble along rails on the far side of the lake. Like he remembered. He'd always loved that sound—the sense of a traveler passing through to some distant place in this great big land.

His heart beat softly.

Stay away from Quinn. That's understood, right . . .

"You got hurt," she said finally, coming closer.

"Not badly."

She reached out and tentatively touched the bandage on his brow.

"Was it the fire?"

His mind raced. He never wanted to lie to her. He had to protect her. These things were mutually exclusive right now. Jeb eased himself into a sitting position, sucking air in sharply as pain sparked across his torso. The beat of his blood hammered against the gash on his brow.

"Nah," he said. "I got away from the fire. Just tripped and fell."

Her eyes narrowed sharply and Jeb got a sense she didn't believe him.

"That's my granddad's shirt," she said.

Jeb glanced down at the lumberjack flannel and a smile pulled over his mouth. "Yeah, it is. How does it look on me?"

She pursed her lips. "Okay." She glanced at his leather jacket draped over the back of the chair, then her eyes went back to the bandage on his head. "Rachel had blood on her pants. Was it yours? Did she save you?"

Jeb felt his smile deepen. The movement pulled at the edges of his wound, making his whole face hurt. His stomach hurt too, where he'd been kicked. He felt as though he'd been dragged through the bush behind a team of Clydesdales.

"Yeah, Rachel saved me. She's my hero."

Quinn studied him seriously, thinking about this. "I hit her with my backpack."

"Oh, did you?"

She nodded.

"Why?"

She looked away, suddenly unable to meet his eyes.

Jeb waited. Tense. Unsure.

Quinn glanced up suddenly. "What were you and Rachel fighting about last night?"

"We were just discussing something."

"I heard you outside the door. It was a fight."

He leveled a mock glare. "Then you would know what we said, if you heard, wouldn't you?" Swinging his legs off the bed, he reached for his boots.

She watched him put them on. He could smell the fabric softener in her soft pink fleece sweater, fruit shampoo in her wild curls. His heart swelled so tight against the edges, he thought it would burst.

"Here's the deal, Quinn," he said, hands on his thighs. "Your aunt was worried I followed you at school. She was really mad about that. I came to tell her it was okay, that I don't hurt children, or anybody."

"Where do you come from?"

Shit. He was in a corner here.

"The city," he said. "I have some things I need to do here."

"The city? Like . . . Vancouver?"

"Yep."

"That's where I lived. That's where my house was."

"Really?" Tension wound tighter in Jeb. He shot a glance at the door. He needed Rachel. He needed to step away from Quinn before things started going sideways. He needed distance.

She inhaled deeply. "She sent you, didn't she?"

His gaze shot back to Quinn. "What?"

"Rachel knows. I told her. She knows that my mom sent you."

Confusion raced through Jeb. "She does?"

"Yup." Quinn nodded her head of curls. "From heaven. Like an angel. To watch me. Because I've got nobody."

Jeb stared at her, his heart cracking clean in two. Silence swelled.

Her eyes began to gleam. "That's why Rachel went to save you from the fire. She knows that my mother would have wanted that."

God. Emotion punched into Jeb, thoughts of Sophia tumbling through his mind, his own grief over losing her suddenly acute. She was one of the only people who'd believed in him. A dear friend. She'd given him his life back, given him his daughter, fueled him with a will to live, to return to Snowy Creek and fight for what was his right. He'd loved Sophia and Peter in so many ways. He could only imagine the depths of Quinn's young grief. This angel thing was a survival tool for her right now. A way to cope, to move forward.

Jeb knew what this was like. To imagine things. Good things, in order to block the bad. His whole childhood had been like that—one of self-delusion.

But he was unsure how to handle this. And then she saved him.

"You want breakfast?" she said.

Relief, warmth, rushed through his chest. He smiled. "Yeah, sure," he said. And he knew by sidestepping this angel thing, he was only fueling it. But it was the lesser of many evils right now. They could work through this.

She reached out shyly, yet determinedly, for his hand. He took hers in his. Small, warm. Jeb felt a clutch in his chest so tight it stole his breath.

She tugged. "Come."

"Where to?"

"The kitchen."

"Oh, Quinn, wait, maybe that's not such a good idea."

Hurt flared through her features. "I thought you wanted breakfast."

"I didn't think you meant in the kitchen in the main house."

"That's where breakfast is."

"Your aunt might not be ha—"

"She's sleeping. My aunt doesn't care about me!" Then in a flash, tears misted her eyes and her nose turned pink. "My daddy used to make me pancakes on every Sunday, and on holidays."

Conflict warred softly, dangerously inside Jeb. "I know," he whispered before he could stop the thought, the words. "Your favorite is pineapple pancakes. With marmalade."

Her eyes flared to his, glittering and wide, her mouth forming a perfect O.

"How do you know?" she whispered. Then as something dawned in her features, a smile cracked her gorgeous, eccentric little face in two, showing the gap between her front teeth. "Of course you know!"

And with that she spun round and led him determinedly out the door of the boathouse. "Rachel has pineapple tins. I saw them," she said as she skipped up the garden alongside Jeb, her little hand clutching his. He felt wind against his face. The chill of dawn was tinged with the faint scent of wildfire smoke that lingered, bringing with it a sense of foreboding.

"We better be quiet, okay?" he whispered as they opened the front door.

Trixie wiggled at the sight of them, her tail thumping in her basket. It was warm inside, coals still pulsing softly in the fire. Jeb's eyes ran quickly over the interior. Not much had changed since he'd last been inside here. The sense of homecoming, of traveling full circle, was suddenly surreal.

Quinn was looking up at him.

He smiled.

She grinned. "The tins are in that cupboard up there." She pointed above the microwave. "I can't reach."

Jeb entered the kitchen, feeling invasive. Rachel would kill him, but it was Quinn he couldn't let down now, his daughter. Rachel would have to understand. He opened the cupboard, perused the contents. Rachel's things, her food, her shopping. It had been a long, long time since he'd simply looked inside a grocery cupboard. There were products and labels in here that were totally new to him.

"There." Quinn leaned up on her toes, pointing. "The pineapple chunks."

"Shhh," he said, finger to his lips. He reached for a tin. "We don't want to wake her, 'kay?"

She nodded, fast. And her grin made whatever wrong he was doing feel so damn right, and worth the delight on his daughter's face.

CHAPTER 13

I roll over in my bed, waking slowly to the aroma of coffee and baking drifting up the stairs. I smile sleepily and stretch my arm over to the other side of the bed. It's cool, the sheet still smooth. I sit up with a jolt.

No Trey in my life.

Quinn doesn't make coffee.

Soft wings of panic flutter through my stomach. I hear a noise, a slam . . . a shriek—*Quinn!*

I grab my robe and dash down the stairs, punching my arm into a sleeve. I stop dead on the bottom landing, robe half-on, half-off. My mind doubles in on itself as I try to process the scene.

Through the open-plan dining area I see Quinn perched atop a stool at the kitchen counter, happily swinging her legs, pink socks on her feet. Jeb is behind the stove, my white cooking apron stretched across his torso, tied behind his waist. He's got my cast iron frying pan, and he tosses a pancake high in the air. It plops neatly back in the pan. Quinn chuckles. I can smell the batter cooking, maple syrup. Fresh coffee is in the pot.

My house is filled with the scents and sounds of a home.

I reach for the banister in shock, stare.

He slides the cooked pancake onto Quinn's plate, smiles gently into her eyes. "Let me guess, you like a really big stack."

She nods vigorously. "Yup. Dad always used to pile like eight on."

THE SLOW BURN OF SILENCE

Jeb ruffles her hair. There is affection in the movement and the poignancy of the moment snares my throat. I swallow, then clear my throat.

"What are you doing?" My voice comes out hoarse.

Quinn spins round. Jeb stills and looks up. I come down the last few stairs. His gaze dips, taking in my dishabille. A slow, seductive smile unfurls over his lips.

"Got up in a hurry, did we?" he says.

I grab the other sleeve, thrust my arm through it, and belt my terry robe tightly around my waist. "Quinn, go upstairs."

"Why?"

"I need to talk to Je . . . to him." I glower at Jeb. He stands there in my dad's shirt, my apron comically askew across his front, his dark hair shining, his eyes alight. He's showered, washed out the blood from last night. He looks more gorgeous, more mature, more seductive than in my wildest dreams. I can't think.

"He made pancakes. He's even making you some. We were going to bring you coffee in bed." Accusation, hurt, glitters in Quinn's eyes. The same eyes as his. The two of them—I can see it so clearly now. Daughter and father.

Confusion whips through me. "Quinn, upstairs. Now."

"Pineapple pancakes!" she interjects. "Like Daddy used to make." The glitter in her eyes turns to hatred. Directed at me.

My gaze flares back to Jeb.

He shrugs, cast iron pan still in his hand. *I didn't tell her anything*, he mouths over Quinn's head.

"They're my favorite." A quaver enters her voice.

I push back a fall of sleep-tangled hair. I don't know what to do.

Jeb reaches for the coffeepot, pours a mug, pushes it along the counter in my direction. "Still take one sugar, cream?"

I come slowly forward. Up closer I can now see the shadows under his eyes, the gauntness in his cheeks. The bruises starting to form under his dusky skin. The lumberjack shirt and apron have made him somehow approachable. Mountain-man sexy. But underneath it I detect the pain of injury, the still-simmering intensity. And his aura, the space he takes up in my home, is suddenly overwhelming.

Quinn has gone dead quiet, is watching us like a hawk.

I hold my robe tightly across my chest. He leaves the mug just out of my reach so that I must come right into the kitchen, into his space to get it. I hesitate, then think this is ridiculous. This is my house. He's the damn trespasser. I move in with false bravado, reaching for the sugar pot and cream. He grins, as though he's won. I pull a face, stir my coffee.

He turns back to the stove, plops a dab of butter into the pan. As it begins to smoke, he pours in batter that has chunks of something in it. I spy the empty tin of pineapple next to the stove. As soon as the thin layer starts to bubble, he does another of those fancy tosses into the air. The pancake lands back into the pan with a neat plop.

"Yesss!" says Quinn with a punch into the air, suddenly over her huff with me. I haven't seen her like this since her parents died. She's a different kid.

Jeb brings the pan over to the counter, doing a fake almost-drop along the way. "Oops," he says with a wink, which causes Quinn to erupt in giggles. Jeb's eyes sparkle in response. My heart beats faster. I feel panic licking at me. This is wrong. This is getting out of hand.

Or is it?

He slides the fresh pancake onto Quinn's plate. "Don't forget the marmalade." He nods to the open jar in front of her plate.

I come up behind him as he melts more butter in the pan. "Where did you learn to do this?"

"First few flopped," he says quietly. "Then it came back." He paused. "Some memories die hard."

"Pineapple? *Marmalade?*"

"Her favorite."

"Did she tell you this?" I whisper behind him. I reach up, turn on the stove fan to suck up the butter smoke, but mostly to keep our conversation from Quinn.

"She didn't need to." He turns to look at me. So close. The fine hairs on my body seem to reach for his warmth, energy, like electrical attraction. I feel my cheeks heat and am conscious of the skimpy nightie under my robe.

"God you look good, Rach," he whispers. My stomach swoops.

"You have no right coming into my home like this," I whisper angrily. "I thought you wanted to keep her apart from all of this."

"What are you guys arguing about?" Quinn says loudly.

I swing round. Quinn is staring at us.

"Nothing," says Jeb. "I'm just explaining to Rachel why we crept in here, that I didn't want to wake her." He holds Quinn's gaze. "Your pancakes okay?"

She stares at him a moment longer, weighing his answer, then nods and cuts into her food.

"It was her," Jeb says softly, turning back to the stove. "She came into the boathouse. I woke to find her standing right there by the bed, watching over me while I was sleeping." His gaze lowers to my lips and his eyes darken. My knees turn to water. I reach for the counter.

"She must have seen us go in there last night. I couldn't reject her."

"You're being selfish, you know that. You're not thinking of her. This is about you wanting to be with her."

Guilt flickers through his eyes.

"Who does she think you are?" I whisper close again as he turns to pour more batter into the pan. "What did you say to her?"

He pauses. "She thinks I'm some sort of guardian angel sent by her mom."

I shoot Quinn another quick glance—she's momentarily engrossed with cutting her pancake into small, matching pieces.

"And you did nothing to dissuade this?" Anger threads my voice.

He turns on me. "Did *you*? Quinn said you knew I was an angel sent by her mom, that she told you. What did *you* say to her, then? Or did you let it slide just like I did because it feels like the kinder thing to do right now, while we sort all this other stuff out?"

I look away. *We. This stuff.* We're arguing like a couple, talking like she is our kid. She is, in a way, shared, right now. But what about down the line, the future?

"I'm trying my best," he adds quietly. "There is no manual for this."

"I know." I look down, hesitate. "How do you know they're her favorite?"

"Sophia," he says softly, and a hot-cold sensation quivers down my spine. He knows more about Quinn than I do. From my own sister.

Trixie yips at the glass slider in the living room. Quinn jumps down from the stool and runs on socked feet into the living area to let the dog out. Trixie is the one and only thing Quinn has truly bonded with since I've brought her home to Snowy Creek.

"What else do you know about her? What else did Sophia tell you?" I speak fast now, urgently, before Quinn returns to the kitchen.

He tosses the pancake up, executing another perfect flip in the air.

"I know her favorite stuffy was Mr. Goo." He slides the pancake onto a plate and pushes it toward a vacant stool. "Sit, eat something."

I stare at him. "Mr. Goo?"

"He was a black-and-white panda that squeaked when you pressed his paw. I know that he was left behind in Manning Park during a road trip. Her favorite color is purple and her favorite TV show is *Phineas and Ferb*. She loves Harry Potter and she's rereading *Schooled* by Gordon Korman. She thinks the main character, Cap, is an outsider but this fact also forces him to be a hero." His eyes hold mine. "Her best friend at her old school was Penny James." His gaze ticks toward the sliding door, where Quinn is fussing with the sticking mechanism to let Trixie back in. As he watches his daughter, he reaches into the back pocket of his jeans. "I had this on my cell wall."

I take the thick, folded piece of paper from him and open it. Chalk dust comes off on my hands.

It's a smudged drawing of rainbows over a purple unicorn. At the bottom are the words, *For mommy and daddy. I love you.*

I try to swallow against the ball of emotion that pushes up my throat. Quickly I refold the paper, hand it back to him. Our skin connects. He stills, swallows. Those licks of panic whip harder. My heart starts to race. Jeb jolts suddenly as the pancake behind him catches and acrid smoke curls rapidly up from the pan. He whips the pan off the element.

"Hey! You're burning them!" Quinn says, running over with a laugh, then a nervous look at me as she clambers back up onto her stool.

"So I am." His voice is big, bold, confident. It fills this kitchen, this house, in the same way his physical presence does. "There always has to be at least one sacrificial pancake," he declares. "To appease the pancake gods." He steps on the bin handle, slides the burnt offering in.

"Or to please Ullr, maybe," Quinn says.

"You think that grouchy old Norse god of snow likes *pancakes*? I thought he preferred bonfires and burned skis. And Australians."

A laugh burps into my chest.

"Not if there's still a fire ban," Quinn offers solemnly. "The kids at school said there will be no Ullr bonfire worships this year

'cause of the drought and the ban. The whole town would go *poof!*"
She throws her arms open wide. Mischievous. A little child again.
Something I've not seen in her, not in the past six months since
Sophia and Peter have been gone.

"Well, yes, in that case Ullr might just have to settle for burned
pancakes." Something changes between Jeb and me at the mention
of Ullr bonfires.

It was around Ullr time that we built the big bonfire in the
gravel pit. A time when the resort community traditionally stacks
and burns giant piles of old skis and people dance like pagans
around the flames to the bass beat of rhythmic music, drummers
working up a sweat to appease the Norse god of snow, asking him
to bless the coming season with plenty of white stuff. Because
snow means money. It means adventure, skiers, full restaurants
and hotels, flourishing rental and clothing businesses. Which all
push up property values. And so the economic cog of the small ski
town turns. Snow is our life in Snowy Creek.

Mostly the bonfire burning and celebrations are something to
do in the off season, a way for all the seasonal employees—largely
Australians, Japanese, Brits, Quebecois, and Ontarians who flock
into town anticipating work—to burn off steam and get drunk
while they wait impatiently for the first winter storms.

It was Ullr time that two women had gone missing and our
lives changed.

The whole town could go poof . . .

I think of the wildfire that started last night. It could still happen. The wind could turn and burn down our town. Or storms
could finally blow in, bringing lightning and spot fires.

"How 'bout another stack?" Jeb says, but his cheer is underlaid
with tension.

Quinn's eyes shoot to me, the rule keeper.

"Sure," I say, unwilling to play the role of ogre. "It's vacation." I
reach for my mug of coffee and take a seat on the stool beside her.

I sip as I watch her eating with gusto. I wonder how it ever evolved to put marmalade on pineapple pancakes. "Quinn," I say quietly as I lean over toward her. "I was just wondering . . . what's your favorite color?"

She stops eating. "Why?"

"You've never told me."

"Purple." She cuts into her pancake.

"And your favorite stuffy?" I can feel Jeb's gaze boring hotly into me.

A look of sadness crosses her features. "Mr. Goo." She glances down at her plate, puts down her knife and fork. "Daddy left him in Manning Park." Quinn doesn't look up again for a while, her throat working as she stares hard at her half-eaten pancake, trying not to cry, thinking of her parents. She's a little roller coaster of emotions.

The weight of responsibility swamps over me. I look up at Jeb. He cocks a brow as if to say, yeah, way to go, party pooper.

I take my coffee and walk to the glass doors in the living room. Cradling my mug, I stare out over the lawn toward the water. Afraid. Of the fragility of my niece's situation. Of life and how it can be stolen away so fast. There's been so much living done in Jeb's absence. Lovers have married. Elders have died. Children have been born and grown, but all that time Jeb's life has been stalled. The injustice of it feels so stark, it hurts. Yet somehow Sophia has managed to weave a connection between Jeb and Quinn that I don't have. That hurts, too.

I think of Amy, how Quinn was her child, too. How Amy's life was also snatched away from her that fateful night. I wonder what would have happened if Amy had gone safely home that night. Would she and Jeb have come together to raise the baby?

Behind me in the kitchen, Quinn is now chattering about school and books. For this moment she is *happy*. The sound of her brightness is so welcoming, but this can't be right, surely? It's not normal. Hell, what is normal—or even could be remotely normal—in a situation like this?

I glance over my shoulder and watch them. Father and daughter. I see my goals coalescing with his. He's right. We do want the same things. Happiness and safety for Quinn. Jeb's real freedom. And as I look at this vignette of warmth in my home, I get a sharp glimpse of something I don't even want to begin to articulate. Because I'm still so unsure about him, about what we will learn. Unsure of myself. I feel I'm going to have huge trouble extricating myself from the knots of this relationship if things go sideways.

My thoughts are cut short by the sudden sound of Trixie barking and growling at the door. I move quickly to the front window.

A police cruiser is coming down my driveway.

———

Annie Pirello pulled up near the carport and parked under a tree. She was still pissed to have been partnered with Sam Novak. He was a Luddite. An old jerk on the verge of retirement. She turned off the engine and took in the Salonen house. It was big, rustic, an eclectic mix of old and new that seemed to define much of the architecture in this town. She got out of the cruiser, adjusted her heavy utility belt on her hips.

"You do that for courage?" Novak asked with a slam of the passenger door.

"Do what?" Annie said, walking down the path to the front door.

"Hitch up your gun belt."

"You going to stand there watching my ass all day, Novak? Or you going to try get a look round the side of the house, or maybe the boathouse."

She went up to the front door while her partner ambled round the side of the house.

Annie had spent the dark hours of the morning reading up on the Jeb Cullen affair. She'd also seen the impounded bike, the tire iron with blood, the burned helmet, gas cans. Something struck her as off. She didn't think Cullen was good for the fire. She rapped sharply on the door and squared her shoulders.

The door opened right away, the kid from school glaring up at her as she held it open a crack. Annie smiled. Something about this stubborn little tough-ass kid reminded her of herself at that age. The crazy dark curls, the gap between her front teeth. The soft smattering of freckles. Her defiance. Annie would also have beaten up some of the girls at her old school if she'd been given half a chance. She wouldn't have told the teachers why, either.

"Hey," Annie said, dropping down so that she was eye level with the child. A dog wiggled out, barked, hackles raised, half-friendly, half-wary. Old. Border collie mix. Annie reached out, ruffled the dog's fur. "How're you doing, Quinn? You remember me from school yesterday?"

The kid didn't reply.

"Quinn—get back in here!" Someone was coming. Female.

Annie quickly took the printout from her pocket. "We're looking for this man. Have you seen him? Is he the same guy you saw at school yesterday? Did you see this tattoo?" She pointed to the fish tattoo on Cullen's neck.

The kid's eyes went wide. "No," she said, staring intently at the mug shot. Annie could see she was lying.

"Why are you looking for him?" Quinn said.

Rachel Salonen, the aunt, appeared in a white terry robe at the kid's side. Her hair was disheveled, her face pale. It looked like she'd just woken up after one helluva night.

"Quinn, get inside." Salonen grabbed her niece by the arm and drew her back into the house. She stepped outside, shut the door behind her. Annie rose to her feet, taking in the woman's defensive stance in front of the door.

"Ms. Salonen. Morning."

"Constable Pirello," the woman said with a curt nod, pulling the tie around her robe tighter. "What do you want?"

Annie glanced at the barred door. Cullen was here, she felt certain of it. And this woman and kid were protecting him. Interesting change of tone since Salonen's visit to the station yesterday.

"We're looking for Jebbediah Cullen, this man." She held out the photocopied mug shot that clearly showed the tattoo down the side of Cullen's neck.

Salonen didn't even look at the printout. "No, I haven't seen him. And please do not question my niece without my approval," she said coolly. "She's been through an incredibly rough time losing her parents."

Annie met the woman's brown eyes. Was that a hint of fear she could read in them? "If he's inside, threatening you, ma'am—"

"He's not."

"Would it be all right if we take a look?"

"We?" Salonen's gaze darted to the squad car, then she stepped forward, catching sight of Novak round the side. "Hey! Excuse me!" she yelled. "This is private property—you got a warrant there, Officer?"

Novak raised his hands in mock apology and moved back toward the cruiser.

Calmly, Annie said, "You came to us yesterday about the incident at school, ma'am. We believe the person who came onto school property and followed your niece is this man. Jebbediah Cullen."

Salonen's eyes finally flickered to the mug shot, then narrowed sharply back on Annie. "Are you looking for him because of the school incident?"

"We're looking for him as a person of interest in an arson investigation."

"The Wolf River fire? What makes you think he's involved?"

"Bike registered to him was found last night at the scene, along with a bedroll and sleeping bag."

Salonen's gaze returned slowly to the mug shot.

"Thing is, we saw his bike leaving your house around 10:42 p.m. last night," Annie said.

Her attention flared sharply back to Annie. "Adam had my house watched?"

"For your protection, ma'am, after you came to the station yesterday. We also have several witnesses placing you at the arson scene last night." She paused. "I understand you have some history with Cullen."

"The whole damn town has history with Jebbediah Cullen, Constable Pirello. Maybe you should be looking for three men in ski masks driving a silver SUV and a dark truck with a long bed. Because those three men attacked him last night, and it was them who set the place on fire. Perhaps you should take a look at the blood you might have found on a tire iron. Because it's Jeb's blood. If he really wanted to burn down Snowy Creek, he's not dumb enough to start a blaze on the west side of the valley in a strong westerly. And he's not going to beat the crap out of himself with a tire iron. Now, unless you want to arrest me or something, I'd appreciate it if you left my property." Challenge crackled in her eyes, and two hot spots had formed high on her cheekbones.

"Three men?"

"If your forensics ident team is doing their job, they'll find vehicle tracks, maybe some boot prints from those men. The truck plate had a *D* on it."

Annie hadn't heard anything in this vein. "Cullen claims this?"

Salonen said nothing.

"Can he come into the station, make a statement?"

"I don't know where he is."

Annie glanced at the door. She nodded slowly and took a card out of her pocket. "Here." She offered her card to Salonen, holding her gaze. "In case you want to talk to me about something."

Salonen didn't take the card.

"Please." Annie held the woman's gaze for a few beats, then added, "I read up on the Cullen case last night." She spoke quietly so Novak wouldn't hear. "I know who all testified against him. Why the conviction was overturned. Things might not be what they seem here. I'm new in town; I don't have a vested interest."

Salonen swallowed. Reluctantly she took the card.

Pirello went back to her squad car, got in the driver's side, and belted up. Novak was already in the passenger seat. She keyed the ignition and drove up the rutted driveway, branches scraping at the paintwork.

"There was a guy inside the house," Novak said. "Saw him briefly through the side window. It's him. I'd bet my new sled on it."

Pirello chewed the side of her cheek, thinking as she drove out onto the highway.

He'd been here last night, that much she knew. She'd witnessed an uneasy intimacy of sorts between Salonen and Cullen. Then he'd left, headed north. She'd called it in, been told to stand down. A few hours later fire broke out. His bike was left damaged and lying on its side, stand kicked up. A bloodied tire iron was found nearby. Bedroll down under a tree near the water, as though he might have been sleeping when shit broke loose.

Maybe you should be looking for three men in ski masks driving a silver SUV and a dark truck with a long bed . . .

"So why would he come back to town, burn his own land, you think?" she said.

Novak peeled open a Snickers bar. "Hell if I know. He's a psycho. What he did to those girls . . ." He bit into the chocolate bar, chewed. "Probably intoxicated, if you ask me. They're all drunks."

"Excuse me?"

But before Novak could answer, a call came through. Blue Ford Focus was driving erratically on Highway 99 north of the municipal helipad.

Annie reached for the radio mike. "Car Thirty-Seven responding." She flicked on the siren, hit the gas.

Novak pulled down the visor as sun hit them directly in their eyes. The photo Annie kept in there fell out. He picked it up off his knees. "What's this?"

Annie tensed.

"Nothing. Put it back."

"She looks like you."

Hands tight on the wheel, Annie negotiated a turn on the twisting highway. Peaks rose sharply on either side of the mountain pass, the siren echoing off the rocks.

"That's because she's my sister."

"You keep a photo of your sister in your visor?"

She cursed under her breath. "She's gone, okay?" The cruiser squealed around another bend.

"What do you mean gone? Like, dead?"

Annie tapped the brakes, then stepped on the gas again as she cut into the next curve. She could see the Ford Focus up ahead, weaving.

"Missing. She went hiking into the mountains with her husband on their honeymoon. They never came back." She beeped the siren. Then again. The Ford finally pulled over. Annie drew up behind it, tires crunching on the gravel verge.

"Which mountains?"

"These mountains, up near Cayoosh. Four years ago."

"Shit. *That* was your sister? Claudette Lepine?" He turned in his seat, faced her square. "So that's why you took this job, came west—you're still looking for her."

"You want to put your big mouth to some use and handle this DUI, Novak? Or you want me to stuff a sock in it?"

I sink onto the ottoman in front of the dead fire. Both Quinn and Jeb are staring at me. What line, what threshold have we just crossed, all three of us together, lying to the police like that?

I scrub my hands hard over my face. Jeb comes over, places his hand on my shoulder. "What did they want?"

I flick my head back up. "What the hell do you think they wanted? They want you."

"The fire?" he whispers.

"Yeah. Fishing expedition, if you ask me. If they really had anything, they'd have come with a warrant. They're circling, sounding us out."

"Is your name Jeb?" Quinn's voice slices like a crystal shard through us both. We jerk round to face her.

She's still standing near the door, her face pale.

"Quinnie," I try to say lightly. "Come over here. Come sit on the sofa next to me."

She hesitates, then sidles slowly over, perches tentatively on the edge. Her eyes are big and dark. She begins to kick the sofa with the back of her heel. *Thump. Thump Thump.*

"Yes," Jeb says suddenly. "My name is Jeb." He comes and sits on the coffee table, facing her. She kicks harder. *Thumpthumpthump.*

My eyes flare to his in warning. This is my house. My territory. But it's his territory, too. The three of us are locked in this together, a dysfunctional family unit trapped on the wrong side of the establishment, possibly even the law now. And there's no turning back. I called him Jeb without thinking when I saw the cop car arriving. Constable Pirello clearly gave Quinn his name when she showed her the mug shot.

"Jeb Cullen," he says.

The kicking stops. Quinn goes frighteningly still. When she speaks, her voice is tight.

"Why do the police want you? Is it because of me? Because I hit Missy Sedgefield?"

"Quinn." I lean forward quickly and place my hand on her knee. "The police have got a mixed-up message about Jeb. We need to sort that all out before we can let them know he's here. It's okay that you lied to them. Sometimes—" *Crap. What am I saying? How do I do this without shattering her apart?*

"Sometimes a little white lie can be the right thing in the long run. Because right now, it'll give Jeb time to show everyone that he's perfectly innocent."

"Rachel." His eyes narrow. "Stop. We need to talk—"

"What do they think you did?" Quinn's eyes pierce Jeb's.

I see the tension tightening in his jaw, his neck.

"They're confusing him with someone else, that's all," I say, getting to my feet and holding out my hand. "Come. We need to get you upstairs and changed before Brandy arrives. Jeb is leaving anyway." I glare at him.

But Quinn hunkers into the sofa. "My mother sent him. He's not a bad man. He's an angel." Her fists clench at her sides.

I crouch down in front of her. "You're right. Your mother did know Jeb, and was very fond of him. And in some ways she did send him. She really did."

"Rachel," he growls behind me.

I reach for her hand. She's trembling. I force a smile, emotion suddenly tight and overwhelming in my chest. "But sometimes an angel has to face challenges on earth. A test. It's like in books. And that's what Jeb is here to do now. If he—if we—pass the tests and get it all right, then . . ."

"Then we live happy ever after?"

The ball of emotion swells so hard and sharp into my throat, I almost choke. I'm sure I'm committing some terrible sin. That I'll burn in hell, let alone never find any kind of happy ever after.

"Something like that," I whisper.

Her gaze is riveted to mine. She is searching my eyes for the mistruth, the trick. When she can't see it, her eyes pool with tears and shimmer.

"It'll be our secret, okay?" I whisper. "For the meantime."

Her gaze darts to Jeb. She holds his eyes a moment, too, then she nods. The tears spill over and shine down her cheeks.

"Come," I say softly, helping her off the sofa and ushering her toward the stairs. "Brandy will be here and loading your bike into her truck any minute. We need to get you geared up before she comes."

"I don't want to go to bike camp."

"Yes, you do. It'll make you feel better, honest. And I need to go to work, and Jeb needs to go sort some things out."

As I lead her up the stairs I feel Jeb's eyes boring hotly into my back.

———

When I come downstairs, Jeb is pacing like a caged bear.

"Where is she?"

"Brushing her teeth. She'll be down in a minute."

"What in hell did you do that for?" he demands. "Going on about proving my innocence? Passing some test on earth? Christ, Rachel."

"Oh, and what did you want me to say? That the cops are looking for you because they think you raped her birth mother?"

Anger flares through him.

I touch his arm. "Look, we have to hew as close to the truth as we can. It'll be easier in the long run when it all comes out. She's not the only kid in this town who's going to be messed up with this. Today you're going to publicly accuse four men of perjury, three of whom have children of their own, one of them around the same age as Quinn. You knew this wasn't going to be easy."

He turns away.

"Jeb, look at me, I don't know how to do this, either. We can only feel our way as best we can, guided by our morals, by the worldview we do have." I hesitate. "Remember? We used to share a worldview. You helped me see things in new ways."

"And yet," he says, very quietly, "in your view you believed I was capable of raping two young women. Murdering one of them."

My eyes flicker and my face goes hot with shame. I drop my hand back to my side.

"It's because of what happened with my father, wasn't it?" he says. "That's really why you thought I was capable. And when you told the court about me and my father, they all believed I could have done this horrific thing."

Nausea washes up into my chest. "Let's not do this now—"

He swears viciously. "I should never have told you, you know that."

"Listen to me, I—"

"You know why I *did* tell you?" His eyes glitter fiercely. "Because I needed absolution, that's why. Because I could never shake the goddamn guilt. It hounded me every day of my life. I *needed* you to know what happened when I was a kid. I needed someone to understand. I needed forgiveness. From you, Rachel. So I could move forward with you in my own mind. So I could be with you forever with a clean conscience."

His words rip through me. I let him down all those years ago. I hadn't realized what he needed from me back then. And then I betrayed him. The weight of this is suddenly staggering.

I hear the water in the bathroom shutting off, Quinn's footfall on the floor above. She's coming.

"You need to go," I say quickly. "You need to be gone before Brandy arrives."

He holds my gaze in silence for a beat, then spins around and strides for the door, untying the apron as he goes.

"You should stay in the boathouse until the interview," I call after him.

"Like a felon," he says, tossing my apron onto a stool. "Hidden in the barn."

"That's not nec—"

He raises his palm, reaches for the doorknob.

"Jeb—"

He refuses to look back.

"Do not go anywhere until that interview. *Please.*"

He yanks open the door and slams it shut behind him.

"You can't afford to let them take you in!" I yell after him, but he's gone. I don't know if he's heard me. And I feel sick.

CHAPTER 14

I swing open the boardroom door and stride in. The group around the conference table glances up sharply. Behind them, picture windows showcase the ski runs and lift lines up Bear Mountain and the snowcapped glaciers beyond. One wall of the room is painted a sage green and displays a row of British Columbian and Canadian newspaper awards, along with a photo of my grandfather holding the first edition of the *Snowy Creek Leader* hot off the press.

"Good morning," I say, putting a notepad and pen on the table and drawing out a chair. It's Thursday, 9:02 a.m. I am two minutes late for the weekly editorial meeting. Cass Rousseau, my editor, sits at the head of the table. Her back straightens in surprise as she sees me.

"Rachel?"

I seat myself. "I'm going to sit in on the news meeting this morning."

A beat of silence, a flicker of exchanged glances around the table. I don't usually attend the weekly editorial meetings. The news content is essentially Cass's to manage. I meet with her separately from time to time, but I want them all to see firsthand where I come down on this story unfolding beneath us.

"You heard, then," Cass says, "about the call I got from Jebbediah Cullen?"

I nod. "Go ahead, Cass. What've you got? How're you going to handle it?"

Another glance, this time exchanged between Cass and her crime reporter, Jonah Tallingsworth. I know what my editor is thinking. She's fairly new in town, but if she's done her job since receiving Jeb's call yesterday morning, she'll have dug up the sordid details of the old Findlay-Zukanov case. If she didn't already know, she'd have learned I dated Jeb in school, and that I, along with other prominent members of our community, testified against him. And judging by the defensiveness in her posture, the guardedness in her eyes, Cass is expecting me to quash the story. My editor is ready for a fight on journalistic principle.

Cass moistens her lips. "Cullen's release from prison is old news. My fresh angle here is, that after his release, he did not retreat into hiding as one might expect a guilty man to do. Instead he's come straight home to face this community head-on in an attempt to prove his innocence, and he's naming some of the town's top citizens to do it—Levi Banrock, Harvey Zink, Clint Rudiger, and, posthumously, Luke LeFleur, which in turn implicates Luke's mother, who oversaw the original investigation. This by default could also cast a shadow on Deputy Chief Constable Adam LeFleur." Her gaze holds mine. "And then there's Trey Somerland, and you, who also testified against him."

The others watch me. I feel tension in the room. These are big names. Big stakes. And clearly personal for me.

I inhale deeply. "Which is why I'm going to distance myself from the story. I want a Chinese wall of sorts between you and your reporters and me on this, Cass. And I want everything run by legal before it goes to press. It'll still raise eyebrows, but we'll have a clear conscience on our end. Otherwise the shots are yours to call."

Cass raises her brow. The others exchange another glance. I read surprise in their faces.

But I trust Cass's journalistic expertise. I was lucky to hire her. She was a top city reporter who took a lower-paying job in Snowy Creek because she wanted to raise her kid here as a single mom. Like so many others, she believes in the outdoor lifestyle, the access to wilderness, that this is a safe, friendly town. This story will prove there's a dark underbelly to every place, no matter what you see on the surface.

I lean forward. "There is only one thing I want out of this story, and that's the truth. However it plays. Any concerns that arise from the fallout, again, take it straight to our outside legal counsel. I'll let them know you're on this story."

A beat of silence. "This is a big one. The Lower Mainland media is going to pick up on this," Jonah says. "Especially if we make a public spectacle of it all at the Shady Lady. And because we're a weekly, the dailies and TV stations will scoop us before we even hit the streets next week."

"Which is why we take charge. The *Leader* owns this. I want a full multimedia approach on this one, guys. As soon as we're out of this meeting, a teaser goes up on our website. Breaking news— Cullen requests exclusive interview in highly public venue. Name those names. We link this to our social media streams: Twitter, Facebook, Pinterest, Tumblr, the works. Try to turn it viral. And I want all the eyeballs to feed back to our website. I want people anticipating the more in-depth feature that will hit the streets when we go to press next week."

My team doesn't know yet that I'm working with Jeb, but I plan to distance myself from this point forward, because the minute I walk out of this boardroom, I'm pretty damn sure I'm going to become part of this story in an entirely different way. Trey's words echo through my mind.

They're going to look at you as an accessory . . . The cop manning the roadblock saw you there. I saw you there . . .

I run my gaze over at the faces around the table. "Where's Hallie?"

"She was on scene shooting the wildfire last night. She'll be in later. I have her booked for the Cullen interview, though." Cass scribbles something in her notes.

"Good. One more thing." I lean forward. "The police are looking at Cullen as a person of interest in the wildfire that started last night. Apparently it looks like arson. It started on his property and police found his bike there."

Eyes widen.

"How do you know this?" Cass says.

"I was also on scene, and I heard from a personal source this morning. Cass . . ." I pause. "However this plays, go for the gut."

"You were there with Rescue One?" Cass asks.

"No."

A seriousness enters Cass's eyes as she hears the subtext in my words.

"So, we go with however this plays, even if your name comes up in a potentially negative context?" She's testing me.

"Even so." I meet the eyes of each member of my editorial team in turn: Blake, Jonah, Peyton—it's a small team, supplemented by several freelancers and columnists. "Good luck, guys." I smile. "Jonah's right, it's a big one. Let's go rattle some cages."

I leave Cass to run the rest of the editorial meeting. But as I make for my office, I feel the gravity of what has been set in motion, and I feel the tendrils of fear. Snowy Creek might look like a Disney ski village that belongs in a holiday snow globe. But like any small town, the fissures beneath its surface can run dirty and deep. And in them a dark and dangerous evil can lurk.

An evil we might just have shaken free.

"Don't lie to me, dammit!" Lily clutched the T-shirt Adam had worn under his uniform yesterday. Her face was blotchy, red. "Smell it." She shoved it in his face. "That's not my perfume. Who is she? How long has this been going on? Over a year now?"

Adam braced his hands on the kitchen counter, head down, and took a deep breath. "I can't deal with this now."

"*You* can't deal with it? What about *me*, the kids? Does the whole community know you've been screwing another woman? Does everyone know who she is, apart from me? Do they see me for a complete fool? Are they laughing behind my back?"

He could hear the thickness of tears in her slurred words, the old paranoia resurfacing.

"Smell!" she demanded, shoving the shirt under his face.

He spun, grasped her wrist. His eyes lasered hers. "What I can smell is vodka. It's ten in the morning, you're drunk, and I need to get to work." His heart thudded, perspiration beading on his lip. "Where are the boys?"

"Where were *you* all night?"

"The boys, Lily." He was angry. So angry. He thought they'd put this behind them.

"Stacey Sedgefield took them with Missy to bike camp."

"And how are they getting home?"

Her shoulders, her whole body seemed to sag.

"You're fetching them?" he said.

She pulled out of his grip, looked away in sudden shame.

"How can I trust you with them, when you do this?"

Adam knew that despite her problems, her children, her family, their relationship, were everything to Lily. It was how she defined herself.

"I'll be fine by then," she said softy, unable to meet Adam's eyes.

"When did this start again, the drinking?"

She walked unsteadily into the dining room and reached for the back of a chair, her features crumpling, her puffy eyes watery.

"When I smelled her on your clothes again, I . . . I didn't know what to do. I wanted to blot it all out."

He felt sweat beginning to dampen his uniform under his arms now, his blood pressure peaking. "Are you still taking your pills? You shouldn't drink with the antidepressants."

She stared blankly at her open laptop on the table.

"You stopped the pills?"

"They made me feel dead."

Adam shoved his fingers into his hair. He didn't know how to handle this. He was sandwiched between his mother and her early onset dementia on one hand, and his depressive, paranoiac wife on the other. His mother had started going downhill after Luke was killed in action. Lily, meanwhile, had had a rough ride ever since their youngest, Mikey, was born, starting with a bad spate of postpartum blues that had turned clinically serious. Physical stuff Adam could handle. He could wrestle things into place with his muscles, with sheer brute force. But the fragile mechanisms of the human psyche, a woman's mind in particular, this was something arcane to him. Prior to Lily's diagnosis, Adam had believed depression was self-indulgent, something you needed to snap out of. Then she'd started to self-medicate, and a vicious circle began as she alternated between drunkenness and then increasing paranoia during her hangover periods. And all the while she battled to keep up the facade of a good mother and the perfect wife of a top cop. She'd cracked under the weight of it in the end. He'd been forced to see that she needed intervention, medical help. After treatment she'd seemed better. He'd thought it was finally all behind them. Now this.

So much for giving up the career of his dreams and moving to Snowy Creek for his family. Things had gone to shit anyway, no matter how he grappled to hold it all together.

"You need to go back to Dr. Bennett," he said, gently. "I want you to go see him today, okay? Will you do that for me? Will you call me at work when you've made the appointment?"

She drew in a shuddering breath and her body heaved with a dry sob. She gripped the back of the dining room chair tightly.

"Do it for us. For the boys," he said. "You cannot start drinking again. You need to go back on the medication. We can do this. We can hold it all together."

She swallowed. And they stood there, the kitchen clock ticking, loud.

"Please tell me where you were last night, before the fire?" Her voice came out so small. Pleading. He had a sudden glimpse of the young Lily, the woman he'd fallen in love with. Always vulnerable, sensitive. Creative. She'd made him feel so male, so strong, so capable of protecting her. It had been a seductive feeling, one that had appealed to the macho guardian in Adam. The cop.

"I had some admin work to catch up on, then the wildfire broke out," he said. "All agencies responded. And I need to get back to the office now. You need to call Dr. Bennett."

"The *Leader* web page says the fire started sometime between one a.m. and two a.m." She nodded to the open laptop. Adam noticed then that she had the *Snowy Creek Leader*'s breaking news page pulled up. "Where were you before the fire? You couldn't have been in the station the whole time."

"Hey." He went up to her, cupped her face. "Please, don't worry. And yes, I was at the station. There's a lot going on right now . . . it's a bad time."

Her eyes flickered back to her laptop.

"You mean with Jeb Cullen being back."

Adam went stock-still. "What?"

"It's breaking news. It's all over Facebook and Twitter. He's giving an exclusive interview at the Shady Lady Saloon at five today.

He claims he's come to prove his innocence, to find out who really killed Merilee, and where her body is."

Adam lunged for the laptop, spun the screen to face him properly. He quickly scanned the piece. A sharp ringing started in his brain. Cullen was claiming that Luke, his deceased brother, was among those who perjured themselves at the trial. His mouth went dry and he swore. He was going to have a small-town insurrection on his hands come five o'clock—a shitstorm.

"I need to get to work. Now."

He started to move, but she placed her hand on his arm. "How'd you get that bruise on your knuckles?"

His gaze ticked to his hand.

She reached up and gently fingered his cheekbone. "And this cut here?"

"The fire," he said quickly. "I was helping carry some equipment and got a branch across my face. Make that appointment. Call me when you've done it." He moved quickly to the bedroom, opened the gun safe, inserted his sidearm into his holster, and donned his bulletproof vest. In the mudroom he found his uniform cap, jacket.

As he was about to exit the front door, Lily came after him into the mudroom.

"What did your mother mean that night, nine years ago, when I overheard you two arguing after Amy and Merilee went missing?"

He stalled, hand on doorknob. "*What?*"

"When she said all you had to do was say nothing. That you had a career and life to think about."

Silence shimmered hot between them.

"I have no idea what you're talking about."

"Yes, you do. I know you do. Luke borrowed your Jeep that night, didn't he?"

"Listen to me, you keep your mouth shut about this. Now is not the time. Things could be taken out of context, and you could take this whole family down. You, me, the boys. Do you want that?"

She stared at him.

"Right, I didn't think so. Now go see Dr. Bennett. You need to get back on that medication, understand? You're getting paranoid again." He hesitated, then took her by the shoulders. "Look, I love you, Lily LeFleur, you got that? We've stuck together through thick and thin, we're not giving up now."

Tears flooded her eyes. She nodded.

Adam kissed her cheek. His brain recoiled as he caught the strong scent of vodka.

Running lightly down the steps, he swore again under his breath. Cullen had landed in this town like a burning match in a tinder-dry forest. And he had a sense this was only the beginning.

———

Jeb arrived in the skiers' parking lot at three thirty p.m. Rachel had given him the keys to her father's SUV. He turned off the radio, sat for a moment, a warrior preparing his mind. Rachel had done what she'd promised. She'd gone to battle. The news of his return and upcoming meeting with the press had gone viral and had been picked up by the Lower Mainland papers and TV stations, who were tweeting that they would be on location in Snowy Creek at five p.m. to follow the story. Snowy Creek was a high-end destination resort, and there was something salacious in seeing the underbelly of the famous ski town.

As Jeb got out the vehicle, he noticed the wind had died. Everything felt eerily still, dry, like the eye of the storm. He looked up at the sky and felt a sense of pressure building. In the distance, to the west, the sky was clouded by a haze of soft brown smoke.

Pocketing the keys, he walked toward the pedestrian-only village, feeling uneasy that the whole thing might backfire.

The air was cool, leaves bright, as he crossed the plaza at the base of the mountain. Mountain bikers in full helmets and protective body armor bombed down the last run of the terrain park, flying into the air over the final jump, turning somersaults, landing and skidding into base, dust-caked, beaten up, and triumphant.

Others stood around the plaza with bikes, watching, pointing, laughing. Music blared from the Gondola Pub above the gondola building. The chairlift was still operational but not loading bikers, just bringing them down at this hour, along with sightseers and hikers. Jeb paused a moment to watch a rider coming down, hitting the jump, and doing a 360 flip thing off the lip. He felt old, alien. A man who'd been locked away too long. When he'd been taken away in handcuffs, mountain biking was nothing like the daredevil sport it had grown into now, at least not on this scale.

From behind him, music also throbbed from the patio of the Shady Lady Saloon, where people were already crowding around thick wooden tables beneath red umbrellas, servers ferrying out appies and jugs of beer. Later, as it grew darker and colder, the outdoor heaters would be lit.

Jeb moved through the crowds on the plaza and onto the patio area. He pushed through the heavy wooden doors of the saloon and entered the darkened interior. It was quieter inside, most of the patrons still preferring the sunshine on the patio outside, which wouldn't last long this time of year.

He took a table in the far corner, where he could sit with his back to the wall, see the doors and most aspects of the establishment. He ordered a coffee from a waitress with a German accent. There was a woman working the bar who looked vaguely familiar. No sign of the owner, Harvey Zink.

Jeb had come early to avoid any trouble that might gather outside given the social media frenzy over his publicized interview.

Rachel had called him to say comments were being made about how this would hurt Merilee's family, how he should be run out of town. And worse. She'd sounded worried.

The server placed his coffee in front of him. Her body language, the way she regarded him, told Jeb she knew who he was. But she said nothing, and he didn't invite chat. Minutes ticked by slowly. He sipped from his cup, eyes fixed on the saloon doors, which began to swing open more frequently, each time slicing blinding white light into the dim interior and silhouetting the incoming figures. It reminded him of an old Western movie scene.

At 4:42 p.m. the doors swung open wide and three built men entered. Firefighters, by their uniforms. The men surveyed the saloon and stilled as they saw him. Jeb's pulse quickened.

But they did not approach.

They went to sit at a large round table near the bar, all facing in a half-moon in his direction. These would be men under Clint Rudiger. Loyal to their chief. Showing machismo and solidarity. Three more firefighters joined them, including a woman. Then a man about six feet tall entered the saloon. His chest was wide and his arms were those of a weightlifter. His stride was confident as he made his way over to his colleagues. Dark-blond hair, brush cut. Square jaw, handsome profile. A ripple of subtle movement ran through the group at the table as the man approached and pulled out a chair. And as he moved under the light, Jeb recognized him—Clint Rudiger himself. Their boss.

Tension whispered through Jeb. He was outnumbered, out-muscled, no question. His gambit was the publicity he'd already gained; vigilante justice was against the law, and people would be watching those men now.

The saloon doors swung open again. Trey Somerland, wearing his Rescue One jacket. Jeb's blood began to rush in his ears. Somerland, his nemesis. His longtime rival for Rachel's affection.

Somerland, who'd sparked his rage that night, who'd driven him beyond logic to sleep with Amy. Which in turn had created Quinn.

His skin grew hot.

Somerland scanned the interior of the saloon, found Jeb, and met his eyes. He stood stone still for several beats. Then right behind him another man who Jeb did not recognize immediately entered the saloon. A balding dude with a paunch and macho swagger. It took a few beats to place him as Harvey Zink. Not what he was expecting. While Clint had kept himself buff, Zink on the other hand had let himself slide.

Zink and Somerland joined the firefighters at the round table.

Jeb took in a slow, calming breath. The battle lines had been drawn, and they'd come en masse in a show of solidarity. Had one of those men, or several of them, tried to kill him last night? Set fire to the west mountains? Jeb checked his watch. Almost five.

A uniformed cop entered and moved to sit at a table near the door, facing the room, back to wall. Another man seated himself at a table near Jeb. Possibly plainclothes Snowy Creek PD—he had that aura. The circles were closing in, cornering him. He took another sip of his coffee, which was now cold, and checked his watch.

The door opened again, and the noise of an outside crowd drifted in over the music—chanting, some yelling. The sound was swallowed again as the heavy door shut behind two women, one with dark hair in a braid, lugging photographic equipment, another with short, wispy white blonde hair, carrying a tote. The blonde pushed her sunglasses onto the top of her head. Jeb pegged her as Cass Rousseau, the *Leader* editor. The two women saw him almost immediately. But they didn't come right over. They first surveyed the scene, who was sitting where. They exchanged words. The dark-haired photographer nodded, and Cass squared her shoulders, making directly for Jeb's table. The photographer followed.

"Jebbediah Cullen?" She held her hand out, but no smile.

He got to his feet, took her hand. It was slim, cool, her grip firm.

"I'm Cass Rousseau, editor of the *Snowy Creek Leader*, and this is Hallie Sherman."

The photographer leaned forward and shook his hand with a startlingly strong grip. "If you don't mind," said Hallie in a husky voice that brought lounge singers and whiskey bars to mind, "I'll shoot as Cass interviews, then maybe we do some outside shots after?"

"That's fine," Jeb said. "Whatever you need."

Cass pulled out a chair, wooden legs scraping against the stone floor. Jeb reseated himself. From her bag, Cass produced a digital recorder and set it carefully in front of them. "You okay if I record the conversation?"

"I'm good."

She pressed the button. "Let's begin then, shall we?"

CHAPTER 15

Adam caught sight of her long dark hair, a gleaming walnut color in the late afternoon sun. Even in a crowd, Rachel Salonen stood out. She closed the distance across the plaza, weaving through the protesters as she made her way toward him and the saloon. Her limp seemed a little more pronounced than he remembered—she was tired.

He stiffened as he saw a group of local activists closing in around Rachel. She was jostled by a woman holding a placard that declared sex offenders should be castrated. Others started chanting at her. Among the crowd Adam noticed Jacob Zukanov and his sons. A visible ripple of emotion passed through Rachel as Jacob, Merilee's father, personally confronted her. The group circled her and started yelling, pointing fingers in her face. One of Adam's officers intervened, marshaling them aside.

But Rachel hesitated before moving away from Jacob. Instead she bent her head close to his, said something. Merilee's father stiffened, then Rachel moved smartly forward. Someone yelled at her from behind. Her face was tight, bloodless. Adam cursed. She'd created a fucking circus.

As she neared the Shady Lady patio, their eyes met and Adam's chest constricted with anger and something more complicated—a sense of betrayal. She was one of their own. She was Snowy Creek's Golden Girl, and she was complicating things, dividing a town, digging up old graves. Rachel Salonen was giving Jebbediah Cullen power he would otherwise not have, harboring him and giving him airtime like this. Adam knew from both Trey and Zink that she'd gone and fetched Cullen from Wolf River last night, the night of the fire.

Rachel hesitated when she saw him. But she had to approach. He and other officers were blocking her way by forming a cordon of sorts in front of the patio in case the crowd tried to storm inside. Then suddenly, as if she'd made up her mind about something, she came directly at him, aggression in her stride, her gaze pinned on his face.

As she reached him, she said loud and crystal clear, "You trying to stop me from going in, Adam?"

"I'm trying to stop people from getting hurt," he said. "Your paper put word out that he'd be here. That was irresponsible. We're expecting trouble."

"Trouble like last night? Vigilante violence? Attempted murder?"

"I have no idea what you're talking about."

"Then my newspaper will happily throw some light on that for you, because Jeb was not responsible for that fire, and I had nothing to do with it, either. Three men tried to kill him. They left him to burn. He was lucky he rolled into a wet gulley, otherwise someone in this town would have murder on their hands. So, if your Constable Pirello or any of your other officers want to set one more foot on my property, you better come backed by a warrant, otherwise you respect my privacy."

A cameraman from CTV angled closer through the crowd, filming their exchange. Adam lowered his head, furious. "You call this privacy, Rachel?" he said hotly under his breath. "This is a bloody circus you've created. What exactly are you trying to prove here?"

She held his gaze. The chanting grew louder as more protesters with placards entered the square. Cameras flashed, people snapped images with cell phones.

"How did you get that cut on your face, Adam?" she said quietly.

He ignored her question. "Do you remember what that psychiatrist said in the witness box about Cullen? He has the markers of a sociopath. He's a smooth-talking, manipulative liar who was capable of heinous deeds, even as a child."

"You taking lessons from Trey now? Because he just tried to tell me the same thing."

"I'm reminding you he's an adept liar. Always has been."

"You never did know him. You and the other guys judged him by where he came from, not who he was. It's easier to lay blame on an outsider than to look into the mirror and examine one's own friends, family"—she paused—"one's own brother, isn't it?"

Adam clenched his jaw. That damn CTV cameraman was in their faces now, catching one of the town's top cops arguing with the newspaper publisher in public, and now Rachel had gone and mentioned Luke.

"I'm warning you, Rachel," he whispered angrily as she began to push past him.

She stalled dead in her tracks. "*Warning* me?" she said loudly. She stepped toe-to-toe with him. "I want to ask you something, Deputy Chief Constable LeFleur." Her voice was strident, carrying over the chanting, being caught by the CTV camera guy. "Does the Snowy Creek PD condone vigilante violence? Or do you care about the truth?" The camera zoomed in. "Why did you become a cop, sir? Did you once believe in the law, in justice? Because if you don't do something about the attack on Cullen last night, people are going to think you're protecting someone. Is it your mother? Your brother? Old mates? Town vigilantes? Which is it?" And with that, she pushed past him and marched up to the heavy wood doors of the saloon.

Adam swore viciously under his breath.

———

I'm shaking with adrenaline as I place my palms on the saloon doors. But before I can push through them, something splats against the wood near my head. I spin round in shock, just in time to duck another flying tomato, which explodes against the wall, spattering warm juice across my face. My heart jackhammers.

"That's her! Snowy Creek Golden Girl, the publisher giving voice to a murderer! Traitor!" An egg is lobbed into the air. It cracks against the door, slimy contents sliding down the wood.

"Where is the sex pervert! Where is Merilee Zukanov! Where is her body!" A chant starts up.

Where in hell did these people come from?

Quickly I push through the doors as another egg comes flying. The doors swing heavily shut behind me, cutting out the heckling sounds. Momentarily blinded by the dim interior, I stall and wipe warm tomato spittle from my cheek and brow. I feel sick.

As my vision accommodates, I see Jeb and Cass at a table in the far corner. Jeb glances up. Our gazes meet across the room. I swallow, then turn to go sit at the bar. I shouldn't have come.

As I near the long bar counter, I feel eyes on me. Clint Rudiger and his core team of firefighters, including female Assistant Fire Chief Kerrigan Kaye, have taken command of a big round table at the end of the counter. Harvey Zink and Trey are also with them. The group of men and lone woman at the round table stare, hostile. A challenge. My heart punches even harder. I know Kerrigan well. We used to ski together. I know them all. I have made myself their enemy.

Bracing my shoulders, I raise my chin and go take a seat on a stool at the bar.

Olivia Banrock, Shady Lady's manager, is working the bar herself today. I order a gin and tonic from her. I don't usually drink during the day, but I can use one.

"I wish you hadn't done that, Rachel," Olivia says as she slides over a coaster. Her eyes are sparking with a quiet anger. "Advertising this on social media like that, making this bar a hotspot for trouble. I don't like the mood in here, or out there. Thank God the cops arrived or I would've called them myself."

I take a sip, try to calm my slamming heart. "I'm sorry, Liv. I didn't expect this level of . . . passion."

"What in hell did you expect then?"

My eyes flick up in surprise. I know Olivia well. We've always gotten on.

"My paper is just covering the news. Jeb needed to meet in public because he's already been attacked in private, in the dark, by men in masks." My eyes flicker to the table. Zink's gaze is intent on me.

She glowers at me. "So you pick this bar?"

"He'll be done soon." I take another gulp of my drink.

"I can just imagine my father's face when he hears about this. He'll have your ass in a sling."

"Excuse me?"

She flushes. "I mean, he owns half the paper, right? This is going to hurt business."

Adrenaline begins to slam afresh through me.

"Forty-nine percent," I say, coolly. "And it's still a *news*paper Olivia, not a flyer for Banrock ski enterprises and real estate."

Olivia raises a brow. She turns her back on me to take a large plate of nachos from the hatch, which she carries over to the firefighters' table. And it sinks into me just how much this fight for the truth might cost me personally. I raise my glass to my lips. There sure as hell better be proof at the end of it all. And it better be the kind of proof I like.

Out of the corner of my eye I see Zink talking intimately to Olivia. They both look in my direction. She yanks off her apron in a huff and heads into the kitchen. Zink comes over, taking up position behind the bar. Tension tightens like a steel bar across my chest. I position my back to the counter, to him. I don't want to meet Zink's eyes right now. Instead I watch Jeb and Cass in the corner.

The music from the vintage jukebox segues to some country-western tune, and Trey rises from the cabal at the round table. He also comes over. For a moment I can't breathe. I take another sip, not looking his way, either.

Quietly, he says at my shoulder, "What do you think you're doing?"

"Having a drink."

"Jesus, Rachel, those guys at that table . . . they're your team, people who've always had your back, both on SAR missions and in everyday life. Now you're harboring a felon who's going to tear this town apart. Let him go." His voice is smoothness over gravel. Old Trey.

Emotion burns behind my eyes. I still refuse to look at him.

"We all know he did it."

"Do we?" I lurch from my stool, spin round, and glare up at him. I'm slammed with shock—his lip is split. He has a black eye, bruised cheekbone. My heart drops into my stomach like a cold stone as I think of the attack on Jeb last night.

Something in my belly starts to shake as I look into his bruised eyes. "What is *your* goal here, Trey?" I point to the team around the table glaring at me. "What do *they* want? To beat Jeb up? Kill him so the real rapist and killer is not exposed? Why are you even fighting this if there's nothing to hide?"

His face darkens, tightens. Tension rolls off him in waves. I'm scared. I don't know this Trey. This is not the man I almost married.

But I continue in spite of my growing fear. "Because I'll tell you what *my* motivations are right now. I want the truth, however it comes, even if he is guilty. And I want Merilee found. I want closure. So, while everyone out there vilifies me as some enemy tearing this town apart, the bottom line is I want what they all want. What Jacob Zukanov and his sons want, what they deserve. And I told Jacob as much."

Before my voice breaks, before I start trembling like a leaf, I spin round and aim for the door. It was a damn stupid move to have come. And yeah, I can be stupid with the best of them. Especially when it comes to libido. I hope to hell it's not a subterranean driver in me right now, that this is not why I am fighting for Jeb.

Trey lunges forward, grabs my arm, forcing me back to face him. I suck air in sharply in surprise.

Jeb rises instantly at his table. Cass turns, watches. The entire saloon goes dead quiet under the country tune.

Trey draws me closer, gripping my arm like a vise. He lowers his voice to a soft growl. "If you need help, if he's gotten to you—"

My voice comes out shaky. "You know what will help? To know you had nothing to do with the attack on Jeb last night."

"What do you mean?"

"How did you get that split lip? You take a punch from Jeb?"

His eyes flicker. He's hiding something, I can see. Cold sinks into my bones.

"I don't know about any attack."

"Read about it in the *Leader*, then. He'll describe in detail how three men in ski masks set fire to his land, then tried to kill him."

He glowers at me, his hand tightening on my arm. I can see thoughts rushing behind his eyes. "It was Stacey," he says finally. "She hit me."

A snort erupts from me. "Good one. Now let me go unless you want to start a bar brawl in your buddy Zink's pub, because Jeb is about to come over and lay into you, and there are two cops watching us right now."

He releases my arm, slowly. I walk to the door but my legs feel like water.

I shove through the doors. The bright light of the setting sun slices through my eyes right into the back of my skull.

"You're no better than an undertaker, Salonen!" someone yells at me.

"Castrate the bastard!"

"Make him tell where Merilee is!"

I face forward and walk without looking. The cops keep the hordes at bay. My heart is a bass drum in my chest, my mouth bone dry. I'm fully expecting the slap of another tomato on my body.

Once through the crowd, I run up the flight of concrete stairs leading to the road. I cross and find my truck in the skiers' parking lot. Someone has stuck a scrawled message on a piece of paper under my windshield wiper. I yank it out.

Bitch! traitor!

I sit in my truck clutching the balled-up note in my fist. I did this. I expected this. So now I have to suck it up. Reaching forward, I fire the ignition, then I see my dad's SUV parked a few cars down. There is no way Jeb is going to get out of here now without being accosted. I don't even trust the police will stop it.

———

Annie Pirello watched Rachel Salonen running up the stairs. Her gaze shifted to her boss, Adam, on other end of the plaza near the saloon doors. He was in uniform and wearing a bulletproof vest like the rest of them. Hal "the Rock" Banrock had gone over and was talking to him. Their body language was intense. Annie frowned as she watched them.

Hal's son, Levi Banrock, was among the four Jeb Cullen was accusing of perjury in the Shady Lady right now, and it looked as though the Rock was none too happy about this.

A CBC van joined the Global and CTV television vans. The media was arriving en force, lapping up the dirt in this famous little ski town. The fact Cullen was targeting top community members was only fueling the news value.

Annie had downloaded and watched the docudrama that Piper Smith had aired on the case. It had been riveting, *Twin Peaks*–ish stuff. Now it was all coming to life again with the return of Cullen, and it was just as compelling the second time around. From where Annie stood, there was definitely unresolved history between her boss and Salonen. Was it because Luke LeFleur was Adam's little brother? Because his mother had led the investigative charge against Cullen? And what interest did Rock Banrock have? How far might someone go to keep a secret buried?

She'd seen Cullen walking into the Shady Lady Saloon earlier. He had looked like he'd been worked over good. As Salonen had claimed. The bandage on his brow matched the story of blood on the tire iron. Cullen committing arson, burning down his own place, didn't make sense.

She thought of the cut on her boss's face. Trey Somerland also looked like he'd been in a dustup, and very recently.

"What you looking at, Pirello?" It was Novak.

She turned. "Salonen's cute ass. How about you?"

Quinn was lagging at the back of the biker pack as they bombed down the single-track trail between trees. The wind was cold against her ears, and her eyes were streaming, her legs shaking from standing on pedals. They'd done a descent of the whole of Bear Mountain today.

As they whizzed into a sharp downhill switchback, her pedal caught on a root. Quinn slammed on the brakes too fast and went right over the handlebars in a complete somersault. She landed with a thud on her back. The pain was so big she couldn't breathe. She stared up at the dark canopy, the slices of sky between the branches, tears leaking into her ears. Slowly her breathing came back and she rolled over, getting to her hands and knees. But she froze as she heard something in the forest. Her heart jumped into her throat. She was all alone.

A chipmunk broke the silence with angry stabs of sound.

Then Brandy cycled back up the trail. "Hey, kiddo," she said, dropping her bike. "You okay? Let me see that knee." That was when Quinn noticed it was bleeding. Brandy helped her sit on a rock, then she unzipped the first aid kit around her waist.

After she'd cleaned Quinn's knee, she applied a Band-Aid. "You all right now?"

Quinn squeezed her mouth tight and nodded. She wanted Rachel.

Brandy picked up Quinn's bike, checked it, then brought it over. But she paused, a funny look entering her eyes. "Did you get to see who was in the boathouse, Quinn?" she asked quietly, holding on to Quinn's bike.

Quinn's heart began to *whump*. She felt trapped. She thought of the police who'd come looking for him. "No."

Brandy stared at her for what seemed like a long time. The chipmunk's shrieking grew loud.

"Are you sure?"

Quinn looked down and nodded her head quickly.

"Because the cops would want to know, you know that?"

Quinn said nothing. Her aunt's words circled around in her head. *Sometimes a little white lie can be the right thing in the long run. Because right now, it will give Jeb time to show everyone that he's perfectly innocent . . .*

"There's a man who started the fire out at Wolf River last night on purpose," Brandy said quietly, still watching Quinn, still holding on to her bike. "The police are looking for him because he could have burned down that First Nations village in the other valley. He could have killed people."

Fire.

It made Quinn shake inside. It made her eyes burn. Her angel would never have started that fire. But Brandy was making her scared. Quinn looked up.

Brandy smiled gently, held out her hand, and suddenly that funny look in her eyes was gone. "Come, let's get you home."

They rode into the camp base together, near the skiers' warming hut. As they came to a stop, Brandy got off her bike and said, "The cops are good people, Quinn. You can trust them. You can trust me."

Quinn nodded and clutched her handlebars tightly. She couldn't meet Brandy's eyes.

"I wanted to be a cop once, you know. I even did the basic training at Depot Division in Regina, to become a Mountie."

Quinn sneaked a peek at Brandy's face, curiosity getting the better of her. "What happened? Why aren't you a Mountie then?"

"They didn't know a good thing when they saw it." Brandy smiled broadly but her eyes looked cold again and her voice had gone weird. "You see, that's another thing we learn in life. Even adults, authorities, one's own parents and family, can make bad judgments." She bent down and spoke softly. "But you can trust me. You can tell me about that man, okay? If your aunt is putting pressure on you, I have a very good friend who can help."

—

Lily LeFleur waited at the base near the cross-country skiers' warming hut for her sons to come in with the younger boys' group. She'd been to see Dr. Bennett—he'd taken her in right away as an emergency—and she felt a lot better after talking to him. He made her feel she had nothing to be ashamed of. It was an illness to which she was prone when things got out of whack in her body. Some people had to worry about stomach upsets, or insomnia, or neck pain, or high blood pressure when facing stress. Her weakness, her health Achilles' heel, was depression. She needed to be more watchful. Taking that first drink last night while worrying about Adam and another woman had been a mistake.

She stood next to Beppie Rudiger, Clint's wife; Stacey Sedgefield, a single mom who was dating Trey; and Vickie St. John, Levi Banrock's personal assistant. They'd gravitated together today because they shared an uneasy bond with the men in their lives being raked through the mud via the press and social media. Jebbediah Cullen was back and he was causing trouble.

"That's the kid who attacked Missy at school," Stacey said with a nod of her chin as a slight girl with dark curls sticking out from under her helmet came riding in with Brandy, one of the group leaders. Stacey was in an especially foul and weird mood. She'd hurt her hand; it was in a bandage, but she hadn't said how it happened.

"Was it really Jeb Cullen who broke up that fight between them?" Vickie said, watching the kid.

Lily frowned. "Who claims it was Jeb?"

"That's what Levi told me," Vickie said. "He also said the cops were looking at Jeb for starting that wildfire."

"Adam never told me that," Lily said quietly, feeling betrayed somehow all over again. It seemed like everyone in town knew things she didn't, and her husband was one of the top cops. She should be the first to know these things.

"That's because Adam is a professional," Beppie offered kindly.

"Jeb's back for revenge, if you ask me," Vickie said. "Revenge against the people who put him away."

"But why would he follow Rachel's niece and step in to help her with the fight, then?" Lily said.

"Yeah, that's what I want to know. And why is Rachel defending Jeb now, stirring up crap with her paper, when she was one who helped put him away?" Vickie said. "There's something weird going on there."

"Maybe it's Rachel's way of getting back at Trey for breaking off the engagement or something," Lily offered. "Who knows with people sometimes. This just doesn't seem like her, though."

They stood in silence, watching the other kids coming in on their bikes, a quiet sense of collusion forming among these women who'd grown up in this town. There was an unspoken understanding they would stick together in the face of this looming adversity.

Stacey, however, was still oddly fixated on Rachel's niece. She rubbed her bandaged hand as she stared at the kid, a strange, distant look on her face.

"Stacey," Lily said gently. "Is your hand okay?"

Stacey swung round suddenly to face the group. She stared at them in silence for several beats, as if weighing a heavy decision. Then she drew in her breath and said, "You guys are not going to believe what I heard. It . . . it changes everything."

———

Jeb's cell rang.

"Go ahead, answer it," said Cass. "We're good to go here."

He keyed his phone. "Jeb."

"It's Rachel. I'm parked in the loading zone right out back. If you go down that passage behind your table, past the men's restroom, there's a fire exit at the end. It's usually unlocked from the inside; fire regulations. Olivia uses it as a delivery entrance so the alarm is usually unarmed during the day." She paused. "Jeb, it's a mess out front. You don't want to go that way."

He leaned forward, whispered to Cass and Hallie across the table that he was going to make a duck for it out back. Hallie nodded. "That's fine. I got what we need. I'm going to head out front, take some shots of the crowd gathering out there."

Diversion. Good.

Hallie gathered her camera bag and made for the saloon doors.

The men across the room watched her go. Jeb took the moment to get up and slip down the corridor out back, as if he were going to the men's room. Cass remained seated as if awaiting his return.

The corridor was dark past the washrooms. He found the door at the end, pushed the fire lever across the back. It opened. No alarm.

Rachel was outside, reversed in beside a Dumpster, engine running, door open. He moved quickly to the truck, climbed into the passenger seat. She started driving before he could even close the door.

He took in her white face, tight jaw. "You're shaking."

She bit her lip, emotion glittering fierce in her eyes.

He reached out, put his hand on her knee. "What happened to Bonnie and Clyde?"

"Bonnie needs a goddamn stiff drink, that's what. She's not up for this."

He snorted. "Quite the reception, huh."

"That's an understatement. Did it go okay with Cass?"

"I said what I wanted to. We'll see how she handles it now."

"She's good," Rachel said, casting him a quick glance. "She'll go for the truth, Jeb."

He nodded.

Silence. The weight, the repercussions of it all, vibrated darkly between them.

"It better be out there, Jeb Cullen," she said. "The proof. Because now I goddamn *need* you to be innocent."

"I don't know how many ways to tell you this, but I did not hurt those young women. I went to the pit that night because I wanted to protect you."

Rachel fisted the steering wheel, her jaw tight. They crossed through an intersection and headed north. But she swerved off the road suddenly, bumping her truck up onto a grass verge alongside a row of trees. She slammed on the brakes.

"What—"

She leaned over, put her hand around his neck, pulled him close, and pressed her mouth over his, kissing him hard, angry, her hand going down his stomach. She slid her hand between his legs and he was hard instantly. Poundingly, blindingly hard.

Jeb couldn't breathe. It was as if she'd fired a twelve-gauge slug into his chest at short range.

Angling her head, she forced her tongue into his mouth, kissing him wide-mouthed, slick, aggressive, digging deep for something she seemed unable to find.

She pulled back suddenly, eyes dark, wild, like a hungry, enraged lioness. Her hair was a soft tangle, lids sultry and low. She was panting, breathless. He could read confusion in her face.

He couldn't think straight, either.

"What was that?" he whispered, voice hoarse.

"That is what you do to me, you bastard. And you better be telling me the truth. Everything. Because you're fucking up my life."

She sat up straight, yanked her seat belt back over her chest, and put her truck in gear.

"I didn't ask for my life to be fucked up, either, Rachel."

She didn't respond, just drove too fast. And Jeb knew there was no turning back now. They were on this road together, come hell or high water.

CHAPTER 16

"Slow down, Rach."

With a start, I realize what speed we're traveling.

"Don't give them reason to pull us over. Don't give them anything."

I ease off the gas and it's like grinding against the gears of my racing adrenaline. I *need* him to be innocent for so many reasons. My heart is cracking wide open, and I'm so afraid of letting go, falling into him again. I want to know who did this. I want to know where Merilee's remains are, before I let go fully, yet I'm unable to stop myself.

"I don't think you should see Quinn again," I say suddenly, as we near the turnoff to my house. "Until this is sorted."

He regards me in silence, tension coming from him in waves.

"I think that's also my decision to make," he says.

My gaze shoots to him in surprise. Something in him has shifted concerning Quinn. I wonder again how the legalities will play out down the road. Now that he's been cleared of his conviction, will the reassertion of his paternal rights be automatic? Or will he have to retain a lawyer to redress that?

"You're going to take her from me, aren't you?" The words just come out.

"*Take* her from you?"

I turn onto the treed peninsula. He's watching my profile. I wish I hadn't raised this. Then, as I enter my driveway, I see Brandy's dark-blue beater of a truck parked near the carport.

"Brandy's already here with Quinn." I drive right past the carport and take my truck down the rutted path and over the grass to the boathouse, parking where I did last night, behind a hedgerow, out of sight from the main house. I swallow.

"Right," he says, opening the passenger door. "Maybe we can talk about this later, then."

For a moment I can't look at him. I hate this. Him having to hide in the boathouse. When his daughter is with me in the house. I hate the possessiveness I'm feeling over Quinn.

"I'll bring supper later," I say. "Once Quinn has settled."

He startles me by leaning over and brushing his lips against my cheek at the corner of my mouth. My eyes flash to his. He holds my gaze a moment.

"Jeb—"

But he's gone, out the truck, door slamming closed. I watch him stride over the lawn. Tall. Strong. Alone. His black hair gleams like a raven's feathers in the evening light, and my heart hurts.

—

"You want to talk about yesterday, Quinnie?" I say as I set a bowl of pasta on the table. "About . . . being adopted?"

Quinn glances down. "No."

"Sometimes it's good, you know, just to keep talking."

"Why can't he come for dinner? Why is he in the boathouse while we're in here, eating?"

It's no use trying to hide it from her. She saw my truck down there, has seen the lights in the boathouse go on. I moisten my lips. I'm edgy as hell. The air outside has grown still and crackles with electricity and pressure. I want to put the radio on, listen to news of the wildfire, hear the weather report. I'm itching to see if there's anything on television yet after our showdown at the Shady Lady Saloon this afternoon. But I'm trying to keep everything as routine as possible for Quinn, and I'd rather she not come across any news at all if I can help it.

I made sure she had a nice soak in bubbles in the tub, and I put a fresh Band-Aid on her knee. I asked her about her bike descent and we chatted about her crash and the fact Brandy said she was lucky her bike didn't get all bent out of shape. I showed her my gold medal and told her about my own crash during the Olympics, and what fun she could have learning to ski this coming winter. I promised I would teach her if she liked, and it made me quietly yearn again for the feel of skis under my boots. I haven't tackled the slopes since my crash, and I realize it's left a deep hole in my soul somewhere. I realize that this child, and Jeb's return, is slowly changing something fundamental in me.

But all Quinn is interested in is what's going on down in the boathouse.

"He's there because it's a nice place to stay," I say. "He's a guest and he wants some privacy, too."

"Is it because the police are looking for him? Is he hiding?"

I inhale deeply. "Please, eat something."

"*You're* not eating," she accuses.

I curl spaghetti around my fork and deliver it halfheartedly to my mouth, chew. I'm not hungry, either. I feel vaguely nauseous. As though I've overdosed on caffeine. What I really want is a drink, to put the TV on.

Quinn suddenly pushes her chair back, grabs her bowl, and goes into the kitchen. She scrapes her food into Trixie's bowl.

I stiffen but bite back a sharp retort.

"I'm tired," Quinn says, dumping her plate in the sink. "Going to bed."

I let her go and I clean up the dishes. There is no sound upstairs.

At eight p.m. I go up to her room. Quinn is pretending to be asleep. I click on the bedside light.

"Want me to read?"

Silence, but I know she's heard. I look through the books on her shelf and find *Schooled*, the book Jeb mentioned. I want to be let into her life, too. I sit quietly on the edge of her bed, open the book, and start reading out loud.

Slowly her eyes open and she edges up the pillow a little, watching me intently. I read for a whole hour, until her eyelids are drooping and she is genuinely exhausted and ready for sleep.

"Night, sweetie." I kiss her softly on her brow.

She holds my gaze for a moment, then says, "My mom used to read to me."

I force a swallow. "I know," I whisper. But I don't really know. There is so little I know about my niece, even now. I want to change that with a passion that hurts. I realize I've fallen in love with her.

I go downstairs to get some food ready to take to Jeb, and it strikes me that I've put everything I have on the line today. Everything. And I've done it via my heart if not my head. Will there be anything left of me once this has all blown over? I think again of ripples in a pond, of where things begin and end.

——

Outside the air is cold and papery dry. The snowcapped peaks glow an eerie white as the moon rises over the range. The lake surface is a black mirror, and there's a sense of electrical weight pressing down over the valley.

I have food in a basket, which I carry along with a bag that holds my laptop and some more of my father's clothes for Jeb. On my way down to the boathouse, I plug the outdoor extension cord that I usually use for Christmas lights into the electrical outlet in the carport. While the boathouse has plumbing, it does not have electricity. I unravel the cord as I go. When it stops short, I connect it to a second cord, which in turn reaches the boathouse.

I knock on the door but there is no answer. I open it. It's warm as toast inside, with logs crackling in the stove. The kerosene lamps have been lit, and three fat white candles flicker in holders on the coffee table. I enter, leading the extension cord in, and shut the door against the cold. I can hear water splashing in the small bathroom. Jeb is in the shower.

Removing my gum boots, I set my bag and basket on the small dining table. From the food basket I extract a bottle of cabernet, glasses, and the pasta that I've warmed for Jeb. I pour myself a glass of wine and take a deep sip. Warmth, relaxation, blooms softly through my chest. A measure of relief.

I set my laptop on the coffee table, plug in the extension cord, and am powering it up when Jeb exits the bathroom, rubbing his hair with a towel. No shirt. Just jeans, slung low on lean hips. Everything in my body goes quiet. I cannot help but stare.

He lowers his towel slowly, holding my eyes. His hair hangs damp onto his shoulders. His skin is supple looking, dusky. The fish tattoo is dramatic in the flickering light, and his pecs, abs are honed to perfection. Across the left side of his chest runs the jagged scar I noticed earlier. On the right side of his torso is the blue medical tape I used to hold his ribs in place. The tape is sticking well after his shower, but it will likely have to be redone after it gets wet a few more times.

My cheeks go warm and I try to swallow against the sudden dryness in my throat. I hate myself for being so damn readable.

"How did it happen, that scar?" I ask again in an attempt to deflect attention from my fixation with his bare chest, the flush in my face.

"Cell mate."

Surprise washes softly through me. "He . . . cut you?"

"With a sharpened pen. We didn't get on that well." He tosses the white towel over the back of the dining table chair. "That kind of thing happens when people think you sexually molest and kill innocent schoolgirls."

"I . . . thought you were alone in a cell."

"He was a snitch. Cops put him in. He was fishing for where I might have left Merilee."

A cold sensation drops through my stomach. "Jesus, Jeb."

He gives a half shrug. "What did you bring? I'm famished."

I get up and move quickly back to the table. "Spaghetti, home-made Bolognese. I warmed it. I'm sorry I took so long." I hesitate. "Quinn didn't seem to want to settle, and I couldn't shortchange her. Not now."

He holds my eyes, our earlier conversation resurfacing silently between us. "Thanks." He pauses. "You make a great mother, Rachel."

Is this his way of saying he doesn't want to take Quinn from me? I turn away from this line of thought, unwilling to probe it further right now. Because one way for us both to keep Quinn would be if we came together as a family, and I'm afraid to even begin to contemplate this when we still all have so much to lose, with so much hanging precariously in the wind.

I take the bowl of pasta from the basket and remove the lid. "Where do you want to eat?"

He looks at my glass of wine on the coffee table. "There by the fire is good."

I take a spoon, fork, and knife from the drawer in the small kitchenette and place them on a napkin along with his bowl of pasta on the coffee table. Reseating myself on the sofa, I reach for my glass, take another deep sip of wine.

He sits easily on the rug. The candles flicker in the wake of his movement. "You're not going to join me?"

I'm staring at him again, my mind going to dark, hot places, the candlelight too intimate, his naked torso, damp hair too seductive.

"Rachel?"

"I . . . uh . . . ate already." I feel myself flush again. "Do you want to watch the news? Shall I stream it now?" I say quickly, fiddling with my keyboard to bring up the CBC website.

"A little later." He curls pasta around his fork. "I just want to enjoy this."

"You serious? You want to wait?" I can't believe it. I've been waiting hours myself. I'm itching to see what we've done, where the networks have gone with this.

"I want to eat, Rachel," he says simply. "I want you to enjoy your wine. Relax for a minute. You need it." He delivers the food to his mouth, closes his eyes, his dark lashes a thick fringe against his cheeks, and he groans softly.

"God, this is good." Opening his eyes, he quickly winds more noodles onto his fork. "I haven't had anything this good in years."

It hits me then, what this freedom to just sit and eat a home-cooked meal must mean to him after being locked away so long, this simple pleasure. I feel embarrassed for rushing him suddenly. Embarrassed by his compassion for me, by my own self-indulgence.

Jeb has waited in a tiny cell for almost a decade to get out. Time must have a very different meaning for him. And this moment in the boathouse—safe, warm, suspended from the rest of the world—I can see why he might want to savor it for a few minutes before allowing the harshness of reality to flood back in, before finding out what havoc we might have wreaked by our actions today.

I curl my socked feet under myself and sip my wine as I watch him eat, as the alcohol eases my wire-tight muscles, calms my mind. He hasn't bothered with his shirt—the room is toasty. Muscles roll smoothly under his supple skin as he moves, the tattoo aggressive up the side of his neck. I allow myself the luxury of fully absorbing his features—those perfectly arched brows, almond-shaped eyes of liquid obsidian. Those long lashes that would make any woman envious. His wide mouth, firm, sculpted lips.

Lips that I kissed not long ago.

The taste of him, the sensation of his body against mine, is suddenly fresh in my mind, and heat stirs low in my belly. As I take another sip, he glances up, catching the intensity in my gaze; how could he not? Again warmth flushes up my neck, into my cheeks.

He stills for a moment, his black eyes darkening at the interest he's detected in mine. "You didn't have to go to bat so heavily for me, Rach."

I blow out a heavy breath. "It almost backfired. I hope it doesn't yet."

"You put everything on the line for me—your paper, your own standing in this community." Sensual tension shimmers, dark and layered. Dangerous and fragile. I wonder if we're ready for the damage that might be caused by the bombshell we dropped today. I glance at the laptop, almost scared to look now.

"No," I say softly. "Not just for you. For something bigger than us. For truth. For justice. For Quinn and Sophia and Peter. This is about the town healing, about the Zukanov family finding closure. It's about me doing the right thing with the newspaper, the thing my grandfather would have done." I push hair back that has fallen over my eye. "Ironically," I say with a soft laugh, "it means being vilified in the process. And while justice and closure might come of it, there's no way this can happen without some kind of collateral damage. And that sucks. I don't want to tear lives apart, either."

"Whoever committed this crime is the one tearing lives apart, not you. It's something they put in motion themselves a long time ago."

"Right." Ripples in a pond. Sometimes they take time to reach a distant shore. Sometimes they grow in power as they travel, a silent, insidious surge.

He's silent for several beats, then a smile curves slowly over his beautiful mouth, and his eyes catch the candlelight. "We'll make a crusader out of you yet. Sophia would be proud."

I stick my tongue out at him. And suddenly we're kids again. Teens. In love. The years overlapping. The force of it all is too much and I get up abruptly, go to the window. Wineglass in hand, I stare over the moonlit lake.

"You really think it was one of them?" I say. "One of those guys at the Shady Lady today, who killed Merilee, raped Amy?"

He's silent. I glance over my shoulder. He's watching me with a feral intensity. I know what he's thinking. I know what he wants. I can see the desire sharpening his features. I can see it in the deep blackness of his eyes. My body wants him, too. The heat, the ache for him coils tighter and tighter in my stomach, like a spring that's going to snap. I break the gaze, turn back to the lake. But my heart is racing and my legs are jelly.

"It's the only place I can think to start." Jeb pushes his empty bowl away and leans back on his hands, the firelight playing over his chest, the angry scar. "One of them, or all of them. I'm hoping that if one or more of them is innocent, they'll crack and turn on the others to save their own skin. Or their family members, friends, might buckle under the weight of secrets."

He gets up, sits on the sofa, pats the seat next to him. "Come, let's see what we've done."

I take a seat beside him, and for a minute I can't focus with his bare skin so close. I can scent the soap and shampoo he's used. I lean forward to click on the laptop. But he places his hand on my arm, stopping me.

"Wait. I . . . need to ask you something first, Rachel."

My pulse spikes. "What?"

He glances away for a minute, then says, "Will you tell me about my mother, how it happened? Do you know?"

I go dead still inside. "You don't know how she died?"

"Only that it was her heart. All Sophia could tell me was that she was found dead on the property. I don't even know who exactly found her."

His eyes, the emotion in them, is both fierce and tender. All the old love I've ever felt for him as a boy, then a young man, resurfaces, the memories swirling thick. I am reminded of the day he rescued an injured robin, how gentle his hands were. And of another day when he took me hunting and I asked him at the very last moment not to shoot the deer. How he lowered his rifle without question. This man was sensitive and empathetic, and he hid it deep from most people under a tough-ass shell. I'm reminded of how deeply I hurt him by telling the lawyers what he confessed to me about his father. Guilt slices sharp and cruel through me. For a moment I cannot speak.

"Rachel?" he says softly.

Tension builds in my muscles and my mouth goes dry. I inhale deeply. "She died right by the river."

"She was outside? By the water?"

I clear my throat. "It looks as though she was hanging salmon . . ." I force myself to meet the intensity in his eyes. "It was two weeks before they found her."

"Two weeks? How do you know this? Through Rescue One?"

"First responders—they talk privately."

He stares. I can see the pounding of his pulse in the carotid at his neck, under the coho. It makes the fish appear alive, as if it has its own racing heart.

"Go on," he says.

"There'd been some wildlife activity. Bear. Probably attracted by the salmon."

He inhales, slowly, deeply, that dangerous edge in him surfacing. The whole cabin seems to shimmer with his quiet ferocity.

"A whole two weeks, and no one called her? No one went to check on her? No one missed her? They let a bear eat her?"

I remain silent.

He surges to his feet, drags both hands over his hair, paces, his muscles rippling bronze in firelight. He's suddenly a caged beast of a man, the cabin too small. I swallow. I cannot imagine him in a tiny cell all these years.

He stops in front of the window overlooking the lake and just stands there with his back to me. A man broken but not bowed. Compassion slices through me.

I get up, touch his shoulder. His skin quivers under my touch. Supple, and warm.

"I did this to her," he says. His voice is strange. Distant. Husky. "I became a pariah that night, and by default, so did she."

"No," I whisper. "If what you say is true, someone else did this to you, to her."

He spins around, eyes sparking with fierce emotion. "*If* . . . it's always *if*."

"That's why we need to prove it. So there is no doubt in anyone's mind."

"But you, Rachel, *you* still say *if*."

"What am I supposed to say?"

His face darkens. "Not one goddamn person on this earth ever just believed in me, apart from her, my mother. Do you know that? Not even you. Not when it truly mattered."

His words deliver a gut punch so powerful I step back, winded. "I was eighteen. It was . . . I . . ." But explanation fails me. We've been here. I suspect we'll revisit this place many more times yet, because even in my own heart I've not managed to come to terms with the role I played in his conviction.

He's breathing hard, a vein swelling on his temple under the butterfly sutures I applied earlier. It makes his cut look angry.

"I'm sorry," he says finally. "Jesus, I am sorry. I . . ." He walks away, then spins back, pointing his powerful arm in the direction of my house. "But this is why I have to fix things before

Quinn finds out who I am. I can never let this same thing happen to my daughter, let her become a pariah like me. Like my mother. Do you see? She'd be forced to wear my history like a label. A label she might not be able to shake for the rest of her life. That's what happens when you put people in a box, Rachel. You judge them. You force them to wear a label. You force them to begin to think that they're somehow deficient and, because of it, they make the wrong choices in life. Choices you can't undo. This is what Sophia was trying to set right. This was why she and Peter were help—"

I touch his arm. His skin is hot, damp. The connection is electric and stops him instantly. He glowers at my hand on his skin, my pale tone against his dark. Slowly he looks up at me. Heat floods to my groin, my nipples going tight. Suddenly I cannot breathe.

He grabs me, yanks my body hard against his. His hand slides brusquely up my neck, his fingers digging, fisting into my thick hair. He pulls my head back, forcing me to look up, and he presses his mouth down hard over mine. I melt instantly, going hot and wet and boneless as I open my mouth to him. His tongue enters, tangles with mine, and I feel his other hand sliding down my waist, going round my hip, cupping my butt. He jerks my pelvis against his thigh. The length of his erection presses hard and hot against my stomach.

My mind goes blank as fire erupts inside me. I fumble desperately with the buckle of his jeans as he kisses me. I undo the zipper, and his erection swells hot and hard into my hands. A soft groan of pleasure escapes my throat as I massage him.

Jeb edges me back toward the woodstove, a moan coming from deep in his chest as I work his erection, and he lowers me to the rag rug in front of the fire. He breaks our kiss, looks into my eyes.

"Protection." His voice is thick.

"Bathroom cabinet," I manage to whisper, my voice hoarse. "Close the drapes."

He leaves me lying there, blood pounding, as he goes to fetch the condoms Trey left down here. Things had been going bad between us with Quinn in the house. We'd tried a romantic tryst in the boathouse, but it hadn't salvaged a thing. I hear Jeb in the bathroom. I have time to change my mind. I can't—I've ached for this on some level since I was a teen.

He wanted me back then, too. I know it now. But he refused because I was drunk, and young, because he wanted even more, my promise to be with him for life. He wanted our first time to be special and with ceremony. He was more chivalrous and noble than any of the guys out here, yet he was the one vilified.

. He comes out of the bathroom. Naked. His erection sheathed and gleaming in a condom. His thighs muscular. My throat goes bone-dry as he pulls the drapes shut over the windows facing the house. Somehow he seems even more powerful unclothed. He's the most beautiful thing I've ever seen.

He kneels naked before me. The years between then and now melt away as he reaches for the hem of my sweater, lifts it over my head. I undo my bra, let it drop. He stares at my breasts. My nipples are so tight they hurt, they ache, with the desire that pulses between my thighs. Every molecule in my body is screaming. I want him. All of him. Deep inside, his body, hair, chafing against me. My vision starts to blur as he lowers me onto my back, takes my nipple in his mouth, sucks, scores with his teeth, nipping. A scream, a pressure, builds low in my chest as I arch into him, desperate for more. He moves his tongue down my belly, slow, tortuous, slick, warm. Molten liquid flares through my groin. I feel like I'm going to blow apart. He unzips my jeans, sliding them down my hips, and he groans with pleasure as he sees my lace panties.

He slides his hand into them, cupping me warmly between the legs. I feel as though I will come just like that. I try to breathe. Try to make it last. His fingers part me and he slides one inside, then another. Moving his fingers rhythmically up inside me, he lowers his body over mine, starts kissing me again, his tongue slicking with mine as his fingers move inside me, his thumb rubbing my sensitive nub. I start to tremble. I open my legs wider, arching into his touch, wanting to feel him deeper, becoming aggressive with my kiss, biting his lips, and something snaps in him.

He yanks my panties off and we're rolling, tangling on the rug in front of the fire. He's between my thighs, kneeing me open even wider . . . and he plunges into me. To the hilt. Hot, hard, quivering. I gasp, my fingers digging into his back as my body accommodates to the size of him. I can feel his balls, soft against my skin. Then he's moving, sliding, driving into me. Hotter, harder, faster. I'm arching, sweating, shaking, desperate to have him even deeper yet, I'm aching for something even more than the sensation inside of me. More than sex. I'm aching to be whole. To be released.

I gasp in shock as he suddenly withdraws and flips me round onto all fours in front of the fire. I'm panting. I brace my hands and knees far apart, dipping my spine, arching my buttocks toward him, wanting him. He mounts me from behind, cupping my breasts tightly as he thrusts against me with a slapping sound, his erection hitting a sweet spot oh so deep inside me. My muscles wind tighter, tighter, I grow slicker, wetter, hotter as he slides inside me. I pant harder . . . and suddenly I am frozen. Every muscle in my body is gripped in some kind of invisible vise. I can't breathe, even my heart seems to stop.

I shatter with a scream that seems to come from someone else, not me. I'm gasping for air as wave after wave of contractions seize control of me, rippling through my insides, rippling over the length of his erection. He grips me tight against his groin, holding dead still as I come apart around his hard cock. When I sag forward, limp with release, he pulls out of me, spins me onto my back, and I flop loosely onto the rug, legs open where I am wet and hot and swollen and still pulsing. He looks down into my eyes. His features are feral, aggressive. His hair glistens on his shoulders in the firelight, and his pulse pumps at his neck under his tattoo. He runs his gaze slowly down my body.

CHAPTER 17

Rachel was sprawled naked on the rug in front of him. Real. Not a dream. But full of warm, pulsing life, her dark hair spread in a tangle around her face as she looked up at him with shining eyes, swollen lips. Her cheeks were pink, her skin painted pale gold by the firelight. Her nipples, a dark-rose color, were still tight. Jeb allowed his gaze to travel slowly down the length of her body to the dark flare of hair between her legs, damp and inviting. Her thighs lean, creamy. A serious surgical scar cut up between her groin and the apex of her thigh. Another round her hip. The skiing accident had almost torn her leg from her torso, he'd read. His chest crunched with emotion, with something he could only describe as love.

She smiled at him, a slow, seductive smile that invited him in, that clawed back the years, made every terrible thing just melt away. She reached up, taking his waist and raising her knees, opening to him. Jeb's vision swirled into shades of scarlet and red as he lowered himself and slowly thrust his cock back into her. She was hot, tight, her muscles humming. And as he sank into her, he felt as though he'd somehow come home. Like he fit, belonged.

She wrapped her legs tightly around him, hooking her ankles behind his butt, and she raised her pelvis up, meeting him thrust for thrust, rotating her hips, rubbing him, increasing friction, heat. The ferocity of her desire, the intensity of his pleasure were blinding. His ribs hurt. He felt the thud of blood under the cut on his head. The pain didn't matter. It had become delicious. He wanted it all and he welcomed the realness of it.

Jeb sank deeper, and even deeper, plumbing her core for something he couldn't seem to touch. And suddenly he came. He shattered into her with explosive, blinding release, and he collapsed down into her arms. They held each other tight, and there were tears in his eyes at the sheer incredible pain and pleasure of sexual relief.

He had not made love to a woman since Amy. Since he was nineteen. And it had not been pleasant. Nothing could describe what this meant to him now. To have Rachel, finally, in his arms. The only woman he ever loved in this way. Ever wanted.

And as he held on to her, she kissed his neck, his tears, and she pushed damp hair back from his brow. She looked into his eyes, and something silent passed between them.

The moment was both so powerful and fragile. In his arms he held his future. Dreams. Her. She was open to him. She wanted him. It could happen. Yet at the very same time, it had shown Jeb just how much he really stood to lose now.

The stakes had just shot sky-high. Rachel. His daughter. His innocence.

Home.

Jeb could barely breathe.

He rolled onto his side and pulled a blanket down from the back of the sofa to cover them. They lay there together in silence, fingers entwined, listening to the crack and pop of the fire, watching moonlight behind the bare fingers of trees outside the window. It was hauntingly quiet outside after all that wind. Even inside he could feel the oppressive, crackling quietness that preceded a big storm.

"What are you thinking?" he said to her.

She turned her head to face him and smiled. "I thought it was the woman in a relationship who got to say that."

A relationship.

"I'm scared," she said finally. "To love you again. And I don't know how to stop this now. I love Quinn, too. I . . . it all feels so fragile."

He leaned forward, kissed her mouth. "Do you believe in fate, Rachel?" he whispered over her lips. "Do you believe that patterns are prewritten into the fabric of our universe, and we can't escape them?"

She stared up at the rafters. "I don't know what I believe."

"Maybe this was always meant to be. Us. But the pattern was broken. We need to find a way to put it back together again."

She inhaled deeply. "I feel something bad is coming."

He moved the hair back from her eyes. He was afraid, too. This meant everything to him. He was going to keep shaking things up in Snowy Creek, but he hoped the cracks that opened weren't going to swallow them both up, too.

They lay together for a long while, and Jeb felt it too, a sense of something evil coming. That they were presently in the quiet eye of the storm, and things were going to hit hard, in more ways than one.

—

Quinn knelt on her bed in the dark, watching the boathouse. The drapes had been drawn on the side of the building that faced the main house, but light glowed behind the drapes and she knew Rachel was in there. With him. A strange feeling of jealousy filled her. She missed her mom and dad so much it hurt. She missed her mom's smell, and the cool touch of her hand on her forehead, the comfort of her voice. The sound of her laughing. She missed her dad's grunts, like a big old bear, when he listened to her tell stories about school. It felt like there was a sock in her throat again and her eyes burned. She dived back into her bed and pulled her duvet over her head. She lay there in a tight ball, refusing to cry. It was easier to be angry.

———

A flat, predawn grayness bled into the sky. Rachel stirred, then sat up suddenly and scrabbled among the pile of clothes for her watch.

"God, look at the time!" She lurched up and grabbed one of the warm flannel shirts she'd brought down to the boathouse for him. "We need to watch the coverage quickly—I don't want Quinn to wake up in the house without me." She pulled the shirt on and hastily buttoned it over her bare breasts.

Jeb propped himself up onto his arm, smiling as he watched her locate her lace panties, pull them on, her muscles moving smooth and long and lean in her legs. He felt himself stir in the groin all over again. She was the most beautiful thing he knew.

She sat on the couch. "Come."

He joined her, and side by side they watched the newsfeeds from CBC, then CTV, then Global Television. Rachel's body stiffened at the clip of her arguing with Adam.

She pulled up the *Leader* web page, and together they read what Cass had written. Highlighted in a pull quote was the thrust of the article.

Jeb Cullen claims in an exclusive interview with the Snowy Creek Leader *that four men who testified against him in court almost ten years ago lied in an effort to frame him for sexual assault and murder. Cullen alleges Harvey Zink, Levi Banrock, Clint Rudiger, and Luke LeFleur all perjured themselves because they either have something to hide, or they are protecting the real killer of Merilee Zukanov, and Cullen's back in town to prove it.*

"She did a fine job," Rachel said. She opened up the comment threads, starting with the ones following the *Leader* article, then going to the comments on the Twitter and Facebook feeds. This thing was going viral. It was blowing up. There were comments on the pages of CBC, Global, and CTV. And the *Sun* and *Province* newspapers. Hundreds of comments, and several camps forming. There was vitriol and hate being directed toward both her and Jeb, but heavy support was also coming from several key quarters, including the civil liberties society, prisoner's rights groups, plus the Lower Mainland Restorative Society and supporters of the UBC Innocence Project. There were hate comments being expressed toward the local SCPD cops and police in general. Others were calling for the "liars" and "perjurers" to come forward and tell the truth. Yet more comments called on the wives and families of these men who allegedly beat Jeb up to look for signs and to do the right thing. Others demanded closure for the Zukanov family.

Jeb whistled.

She turned to him. "You got what you wanted, Jeb."

"I couldn't have done that—not at that level—without your support."

She dragged her hand through her hair, and for a moment they sat in silence on that little sofa in the warm cabin, trying to digest the impact of what they'd done.

"I wonder when the other shoe will drop." She glanced at the window. "I should get back to the house before Quinn wakes."

"Rachel—"

She turned. He kissed her hard and sudden, holding her face in both hands. "Thank you."

Her gaze flickered, and Jeb saw that she understood; he was thanking her for a lot more than the story.

"What now?" she said. "We just wait?"

"I want to go see the house where Amy shot herself."

"Why?"

"I just want to see it."

She frowned slightly. "You are telling me everything, right?"

"I'm not lying, Rachel." A twinge of guilt quivered through him as he said the words. But he wasn't going to voice his suspicions. Not until he was certain. She'd dealt with enough since his arrival.

She regarded him in silence, something unreadable entering her eyes. "I'm coming with you," she said.

"No. You've done enough."

She got to her feet. "I'm coming, whether you like it or not. I'll fetch you and we'll go over once Brandy has taken Quinn to bike camp. I'll leave you my laptop in the meanwhile."

"I mean it—I want you to step back now. You're in deep enough."

Her frown deepened as a cool glimmer of suspicion entered her eyes. "That's just it—I'm in too deep to step back. This is my fight, too, now. There's no debate, I'm going with you."

Silence hung for a beat. He inhaled deeply.

"You're holding something back, aren't you, Jeb? Is it because I betrayed your confidence before, because you can't fully trust—"

"Fine," he snapped, memories of his father suddenly swirling sickeningly through his brain. With the memories came the familiar, nauseating crush of remorse. "Come if you want. After that I want to go see Piper Smith."

"Piper? What the hell for?"

"Because Piper was the catalyst. She's the one who first got that lab tech to talk about the evidence that wasn't presented at trial. She's the one who got into Sophia's and Amy's heads that Amy might have remembered something. She inspired Sophia to start the hypnosis with Amy. Amy was . . . starting to remember things."

He avoided the next train of thought. He got up and went instead into the small kitchenette to put some coffee on.

She stared after him. "Jeb," she said quietly, darkly. "You promised me that you'd be open. I want—I *need*—to trust you one hundred percent."

A complex mix of guilt and determination wormed deeper. He nodded, filled the coffeepot. "Want some coffee?"

"No, I told you, I need to get back before Quinn wakes."

As she reached for her jeans, he asked, "Did Quinn ever say why she hit that kid?"

Rachel stilled, jeans in hand. He turned to face her. He could see in her eyes she knew why the fight had happened between the girls.

"Trust—it cuts both ways, you know."

She hesitated. "The kid told Quinn she was adopted."

It went through him like an ice shaft. Slowly, he set the pot of water down on the counter. "Why didn't you tell me this?"

"I just did, Jeb."

"Just that was she adopted, nothing else?"

"Nothing more," she said too quickly. "Nothing about you being her father. No one knows that."

"Sit down," he said. "Tell me. All of it. What exactly happened at the school? Who's the kid?"

For a moment she didn't meet his eyes. Then she sat slowly, her face tightening. Her jeans were clutched in her hands. "Missy Sedgefield."

"Sedgefield? As in Stacey Sedgefield, from back in our school days?"

"Yes. Stacey is Missy's mother. A single mother. She was already pregnant the night of the pit party. Father never stepped up." Rachel paused. Then said quietly, "Trey and Stacey are seeing each other. They're living together."

Jeb narrowed his eyes. "Did Missy learn from Trey that Quinn was adopted?"

"A lot of people know my sister adopted a baby, Jeb. That in itself was never a secret."

Tension, dark, rose between them. And Jeb suddenly understood the reticence, the look of disquiet and guilt, in Rachel's eyes. "Trey knows, doesn't he? He knows I am Quinn's birth father. Jesus. I never thought of it. The two of you were engaged. You were going to get married. You brought Quinn home together . . . you told him."

"I had to."

Why did this grate him so? Because it was Trey? His nemesis since school. His rival for Rachel's affection. The A-hole who drunkenly called him a half-breed that night when his hand was up Rachel's shirt. The guy who then sat in the witness box telling the jury he'd seen Jeb drive off with Merilee and Amy, that Jeb had threatened both him and Rachel.

The taste of that night was suddenly fresh in his mouth again. His heart began to thud.

"So, he knows," he said quietly. "Which means Stacey might know also, now."

"He promised me he wouldn't tell anyone, ever. Trey wouldn't hurt a kid, no matter how much he despises you. He's not like that."

"And you trust him? That much? Do you still feel something for him?"

Anger flared hot and sharp and sudden in her eyes, and she lurched to her feet, clutching her jeans in a ball at her hip.

"You sound like him now. I don't have time for this. This is not you, Jeb."

"I saw Trey approach you outside the police station. That SUV he was in—it was silver. It's the same shape as the model that came onto my property with the masked men. I have valid reason to ask, dammit."

Silence simmered between them.

"There are a lot of vehicles out there exactly like that one. You're being . . . you're being paranoid."

"Oh, that is rich. I'll tell you what I'm being. Protective. Of my kid. This is our secret. And he *knows*. How did that Missy kid find out about the adoption anyway? Think about that—they must have been talking about Quinn in Missy's presence for her to know. What else haven't you told me? You do still hold a candle for him, don't you?"

She stormed toward the door and grabbed her gum boots. She rammed her feet into the boots, affording him a glimpse of her lace-covered ass.

"Trust, like I said, slices both ways," he called after her.

"This was a mistake, you know that." She swung her hair back over her shoulder, pointed at the rug in front of the fire where they'd made love. "Being with you like this, I . . . fuck it." Her eyes shimmered with emotion. "This could all still go to hell in a hand-basket." She grabbed the doorknob.

He went to her. "Rachel—"

Her palm flew up. "Don't. Do not touch me." Her voice caught. "I . . . I made a mistake. That's all."

She swung open the door, faltered. "And don't you dare leave this boathouse, Jeb, not until Quinn is gone for the day. Don't think you're going to Amy's house and to see Piper without me."

"Maybe you should let me do this alone now—"

"You think you can control this alone now? Or even with me? Shake them loose, you said. Play with their heads. Rattle their cages. Well, we did more than that yesterday. We've stuck a stick of freaking dynamite into a pond and detonated it, and now all the dead fish are going to be floating to the surface, if what you claim is true."

If. She said it again. His hands fisted.

"This is *my* business at stake now. My reputation. Quinn's future. So, yes, dammit. I'm coming." She marched out the door, slammed it behind her.

Jeb cursed and went to the back window. He yanked open the drapes and watched her stomping up the garden in the predawn light—the long plaid shirt, bare legs, gum boots, hair a wild tangle. She was still clutching her jeans. And God he loved her just about more than anything on this earth. He knew why she'd flipped. She was scared and fraying at the edges. He was scared, too, after tasting her love, being shown what he *could* have. How much was at stake.

He needed to find a way to forgive her for telling the lawyers and cops about what happened with his dad, because it was going to keep coming up in unspoken ways, like he believed it just had in this argument about trust. Rationally he understood why Rachel had done it, but it had cut him irreparably. He'd laid his heart bare to her, and she'd torn it out. His memory slid back to that fateful night when he was nine.

He'd been at Snowy Creek Elementary for almost four months. He was having trouble adjusting. The snows had started to blanket the valley and Christmas was near. Not in his house, though. In his house his father had already hit the whiskey, hard. Jeb understood on some level there would be no Christmas for them that year. His mother had also grown sick, weak, in ways he couldn't understand. She'd lost so much weight, had developed black circles under her eyes. She had bruises, and sometimes her lips were swollen and split. She wouldn't talk to Jeb about it, and he stopped asking because he was afraid to hear the truth.

One day, shortly before Christmas break, she didn't come pick him up from school. He had to ride the yellow school bus as far as Green Lake, which was the last stop, then walk the eight miles down the Wolf River logging road alone. By that time of year the day was dark, and the snow base was growing thick. As he slogged along that road through the dark, snowy forest, he knew something terrible was coming with every fiber of his nine-year-old being, because his mother would never ordinarily have left him to do this. She'd given up. She hadn't made lunch for him that morning, either, and lately she was barely speaking to him at all. She was slipping away, and he didn't know who to turn to.

He made it home alone, and that night a blizzard came. He woke to thuds. He thought it was snow *whumping* off the roof and branches. But then he heard a thin cry. Heavy breathing. Cursing. A cracking sound that sent bile to his throat. Jeb crept out of his room.

His mother and father were in the living room. His father's face was purplish red, shining with sweat. His pants were off and his mother was on the sofa. Blood glistened down her face.

"Bitch!" His father raised his hand and cracked it hard across his mother's cheek. She sobbed softly. His father pushed his mother's skirt up her thighs. She moaned, trying to crawl away. But he grabbed a fistful of her hair and yanked her upright, then he hit her so hard again, her head flew to the side and a tooth came out.

"Stop!" Jeb screeched as he barreled into the room. He grabbed his father's arm, yanking him. "Stop. Stop! Stop it!"

His father lifted his beefy arm up and flung him into the corner of the living room like a useless flea.

"You—" He pointed at Jeb, his eyes shining, wild, his hair all over the place.

He had an erection. Jeb knew what an erection was. He felt sick. He was going to throw up.

"You get back in your room where you belong, or I'll take the belt to you, do you understand? Get!"

His mother moaned. "Leave him . . . leave . . ." She tried to crawl off the sofa. His father turned on his mother again, raising his ham of a fist and punching her in the face.

THE SLOW BURN OF SILENCE

A ferocity Jeb didn't even comprehend overtook him. He grabbed the heavy iron poker from the side of the fire with two hands and he rushed at his father, wailing, "*Stop it stop it stop it!*" He cracked the poker down across his father's back.

His drunk dad tumbled forward from the impact, then rolled onto his back, glaring at Jeb. The fire in his father's eyes was not human. That beast was not his dad; he'd become an animal. His father lurched off the couch and barged at him.

He raised the poker. "No, Daddy, no! Please, no!" But his dad kept coming. In abject terror, Jeb swung the poker at his dad's face. It hit with a kind of wet crunch across his temple and nose.

His father went still, like an elk stopped by gunshot to the heart. He staggered sideways a little, and his face went funny looking. His knees folded, and he slumped forward. His face hit the ground. Dark blood leaked out from under his head.

Panic whipped through Jeb. Poker in hand, he stared at his dad, his whole body shaking like a little leaf, bile in his throat. His gaze shot to his mother. She was not moving. He dropped the poker, ran to her. "Mom! Mommy!" He shook her. She wouldn't move.

Jeb left her on the sofa and went to his dad. He rolled him over onto his back. His eyes stared up, empty. Jeb had hunted. He knew death when he saw it.

That night, he'd killed his own father.

Jeb inhaled deeply, pulling his thoughts back to the present. He left the window and slumped down onto the boathouse sofa. His mother, when she'd recovered, had protected him. She'd lied, saying she'd struck her husband when he tried to beat her, and he'd fallen and hit his head because he'd been so inebriated. The cops had bought it—drunk natives and all.

A social worker came out to see Jeb, but he didn't talk to the worker. He told no one anything.

It had finally died down. Jeb went back to school in the spring.

The only person he ever did tell was Rachel, years later.

He put his head into his hands. Reliving it made him physically ill. The guilt . . . it would never go away. God, he wished he could have spoken to his mother before she had died. He wished she could have lived long enough to see the judge set him free.

He looked up, tears pricking into his eyes.

I'm going to prove this still, for you, too. I know you're out there. I know you will be able to see . . .

But the tears burned down his face anyway. Because who the fuck was he kidding? It was too late. That was all.

Men don't cry, you asshole . . .

That was something his father had said to him, too. This was his legacy. And this was something Jeb had to find a way to live with.

CHAPTER 18

I barge through my front door and stop dead in my tracks. Quinn is sitting at the kitchen counter, face pale. The house feels cold, empty.

"Quinn? What are you doing up so early? It's not even fully light yet."

She glares in sullen silence at my bare legs in gum boots. Guilt washes through me. "Would you like some breakfast? Oatmeal, bacon, and eggs?"

Quinn's gaze goes from my legs to my mussed hair.

"French toast, maybe? Pancakes?" My voice comes out too high.

She slides off the stool and clatters up the stairs. Her door slams hard, skewing a picture on the downstairs wall. Trixie whines.

I feel gutted.

And I'm awash with remorse, for starting a fight with Jeb. For not trusting him all those years ago. For betraying his confidence and relaying that awful story of his youth. I can't even breathe for a moment as I think about the gravity of what I did. We're all unraveling at the edges. And truth be told, I'm terrified. About my feelings for him. About what might give now. I switch the radio on to the weather station. A meteorologist is talking about a big multi-cell storm cluster that is heading north into the mountains. Snowy Creek is directly in its path.

Quickly, I turn up the volume. The meteorologist explains in lay speak that this is the most common type of storm cell development in these mountains. Mature thunderstorms are typically found at the center of these cell clusters, while dissipating thunderstorms exist on their downwind side. These big clusters can also evolve into one or more squall lines that could bring extremely heavy precipitation, hail, frequent lightning, and gale-force winds.

I look out the window at the dead-calm waters of Green Lake, the tinder-dry brush and crisp dead leaves, the brown-tipped conifers. We need rain. We need snow higher up. But lightning could be a killer. And if the winds do switch suddenly, the Wolf River fire could grow aggressively within minutes and turn this way. If other fires are sparked by lightning strikes elsewhere, and these fires join the Wolf River wildfire . . . we could be looking at a perfect firestorm. I have a real bad feeling about this.

Before anything else, I go quickly up the stairs to make sure both Quinn and I have emergency bags packed, and that Trixie's kennel, water bowl, kibble, and leash are also ready.

———

Beppie was making breakfast. It was Clint's Friday off. The Wolf River fire had finally been brought under control using water bombers, but it was still burning and the air outside was static with the crackling quiet that often heralded a severe thunderstorm. Clint's gear was packed and he remained on standby, his pager and radio with him as he worked down in his shed.

The washing machine chugged downstairs, a comforting sound. Beppie was reading a novel as she stirred a pot of steel-cut oats on the stove, the steam rising up and misting her glasses; she'd never been able to wear contacts. It used to worry her at school, but not anymore. She removed her glasses and glanced at Susie, who was struggling with her knitting at an antique wooden table.

Janis, her middle daughter, was upstairs reading. Holly was playing with her dolls. Beppie homeschooled and tried to grow as much of their own food as she could. She liked to be in control of what was going into her children's minds and bodies, and she wanted them to learn in the spirit of the Lord.

The windows were misting up, too. Blackstone, their Labrador, slept in front of the hearth where Beppie had lit a fire that morning. When the timer buzzed, she set down her book and carried the steaming pot to the table, where there was fresh farm cream and fruit preserves. The weather guy on their small television set near the table was talking about how a change in wind direction could cause the Wolf River fire to flare up again, turning it toward the high-end real estate of Snowy Creek.

TV was Beppie's weakness.

While she limited viewing in the house, she had not managed to go so far as doing without a television completely. It was addictive, and she liked the news. She'd gotten used to it, the company it had provided when Clint was away on tours with the army and she had been raising the girls on her own.

"And speaking of Snowy Creek," the anchor was saying, "a storm of another kind has been brewing in the popular ski resort, one that ties back to a vicious sexual assault almost ten years ago, and the mystery of a missing young woman who has never been found."

Beppie stilled, the pot clutched in her oven gloves.

The news anchor started recapping the story that had broken last night after Jeb and Rachel's publicity stunt at the Shady Lady. As the news footage segued to the skiers' plaza outside the saloon, Beppie saw her husband coming out of the saloon with a group of his firefighters.

The anchor was saying that Jebbediah Cullen had accused the fire chief, among other men, of perjury. The camera zoomed right into her husband's rugged face. Beppie's pulse quickened. She moved closer. The file footage cut quickly to a shot of Adam, his face twisted and angry as he argued with Rachel outside the saloon. There was chanting, yelling, in the background, but the sound bite that followed played clear.

"I'm warning you, Rachel."

She spun round, the camera catching the fierceness in her eyes.

"I want to ask you something, Deputy Chief Constable LeFleur," she said, as though she was saying it especially for the cameraman. "Why did you become a cop, sir? Did you once believe in the law, in justice? Because if you don't do something about the attack on Cullen last night, people are going to think you're protecting someone. Is it your mother? Your brother? Old mates? Town vigilantes?"

"The community is enraged," one protestor said into the reporter's mike. "A dangerous man, a rapist, is out free."

The footage cut away from the taped segment to a reporter standing in the plaza. "Clearly, wounds from an event ten years ago are still raw here in Snowy Creek."

The anchor cut in with a question. "Can you tell us more about this alleged attack on Jebbediah Cullen?"

The reporter held her earpiece for a moment, listening to the question. She nodded. "Yes, Cullen claimed yesterday that he was attacked the night before by three men in ski masks. He would not speak with us directly, but according to the *Snowy Creek Leader*, the men arrived in two vehicles. One was a silver SUV, the other a dark-blue truck with an extended cab and a long box. Cullen claims he could make out the letter *D* on the plate. These three men allegedly set fire to his land and attacked him with a tire iron. He says he has no doubt they would have killed him had a propane tank not exploded near their vehicle, wherein they basically fled and left him to burn. Cullen told the *Leader* that he landed a few punches of his own, hitting one of the masked men in the face. He says the community should take note of vehicles matching those described, and be aware of injuries and possibly even ski masks with bloodstains on them, or which smell of smoke."

"He's stirring an atmosphere of suspicion, a witch hunt?" asked the anchor.

"Yes, and it's upsetting a lot of people. But Cullen claims someone here in Snowy Creek is hiding the truth and is prepared to kill him in order to stop him from digging further."

"Heavy stuff for the small ski town," said the anchor.

The pot burned suddenly through her oven gloves. Beppie quickly set it down on the table, heart racing.

"What's a rapist?" Susie asked, looking up from her knitting.

Beppie reached over and turned the television off. "Go tell your father breakfast is ready. He's down in his work shed."

"Why me?" she whined.

Beppie cast her The Look. Susie sighed dramatically. "He's *always* in that shed. I hate that shed," she said, stomping to the door. Blackstone lifted his big, square Labrador head, but slumped back, deciding to remain by the fire.

The door thudded closed.

Beppie quickly put the news back on, Stacey's shocking revelation about what she'd overheard playing through her mind. She glanced up through the misted window and watched her daughter going down the path to the shed. Susie was only a year younger than Quinn.

What would she do for her own children?

Was it possible—that someone other than Jeb Cullen took those girls? No, of course not. That would mean Clint and the others lied, that they'd knowingly sent the wrong man to prison. Jeb had to be the one lying. He was messing with their heads, that's all this was. Some kind of twisted revenge.

Susie skipped down the path. Mist was rising in wavy wisps from the river in the gulley, and the sun was just starting to spill over the high granite mountains. The light from the sun was a weird sort of orange, and she could smell smoke. A scarecrow stood silent in their veggie field. It was being watched by black crows that lined the wire between telephone poles. The trees had lost most of their leaves in the last winds, and their branches reminded Susie of a skeleton's fingers pointing into the sky. Pumpkins big, and fat, and orange dotted their neighbor's field.

She stilled suddenly as something caught her eye. *A ghost.* Sifting through the grove of alders on the neighboring farm. Strings of panic wrapped around her throat before she realized it was Mr. Davis in his bee suit, smoke coming from the smoker thing he used to calm the bees. The mist from the river had played tricks with her mind. She gave a little shiver, wishing Blackstone had come with her. She fisted her hands at her sides and tromped smartly down the path to her dad's workshop, dead leaves crunching under her feet.

She opened the door. It creaked against the hinges.

Her dad glanced up. "Hey, hon."

Susie's eyes went immediately to the bearskin on the wall, the giant claws. She swallowed and her gaze was pulled, inexorably, as it always was, away from the grizzly pelt to the bottles of weird things floating in formaldehyde on the top shelf. She felt a skitter in her stomach. She hated this shed.

Her sister, Janis, loved it. Janis thought it was cool that their dad had a big walk-in meat locker with hanging carcasses and a freezer full of animal parts, stuff that went into the pot that reached their table, like the moose that her mother was going to stew for tonight. Janis also thought it was awesome that their dad stuffed animals as a hobby, sometimes for nice commissions.

But it made Susie feel . . . she wasn't quite sure. She forced her attention back to her father, who was busy with a raccoon.

She smiled shakily. Her father didn't like it when she got squeamish or frightened. He liked her to be adept in the wilderness, confident in herself. And she liked to make him happy.

Susie cleared her throat. "Mom says breakfast is ready."

"Well, this is good, because I'm starved," he said with a grin.

Her father washed his hands in a deep metal sink in the corner. The knuckles on his right hand were red and scraped. His sleeves were rolled up, his arms big and strong. She could see part of one of his tattoos—he had a few, some from school even. He made sure he scrubbed under his nails with a brush. Then he dried his big hands carefully on a towel hanging neatly next to the sink. He reached for her hand. "Come on, then, poppet, let's go eat!"

Susie clutched her father's hand tightly as they made their way back up the path to the house. She cast a furtive look into the misty trees, but Mr. Davis in his ghostly suit was gone. And her dad's hand was warm and strong. He made her feel safe. A slight bounce, then a skip, reentered her step. Mom had promised they could bake muffins today. She loved muffins.

"When are you going on your fall hunt, Dad?" He went on several long hunts alone each year. Always one in the late fall. He'd bring home meat enough to last the winter.

He smiled down at her. She loved her dad's smile, the little twinkle that entered his blue eyes. "Soon as all this fire worry has died down and the rains have come good and proper," he said as they reached the door.

———

Beppie glanced up from the television as her husband entered.

"He named you," she said. "He claims he was attacked and beaten by vigilantes who started that wildfire."

Clint came up to her and kissed her on the cheek. He turned off the television. "He doesn't deserve airtime." He ruffled Susie's hair. "Smells good. Let's eat, shall we?"

"Susie, go get Janis and Holly."

As Susie skittered up the stairs, Beppie lowered her voice. "Do you think this is some kind of vengeance, that he wants to mess with our minds? What else could he want?"

"The man is a psychopath. Don't worry, he'll do something stupid. The cops will put him back where he belongs."

"He's maligning your name. And the others."

"When has that sort of thing ever worried you, Beps?" He gave her a smile that lit his eyes, and he kissed her on the mouth, his big, square, calloused hands holding her face. Solid. Everything about Clint was solid. Capable. "Relax, this will go away. Nothing for you to worry yourself about."

"How will it go away?"

"I told you, Cullen will make a slip. Adam's guys are watching him. He might even go out to where he left Merilee, and they'll be on him like stink on a skunk. Then they'll nail him for good, put him away for murder this time."

They sat to eat as usual.

The washing machine downstairs entered a spin cycle. Everything normal. But something had somehow shifted. Clint was watching her. Beppie felt uneasy. She thought again about what Stacey had said.

When the girls were washing up, Beppie went to fetch the laundry. She came upstairs, clutching the basket of wet washing. "Why do you think Rachel is helping him?"

Clint came up to her, drying his hands on a dishtowel. Her gaze flicked to the grazed knuckles on his right hand. He'd said he hurt his hand fighting the fire in the early hours of Thursday morning.

"I don't know," he said. "The guys think she still has something for him."

She swallowed. Her gaze darted to her girls laughing and busy at the sink, Susie standing on a special box Clint had made so she could reach easily, the other two drying.

"Did you know," she whispered quietly so her girls wouldn't hear, "that Quinn MacLean is Jeb's daughter? The rape baby."

"What?"

"You don't know?"

"Where did you hear this?"

"Stacey Sedgefield overheard Trey talking to Rachel on the phone Wednesday night, late, around midnight. Rachel's sister and brother-in-law adopted Amy and Jeb's baby. Trey was promising Rachel he wouldn't tell anyone, no matter what happened."

Clint stared at her, his pulse suddenly hammering at his neck. "Trey *knew* this?"

"That's what Stacey told me, Lily, and Vickie at the bike camp. They think this could be why Jeb has come back to town. And maybe it's why Rachel is helping him."

A darkness twisted through her husband's face. "And how long has Trey known this?"

Worry flickered through Beppie. "I don't know. I assume since Rachel became her guardian, after the fire killed her parents. They were engaged, after all."

"Fuck," he said quietly. "Trey never breathed a word to us. And now you tell me he's making promises to Rachel?"

"Don't," she warned, her voice low. "I will not have that language in front of the girls. Not in this house."

He cupped her face. "Look, whatever they're all up to, it's not our worry. Okay?"

"But he's dragged us into it."

"He's dragged the whole town into it. He's just playing head games. Don't give him any power over your thoughts, because then he wins. Like I said, he'll do something stupid. They'll lock him away." He hooked his knuckle under her chin, held her gaze. "It's going to be fine. Now, you go hang that laundry, I'll help the girls finish the breakfast dishes."

Beppie made her way down to the washing line, clutching the basket of wet clothes. She began to hang the laundry with wooden pegs even though the air was tinged with smoke. She didn't own a dryer, didn't believe in them.

Shaking out a heavy pair of black jeans, she pegged them, then reached back into the basket, and took out a wet black ski mask. Something inside her went ice-cold.

Glancing over her shoulder, she saw Clint in the kitchen window above the sink, watching her.

Beppie turned and pegged the ski mask to the line. She felt a shift in the air. The wind was turning. She hung up the next thing in the basket, a thick black long-sleeved T-shirt.

Her gaze drifted toward her blue truck, which Clint had borrowed Wednesday while his had been in the shop. Her heart started to hammer.

CHAPTER 19

Assistant Fire Chief Kerrigan Kaye kept half an eye on the small television screen above her desk as she worked on the time sheets. The news was on and it was mostly a recap of the shitstorm that had erupted last night around Jeb Cullen. She and some of the guys from the station had been at the Shady Lady to support Chief Rudiger, but the anger, the sheer depth of the animosity among her colleagues niggled at her.

The clip of Rachel arguing with Adam LeFleur played again. Kerrigan stilled, watched it for a second time. She knew both Rachel and Adam well. Adam through work, Rachel from skiing with her on the provincial team way back. Tension rustled through Kerrigan as she watched the altercation. This thing had cleaved the town in two, and it was causing additional friction here at the fire hall.

She wondered for a moment if one or more of them could even have attacked Jeb. But she rebuffed the idea—none of her guys would risk starting a wildfire in these conditions. Would they?

That was the trouble with stirring things up like this—it started a witch hunt. People started doubting each other. If Jeb and Rachel had achieved one thing with their stunt, they'd sown doubt. Possibly even fear. And it wasn't just the surrounding forest that was like a tinderbox right now. Whole damn place felt like a powder keg itching to blow.

Kerrigan glanced at the firefighters' calendar hanging next to her desk. The date for her flight was circled in red—two days away. She had a sinking feeling that with all this shit going down, her big Mexico vacation was not going to happen. Again.

She returned her attention to the time sheets as the newscast cut to commercial. It was Clint's regular Friday off. He'd also put in long hours with the wildfire crews. While the Wolf River fire had been contained with the use of heavy machinery, air tankers, five helicopters, and fire retardant, the weather forecast had turned ominous. Kerrigan was making certain they had enough staff and reservists on call in case things went to hell.

———

Margot Rietmann was watching the news as she watered her bonsai in the bay window overlooking the distant waters of the Burrard Inlet. Vancouver on a day like this was a shining jewel. It was why they'd bought this West Van house, for the view. She stilled as the news anchor started talking about Snowy Creek. Sophia and Peter, their neighbors, were originally from Snowy Creek. She watched, water dripping from the spout of her watering can, as footage showed faces in a crowd of protesters gathered outside the Shady Lady Saloon at the base of Bear Mountain. A bolt of recognition went through her as she caught sight of a man putting on a ball cap. The camera zoomed in on his face for a moment.

She dropped the watering jug and lunged for the remote, her cat skittering away in surprise. She paused her DVR, rewound. Hit "Stop."

Her pulse raced.

"Harry!" she called. "Over here!"

Her husband came hurrying in. "What is it?"

"That man . . ." She pointed at the screen. "Where did you put that fire investigator's card, the one he gave us?"

"In my desk drawer."

"Get it for me."

"What is it?"

"It's *him*." She pointed. "That's the same guy I saw lurking in the crowd outside Sophia's and Peter's house when it was burning, that big guy there. Remember when the cops asked if we saw anyone or anything unusual? I mentioned that guy because I'd never seen him around here before. But no one questioned by the Mounties knew who he was."

"Are you certain?"

"He's got the same walk, Harry, the same profile. He's the right shape, size. Big like that. Same cap."

Harry scrabbled in his drawer, came out with the card.

———

The atmosphere in the truck is charged as Jeb and I drive in silence to collect my father's vehicle from the skiers' parking lot. Jeb drives it back to my house and I follow in convoy. Once the SUV is safely back home, I let Jeb take the wheel of my truck for the trip to the house where Amy died.

I glance at his profile, the aristocratic lines of his brow and nose, the sharp angle of his cheekbones. My body warms involuntarily as I recall our lovemaking in front of the fire, and my heart twists. I feel so damn vulnerable. I'm falling so hard, so deep for him all over again, and I just know some other shoe has to drop. I fear he's keeping something from me, too, and this unnerves me further.

My cell vibrates in my pocket, making me jump. Quickly, I check the incoming number. *Rock Banrock.*

"Hal," I say, nerves skittering through my chest.

"What in God's name do you think you're doing?"

My pulse quickens. I wondered how long it would take him to call. I glance at Jeb and mouth the words, *It's the Rock.*

"This story has even made the *National* now, and right on the cusp of the winter season—you had better pull the plug on this, stat, before the whole town goes to bloody hell in a handbasket."

"Hal," I try to say calmly, "if we kill this story now, that's going to make even bigger news. Journalists will start asking what it is we're trying to censor, and why." My blood pounds as I counter the patriarch of Snowy Creek. He's powerful not only locally, but on a provincial and national level. He has politicians in his pockets. He holds business interests in the palm of his rugged hand. He could sink me in the blink of an eye. But I'm also thinking of Jaako, my grandfather, and why I committed to this story in the first place.

"You should never have pulled such a goddamn stupid stunt to begin with. It's—"

"It's what Jaako would have done," I say. "He founded the paper based on a set of philosophical and journalistic principles and I—"

"It's a small-town rag, for God's sake, Rachel. Don't go talking to me about principles and ethics. This is not some global conspiracy or crisis of democracy you're facing. Have you forgotten I own half your company?"

Anger coalesces cold and tight in my gut. "Forty-nine percent," I say coolly. "It's still mine."

Jeb shoots me a glance.

"Listen to me, kid." The Rock's tone turns soft and patronizing. "As a publisher in a small town, you have a responsibility to balance the economic needs of the community along with the editorial content. What are you now, twenty-five, twenty-six? You need a guiding hand here. And this is bad for business. It's bad for local morale."

I point to the street sign as Jeb nears the subdivision where Amy's duplex is. He swings the wheel.

"Twenty-seven. And you're wrong." I watch for Amy's place. "The coverage has been excellent for our business. We've received the kind of publicity you can't buy. I spoke with our sales manager earlier this morning and already ad bookings are up." I hesitate as I see the house where Amy died coming up on the corner. "Tell me honestly," I say as I stare at the brooding dark-brown walls of the old duplex, "that your wanting to kill this story is not about protecting Levi."

"Christ, Rachel—"

"It was you who hired the lawyer who helped coach us all for the witness box. It was your lawyer who first got me to talk about Jeb's childhood and what he did to his father." I can feel the anger rising in my voice. I feel Jeb's tension at my mention of this. "Does Levi have something to hide?"

"Damn you," he growls. "You don't want to go making an enemy of me, girl—"

I kill the call midsentence, adrenaline thumping through my veins. I've taken a step in setting right the wrong I did to Jeb in betraying his confession. I've fired a salvo at goddamn Hal Banrock. I'm toast, and I don't care.

"That's the house," I say to Jeb. He crooks a brow at me and pulls up onto the grassy curb. I put my head back against the seat. There's a dull roar inside of my skull.

"I just made Banrock my enemy."

The corner of Jeb's mouth curves into a strange sort of smile. "And who said Rachel Salonen was no crusader?"

"Oh, shut up. How do you want to handle this?" I jerk my chin toward the brooding brown duplex.

But he holds my eyes for several seconds. "I love you, Rachel," he says.

The roar inside my brain grows louder. I can't breathe. But before I can even think of a reply, he's already turned and gotten out, door slamming shut.

"Oh, fuck," I whisper to the interior of the truck cab. It's the second time he's said he loves me, not that I'm counting or anything. He raps on the window. "You coming, or what?"

———

Snowy Creek PD Chief Constable Rob Mackin replaced the phone receiver and sat back in his chair. First a call from Rock Banrock demanding an end to this madness. Then a call from Mayor Thompson saying the Snowy Creek Police Board wanted a meeting ASAP. Now a call from the West Vancouver arson investigator looking into a fire that had consumed the house and lives of Rachel Salonen's sister and brother-in-law. The investigator had just this second informed Mackin he was coming up to Snowy Creek with some new video evidence. He wanted to meet with Mackin tomorrow. Apparently a woman named Margot Rietmann who had witnessed the fire had recognized a man on the news footage filmed outside the Shady Lady yesterday. She claimed the same man had been acting suspiciously in the crowd outside the burning MacLean house.

Mackin drew his hand down hard over his mouth, thinking. Then there was Adam LeFleur. His second in command. The image of LeFleur arguing with Rachel Salonen on the news played through in his mind. LeFleur's brother had been linked to this. LeFleur's mother had sat in this very chair, in this office, nine years ago. She'd led the charge against Jeb Cullen. Whatever was at the bottom of all this, perception was everything.

He reached for his phone, buzzed LeFleur.

When LeFleur entered his office, Mackin asked him to close the door and take a seat.

"This about Cullen?" LeFleur said, continuing to stand.

"The door, please."

THE SLOW BURN OF SILENCE

LeFleur bristled, shut the door, met his boss's eyes, still refusing to take a seat.

"I'm going to need you to step back from this one, LeFleur."

He opened his mouth but the chief constable raised his hand. "Perception is everything right now. Cullen has accused your brother of perjuring himself. You took a bad tack with Salonen in front of a camera. Your mother was on this case, and a judge has recently thrown out a conviction based in part on a policing error made on her watch. You need distance. I'd like you to take a few weeks of paid leave, starting now."

LeFleur's jaw dropped. "Cullen opens his mouth in public, makes some false accusations that border on libelous, and I'm *sidelined*?"

Mackin placed his hand firmly atop a printout of the *Leader* interview on his desk. "Cullen claimed three men in ski masks tried to kill him and started that wildfire. My understanding is that you're looking at him for arson, not these men?"

LeFleur's body went still, his face darkening. "You're not serious."

Mackin said, "How'd you get that cut on your face?"

"Helping with the fire, branch snapped back. Christ, you can't—"

"Adam," Mackin said, using the man's first name, bringing him down, into focus. "Perception. That's all this is. Because these questions I just asked you *will* be asked by the media. Let the investigation unfold without you. Take some time."

"You talk about perception? This is going to damage the public's perception of *me*. Being sidelined like this is going to make it look like I do have something to hide."

"You need a holiday. Take that nice wife and those kids of yours, get out of Dodge for a while, for the Thanksgiving break at least."

LeFleur stared at him, fire burning in his eyes. Several beats of silence pulsed between them. He turned abruptly to leave.

"Your weapon, Adam."

He spun round. "You've got to be kidding me?"

Silence.

Adam LeFleur unsheathed his Smith and Wesson, laid it on the top cop's desk. "You know what you're doing? You're giving Jebbediah Cullen power. You're playing right into his hands, all of you are—Banrock, the mayor, the police board, town council, tourism board. *This* is exactly what he wanted."

"Let us prove him wrong."

LeFleur slammed the glass door on his way out.

The chief waited until he saw LeFleur actually leaving the station. He went to his door, held it open. "Pirello! Novak!"

The two constables exchanged a glance, got up, and answered the chief's summons into his office.

Once they'd closed the door and seated themselves in front of his desk, Mackin said, "We already have a full complement of investigators handling the Wolf River arson. But I want you two to keep an extra eye on this whole Cullen thing. And keep it quiet." Mackin held the gaze of his two constables. He then told them about the call he'd just received from Vancouver.

"You're saying the Vancouver arson investigators believe someone *here*, in Snowy Creek, could be good for the fire that killed Salonen's sister and brother-in-law?" Annie said.

"I'm saying I want a very subtle extra eye on this whole thing." He paused, his gaze lasering each of theirs in turn. "Deputy Chief Constable Adam LeFleur is taking some time off. Report directly to me."

"Shit," Annie whispered.

———

Adam sat in his truck outside the SCPD station, engine running, Lily's words echoing through his head . . .

What did your mother mean that night, nine years ago, when I overheard you two arguing after Amy and Merilee went missing . . . When she said all you had to do was say nothing?

Adam put his truck in gear and drove up to his mother's condo in the benchlands.

CHAPTER 20

I rub my face hard, then get out of the truck.

Jeb is waiting for me next to a "For Sale" sign that has been stuck crookedly into the grass on the verge.

"Looks like her aunt is trying to offload the place," I say with a nod to the sign as I approach. He's watching me intently. His words echo through my mind, and panic flutters through my stomach all over again.

I love you, Rachel . . .

I clear my throat. "Her aunt lives next door, over there." I jut my chin toward the neighboring property. "She owns this duplex as well. Amy had open-ended use of the left half for whenever she wanted to come up to Snowy Creek. The other half was rented out."

He nods. As if he knows it all. The suspicion that he's withholding something from me deepens. "What exactly did you want to see here, Jeb?"

"I called the tenant early this morning, while you were with Quinn. He's a young snowboarder from Toronto. He and his mates have taken over both sides of the duplex now. I asked if we could look inside Amy's place, talk to him. He's expecting us. I also called Piper Smith. She said we can go round anytime this morning."

"How did you get the tenant's number?"

"You left me your laptop, remember. I looked up the articles the *Leader* ran on Amy's suicide. The tenant's name was in one of them—Doug Tollet. He found her body."

I reel at the fact I didn't know this. I try to remember what ran in my own paper on the suicide. But I'd been publisher only four months by the time Amy shot herself. I was in Bali with Trey when it happened, a prearranged trip to celebrate our engagement. Cass was newly hired and I'd left her in charge of the editorial side of things. It was also in Bali that I received news of Sophia's and Peter's deaths. Next there was Quinn coming into our lives. No wonder it's blurry in my mind.

My gaze flashes to the duplex. An Australian flag now hangs in the front window of what was Amy's half. The place looks sad. But it's the feeling in my stomach, an anxiety, that distracts me. The fact that Amy shot herself right around the time of my sister's house fire is beginning to bother me.

The front door of the tenant's side opens, and a young man steps out. "Hoi," he calls across the lawn. "You the Cullen guy?"

Jeb takes my arm. "Come."

As we approach the door, a white Subaru station wagon draws into the adjacent driveway. My pulse quickens.

"It's Rebecca Findlay," I say to Jeb. "Amy's aunt."

"We're within our rights to be here. Tenant invited us. Just keep walking."

The woman gets out of her car. "Hey!" she yells, running over her lawn toward us, leaving the driver's door open, engine still running. "What do you want here? This is private property!"

"Go ahead," I say quietly to Jeb. "I'll handle this."

I move quickly toward the woman. "Mrs. Findlay, I'm Rachel Salonen, a friend of Amy's—"

"I know who you are. Saw you all over the damn news. Digging up muck, dragging our family through hell again. What on earth do you think you're doing? Do you know how much pain that . . . that man"—she points at Jeb, her voice quavering—"has caused our family? *He* killed our Amy. She shot herself because of *him*, because she couldn't go on living with all that weight on her mind, because he sucked all the life out of her, all that was good and true. What do you think you're doing here?"

"We just want to talk to the tenant, about Amy."

She staggers backward, face red, her hand going to her throat. "I don't believe this. The audacity. Get off now. This is my property!"

"Mrs. Findlay, Rebecca, we just—"

"I'm calling the cops. I'm calling 9-1-1." She scurries back to her car, leans inside, and scrabbles in her purse for her phone.

"Mrs. Findlay!"

But the woman climbs back into her Subaru, slams and locks the door. I can see her punching the keypad of her phone, head bent forward.

I jog over to Jeb. He's at the door, talking to a lean guy with long, dirty-blond dreadlocks and baggy striped pants.

"We better move fast," I whisper, placing my hand on his arm. "She's calling in the cavalry. They'll be here any minute."

Doug Tollet introduces himself as DJ PeaceWorld. As he lets us in, he informs us he works at The Base, an underground nightclub in the village.

"This is so sick, man. I saw you both on TV." He's staring at Jeb as if he's some celebrity. "Me and a bunch of eight others have the whole duplex to ourselves now. She—the landlady—was having hassles renting out the left half after the shooting. But we're like, no problem, man, if the rent is real low, it doesn't matter there was a death in there. She's trying to sell the place now. It's been on the market ever since the shooting, but no takers yet. Until she does sell, the rent is supercheap."

He shows us to a door that leads into the other half of the duplex. "When I had just the one half, this connecting door was permanently locked. Basically it's plywood, thin. Soundproofing is crap in the adjoining walls, too. The place was built back in the late seventies on the cheap as a ski cabin, you know, before Bear Mountain really took off. Before the fancy village was built."

Before Banrock's money . . .

I shoot a glance out the window, expecting sirens and police cruisers any second now.

"So you were home that night," Jeb says. "You heard the shot through the door and walls?"

Something chases through DJ PeaceWorld's features. Amy's death has affected him in spite of his cool-dude machismo.

"Yeah. She arrived from Vancouver two days before it happened. I saw her going inside with her bags and shit. I saw her again the following afternoon, carrying grocery bags. She'd been to the liquor store—I could see from the logo on one of the bags she was carrying, the tops of bottles sticking out. Then, in the evening, she started playing this music real loud."

"What music?"

"Reggae shit. Old shit. Here—" He goes to a shelf, rummages through a pile of CDs, finds what he's looking for. "Landlady didn't want to keep it." He hands us the CD.

Jeb reads the title out loud, a frown lowering his brow. "*The Philistines: The Best of Damani Jakeel?*"

"Yeah. Old Jamaican reggae. Amy was playing it over and over. Louder and louder. I could smell dope. You can keep it," he says, nodding at the CD. "Not my thing."

DJ PeaceWorld shows us through the connecting door into the other half of the duplex.

"That's where I found her." He points. "There was a chair against the wall over there. She was slumped in it. Gun was lying on the floor, her hand hanging over it. Shot herself through her mouth." He jerks his chin toward the wall. "There was blood and . . . stuff . . . spattered across that wall behind her. Came out the back of her head."

Nausea washes through my stomach as I stare at the wall. The paint has clearly been scrubbed clean.

"So you heard the shot," Jeb says.

"Yeah." PeaceWorld rubs his brow. "Like I said, you can basically hear anything through these walls. Even when there's no one home and the answering machine clicks on, you can hear the message, everything. Before the shot was fired, Amy turned the music down and she made two calls. The first one, she was yelling, slurring at some guy."

"A guy?" I say.

He gives a shrug. "It sounded like it was a guy from the way she was talking. She called him an effing bastard. Some dude came round right after."

Jeb and I exchange a fast glance. "You told this to the police?" Jeb says.

"Look, I was out of it, stoned, basically. The cops . . . I don't know. They didn't think my timeline was reliable or something. But yeah, I told them."

"Which cops?" I say.

DJ PeaceWorld looks at me. "You know, the tall dark one, the one you were arguing with on the television. Thick hair. Movie star face. That one."

"The deputy chief handled this himself?"

"Yeah. He came and took over from the officers who were first on scene. This is *so* sick, man. Seeing him and you on the news like that. And now you're here." He's still staring at me. I wonder if DJ PeaceWorld is out of it now, too. But a movement outside the front window snares my attention.

A police cruiser is pulling up behind my truck on the opposite side of the street. Rebecca Findlay runs over her lawn toward the cruiser. That dark-haired female cop and her partner get out. "We need to hurry," I whisper to Jeb.

"We're within our rights, Rachel." But I can see he's tense from the way his neck muscles tighten. "And you saw this guy who came over after the phone call?" Jeb asks PeaceWorld.

"Big dude. Maybe just over six feet, wearing a ball cap pulled low over his eyes, and a blue jacket. It was already dark out by then. I didn't see his face."

My pulse kicks.

"When did this guy leave?" says Jeb.

He scratches his head. "That's where it kinda gets fuzzy, dude."

"Fuzzy?"

Pirello is coming up the path now, hands on her gun belt. Her partner remains talking to Mrs. Findlay at the car.

"I didn't actually, like, see him leaving before Amy shot herself. Maybe I passed out for a moment or something and missed it. But the shot startled me right up. There was no music. Just dead silence. I banged on the door, then went round to the front window to look in. That small light was on near the chair. I could see her. Amy." An involuntary shiver chases over the guy and he looks pale suddenly. "I ran next door, to the landlady's place, banged on her door. She came with keys. We went in together. She called 9-1-1."

"So this man who visited Amy, he could have left *after* the shot? Gone out the kitchen slider at the back, maybe?" Jeb says, studying the layout of the place.

PeaceWorld nods. "I suppose, yeah."

"Did you see if she left any note?" says Jeb.

"Just a piece of paper with phone numbers. On that little round table there, which was next to the chair we found her in."

Constable Pirello is at the door.

"There was also an open newspaper on the floor by her feet. *Snowy Creek Leader.*"

A banging sounds on the door.

Jeb stiffens. "Open on a particular page?"

"It was open on a full-page advertisement for a firefighters' fundraiser. It had pictures from their new calendar."

"You remember this?"

"Shit, man, from that point, from the time I saw her in that chair like that—it's burned into my brain. The whole scene. I can't get rid of it."

The banging sounds louder. I glance at Jeb. He nods, telling me to get it. I go to the front door.

"You mentioned Amy made a second call, before this man came around," Jeb says quickly.

"Yeah, right after I heard Amy arguing with some dude on the first call, she made the second one. But it was short. It sounded like she was just leaving a message. I couldn't hear the exact words, just a name. Sophia. Then Amy said something like, 'I spoke to him. I know who did it.'"

I freeze in my tracks. *"Sophia?"*

More banging. "Police, open up!"

"What time was this?" Jeb says, holding my eyes. Deep inside my belly, I start to shake. My skin grows hot.

"Maybe around seven?"

"Then after Amy left the message, the guy showed up?"

"Yeah. They started talking. Then arguing."

"What about?"

He glances down. "Man, I took a hit of acid. I didn't kind of register. Like I said, it was the shot that woke me right up again."

"Police. Can you open up, please?"

I swallow, reach for the door, open it.

Constable Pirello's cheeks are flushed, her violet eyes flashing. Her gaze shoots over my shoulder at DJ PeaceWorld. "Everything okay in here?"

"Thank you, Officer Pirello," I say. "We were invited by the tenant to see the place."

THE SLOW BURN OF SILENCE

She studies my face intently. "We received a complaint of trespassing from the landlady."

"It's cool, man," says PeaceWorld, coming up beside me. "I did invite them. I have a right to invite people. Says so in my lease. Tenants' Act and all."

"It's all good," I say. "We're just leaving anyway."

Pirello steps aside as we exit. Jeb walks ahead but I hesitate, holding back as I recall Pirello's words when she handed me her business card . . .

I know who all testified against him. Why the conviction was overturned. Things might not be what they seem here. I'm new in town; I don't have a vested interest . . .

"It was Adam LeFleur who signed off on Amy Findlay's death as a suicide," I say suddenly, taking the gamble, hopefully sowing a seed of doubt in her head. "Are you all so certain it was suicide?"

"Excuse me, ma'am?"

"Did you know that Amy was visited by a big guy in a ball cap and a blue jacket just before the shot was fired? And that no one actually saw him leave before the shot was heard?"

Her features remain emotionless. Her gaze is unwavering, but I believe I see a flicker of interest in her beautiful big eyes.

"And before Amy was visited by this guy, she made two calls, did you know that?"

She says nothing, waits for me to continue.

"One call might have been made to the guy who showed up. The second call might not have been answered. She might have left a message." I'm shaking slightly now with the intensity of the thoughts charging through my head. "Do you know who she might have left that message with? *My sister.* The victim's services worker who first treated Amy after the rape nine years ago. What message do you think Amy might have left my sister? Has anyone tried to look into that, retrieve the message?"

"It wasn't my case, ma'am." Her voice is deadpan. "I joined the SCPD only three months ago."

I hold her eyes. "Right. It became Adam LeFleur's case. The deputy chief took it over himself."

I turn and leave Constable Annie Pirello standing there.

Her partner is leaning against the cruiser, and he watches me as I march toward my truck. Jeb is already in the driver's seat. I climb in.

"What was that about?" he says.

I ignore him. My mind is reeling. I know both Amy and my sister died while I was in Bali, but I'd been focused solely on my family. Amy was in the buried past for me. Not relevant at the time of my loss. But now . . .

"What was the date?"

"The date?"

"Yes, dammit, the exact date of Amy's death!"

He inhales deeply. "April eighth."

"The day before my sister's fire?"

He says nothing.

I feel like I'm going to throw up. "And Amy could have called Sophia? Saying she knew who did it?"

He still doesn't reply. Anger mushrooms inside me.

"You knew," I say, very quietly. "You didn't believe Amy's death was a suicide. You believed there was a connection between her death and my sister's death."

"I didn't know. I had a feeling."

"A *feeling*?" I glare at him. "You had a feeling Amy was murdered, a feeling it was somehow connected to my sister, and you said nothing."

He starts the engine and pulls into the road. Amy's aunt is watching from her window. The wind has suddenly picked up again, dead leaves blowing across her lawn.

Jeb drives for Piper's house, hands fisted on the wheel.

"Talk to me, dammit. I told you, no secrets. How can I trust you when you do this to me? This . . . this is my sister we're talking about." My whole body is shaking.

He refuses to meet my eyes. He inhales deeply and slowly. "Sophia called me in prison the night Amy left that message."

I go stone cold. I reach for the door handle, clench it. Terrified at what is going to come next.

He glances at me. "Sophia and Peter went out for dinner that night, which is why they missed her call. They came home to the message. Sophia said Amy sounded very drunk, but that she said she knew who did it."

"Stop."

He shoots me another glance.

"Stop the car! Right now!"

He slows down, draws over to the curb, comes to a halt. I swing round in my seat, face him square. Anger, hurt, fear, it's a violent cocktail swirling in my gut, pounding through my blood.

"From the beginning. Every damn detail. You tell it to me now or you get out of my truck and stay the hell away from me and Quinn."

His features tighten, eyes darkening. Even as I say the words, I know he has rights to Quinn no matter what I say. I feel ill. We're locked together, whether I like it or not.

"Rachel—"

"From the beginning."

He turns off the engine, scrubs his hand hard over his face. "It started with Piper. Five years ago. She was interviewing people for the CBC *True Crime* docudrama—"

"I know all this. She tried to interview me, too. I refused."

He nods, holding my gaze. "You also know Piper has an ability to see things that haunt people, especially people who've experienced a deep psychological trauma."

I give a harsh snort. "Yeah. So-called psychic."

"Whatever you want to think of her ability, when Piper met Amy and shook her hand, she got a vivid image of several young men assaulting a screaming woman. Piper told Amy about this vision, and she questioned Amy about the possibility of there being more than one rapist. Amy completely shut down."

"How do you know this?" My voice is going shrill and I hate it.

"I know from Sophia."

I tighten up. I feel so left out, so betrayed in a way, by my own sister.

"The initial thinking was that Amy was so drugged she was not able to form memories of the event. But Piper felt that because she'd received this vision from Amy herself, that the memories were actually there, locked in Amy's brain, and subconsciously haunting her."

He clears his throat and raises his hand slightly, as if to touch me. But I recoil, pushing my back into the truck seat. I'm a dangerous mess. I'm ready to implode. "Go on."

"Piper met with Sophia and told her about the vision she received when she touched Amy. Sophia decided to ask Amy whether she'd be willing to try a new form of hypnosis to prompt potentially locked-down memories."

"All based on a psychic experience?"

"There was also the DNA evidence from the hoodie that indicated there might be at least one other male involved. Amy agreed. She and Sophia had several sessions. Amy started to recall some things—"

"Autosuggestion. From Piper. That's what it could have been."

"It's possible. However, the few images that Amy did recall prompted Sophia to visit me at Kent. She came first under the pretext she was doing research for a series of case studies. She said she wanted to talk to me about that night."

"And you agreed."

"I was prepared to tell my story to anyone who might actually listen. Yes. I agreed."

"So that's how it started, five years ago, the bond between you and Sophia, because of some psychic. And then Sophia told you about Quinn?"

"Because of what the lab tech revealed about there being an unidentified DNA profile, and because of Amy's growing self-doubt, because of her snippets of returning memory. And because of me. After visiting with me on several occasions, Sophia began to believe I was telling the truth. She took on my cause, for Quinn. For truth, justice. She approached the UBC Innocence Project."

I curse softly under my breath. "And what did Amy allegedly remember in those hypnosis sessions?"

"More than one rapist. A group of guys. Repetitive music. A cold place with a musty smell, darkness, a low ceiling or sense of heaviness overhead. The smell of soil and marijuana. The sound of water rushing. Like a river."

"The old trapper's cabin they traced Amy's tracks back to, after she was found, was near a river. It had a low roof."

He nods. "Amy also recalled an odd phrase that seemed to go round and round in her brain: *Lewd boy brain is coming crashing now.*"

"What?"

"I don't know what it means. Sophia believed more context would come with further hypnosis sessions. She felt they were getting close. But Amy started to get scared and stopped the sessions. Sophia let it ride; we had enough with the DNA and the tech's testimony at that point to appeal my case. Sophia felt Amy might grow more courageous once the judge ruled in my favor. And when it looked like he really was going to rule in my favor, Amy agreed to try again. That was six months ago. But she missed her appointment with Sophia, and two days later she called from

Snowy Creek, leaving that message on Sophia's home phone. By the time Sophia got it, Amy was dead."

"Oh, God," I whisper as I look down at my hands. My brain is spinning. I can't seem to absorb it all at once.

He lets me sit in silence awhile. Then he places his hand gently over mine. I allow it. I need him. As much as I resist, I need Jeb. I love Jeb. I want Jeb. I hate that he's had this intimate relationship with my own sister. That I was not a part of any of it. Logically I can see why. But it doesn't stop the hurt. The sense of aloneness.

Emotion burns into my eyes.

"I can't believe you didn't tell me all this."

"It was too much at once, Rach."

"That's not for you to decide."

Again, he remains silent for several beats. Then, quietly, he says, "Sophia also told me that Amy recalled an image of a dragon, an undulating dragon."

I look up slowly. "A dragon?"

"That's all I know. Every time this image of a dragon came into her mind, the rest of the memories went blank."

I take my hands out from under his and rub my brow. "Did Sophia go to the cops with this?"

"She didn't trust the cops who had handled the case, or the original defense counsel. She took the information to the Innocence Project lawyers instead. There was enough for the judge to rule last week that I didn't get a fair trial."

Last week.

He hasn't even been out a week. It feels like a lifetime has passed in just a few days.

"Sophia's been gone *six months*," I whisper. "She never got to hear the final verdict. She died before she could see what she'd done."

"These wheels turn slowly. The judge took his time. But six months ago we were all feeling good about it, positive it was going to come down in our favor."

"It must have been hell, remaining in prison those last six months, waiting. Especially with the news Sophia was gone."

"It was the longest time of my life. I miss her more than you can know."

I hold his eyes. "I'm sorry, Jeb."

"I'm sorry, too. She left a big hole in a lot of lives."

I turn and look out the window.

"When she called you in prison," I say, my voice coming out thick, "the night before the fire, did she say anything else?"

"Only that Amy had left the message saying she was in Snowy Creek and that she knew who did it. As soon as Sophia got the message, she tried to return the call, but there was no reply. She said she was going to drive up to Snowy Creek first thing in the morning, to see Amy. She called me because she was excited. She told me this could be it, we might finally learn who did it. But the next morning the fire took her life."

Ice forms in my veins.

"Jeb," I say, very quietly, "if—just if—Amy was killed by this guy in a ball cap, do you think this same guy might have learned from Amy that she'd called my sister and left a message? Do you think my sister was murdered?"

He says nothing.

"Fuck!" I reach into my pocket, take out my smart phone. I call Jonah Tallingsworth, my crime reporter. He would have been the one to write the stories on Amy's suicide.

He answers and I waste no time with pleasantries. "Jonah, it's Rachel. The Amy Findlay suicide story in April this year, do you still have your files for that?"

He asks me to wait as he pulls out his notes. I hear paper rustling.

"I have copies of the coroner's report," he says. "And the police report."

"Was the gun Amy used registered to anyone?"

He pauses, going through his notes. "Serial number was filed off. The cops figured she obtained it on the black market."

"Any mention of phone calls she made the night she died?"

He's quiet for a few beats. "Yes, the report mentions she made two calls that matched the numbers left on a piece of paper on the table. First call was to the Snowy Creek Fire Hall. The second to her therapist in West Van, Dr. Sophia MacLean." He hesitates. "Your sister."

My mouth goes dry. "She called the fire hall?" I glance at Jeb. "Do you know who she connected with at the hall? How long the call was?"

More papers rustle. "There's no record here of who she spoke to at the hall. Just the fact she dialed the number."

"Can you give it to me?"

"You mean the fire hall number?"

"Yes."

He recites it, including an extension number. My pulse quickens. "Whose extension is that?"

"I don't know. I didn't follow it up. It was ruled a suicide. The case was closed."

"And you just dropped the story there?"

"I had no reason to pursue it further. We had a lot on our plates at that time."

"Thank you, Jonah." I kill the call. Immediately, I dial the fire hall plus the extension. The phone rings twice, then clicks over to a generic fire hall voice mail.

I hang up, heart racing. "I want to go there," I say. "When we're done with Piper."

"The hall?"

"Yes. Kerrigan Kaye works Fridays—she's an old friend of mine." *Or used to be.* "I can ask her who the extension belongs to. I want to know who has access to that phone, and who was on duty at the time Amy called."

———

When Annie Pirello returned to the station, she pulled the Findlay suicide file. Rachel Salonen's insinuations had piqued her interest.

In the file, Annie found the two numbers Findlay called before she died. She jotted them down. One was for the Snowy Creek Fire Hall, with an extension. The other belonged to Dr. Sophia MacLean. Annie double-checked the dates. Salonen was right. The MacLean house fire had broken out the morning after Findlay died.

She sat back, thinking.

A woman like Amy Findlay? She doesn't eat a gun. She takes pills, an overdose. Annie pulled out the photos of the scene, laid them out on her desk. She pursed her lips as she studied them. She leaned forward suddenly as she caught sight of the open newspaper at Findlay's feet in one of the photos. The paper was open on a full-page advertisement for a firefighters' fundraiser. Included in the ad were two pictures from the new firefighters' calendar. One was a photo of a man's muscled back as he worked an old-fashioned water pump. She knew who the man was because she had the same calendar at home; she'd read the small caption underneath.

Quickly Annie turned to her computer and ran a cursory background check that set her spidey senses tingling.

She got to her feet, reached for her jacket. "Novak."

Her partner looked up from his desk.

"We're taking a drive to Pemberton."

CHAPTER 21

Piper was wearing a long, flowing dress, soft Ugg boots, her hair a tumble of honey-colored curls around her face. She was beautiful, thought Jeb, but in a way that was very different from Rachel's looks. Rachel still did it for him.

"Come in." Piper's voice was warm, husky, as she invited Jeb and Rachel into her home on the west side of Pine Cone Lake.

A striking dark-haired man with angular features, olive skin, and hooked brows got up from the table at which he was sitting, in front of a window overlooking the lake. In front of him on the table were a laptop, notebook, scattered papers—he was working. A toddler sat in a high chair at the table beside him. A girl of around four was drawing pictures in front of a crackling fire in the hearth. The dark-haired child got up quickly and went to hug her mother's skirts while spying curiously up at Jeb and Rachel.

Jeb's heart did a funny squeeze as he imagined Quinn at that age, holding on to Sophia's legs. Emotion suddenly rode hard through him. This was taking its toll.

"This is my husband, Dracon, the horror writer, as everyone refers to him here," Piper said with a smile. "Dracon also lectures at the new private university in Snowy Creek." She had an aura of happiness, contentment. Their home exuded a sense of family, of peace. Suddenly it was everything Jeb craved, and more. He glanced at Rachel and she met his gaze. She was seeing the same thing he was, but she looked uneasy.

Jeb moved forward and shook the hand that Dracon offered. The man's eyes were black as night. He had a silver streak at his widow's peak that Jeb guessed had little to do with age and more to do with genetics. He looked as mysterious and haunting as the kinds of books he wrote. Historical gothics and horror novels set in the Pacific Northwest. Jeb had read a couple in prison.

"We finally meet," Dracon said, shaking Jeb's hand with a solid grip. He exuded a casual confidence, the kind of ease that came with wealth.

"You're Merilee's half brother," Jeb said.

"Older half brother, yes," he added with a smile. "Hence the different last names."

"And you hold no animosity toward me?" Jeb needed to clear it out of the way.

Dracon glanced at his wife. "I've learned the hard way to trust Piper's intuition. I've believed for some time now that you're not the one who knows where Merilee is, or the one who did this."

Jeb stared at Dracon. To be so openly accepted at face value, to not have to erect walls of defense . . . it turned his bones to a feeling of water for a moment.

"And this is Crystal," Piper said, smoothing the hair of the girl hugging her skirts. "Sage is the little monster eyeing you from his high chair with cereal on his mouth."

Rachel took Dracon's hand. "We've met."

"We have indeed. Thank you for the coverage and reviews in your newspaper."

"Your books speak for themselves," she said with a smile that belied the wariness in her eyes. "I'm a fan."

"And we've met, too, of course," Rachel said to Piper. Jeb noticed Rachel did not take Piper's hand. She was keeping a physical distance from the psychic.

"I tried to interview Rachel for the docudrama," Piper offered in way of explanation for Jeb. "But I understand the reasons for declining."

"Yeah, well, I'm not into all that rehashing true crime stuff. I'm sorry." Rachel rubbed her arm. It was a nervous habit. "However, I can see that in this case the show offered something really valuable. Jeb's freedom. We're hoping it'll now all lead to the truth somehow."

Piper eased the tension with a grin. "Come, take a seat in the living room. Anyone want tea?"

Both Jeb and Rachel declined.

They sat on overstuffed sofas surrounded by artsy decor. The view over the lake was stunning from the living room's large picture windows. Shelves lined the one wall and were packed floor to ceiling with books and magazines.

"What can we help you with?" Piper said.

Jeb leaned forward, resting his arms on his knees. "You had a vision when you first touched Amy all those years ago. Are you able to tell us exactly what you saw? Can you still remember it?"

Piper nodded. "Indelibly. I saw two distinct figures, males—"

"You saw their features?" Rachel interrupted.

"It doesn't always work like that," Piper explained. "I didn't see their faces in this case, but rather the shadowy forms of two distinct males, which is likely what Amy remembered, and what I was picking up from her subconscious. However, I also had a sense of there being two or more other guys as well, in a peripheral way."

Rachel's mouth flattened and her eyes narrowed slightly. Jeb could see doubt written all over her. "How can you be sure? I mean, if you don't see faces?"

"It's a sense of separate souls, individuals. Distinct."

"I see," Rachel said.

"I know it's difficult for some people to grasp." Piper bent down, spoke softly to her daughter. "Crystal, can you go fetch the cookie tin in the kitchen?" She waited while her child slid off the sofa and left the room, then said, "The two males in the foreground of my vision were attacking, raping a screaming woman. I got an image of a handgun, and one of them was . . ." She glanced toward the door, making sure Crystal had disappeared. "He was using it to rape the woman."

Rachel swallowed hard, her face going markedly pale. Jeb felt ill. No matter how many times he heard this stuff, it affected him physically. It had come out in court that Amy had been sexually assaulted with a foreign object, front and back.

"Was it Amy who these two guys were attacking in your vision?" Rachel asked, her voice tight.

"I believe what I was picking up was Amy's suppressed and horrific memory of watching her friend Merilee being raped by at least two guys."

Dracon looked away, out the window, features tight.

Piper reached over and placed her hand over her husband's knee. "That's how it works for me. I can see people's nightmares, the ghosts, memories that haunt them. Often those hauntings are vivid images locked in the subconscious. I can bring them out in starker detail sometimes if I sit down and draw the person being affected by the image. The act of drawing seems to open a channel in my mind and connect me more deeply." She glanced at Dracon as she spoke.

Crystal came scurrying back with a red cookie tin covered in white hearts.

"Why don't you offer them around," Piper said gently, removing the lid.

The child glanced shyly at Jeb, then Rachel. She slowly approached with the cookie tin held between both hands. Jeb took one. "Thank you."

Again he couldn't help thinking of Quinn. The lost years. How foreign it was to simply be inside a home like this, be accepted and free to go where he pleased. To be able to dream again. But he reminded himself that, while Piper and Dracon accepted him, the rest of the town didn't. He was not truly free. Not until he had proof that could be used in a court of law.

"Is there anything else you can recall about the vision?" he said as he bit into his cookie. "Anything about the setting?"

"Well, I got a sense from Amy of oppressive weight overhead. As if the place where this crime happened was under something, lots of earth pressing down, maybe. At the time I had a feeling . . . of being underground."

"Not in a cabin?" Rachel said.

"It didn't feel like a cabin, no."

Jeb cleared his throat. "Sophia mentioned that during hypnosis Amy experienced a sensation of cold, dankness, and she could scent dirt along with marijuana smoke. Do you feel the crime could have happened in . . . some sort of cave, maybe? Would this fit with what you saw and felt?"

"It would, yes, absolutely."

Rachel suddenly sat forward on the couch. "Jeb, the mine!" Her eyes glittered. "The old copper mine above the gravel pit, near the trailhead to Mount Rogue. Rogue Falls comes down near the mine entrance. You said Amy heard water rushing. Back then you used to be able to drive the trestle bridge over the Rogue Falls gorge. A car could have been taken right to the mine opening." She paused. "It could have happened right there, up above the gravel pit. The music Amy heard—the rhythmic repetitive music—could have been coming from a car parked outside, perhaps with the doors open."

Adrenaline punched through Jeb. It was possible. But it didn't explain why Amy was found wandering on railway tracks over twenty miles north.

"Piper," he said, "before Amy died, she was listening to music, a CD called *The Philistines: The Best of Damani Jakeel*, and she was

THE SLOW BURN OF SILENCE

apparently smoking dope. Do you think she might have been trying to re-create the events of that night by using the stimuli she
was starting to recall, including the scent of marijuana? Because
this is the kind of thing Sophia had been trying with the retrograde
hypnosis."

"It would make sense," Piper said. "What else did Sophia say
Amy remembered during the hypnosis sessions?"

"An odd string of words: *lewd boy brain is coming crashing now.*
Sophia said these words would go round and round and round
in Amy's brain. Then everything would come to halt as an image
of a dragon came into her mind. An undulating dragon. *Pumping
dragon* were the words she used."

Piper's gaze shot to her husband, a frown furrowing into her
brow. "Dracon, your name means dragon. Does this mean anything to you? Could it have meant anything to Merilee, perhaps,
something Amy might have been aware of?"

He pursed his lips. "By the time Merilee was in high school,
I hardly knew my sister. You know how a gap of a few years can
seem monumental at that age? And when she disappeared, I'd been
out of school for four years already, living in Victoria and working
toward my doctorate." He gave a slight shrug. "The word *dragon*
means nothing to me apart from the fact that's what my name
translates to. It's a family name. My great-grandfather was called
Dracon." He hesitated. "What did you say those other words were
again?"

"Lewd boy brain is coming crashing now."

"And you said she was listening to a Damani Jakeel CD?"

"Do you know of him?"

He got up, went over to a shelf containing racks of CDs. He
pulled out one, held it up. It was the same CD that DJ PeaceWorld
had given them.

"They were selling these at the annual Snowy Creek spring
music festival last April. Damani Jakeel and the Toots performed

at the festival this year—they're one of the oldest original ska and rocksteady Jamaican bands still around. Jakeel himself had just turned seventy and the spring concert in Snowy Creek was part of their finale tour. The band formed in the early sixties when ska was hot. Their first performance in Snowy Creek was thirteen years ago, at the premiere Snowy Creek music festival. It was a coup for the festival organizers to bring them back again. I went to the concert for old times' sake. Picked one of these up." He brought it over to Jeb.

"Take a look at the lyrics from that track." Dracon pointed to a song titled "Rude Boy" on the back.

Jeb took the CD, opened the box, removed the CD booklet, and turned to the song labeled "Rude Boy." He read the lyrics, a chill sliding down the groove of his spine.

C'mon all you crashers . . . c'mon you all rude boys and girls
The rude boy train is coming crashing now
Coming now
Ticky ticky tick
Rude boy train is coming crashing now
Rude boy train is coming crashing now
You dance hall crashers
You all hypocrite, you . . . rude boys and girls . . .

He glanced up, pulse racing.

"The songs are repetitive like that," Dracon said. "Kind of gives one an earworm. I can imagine it going round and round in Amy's head if it was something that was playing during a traumatic event."

"*Rude boy*. Not *lewd boy*. Amy misheard the lyrics."

"Wouldn't be the first time someone remembered the wrong lyrics of a song. I certainly have. *Rude boy* was a slang term that originated in 1960s Jamaican street culture. It was associated with violent youths and ska and rocksteady music. A lot of the ska and rocksteady music of that period either supported or criticized the rude boy violence. Like this one by Jakeel and the Toots."

Several beats of silence ensued before Rachel said, "But who would have played a CD like that nine years ago, while Amy was assaulted? Who at the time liked old ska, rocksteady reggae music from the sixties? I mean, kids like trendy stuff."

Dracon snorted. "After Jakeel and the Toots' first tour to Snowy Creek, there was at least one fan I know of, including myself. We kind of bonded over the music interest at the time. He was in the class below me."

Everyone's gaze was suddenly riveted on Dracon.

"Who?" Jeb said, his pulse quickening even further.

"Adam LeFleur."

Rachel's mouth dropped open.

"You're kidding," Jeb said.

"Adam became a die-hard fan of the old Jamaican stuff. And it started with that concert here in Snowy Creek thirteen years ago."

"What day did Jakeel perform last April?" Rachel asked quickly.

Dracon's brow furrowed. "The festival is always held during the spring break, which falls around the second weekend of April. Hang on." He pulled his smart phone out of his pocket, scrolled. "The performance was April seventh. A Wednesday."

"Jeb." Rachel's voice was hoarse suddenly. "That was the day before Amy died. She was shot April eighth. Do you think that's why she came up here and missed her appointment with Sophia? Because she'd learned Jakeel was playing, and she wanted to re-create something? Do you think she was remembering, and that's why she bought the CD, went back to her place, kept playing the music?"

Jeb stared at her. "Jesus, it's possible."

"We need to go back to the gravel pit," she said, lurching to her feet. "And we need to go up and check out the mine. What if it happened right there, in the old copper mine, just up the road from the pit party? Someone could have driven Amy north and dumped her at the trapper's cabin *after* the assault in order to deflect attention from the mine."

"Which means," Jeb said very quietly, "Merilee could still be down there." He got to his feet. "We should go. We still need to stop by the village."

They both thanked Piper and Dracon. Jeb noticed that Rachel, once again, avoided taking Piper's hand. While they were walking back to the truck, Piper stopped him with a gentle touch on his arm, holding him back.

Startled by the sharp electrical sensation, he glanced down into her eyes. Her intensity was suddenly strange.

"You're reading me?" he said.

Piper smiled. "I can tell she consumes you, Jeb. You don't need to be psychic to see that."

"Yeah, well—" He glanced at Rachel, who was already at the top of the driveway, opening the door of the truck. "She does. Always has." He gave a soft snort. "It's not like I met a lot of other women in the joint, you know."

"I want you to know why Rachel was steering clear of me inside," Piper said. "When I met her for the first time, when I tried to interview her five years ago, I shook her hand." Piper paused. "And I saw you in my mind. It was like a brick to the head. Stark as day. I knew it was you from the photos, from the research I was doing for the docudrama. The intensity was truly overwhelming. You were the ghost that haunted Rachel."

"Five years ago?"

Piper nodded.

Jeb's gaze went to Rachel, now waiting in the truck. She was watching them. His chest was suddenly tight. She hadn't let him go. Not even after his conviction. She had held him in her mind, her heart, and her spirit.

"You're part of her fabric, Jeb. And she's part of yours. I just wanted you to know that."

Jeb swallowed. Unsure.

"I believe in destiny," Piper said. "You both need to fight for this, no matter what happens. Otherwise neither of your lives will ever be right, or whole. Trust me. I know this."

"You and Dracon, it was the same for you?"

She smiled ruefully. "I'll tell you the story someday. When you have more time."

He hesitated, held her eyes. "Thank you. For everything. I truly mean that. I wouldn't be here had it not been for you."

"Go," she said. "Finish it off."

Jeb turned and marched up to the truck where Rachel was waiting.

"What did she say to you?" she asked as he climbed into the drivers' seat.

"Nothing much."

Rachel crooked a brow. "It was that woo-woo stuff of hers, wasn't it?"

He keyed the ignition. "Her woo-woo stuff saved my bacon. It brought Sophia to me. It gave me Quinn. It got me here, with you. I'm not gonna sneeze at Piper Smith's 'woo-woo.'" He geared the truck, drove up the steep driveway and out onto the road that wound around Pine Cone Lake.

"It doesn't make sense, you know," Rachel said after they'd been driving a few minutes.

"What doesn't?"

"Adam. You think those guys could have been protecting *him* by lying in court? I mean, he was already a cop at the time, with the RCMP in Edmonton. He'd been with the Mounties three years and was just home for the Thanksgiving break. Yet I can't see it. Not Adam."

"Easier to believe it was me?"

She shot him a hot glare.

They drove in silence round the lake, back toward the village, to the fire hall.

Dry leaves scattered across the road, and branches swayed in the mounting wind. A sense of something about to break whispered around them, like the storm electricity in the air.

———

"She's out in the sunroom," Rubella said with a smile as she opened the condo door to Adam. "She's having a good day. Go on through. I'll bring some tea out."

"I can do the tea, Rubella," Adam told his mother's home-care nurse. "If you want to run some errands, I'll be here for an hour or so."

"You sure?"

"Yeah, yeah. Of course. Go." Adam would rather be here than breaking news to Lily that he'd been placed on mandatory leave. He found his mother in the glassed-in sunroom off the living room. She was sitting in her wicker rocker, bent like a question mark, a fleece blanket over her lap. Her blonde hair had been worked into a braid, which Rubella had tied with a small pink ribbon. It looked absurdly girlish. His mom had been a tough top cop, never girlish.

Dementia had a way of doing that, robbing people of dignity, pride, making them helpless babies again. Not cute babies that called out to be touched and cuddled, but clumsy old babies who smelled and needed diaper changes and help being fed. Adam would rather terminate his own life than end up like this.

He went through the French doors. It was pretty out here, the glassed-in alcove surrounded by clematis, the desiccated blooms still hanging like fragile ghosts on the autumn vines. Birds darted to and from a feeder hanging outside. His mother was watching them. Bird feeders were deemed bear attractants out here, but

Adam didn't have the heart to remove it. His mother loved the hummingbirds especially.

"Mom?"

She looked up. Confusion creased her brow. She was still handsome; the echoes of a beautiful, strong young woman were yet evident in the lines of her face. Sheila Copeland LeFleur was not so much old as robbed of her brain. Early onset dementia, they called it. Hereditary, they said. It had been compounded by a stroke that left one side of her face out of sync with the other. The shock of Luke's disappearance, they said, could have precipitated things.

"Rafe," she said, recognition suddenly lighting her eyes. "Where have you been?"

He lowered himself onto the wicker ottoman in front of her. "It's Adam, Mom."

The frown etched back into her brow. She started to pat her knee lightly. A nervous tick. Fear. Of not knowing things.

"I know," he offered. "I look a lot like Dad."

"Where is he? Rafe should be home by now. I get so worried."

How many times could she bear the pain of being told her husband was dead, never coming back, that he'd died at age thirty-two? Almost the same age Adam was now. Each time she was told, it wounded afresh, as if she were hearing it for the first time.

"He's out," Adam said finally. "He'll be back later."

He waited until he heard the front door close behind the nurse. Then he leaned closer and said, "Mom, do you remember the Zukanov-Findlay case, the missing girls?"

Her face twisted into a range of expressions as she sent her mind scurrying down neural pathways only to find holes, missing links. Dead ends. It was like watching the face of someone whose features were being sparked by electrodes planted in the brain, and the scientist in control was randomly testing which connection activated which muscle.

The UBC Innocence Project lawyers had tried to bring his mother in to testify about the evidence log, the additional DNA found on the bloodied shirt. But she'd been deemed medically, mentally unsound. Adam had wondered at the time if she might have been trying to hide behind the illness that was progressively ravaging her brain. Or if she'd truly slipped into a forgotten place. Perhaps it was a bit of both.

He placed his hand over hers to stop the knee patting. "Mom. Sheila?"

Her eyes flickered at the use of her name.

"Do you remember, when the girls went missing, we had an argument about a small gold Saint Christopher medallion. I found the medallion in my Jeep after Luke borrowed it the night the girls vanished. I put the medallion in an envelope in my top drawer. Someone took it two days later. I thought it was Luke who'd done it. He denied it, and he and I had a huge row. You heard us. Afterward you came to me, and you told me to let things rest—do you remember that?"

She looked out the window. "When will Rafe be home?"

Frustration tightened in Adam. He blew out a long, controlled breath. There was no harm now in just shooting it from the hip. The longer he left this, the more she would forget. "Mom, that medallion, it was like the one Merilee was wearing when she went missing from the gravel pit."

"It's late. Rafe should be here by now."

"The bloodied hoodie with the empty Rohypnol pack in the pocket, your officers didn't find it in Jebbediah Cullen's car, did they? It was Luke's shirt, wasn't it? It came from our house. You put it directly into evidence and logged it as having come from Cullen's vehicle, didn't you?"

A distant, soft smile crossed her face, and her eyes turned misty. "Adam is such a good boy, Rafe. He's following in your footsteps. He's a Mountie, like you are. He's going to make a great cop someday. Luke . . ." She shook her head sadly. "He's not strong-minded like our Adam. Sometimes Luke gets in with a bad crowd, that's all. He has no malice, though. It won't happen again. He's going straight into the army, where he can stay focused." She clasped Adam's hand tightly and leaned suddenly forward.

"You see, Rafe, I can't allow Luke to ruin Adam's career, his life, before it's even started. It was Adam's Jeep, you see, that Luke borrowed that night. It was that girl's blood on Luke's shirt; that's what the lab showed in the end."

Adam's heart stuttered. Sweat slicked down the groove of his spine. "Mom—*Sheila*—"

"Yes, Rafe," she said with another girlish smile.

"You're saying the male DNA found on the hoodie would match Luke's profile?"

Her face crumpled. She withdrew her hand, started tapping her knee again, fast.

Adam sat back, dragged his hands through his hair. His shirt was soaked under his armpits, his mouth dust dry.

"It's so tough being a single mother of two sons, Rafe. I . . . I have to protect my boys. Once Luke is in the army, it's going to be okay. And Adam will have a clear record. I can't have this thing touching him. I told him so, Rafe, to let it be. Because he has to make a choice. Either he goes after his own brother and mother. Or he keeps quiet. And what evidence is he going to go after his own brother with? Those boys already made a pact. Adam's got nothing concrete on them. It's better this way." Her eyes went distant. "Jebbediah's an evil boy," she whispered. "He killed his own father. It was right. I did what a mother had to do."

Nausea pushed up into Adam's throat. He had to stand abruptly to prevent himself from throwing up.

"What happened to the medallion?" he said coldly.

She rubbed her temple, moistened her lips, then a flicker of brightness sparked through her eyes. "Yes," she said. Then her face collapsed again in a wash of sadness and lost memories as she disappeared into herself once more, somewhere in the past.

Adam went to the windows, watched the birds pecking through the dead leaves. Sometimes, when parents didn't find what they were looking for in their child, they planted seeds for what they'd like to grow there instead. They tried to create in their children the lives they themselves missed. His mother had been trying to turn him into his father.

Rachel's words washed into his mind. *Why did you become a cop, sir? Did you once believe in the law, in justice?*

"Rafe?"

He jumped, spun round.

"Is that you? Where have you been?"

"Rafe is gone, Mom. It's me, Adam. Your son."

"Adam?" An odd expression twisted her features. "Bring me that box from my bedroom, won't you? The one with the seashells on the top. My windup jewelry box. It's on my dresser."

"What's in the box?"

"Please, Rafe, just bring it."

Adam went to the room, found the box, and came back. He handed it to his mother.

She opened it slowly and a little ballerina popped up from her spring on her pedestal. Music tinkled and the ballerina started to spiral in front the mirror inside. The interior of the box was lined with velvety red cloth, and it was filled with silver and gold jewelry and other trinkets. His mother suddenly seemed like a little girl again as she sifted through the contents. She removed a small, flat gold medallion from among the contents. It had a filigree edge, like golden lace. She offered it to Adam, hand shaking slightly.

His heart stopped as a blade of recognition sliced through him. He met her eyes. She was looking at him, into him.

It was Merilee Zukanov's pendant.

A Saint Christopher traditionally worn by travelers to keep them safe. It had not kept Merilee Zukanov safe at all.

Slowly Adam reached out, took it from her. It lay flat on his palm.

"You took it?" he whispered. "From my drawer."

Silence.

All these years he'd thought Luke had taken it. He thought Luke had erased the GPS route in his Jeep. All these years he'd hoped it had been a coincidence that the hoodie found bloodied in Jeb Cullen's car had matched the hoodie that Luke had arrived home in during the early hours of that fateful day.

Tears filled his mother's pale-blue eyes.

Adam stared at her.

"Are you going to make tea, Rafe? I'd love some tea with one of those ginger snaps."

Adam went into the bathroom, pocketed the medallion, and threw up. He ran the tap water until it was ice-cold, and he rinsed his face, stopping as he caught sight of his reflection in the mirror. For a split second he saw his father. Likeness lies in wait, he thought. And now that he was the same age his father was when he was killed, he could see the man in his own face.

He remembered the night they'd received the news of his dad's death, the look on his mother's face. He'd been eight years old. Luke had been only five. Almost the same ages that his and Lily's boys—Tyler and Mikey—were now.

His mother had tried to protect her sons.

How far would he go to protect his own sons?

The things that were done for love. For family. How wrong it could all go.

His mother had left the RCMP to take the top cop job here in Snowy Creek, where she believed it might be safer, easier, to raise her boys alone. Adam remembered his mother's pride in becoming the first woman to hold down the chief position with the Snowy

Creek PD. But later that night he'd heard her crying in her room. He'd opened the door to find her holding a framed photo of his dad. She had been furious with him for finding her in that state.

He gripped the sink with both hands, hung his head down.

He'd also left the RCMP to come raise his boys here. To make Lily happy.

Why did you become a cop, Adam . . . Was it because you believed once in justice, the law . . .

He dried his face and went into the kitchen, where he made tea and put shortbread cookies on a plate because he could find no gingersnaps.

He sat with his mother while she sipped from her cup, and he wiped her mouth. Because of the stroke she dribbled when she ate or drank. His mom had always taken care of him and his brother. Now here he was taking care of her. And he was looking after his wife. His world was crumbling around him.

He waited for Rubella to return. Then he went back to his truck and put on his music—old Jamaican ska. He inhaled deeply. His alter ego had wanted to visit Jamaica. As a kid, instead of snowboarding, he'd wanted to surf in the warm sun. It was why he'd stuck a Hawaiian surf sticker on the back of his Jeep all those years ago, after a visit to the islands.

He had a choice to make.

His mother was gone, inside her own head.

His brother was gone.

His choice could not hurt them.

Why did you become a cop . . .

He had become a cop because his parents were cops, because they had both wanted their sons to be cops. They'd planted the seed in him. They'd watered that seed with tales of the legendary Sam Steele of the North West Mounted Police. A quintessential Victorian, imperial hero, a big barrel-chested bear of a man with a grand, sweeping mustache who cleaned up the gold rush saloons, brothels, and gambling dens of the wild Pacific Northwest, who kept the American whiskey traders at bay.

Adam had believed in justice, retribution. The law. Childishly so.

Until that night the girls had gone missing.

Until he had turned a quiet blind eye and everything turned subtle shades of gray.

He'd thought the grayness was part of becoming an adult, seeing life for what it truly was in all its tricky nuances. But then had come the conviction and incarceration of an innocent man. Adam knew his inaction had been key to that conviction. He was as guilty as the rest who had perjured themselves. And he knew deep down they had. Now he was back here. Snowy Creek. With sons of his own. Full circle. To face the role he had played in his own mother's and brother's criminal actions all those years ago. To face his own guilt.

Adam reached for his phone. Dialed.

She answered on the third ring, sounding breathless.

"I need to see you this evening," he said. "I just . . . need to be with you, talk to you. Can I come round?"

She laughed and whispered dirty things in his ear. Her voice was a salve. She was his addiction. She was the reason he coped with Lily, with being in Snowy Creek, with everything.

Adam hung up, started the engine. This was the beginning of the end. He had to do this. And he would do it for his sons.

———

Annie drove up the rutted driveway to the Rudiger house.

"Check that out," she said to Novak with a tilt of her head as they passed a wash line full of laundry. "Black toque. Black men's sweater. Black jeans."

Round the side of the house, a blue truck was parked.

"See if you can take a look at that truck while I speak to the occupants."

Annie went up the steps to the front door, knocked while Novak ambled round the side of the house.

A plumpish woman opened the door, cheeks flushed. She had a white apron on, flour on her hands.

"Beppie Rudiger?" Annie said. "I'm Constable Pirello, with the Snowy Creek PD."

"What is it?" The woman's gaze shot immediately toward a shed down the yard. Annie turned, following her gaze. She waited a beat, then said. "Is your husband home, Mrs. Rudiger?"

"No. He . . . he's out. Why?"

"He's not in that shed?"

"No."

"Is that his truck round the side?"

Something hot flickered through the woman's face. A blonde child appeared at her side. "Susie, go inside," Beppie Rudiger said as she stepped out, closing the door behind her. "It's my truck. Clint drives a Dodge Ram. Red."

"He take the Dodge Ram to work on Wednesday?"

"What's this about?"

"Your truck matches the description of a vehicle that was placed at an arson scene, ma'am."

Blood drained from her cheeks. She swallowed, looking nervous.

"Did your husband perhaps borrow your vehicle Wednesday?"

Beppie reached for the banister on the side of the stairs. "I . . . I don't recall. You'd need to speak to him."

Annie nodded, holding the woman's eyes. Novak meanwhile popped back from around the side and Beppie Rudiger jerked in surprise.

"Plate has a *D*," Novak called up to Annie.

"Do you mind if we take a look inside the truck, Mrs. Rudiger?"

"Yes, I do mind. I don't like the insinuation here. I . . . I'd like for you both to leave. Now."

Annie turned her back on Beppie and made a show of taking in the landscape. "Nice place. Rural. I also grew up on a farm, in Quebec. My mother liked to air-dry the laundry, too." She turned back to face Beppie. The woman looked ill suddenly. "When did you last do a wash, Mrs. Rudiger?"

"What's that got to do with anything?"

"Black toque," Annie said with a nod toward the washing line.

"It's getting cold," Beppie snapped. "People wear toques when it's cold."

Annie's pulse quickened slightly at the woman's reaction. They were on to something here, she was sure of it.

"What's in the shed down there ma'am?"

"That's my husband's shed. It's where he does his taxidermy."

Annie raised a brow. "Taxidermy? He likes to hunt?"

"Goes on two long hunts a year. We store the meat in the freezer down there."

"Might we take a look?"

"No." She wiped her hands on her apron suddenly, as if they were sweating. "I mean, it's Clint's space. Not for me to say who goes in there. Look, if you want my husband, you can get him at the fire hall. He's the fire chief in Snowy Creek."

Annie nodded again and smiled broadly. "It's his day off today, I believe."

Beppie said nothing.

"You sure he's not around? Out back maybe?"

"He's getting hay from one of the farms down valley. For winterizing the garden."

"He keep his hunting weapons in that shed?"

"In a safe. In the house."

"Rifles, shotguns?"

Beppie's mouth formed a tight line. "That's what he hunts with."

"Any handguns in there?"

She swallowed. "I wouldn't know."

"Well, thank you for your time, Mrs. Rudiger." Annie started down the stairs to join Novak, but stopped halfway down and turned around once more to face Beppie Rudiger.

"Your husband was discharged from the army, is that correct?"

"He left the army to spend more time with his family."

"Dishonorable discharge, right?"

Beppie Rudiger went even whiter. The wind ruffled her curls.

"Something to do with a sexual assault allegation," Annie said, "but it was later dropped?"

Silence.

"Where was your husband April ninth, ma'am?"

Beppie opened her mouth. Then closed it again.

"I know, six months ago is a long time to recall something specific like that. No worries. We'll ask him when we connect with him."

"Religious," Annie murmured quietly as she walked with Novak back to the cruiser. "Crucifix around her neck."

"Doesn't mean she's religious."

"Good chance it does." She opened the door. Beppie was still standing sentry at the top of the steps, watching them.

As they exited the driveway and turned down the farm road, Novak said, "Shit, I'm thinking there might actually be something to Cullen's claims."

Annie snorted, stealing a glance up at the sheer rock slopes and avalanche chutes of Mount Currie as she drove. It was not far from here that her sister had gone missing. "Cat among the proverbial pigeons," she said softly.

"What?"

"I said, Cullen is like a cat put in among the pigeons."

Novak stared blankly.

"You know; scattering everyone, getting them running scared. Jesus, Novak, where'd they find you, anyways?"

He was silent awhile. "Can I ask you something, smart-ass?"

"What?"

"Why do you think Chief Mackin put you and me on this case? I mean, look at us, nosing around the head honchos in town when there is already an official investigation into the arson."

She glanced at him.

"You're brand-new. Easy scapegoat if this all goes to hell. Me? I'm up for retirement next year. If this goes to shit, Mackin sends me out to pasture early and he kicks your ass right out of the valley. He tells the police board you were a loose fucking cannon. He claims he didn't even know we were sniffing around the case. However this shit hits the fan, Mackin has his ass covered all ways to Sunday."

Annie swallowed.

"So, yeah, who's the smart-ass, now?" Novak said, removing a half-eaten Snickers bar from his pocket.

CHAPTER 22

"Rachel?" Kerrigan jerks her head up as I enter her office. She gets up and quickly closes the door behind me.

"Guess I'm not that welcome here, huh?"

"I'm sorry, Rach, but that stunt at the Shady Lady has everyone here kinda steamed."

"Stunt?"

"You know what I mean. It's . . . your paper that gave him a voice, okay? He accused our chief of perjury. You know how things work among first responders, We're tight, have each other's backs." Kerrigan looks as though she wants to say more but bites her tongue. "What can I do for you?"

I inhale deeply and decide to just go for it. "Before Amy Findlay shot herself, she called the fire hall."

"She did?"

"This number here." I push the piece of paper on which I've written the number toward Kerrigan. "Do you know whose extension that is?"

She looks up, meets my eyes. Silence hangs for a moment.

"Look, Kerri, you know me. I don't want trouble any more than anyone else does, but a man's life is at stake."

"A man's life? Christ, Rachel, hardly. He's not in prison anymore. He's free. I don't know why you're doing this." She shoves the piece of paper back at me.

"He's *not* free. Not until he can prove he didn't commit that crime. Look at how the town's reacted to his return. Look at your own reaction."

Her eyes flicker. "That's because of your newspaper, him naming names."

I lean forward. "Three men tried to kill him before he even went to the paper. They burned his place down, and I don't believe they would have stopped there unless he *had* gone to the papers and spooked them. You can't honestly think Jeb razed his own property and somehow managed to beat himself up with a tire iron? Please, tell me whose extension that is."

Kerrigan's jaw tightens.

Frustration flares in me. "Okay, can you at least let me know who was on duty the evening of April eighth?"

"I'm not sure that's public information."

"Of course it is. You work for the Snowy Creek municipality. The taxpayers are your employers."

"Then go get it from the municipal office."

I stare at her.

"Look, you chose to make yourself the enemy here, Rachel. I have enough trouble as it is bonding with the guys. I'm not going to be the one to hand this information over."

I drag my hand over my hair. "Okay, what about you—were *you* on duty the evening of April eighth?"

She inhales deeply, holding my gaze.

"Please."

She curses under her breath, grabs the firefighter calendar on her wall, unhooks it, and slaps it on her desk. She flips back to April.

I freeze as an image catches my eye. "Wait—" I clap my hand down on her calendar. "That photo, back there, flip back a few pages."

Startled, she lets me take the calendar.

I quickly flick back a few months and come to the photograph. My blood turns cold.

A firefighter. His big muscled back to the camera, his skin oiled and gleaming, fire pants hanging below his hips, exposing the top of his buttocks. He's working an old-style water pump, but it's the tattoo snaking up from the exposed top of his buttocks that rivets me. A tail. A dragon's tail. With an arrowhead shape at the tip.

"Who is this?" I whisper.

Kerrigan looks at me oddly. "A lot of the guys posed for that. It's a fundraising calendar. They do it each year."

"That tattoo, it's a dragon."

Undulating dragon. Amy watching Merilee being raped. *Pumping dragon.*

"A dragon across his butt, yeah, he's had it since school, apparently."

"Who has?"

"Chief Rudiger."

A dull roar sounds in my brain.

"You okay, Rachel? What is it?"

I clear my throat. "Was . . . was Clint Rudiger at work on the evening of April eighth?" I grab the piece of paper from her desk, hold it up. "Is this *his* extension?"

Laughter and men's voices reach us from the next room.

Kerrigan's complexion pales. She gets smartly to her feet, walks around her desk, opens the door. "I think you should leave. Now."

I glare at her. Her reaction has confirmed it for me. The extension belongs to Clint Rudiger. Clint with the dragon tattoo. But Kerrigan has shut down. She stands unflinching by the door. But underneath the flint of her gaze I detect something else, a whisper of uncertainty, fear even.

I get slowly to my feet, go to the door. "I'm not the enemy, Kerri. I just want the truth."

She says nothing. I leave and she shuts her door firmly behind me.

I walk quickly out to where I've left Jeb in the parked truck, get in.

"What happened?"

I explain the photo of Clint, the dragon tattoo, Kerrigan's reaction.

"Jesus," he whispers.

I turn in the seat to face him. "April eighth was a Thursday, Jeb. Fridays are traditionally Clint's days off—it's why Kerrigan always works on a Friday. If he was sticking to his schedule, he had opportunity to be in Vancouver on Friday the ninth, the day my sister's house burned down."

He swallows, eyes narrowing, a vein on his brow beneath the small butterfly sutures swelling.

"Clint also fits the physical description of the man who visited Amy's duplex after those phone calls."

"Fuck," he says quietly.

We both sit stunned for a moment.

I recall what the West Vancouver police told me at the time of Sophia's fire, that a lot of evidence is destroyed by the first responders to a blaze.

"What better person," I say, my voice hoarse, "to set a fire, to try and hide the fact it might be arson, than a firefighter? He could have taken the answering machine tape from the phone, the voice mail Amy left Sophia. He could have silenced Sophia." Something else strikes me. "They never did find her cell phone, Jeb. And her laptop was damaged beyond retrieval."

"It's all circumstantial," Jeb says.

"But it's feasible."

"We need proof. We can't do a damn thing without *proof*."

"Let's go to the pit," I say. "We can take a look at the place again, walk you through that night. Maybe being there will prompt something fresh in your own memory, like that music, the scent of dope, maybe even that newspaper ad for the firefighter's calendar, finally prompted Amy's."

As we drive north we see a dark bank of clouds building over the mountains. The wind has increased, bits of branches now blowing across the road. The first of the storm fronts is approaching.

———

Thinking about Clint Rudiger, the possibilities, Jeb turned the truck off the highway, drove over the bridge, and crossed the train tracks. As the waters of the Green River churned beneath them, a strange feeling wrapped around him. He felt as though they'd just crossed some kind of threshold and were going back in time, things closing around them, past melding with present.

He took the truck across a wide clearing that had once been used as a turning circle for vehicles ferrying basalt from the pit. This was where the two girls had gotten out of his car nine years ago. They'd run back across this clearing toward a grove of alders, while he'd turned south onto the highway and headed home. Engaging four-wheel drive, Jeb entered a narrow, rutted logging road hemmed in by forest on either side. After about a mile, the road opened suddenly into the wide gravel pit on a bench of land above the tracks. It had once been a quarry.

They parked and got out.

Hydro wires were near, and the air hummed with a crackling electricity. Jeb's heart began to hammer and his skin pricked with perspiration.

Nothing had changed. Rocks lined the high bank. Dry grass pushed through the stones in clumps. There were remains of small campfires. Broken bottles, beer cans. Kids still came here. Did the same things.

He turned in a slow circle, his boots crunching over gravel, sun collecting against his leather jacket and black hair. An eagle soared up high, cried.

Rachel slipped her hand into his, cool, slender, strong. He looked down into her eyes, the years suddenly spiraling, kaleidoscoping back to that moment, the night that had changed them all.

"She tried it with me, you know. Retrograde hypnosis. In prison," he said.

"Sophia?"

He nodded. "Well, that's what she called it. She took me back to that night several times. Walked me through to see if I might have missed a detail that could help. We found nothing new. She said at the time that returning here, then trying myself to re-create the events of that night, might spur something."

"How did Sophia do it?"

"She'd induce the hypnotic state, then step-by-step, walk me back as if in real time to re-create a vivid picture of the past, something I could examine." As he spoke, Jeb walked with Rachel up to a blackened circle surrounded by heavily charred logs.

"Here," he said, "was the bonfire. You and Trey were sitting on a sleeping bag against the slight rise over there."

Her hand tightened in his. His face felt hot. The sounds of that night started coming back to him. Music. Someone had a drum. Rachel and Trey laughing, jeering at him. Amy teetering toward him, silhouetted by the orange flames, her high-heeled boots digging in between the tiny stones, low-cut blouse. Amy grabbing his arm. The eerily dancing light from the fire.

"I'm so sorry," Rachel whispered suddenly, pulling him back to the present. "It was my fault."

He turned to her and took her face in both hands, looking deep into her eyes. They were liquid, wide, vulnerable, as if she had nothing left to hide. The fragility of what he held in his hands, right here, suspended between past and present, could not have been more stark to him.

"No, Rachel," he whispered. "We all took actions that night that held consequences." He bent down and kissed her lips, so gently, poignantly, a wild, ferocious rushing in his heart. Rachel melted into him, against him. This was how it should have been that night. This was what he should have left with.

Maybe it was a good thing to confront this place, the past, together like this. To come full circle. There was a lot to be said about closure. She pulled back, looked up at him. "Let's go back to the bridge crossing, Jeb, where they claimed they saw you turn north onto the highway."

———

Jeb stopped the truck in exactly the same place he'd stopped to wait for the train before crossing onto the highway that night. He wound down the window as it had been. He could smell smoke, carrying from the Wolf River fire with the new wind direction. There was a brown haze in the western sky.

"Think back. Walk me through it, Jeb," she said softly.

He closed his eyes, inhaled deeply. "I could smell smoke. Like now. But it was from the bonfire up at the pit. My car was facing the tracks, like this. I was heated. Angry. At you. At myself for having slept with Amy in the backseat. Angry at getting drunk." He swallowed, face going hot. "We had drunken sex in my car while it was parked up at the gravel pit. I hardly even remember it. Then, when I was going to take Amy home, she saw Merilee at the pit, and offered her a ride home with us. My head was spinning. I was unfocused. I shouldn't have been driving, but I did."

He sat silent for a while.

"While the three of us were in my car, waiting here to cross onto the highway, the train came rumbling past. Loud. Screeching wheels against the tracks. Amy was in the passenger seat next to me. She was facing the back, talking to Merilee. She had a fifth of brandy; they were passing it back and forth." Jeb glanced up into the rearview mirror. "I could see Merilee in the mirror, brushing her hair, a gold pendant glimmering in the hollow of her throat."

"That's why they found her hair in your car—she was brushing it."

He nodded. "I guess she might have hooked out the earring they found, too, while brushing. The girls were giggling, saying something, but the sound of their voices was being drowned by the noise of the train. The whistle sounded. It was piercing. The water under the bridge was rushing loud. My brain felt thick."

He closed his eyes again and thought deeper, trying to take his mind back further, trying to force clarity into the fuzziness of his drunken memories. The scent of smoke was stirring something fundamental inside him. Suddenly he could see again the luminescence of moonlight on the frothing white surface of the river. He could feel again the steering wheel of his car clenched in his fists, the tightness in his neck and shoulders. He heard the train coming again. He could smell the booze and cigarette smoke and perfume on the girls. Sweat trickled down his spine. He could taste Amy in his mouth, her lipstick. Shame, remorse, washed through him.

He heard the loud, long whistle of the train. Once. Twice. The screech and rumble. He could feel the vibration in his car.

Jeb realized with a start that a real train was approaching. Rachel touched his thigh. "Go with it, Jeb. Keep your eyes closed. Look back into that rearview mirror in your mind."

He glanced up into rearview mirror of memory, his eyes still shut.

The screeching of the train along the tracks grew deafening. He felt the wind of it. Could smell metal. The wood chips and lumber it was carrying.

"Music," he said suddenly, eyes still closed. "There was music coming from somewhere, drowned by the sound of the train, but I knew it was there. The girls were laughing and Amy told Merilee to look at something behind us."

Jeb went still. In the mirror he saw the shadows of the dark grove of alder trees on the far side of the clearing. Suddenly a light came on in the shadows. It was the interior light of a partially hidden vehicle. And in that brief moment Jeb glimpsed shapes inside the vehicle; several people. He saw the orange flare of a cigarette being lit. Then all went dark again.

A dialogue between the girls sifted into his memory.

It's them.
Do you wanna go?
Is he there?
I think so. They've got the good shit . . .
Better than with Jeb. Hey, Jeb . . .

Laughter. Drunken laughter.

Words formed in his own mind. *Who are you talking about? Who is behind us? I should take you home.* Words he never uttered because another part of him didn't want to know who was behind them. He just wanted the girls gone. He was happy for them to leave.

He felt a tightening in his stomach. Doors opened. The girls got out of his car and turned into silhouettes as they ran toward the hidden vehicle in the trees, where the music was coming from. The train passed. He drove over the tracks, turned left, never looked back.

Jeb's eyes flared open and he spun round, stared out the back window, the memory shattering into a million mirrorlike shards at his feet. His heart was thumping. He was wet under his arms.

"Rachel," he said thickly. "I think there was a vehicle parked in the trees over there."

He got out of the truck and quickly marched over to the clump of trees. Rachel came running behind him.

"There. It was parked right in there, partially hidden, but the interior light came on for a second, and I saw it." He spun to face her. "Those four guys, they said in court they were sitting here, in the copse, smoking, when they saw me turn north onto the highway. I remembered the girls running to join someone behind us, but there was not one mention of a vehicle. Why not?"

"Are you sure?"

He raked his hand over his hair, staring at the trees, doubt whispering around the edges of his drunken memory.

Wind gusted, rustling dead alder leaves. Several clattered down on them.

"Close your eyes again, Jeb." She placed her hand on his arm. "See it. Talk me through it."

He shut his eyes, inhaled deeply.

"Which way was the vehicle facing?"

He thought for a moment of the shape of the vehicle that was so briefly lit up.

"That way." His eyes flared open. "Rachel, it was facing that way, toward the old road leading up to the trestle bridge, to the mine." He stilled as something hit him. "A Jeep," he said. "It was a Jeep."

"How do you know?"

"The shape of the windows."

The wind rustled again through the dry trees and brush. The faint scent of smoke filled their nostrils. Rachel glanced up at the sky. Jeb followed her gaze. The orange haze was moving in fast from the west, while a purple bank of clouds was building over the peaks to east. The sky was darkening.

Thunder growled, soft and distant in the mountains.

"Adam used to own a Jeep," she said softly. "He had a Hawaiian sticker on the back, near the right taillight. White, with a rainbow and a hand making that 'hang loose' surfing sign. I saw it up at the pit earlier that night." Rachel rubbed her hand over her brow. "Oh, God. I remember—Luke was driving the Jeep when I saw it. I never thought of it again, Jeb. I . . . I didn't even think about whose Jeep it was, or where it went. It was irrelevant at the time." Her eyes glittered with emotion. "I should have remembered."

"That's why this technique works. It can help you see pieces you never thought fit at the time. This is not your fault. I didn't recall a Jeep either, until now, until the smell of smoke, the sound of the train, being here with you, taking my mind back."

She looked away, struggling.

He took her arm. "Come. Let's drive up that logging track to the trailhead where the trestle bridge crosses over to the mine. That's the way the Jeep was pointing. Maybe it did go up there that night."

———

They arrived at the trailhead where the track forked. The right-hand fork led to a hiking trail along the flank of Mount Rogue and up to the glacier that fed Rogue Falls. The left fork led to the trestle bridge and mine. But it was barricaded by a row of giant boulders. This was as far as they could take a vehicle. A large yellow sign warned that the road had been decommissioned and was danger-ous. Bridge unstable. No access.

Rachel and Jeb left the truck and continued on foot along what was now a small grassy track. A grouse *whoop whoop whooped* in the woods, the soft sound like a muted owl. A squirrel chucked a shrill warning. The air whispered with the scent of smoke and dry-ness. As they neared the bridge, they could hear the rushing waters of Rogue Falls, and the air grew damp and cool.

They came to the edge of the gorge where the old trestle bridge spanned the plunging chasm and raging waterfall. Mist rose in clouds. Fine droplets began to cling to their hair. Nine years ago they would have been able to drive over this bridge to the old mine on the other side. Now crosspieces of the bridge were missing, gaping maws opening to the gorge below.

Had the Jeep come this far and crossed over to the entrance of the old copper mine? They could see the mine entrance on the other side, a black hole in the red rock of the mountain.

Rachel rubbed her arms. "Amy remembered the sound of rushing water."

"And dirt, cold, dark, damp. Piper mentioned earth, heavy above their heads."

She shivered. Jeb put his arm around her, drawing her close.

"Do you think it's possible that Merilee is down there," she said, "at the bottom of a shaft somewhere? Because if she is, there could be evidence with her. Her body could have been fairly protected down there. She could still tell what happened."

He moistened his lips, staring at the black maw in the red mountain. He could almost sense a presence, something reaching, calling from that hole, from the dark bowels of the mountain. "Every contact leaves a trace," he whispered. "Like in tracking. Wherever a person steps, whatever he touches, it will serve as silent witness against him."

"We could walk across, using the crosspieces," Rachel said. "The side railings still look solid."

"Risky," he said. "No idea how rotten that wood might be. The best way would be to access the mine entrance by coming up from the north side of that gorge. We'd need equipment to get down the shafts."

"Equipment and expertise that Rescue One has," Rachel said. "But I don't see them helping us with this, Jeb. How are we going to do it?"

He looked up at the darkening sky. The wind was blowing harder. Thunder grumbled into the distance again, louder this time, rolling into the peaks. "I don't know. Yet. We need to go fetch Quinn. This weather is not looking good."

Jeb could tell Rachel felt it too, a sense of time closing in. Pressure building. The storm was almost on them.

They hiked quickly back to the truck. Lightning flickered against the puce sky to the east. Thunder clapped. Wind gusted and raindrops began to spit from the sky.

As they drove back down the mountain, Rachel leaned forward, turned the radio on to the local news channel.

They were talking about the Wolf River wildfire. It was burning out of control again, and heading back toward Snowy Creek, fueled by fresh southeasterly winds. Another small fire had also been ignited by a lightning strike below the peak of Mount Barren, and it was burning on the south flank. More strikes were expected to spark many more spot fires as the storm cells moved in.

"There's no time to drop you at home first," Rachel said. "We should go straight to pick up Quinn."

He nodded. It would mean people might see them all in the truck together. But he didn't like the sound of fire on the south side of Barren. Things could get ugly fast.

When they reached the highway, Jeb increased the gas. He was worried about getting his child now. Keeping them all together.

CHAPTER 23

Rain bombs down, fat drops hitting dry ground and rolling like mercurial marbles in the dust. I run with my jacket over my head toward the staging area for Quinn's bike camp. Jeb has parked a small distance away in an effort to remain incognito in my vehicle. Wind gusts in strange, unpredictable eddies fueled by mountain downdrafts and valley crosswinds.

The thought that Merilee could be down there in that mine dogs me. To think of her family tearing themselves apart, suffering so painfully, aching for closure, her mother dying with grief while her daughter's broken body lies down a shaft so close to home. We don't know for certain she's down there. Yet everything fits. I could almost feel in my bones as we stared across that old bridge that her ghost was in that mountain.

As I head into the trees and near the cross-country skiers' hut, I realize there is no longer a whisper of doubt in me that Jeb is innocent. And I'm boiling inside with rage toward the people who have done this to him. Those who have lied, kept this heinous secret, turned a blind eye all these years, stealing his life while they all built their own. Brutal, selfish cowards who set in motion a series of interlocking events that possibly led to even the death of my sister and brother-in-law. To Quinn coming into my home.

I wonder again, when does something really begin, and end? Can you pinpoint the moment you start on a collision course with others destined to cross your path?

I recognize the group of women huddled in rain jackets beneath the boughs of a huge hemlock. There is a sense of urgency in them, too, as they wait for their children. The storm and smoke are growing thick around us. Those kids should have come down already.

They all glance up sharply as I approach—Lily, Beppie, Stacey, Vickie. The emotion in their faces is raw and hostile. I hesitate. Something has changed. But my jaw steels with fight, and aggression pumps through my blood as I go up to them.

Beppie's complexion is white and she glowers at me. Stacey's eyes are narrow and resentful. Lily's face is pugnacious, and Vickie, Levi's personal assistant, stiffens visibly as I reach them.

"How can you do this, Rachel?" Lily demands immediately. "How dare you tear the town apart like this and drag that poor Zukanov family through hell again. You should never have brought his kid back here. Spawn of the devil, that's what she is!"

I freeze dead in my tracks. "*What* did you say?"

"We know," Stacey replies. "From Trey. We know that Quinn is his offspring."

"*Offspring?*" I almost choke. My hands fist at my sides. I now know what it must be like to mentally crack, to kill someone. To feel pure, black hatred. To feel the rush of violence in one's veins.

"We all know," Beppie says darkly, strangely.

"If you hadn't brought his kid back here," says Lily, "he would have stayed away. Now look what you've done."

Thunder cracks above us. They flinch. I feel nothing. Rain bombs harder.

"Trey? *He* told you?"

Stacey smirks.

"I don't believe you people." I'm shaking with the cocktail inside me now. "You're blaming an innocent child for tearing lives apart? You're blaming *me*?"

They stare coldly at me.

"I dare you all to place the blame where it really lies. Do you honestly think what your men said all those years ago is the truth? What if"—I go closer to them, right up to them, my gaze lasering each one of them in turn—"the crime never happened up north? What if someone borrowed a Jeep to go to the party at the gravel pit that night?" My gaze settles on Lily. "And what if that Jeep had a Hawaiian sticker on the bumper and was parked in a copse of alders near the Green River rail crossing when Jeb stopped at the tracks to wait for a train? What if there was old Jamaican ska music blaring from that Jeep, the *Best of Damani Jakeel*, perhaps?"

Lily swallows hard. Her hair is plastering to her cheeks with rain.

"What if the two girls got out of Jeb's car at the tracks and ran back to that Jeep, and the Jeep was then driven up to the old copper mine?"

Lily started to shiver.

"Maybe the girls were brutally assaulted in the mine, and one died. Maybe it was even an accident, but everyone panicked. Maybe they threw her body down a shaft. Perhaps they didn't know what to do with Amy, who was still alive, but they couldn't just kill her there in cold blood. Possibly they drove her north twenty or so miles, in that Jeep, trying to figure out what in hell to do with her. Then they dumped her in that trapper's shed. Perhaps one of the guys tried to strangle her with a rope. Whatever happened, a pact was made. A lie was told. They all said the girls never got out of Jeb's car and that they'd seen him driving north with them. And when Amy was eventually found, still alive, the search for Merilee happened twenty miles north of where she really lay. At the bottom of a mine shaft. That hoodie with the drug packet wasn't Jeb's, so whose was it?"

Thunder booms right above our heads and sheet lightning pulses in the darkening clouds. The sky grows black.

"Where the fuck are you going with this, Rachel?" Stacey snaps suddenly.

"You're frightening me." Lily is sheet white. "You're just trying to wreck our lives."

Beppie reaches out to quiet Lily. But she's listening intently to me, a strange look entering her eyes.

"No," I say. "It's not me or Jeb or my niece wrecking lives. Someone else already did that nine years ago. You're just feeling the ripples of that now, feeling the impact of those lies." My stomach is churning up into my chest. I know on some level I've lost it. I'm heading down a road from which there can be no return. But they already know Quinn is Jeb's child. Thanks to Trey. Goddamn Trey. The whole town must know now. It's over. Urgency pulses through me. I peer through the rain into the dark trees, desperate to see Quinn's shape coming down on her bike through the trails, Brandy in tow.

"You've gone mad," Vickie says. "Stark raving mad."

"Yeah. Yeah, I have," I say, staring into the trees, my clothes starting to stick to my body, my hair plastering to my cheeks. "Mad as hell that people could do this, turn a blind eye, send an innocent man to prison."

"None of those guys could do something like that," Vickie says. "I know Levi, I know he—"

I spin back to face her. "Right. It's easier to believe that the guy from the wrong side of the river did it. Much easier than facing the truth. Because one of you must know something. At least one of you must have come across a black ski mask in a laundry basket, black clothes that smelled of smoke, or maybe even had some blood on them. Someone's husband, or lover, or boss, took a blow to the face in the early hours of Thursday morning, and he has bruises and cuts on a knuckle from beating up Jeb. Someone here drives a silver SUV or dark truck."

I turn on Beppie. "Perhaps someone here is also missing the handgun that shot Amy six months ago. Perhaps someone's husband was in the city on the morning my sister's house burned down. Perhaps someone's husband has a dragon tattoo emblazoned across his ass! Because that's one thing Amy did remember before she was shot dead six months ago—an undulating dragon moving between her friends legs as she was raped."

Lily gasps. Beppie staggers backward. Vickie and Stacey stare, eyes huge.

"But hey, no worries. Because when we get ropes down into that mine, we'll all know for sure."

Lily makes a furious lunge at me. "I wish you'd die! Just go away, leave us all alone! I won't let you do this to Adam, I won't!" Beppie grabs Lily's arm, holds her back.

"I don't know what you're talking about, Rachel," Beppie says with a strange calm. "You need help. This is messing you up. And these accusations will hurt our children."

"Like those lies in court ended up hurting Quinn? You all have a choice to make. And yes, think of your children. Do the right thing. They're the ones who will judge you in the end."

Suddenly the kids are coming, bikes bombing out of the trail. They're spattered with mud and soaked with rain. Panic races across the women's faces as they see the children. They seem trapped between me and their kids.

I catch sight of Quinn and I run to her, grabbing her handlebars before she's even properly stopped. I force a smile. "Hey, how was it?"

Quinn dismounts, takes off her helmet. She looks at me funny.

"Come, let's get out of the rain." I start pushing her bike and we walk smartly toward the truck. My heart is slamming. My throat feels as though it's stuck together from dryness. Quinn has to run to keep up with me.

"Bitch!" I hear someone yell behind me. "Go to hell, Rachel!"

In my peripheral vision I see Brandy heading over to the group of women with Beppie's girls in tow. They all huddle together, talking urgently. Brandy looks our way. She must be wondering why I didn't wait to talk to her, to tell her I was taking Quinn. Right now I don't care. I just want to get Quinn away from those madwomen.

"Why did they yell like that?" Quinn asks, aghast as she trots beside me. "Why did they call you that word?"

I fake another smile. "You mean that word you called me once?"

"I didn't mean it," Quinn said.

"I'm sure they didn't either. Come, let's move faster." The rain is pelting sideways now. I'm drenched to the bone.

As we near the truck, Quinn spots Jeb in the driver's seat, hesitates. "*He's* here? You brought him?"

"He wanted to come see where you ride."

"He did?"

"Yes."

She does a happy skip. And by God I want it to all come out right. I want her to be happy. I want us all to be free just to live in peace.

"Can he come for dinner?"

We reach the truck. Jeb gets out, takes the bike from me, lifts it into the back.

"What happened?" he says. Worry darkens his eyes. "It looked like you were getting into it with those women."

"They called Rachel a . . . really bad word."

"Hey, you." He ruffles Quinn's wet curls, opens the back door. "Hop in."

She clambers up onto the backseat. Jeb closes the door. "What happened back there?" he asks me again.

I reach for the passenger door. "Later. Just drive. I don't want Quinn to hear about it."

He pulls out into the road but keeps glancing at me. I push wet hair back from my face. My hands are trembling like leaves. I finally understand what it means to lose one's temper and fly into a blind rage, to act without logic. I can fully comprehend Jeb attacking his father all those years ago.

Thunder smacks again, almost above us. A jagged yellow streak stabs down from the sky. The wipers clack but have trouble keeping up with the rain.

"Jeb," Quinn says from the backseat.

He tenses. Shoots me another hot glance.

I look away.

"Are you coming for dinner?"

"Yes," I say. "He is."

He drives in silence, hot energy coming off him in waves. He glances every now and then at my hands, which I press down hard on my wet jeans in an effort to hide the shaking.

———

As I boil spaghetti once again, for there has been no thought of grocery shopping, Quinn gets plates. Jeb comes up behind me, and under the rumble of the stove fan, which is sucking up steam from the roiling pot, he says, close to my ear, "What did you say to those women? What happened back at the bike camp?"

"They know," I say quietly as I stir the pasta. "Everyone in town knows you're her father. Lily called her 'spawn of the devil' to my face."

He goes dead still. I glance up at him, nervous.

"Trey. He did this?"

I say nothing. I'm afraid of the fury crackling in his eyes.

"Jesus. I told you, that guy—"

"Enough. She'll hear you."

"You could have told me up front that he knew about her," he growls near my ear.

"You didn't ask, did you? It was obvious he'd know. I was going to marry him, and you were still in prison, supposedly guilty, supposedly unaware of your child's sex let alone where she went." I angrily stir the pasta, steam heating my face.

"Besides," I add. "*You* could have told me you suspected Amy was murdered, that you thought my sister's fire was deliberately set. You could have *told* me you thought there was an active killer lurking out here."

"What are you talking about?" Quinn says behind us. We both jump.

Quinn is staring up at us, a look of worry entering her face.

"It's nothing, Quinnie," I say as brightly as I can, handing Jeb the pasta spoon and leading her to the table. "We were just arguing about how much hot sauce to put into the pasta."

"I hate hot sauce."

"That's what I told him."

"You're not telling me the truth. You were fighting."

"Here, sit." I pull out a chair. "Jeb will bring the pasta."

The radio is on. There is urgent chatter about the fires. Mount Barren is burning aggressively along the south flank now. There is a second storm cell moving in. It sounds as though things could get a lot worse. I make note to turn on my scanner and tune into the emergency channels as soon as we're done eating. There's always a chance the winds will turn away again, and we're in a good place right here on the glacial lake. I hope it will all be okay. Rain hammers down on the metal roof. Wind rattles the window panes, bombing debris down onto the house.

THE SLOW BURN OF SILENCE

Jeb brings the pasta and sets the pot heavily on the table. He's steaming as he takes a seat. I can see his brain is racing.

I dish up, put a plate in front of Quinn.

"Why did my real parents give me away?" Quinn says.

I stiffen. My gaze jerks to Quinn, then Jeb.

Jeb's fork clatters.

Now she wants to talk about the adoption?

"Was there something wrong with me? Who were they?"

Thunder claps above the house. I wince as the lights flicker on and off. The power could go any minute. Clearing my throat, I say, "Maybe right now is not such a good time to talk about it—"

"You said it was good to talk. Now you don't want to tell me, do you?"

Jeb and I exchange a hot glance. I clear my throat. "They're not called 'real' parents, Quinn. They're called birth parents. Sophia and Peter were just as much real parents as your birth parents were. Just in a different way."

"Why did they give me away?" Her voice is going thin.

"There can be many reasons for an adoption. Sometimes, a mother and father can be in a bad position, or even too young to raise a child of their own."

"What about my birth parents? Were they too young?"

It was finally all coming out now. The information has simmered and reached some kind of boiling point in Quinn, and now she is not going to let it drop.

I exchange another nervous glance with Jeb. We're not ready to tell her . . . not yet. Not now. Not this way. It goes against everything he promised Sophia.

"Why didn't my mom and dad tell me I was adopted? Why did they *pretend*?"

"I told you," I say softly, leaning forward. "Sophia and Peter— your mom and dad—wanted to wait just a little while longer before they told you. Until you were a bit older."

"Why?"

"Because they believed that you would understand things differently. "

"How did Missy know that I was adopted, then?"

I clear my throat, brain racing. "I think Missy might have overheard Trey and Stacey talking about it. Remember, Trey and I were going to be married, so he knew you were adopted. And there's a good chance he might have mentioned this fact to Stacey because he's going out with her now."

"So other people know, too?"

We're entering dangerous territory. My thoughts flash to the women. *Spawn of the devil . . .*

Anger rushes hot and instant to my face again. "Maybe a few know, Quinn. It's not a negative thing."

"Will I ever know who my birth parents are? Do you know?"

Jeb's muscles are coiled like a spring. He's not touching his food. I can literally feel his energy across the table and I avoid his eyes, because if I look at him again, Quinn will read me. She will know we are both keeping something from her.

"Is it a secret?" She picks at the frayed edge of her napkin.

Again, I clear my throat. "In certain adoptions, these things can be secret, and it's a bit complicated in your case, but I want to promise you something. Right now. Look at me, Quinn."

She lifts her eyes.

"I'm working on finding out all the details for you, the whole truth about what happened to bring you into Sophia and Peter's arms . . . my arms. And when I know it all, I will tell you. Only the truth. Always the truth. You can trust me—I will not lie about this."

Quinn lurches up from her chair, and she lunges into my arms. I hug her fiercely, stroking her hair.

Jeb surges to his feet. He paces in front of the storm-streaked windows. It's getting dark out.

When I feel Quinn's muscles ease slightly, I hold her shoulders, look into her eyes. "You okay?"

She bites her lip hard. Her eyes are dry and hot looking. Red spots sit high on her cheeks.

"I think we should go upstairs and run a quick bath, how about that? We'll put some bubbles in, okay?" I'm not sure it's wise to bathe in a storm, but it's all I can think of. It's something concrete and comforting.

———

I sit with Quinn while she soaks, then I rub her dry with a big fluffy towel. She remains mute and oddly distant the whole while, and it makes me edgy. I leave her to change, giving her some space, and I go downstairs.

Jeb comes up to me, takes my shoulders. "Is she okay?"

"I hope so. It's going to take time." I hesitate. "We should find a therapist, a professional to help us all through this, because I sure as hell don't know what I'm doing." As I speak I realize we really are forming some kind of dysfunctional family unit. And we're not ready. This is all happening outside of our control, in spite of our best attempts to delay things. In spite of Jeb's goal, Sophia's wish, to clear his name first.

"What else happened at the bike park?" Jeb says quietly. "There's more, isn't there? I saw you going at those women, Rachel. What did you say to them?"

A brilliant white flash of lightning illuminates the lake and thunder booms. I flinch as the power flickers again. The thunder grumbles away into the peaks.

"I told them," I say. "I told them everything we think happened. About Merilee maybe being in the mine, about the Jeep, the ska music."

"You *told* them?"

I say nothing.

"What for?"

"I lost it. I'm sorry, Jeb. I went postal when they called her 'spawn of the devil.' It all came out before I could even think it through."

"What, exactly, did you say?"

I push my hair back off my face. "Everything. I told them we knew Luke borrowed Adam's Jeep, that the girls ran to the guys in the Jeep. I suggested the guys might have driven the girls up to the mine and that maybe Merilee died there. I said they might have tried to take Amy north to deflect attention from the mine. And they might have formed a pact to blame you." I swallow. "I told them Amy remembered a dragon tattoo."

He spins away from me, glares out the black, rain-streaked window. "Fuck," he says quietly.

"You wanted to rattle their cages, Jeb. I rattled."

"Yeah, but—" He turns back to me. "Jesus, if Beppie tells Clint . . ."

"You think he'll come directly after us?"

"I think he went directly after Amy and Sophia and Peter. And fast. I believe it was him." He grabs my shoulders suddenly. "Listen, pack your bags. When Quinn is done changing, I'm taking you both out of here."

"What about the proof, Jeb?"

"The proof is buried deep in a mine, Rachel. It hasn't gone anywhere in nine years, and it's not going anywhere now, fire or not. My priority is now to keep you and Quinn safe, to get you away from these people, this town. We've learned what we can here. We have a lot of information, a lot of possibilities to work with. We can deal with what we have from afar now. We can involve outside agencies. This town is too crooked, too steeped in this to handle it from the inside. It's now become dangerous for you. For my daughter. I'm getting you both out."

"Jeb—"

"I don't like these fires and this weather as it is. We're going. Go upstairs and get your things."

———

When Lily arrived home with the boys, she saw that Adam had been home but was no longer there. His uniform was on the bed and his hiking boots were gone. So was his jacket. With trembling hands, she tried to call his cell, but he was not answering.

She put frozen pizzas in the oven and told the boys to go bathe quickly and change. She turned on the radio, listening to news of the fires. The Mount Barren fire was burning rapidly down the south flank in the alpine. The downdrafts were strong enough that it could jump the Khyber Creek drainage and move on to Bear Mountain. If it did that, the village itself would be in danger. She'd already packed emergency bags, just in case, before fetching the boys from bike camp.

She paced up and down, tried to call Adam again. Still no answer. She thought of the Jeep he had owned all those years ago when they were dating. The ska music he loved. The bumper sticker, what had that sticker looked like? There was a photo somewhere.

Lily went into Adam's office and rummaged on the shelves for the old photo album she knew was there. She found it, flipped through the pages. She froze when she came to the one she was looking for. Adam with his arm around her. He'd been a cop for three years when that was taken. They were standing behind his Jeep, and there was a Hawaiian sticker on the bumper. Just as Rachel had described. She set the album on his desk and quickly flipped through his stack of CDs. Lots of old Jamaican ska, including Damani Jakeel.

She thought of that argument with his mother. The bloody hoodie.

What had Sheila known, or been hiding? Had both she and Adam tried to protect Luke? This would ruin Adam if it came out now. Ruin all of them. Her name would be mud. Her sons would be scorned.

As Lily moved to replace the CDs, she bumped Adam's mouse and the computer screen on the desktop crackled to life. A Word document filled the screen. It was a letter. Addressed to Chief Constable Rob Mackin.

Lily leaned forward, her stomach rising into her throat as she read what her husband had written.

It is with deep regret that I present to you these facts pertaining to the Jebbediah Cullen case nine years ago . . .

A ringing began in Lily's ears.

It was a confession. A full confession that incriminated both him and his mother. And by default accused the group of four guys—Luke, Clint, Harvey, and Levi—of having gang-raped the girls and killing Merilee.

Her hand went to her mouth as she read about the GPS system in his Jeep that had tracked the Jeep's route up to the mine and back down to the Green River rail crossing, then north from the gravel pit that night. About how Adam had found the GPS route erased the next day. How he'd found a gold Saint Christopher medallion in his Jeep after Luke had brought it home, and how his mother had later taken the medallion from his drawer. How Luke had arrived home in a bloodied hoodie. How his mother had added the hoodie to the list of evidence found in Jeb's car.

He wrote in his confession that he was including in the envelope Merilee Zukanov's Saint Christopher medallion, and the GPS route from his Jeep that night, which he'd saved on a flash drive before it had been erased. He said his mother hadn't known he'd saved it.

What did he mean, "including in the envelope"?

Lily scrabbled around in Adam's desk drawers, finding nothing but an open pack of manila envelopes. And it struck her. Her gaze shot to the printer.

He'd printed the confession out already; the printer light was still on. He'd put this confession along with the medallion and a flash drive into an envelope. He must have it with him.

Or worse.

Hands shaking, she tried again to call her husband. The call went to voice mail.

She stared out the rain-streaked window. It was getting dark.

Quickly she called Chief Mackin. They put her through right away.

"Lily, we're busy. Getting ready to upgrade to mandatory evac. You and Adam and the boys, you'll need to get out—"

"Have you seen Adam?"

He hesitated. "This morning, yes."

"You haven't seen him since? He hasn't brought you an envelope?"

"A what?"

"Where is he?"

"Lily, did he tell you?"

"Tell me what?" Her voice came out shrill.

"I placed Adam on mandatory leave, until this Cullen affair is sorted out."

"When?"

"Early this morning."

She hung up.

"Mom! Pizza's burning!"

She rushed through to the kitchen, tap, tap, tap, tapping her wrist with her fingers as she went, like Dr. Bennett said. To relax herself. She yanked the pizzas out the oven and dumped them smoking onto the stovetop. Tears flooded down her face.

"What is it, Mom?" Tyler asked.

This was Rachel's fault. That spawn's fault. Jeb's fault. Evil, they were evil.

"I . . . I need to drive you both over to Vickie's place. She will take you and Mikey down to Vancouver with your bags if there's an evacuation order. I'll follow. Later. Real soon."

"Why? Where are you going, what's the matter?"

She wiped her face quickly with the dishcloth. "Nothing. I need to find your father, I need to fix something. Go upstairs, get Mikey, your bags. Go to the car."

Lily poured a stiff vodka, swallowed it, then poured another big one. She gulped it down, almost gagging. She wiped her mouth, went back to the office, deleted all the files and wiped out the computer's recent history. Then she went to the gun safe in the bedroom. But the spare pistol was gone.

Heart in her throat, she grabbed her coat and rushed outside.

She didn't notice the small white envelope lying on the table, addressed to her.

———

Beppie drove home in the pouring rain, a cold sweat over her skin, wipers clacking. Smoke was dense in the canyon, the road slick after months of no rain. She took a bend too fast in her dark-blue truck with the *D* on the number plate. Tires squealed.

"Mom? You okay, Mom?"

She slowed down, heart hammering. "It's fine, girls, fine. Just worried about Dad and the fire and the storm."

And about what Rachel had said. What that female cop had said. Beppie gagged, tried to breathe, tried to calm herself.

Clint would be back at the fire hall by now with all this going on. She turned on the radio, listening to the news. The possibility of a mandatory evacuation of Snowy Creek was raised. Their ranch was much farther north, a different valley. But it didn't mean they were safe from this lightning and other fires.

When she pulled into the driveway and drove up to the house, the trees were swaying, rain coming sideways. She could smell smoke, thick, coming from another fire somewhere north.

"Go into the house. Get your bags ready," she told the girls. "I'll be right up."

While her girls went into the house, she ran through the rain down to the shed and took the key from under the rock near the door.

Beppie creaked the door open, searching with her hand for the light switch on the wall. Branches scratched and squeaked against the tiny window. As the bulb above the workbench flickered on, animal heads leaped to life and leered. Thunder boomed.

Beppie got down onto her hands and knees and felt under the counter for the metal box. She dragged it out, fetched a crowbar, and stuck it into the padlock. She wrenched hard.

It took two tries to get the correct angle before the lock cracked open.

She got back to her knees, opened the lid.

Her entire world came to a standstill as everything seemed to fade into the distance. It was as if she'd opened the lid to the basement of hell, a place she had known existed, which she'd buried in her own soul. Something she'd never wanted to think about or poke at. The reason she hated coming into the shed.

With shaking hands, she scrabbled through the rings and earrings in the top compartment of the metal box. There were locks of hair tied with wire. Human teeth. It was all here. Trophies. Things he said he found in the woods, that he liked to collect. She glanced up at the bear head, the stuffed bobcat. Trophies from his hunts. Memories of a kill.

Beppie gagged again, bile coming up her throat as she lifted the top compartment off the toolbox. Under it were three photos with time-date stamps. Like ones taken with a cell phone, then printed out.

Time slowed further, and the sounds of the storm and wind completely disappeared as she lifted the first one up. It had been taken nine years ago, according to the stamp. The night the girls had disappeared. It was fading a little, the colors off. It had been taken in a dark place. A picture of a woman's thighs, lily white. A man inserting his penis into her. His fingers digging hard into her skin as he held her steady. A dragon tattoo across his buttocks. In the other two photos he was forcing the muzzle of a handgun into her vagina. There was blood.

Beppie lurched up, retched into the sink. She hunched there while the room spun. She ran water until it was ice-cold. She splashed it all over her face. Her whole body was shaking as another wave of violent stomach contractions bent her over. She threw up again, washed and wiped her face, threw the towel into the sink.

Panting, she grabbed a plastic bag from one of the drawers and stuffed the jewelry and teeth and hair inside. She ran with the bag up to the house.

"Get your bags and get in the car, girls!" she yelled as she ran through the living room into the study and struggled with shaking fingers to unlock the gun safe. She removed a twelve-gauge shotgun and several boxes of slugs.

The girls obeyed, quietly. They were scared of what was happening to their mother.

Once they were all buckled up, Beppie hit the gas and roared down the driveway with the girls and their bags in back. She turned left onto the farm road.

"Where are we going?" Janis said.

"I'm taking you to Mrs. Davis. She's going to watch you guys. I need to do something. If the fires come this way, go with the Davises. Do what they say."

"I don't like Mr. Davis." Susie started crying in the backseat.

"That's because you're scared of his bee suit," taunted Janis.

"Am not!"

"Are too."

"Quiet!" Beppie snapped. The girls jumped.

Susie sniffled louder. "I want my dad. Where's Daddy?"

God will protect us. God will be the final judge . . . God will keep my children from Evil. We must do difficult things for it is God's way, we cannot always understand his way . . . we must purge the Evil . . .

Beppie repeated these mantras in her head as she turned into the Davises' driveway.

CHAPTER 24

His phone was ringing somewhere in the room, in the distance of his mind, buried in his pile of clothes on the floor. On one level Adam knew it was his wife. On another he couldn't seem to absorb it. He lifted up the woman he loved, slammed her back against the wall. She gasped from the impact. Panting, she wrapped her legs around him, hooking her ankles behind his butt. She arched her back, thrusting her pelvis against his, hard, fast, the friction driving them both high, wild.

He staggered sideways, sending her snowboard and bike crashing to the hardwood floor. She gripped his balls, rotating her hips, milking his erection with her tight vaginal muscles. His skin was wet. He was growing dizzy, hotter, as he met her thrust for thrust, grunting, driving as deep as he could. She fisted her hand so tightly in his hair that his eyes burned. She pulled his head back by his hair and kissed him, biting, thrusting with her tongue until he tasted blood but didn't care. Suddenly she froze. With a scream, she threw back her head, exposing the long, creamy column of her neck as she shattered hot and wet and hard around him, contractions seizing control of her body. And he came inside her, a sweet, hot, pulsing release of everything.

Clarity began to sift back into Adam's brain as they lay side by side on a mattress on the floor under the skylight, watching the rain and listening to the wind. The air was cool against his hot, damp skin. His phone rang again. He let it go to voice mail with only a faint twinge of guilt. He'd left instructions in an envelope on the dining room table for Lily. And now it was time to leave the woman he loved. She was the one who had given him his edge, his reason to get up mornings. To look forward to the day. She had made him feel alive again. Brandy was the reason Adam had coped over these past two years.

He rolled over onto his side and traced his finger over her smooth alabaster skin, admiring her honed body. She was young. Perfect. Flame-red hair.

His wife might turn to vodka. He had his Brandy.

"Something's worrying you," she said. "What is it? This Jeb Cullen thing?"

"I went to see my mother," he said. "She gave me the pendant that Merilee Zukanov was wearing the night she disappeared."

A strange look came over her face. She sat up, cross-legged, facing him, her hair falling in a tumble over her pale shoulders. Her nipples were a dusky pink, pointing at him. His gaze wandered down her flat belly, to the flare of red hair between her open thighs, where she was still wet and glistening and sticky from their sex. He put the tip of his finger in her belly button, trailed it slowly down her abdomen, down to the apex between her thighs, then suddenly he stuck his finger up inside her. She gave a gasp, then a small moan of pleasure as he moved his finger inside her, her lids fluttering low as he felt for her G-spot. Adam felt himself grow hard again. He could make love to this woman all day, over and over, like a rutting bull, and get it up each time. He'd never been able to do that with Lily.

Brandy was so at ease with herself, with her own femininity, her strength and sexuality. He slid his finger slowly out of her vagina, watching her face. A slow smile curved over her mouth.

"Careful, Deputy Chief, I could make you suffer." But her smile was not quite lighting her honey-gold eyes. She was worried. She could read him like a book, and she knew something was very different. Very wrong. Slowly he pulled his finger out of her, leaned back.

"Luke borrowed my Jeep that night," he said. "I had time off from the RCMP in Edmonton and had come home for Thanksgiving. I went to see a movie at Lily's place, just up the road, and I let my brother take my Jeep to the pit party. I came home early."

Brandy reached for her denim shirt, put it on, gave a little shiver. She didn't say a word, just waited for him to continue, an odd look in her eyes.

"Luke came home around three a.m. I woke when I heard a thud, like a body against the front door. It was Luke, passed out against the door. He was wearing a gray hoodie and it was covered with blood. I asked about the blood. He said he must have cut himself at the pit. There were a lot of broken bottles there, glass everywhere. I was pissed, thinking he'd driven my Jeep home in that state, but he said that Clint had brought both him and the Jeep back, then walked over to his own place, which was one street up. Luke said that he, Clint, Levi, and Harvey had been at the pit party but had gone to Harvey's house sometime after ten p.m., where they'd had more to drink. I asked Luke where my Jeep keys were, and he said he didn't know, that maybe Clint had them. I helped get him inside, helped him take the hoodie off, but he had no cuts on his body. I left the hoodie in the bathroom, on top of the laundry basket. I never checked the pockets. I fetched my spare keys, went out to check my Jeep."

Brandy didn't look well suddenly. "Why are you telling me this?"

"I need to."

She swallowed, then said quietly. "What was in the Jeep?"

"There was some blood on the backseat. The medallion was there, too. The Jeep was covered in black mud, tires thick with it. There's no mud like that anywhere near the pit. The gas tank was almost empty. I had a GPS mounted on the dash, which I'd left on. I took the GPS inside and downloaded the route from that night. My Jeep had been driven from the pit up to the trailhead and over the trestle bridge, to the old copper mine, then back down, north along Highway 99 for about twenty miles, then up into the Rutherford drainage."

"Where the trapper's cabin was," she said quietly. "Where Amy had been."

Adam nodded. "The Jeep was then driven straight back to our house. Not to Harvey's. The time stamps were not consistent with Luke's story, either. I saved the route to my computer log and put the GPS back into the Jeep, then went to sleep. I didn't think too much of it. Mostly I thought Luke was so wasted he didn't know what he was talking about."

Adam scrubbed his hand over his brow. "Next morning around nine thirty a.m., I went outside and I found my Jeep as clean as a whistle, washed and detailed. Mud gone. Blood had been scrubbed out, just a damp spot on the backseat where it had been. My GPS was also wiped clean."

Brandy looked away. The wind rattled windows and rain slashed at the skylight. The sky was darkening. "Yet you still had the medallion," she said.

"Yeah."

"And the bloody hoodie?"

"It was gone from the laundry. I assumed it was in the wash."

"And then you heard the girls were missing."

"Later that day, yes."

"Shit," she said.

They both sat silent for a moment, just the sound of the storm crashing through trees outside, the flicker of lightning through the skylight above them.

"What happened then?"

"I saw the missing person posters. They used photos of the girls taken earlier that night. Merilee was wearing the medallion in the photo. I confronted Luke, told him I'd found a medallion in my Jeep. He said I was full of shit, I didn't know what I was talking about, and that they'd all seen Jeb Cullen driving off with those girls."

"You believed him?"

"I don't know what I believed. Perhaps I just fooled myself because I didn't want to think what else it might mean. My brother was not a bad guy, just an asshole sometimes. My mother's team questioned everyone who'd been at the pit party. Those four guys all had the same story. All said they'd seen Jeb go north with the girls. Trey and Rachel had also seen Jeb with the girls in his car before he left the pit. So yeah. I started to think Jeb had something to do with it. I put the medallion in an envelope in my drawer."

"Why?"

"Because—" He dragged his hand over his hair. "Because otherwise I'd have to get involved. I didn't think it was that relevant. At that time my GPS route didn't mean much. But then, seven days later, Amy was found staggering along those tracks. Twenty miles north, in the area the GPS said my Jeep went. It's a drainage thick with black mud. God knows how she was still alive. But humans can be resilient, even when lost in snow in the wilds. And Amy was a fighter. She'd have had water from the snow and river, and there were old sacks in the trapper's cabin to wrap herself in. There were rope marks around her neck, and she'd been brutally raped. But too much time had passed to collect viable semen evidence. There was, however, the pregnancy. They arrested Jeb, impounded his vehicle. Later I heard that they found a gray sweatshirt with Merilee's blood in his car, and in the pocket of the hoodie was an empty pack of date-rape drug."

"You thought the hoodie could have been the one Luke came home in?"

"I don't know what I thought. It could have been a coincidence. Gray hoodies were common enough at the time. Jeb and Luke were about the same size. I asked Luke what happened to his hoodie. He said he threw it out. I asked him why my GPS had showed they went north. He said he didn't know what the fuck I was talking about. We got into a yelling match. He stormed out but my mother overheard. She came in and told me to mind my own business. To just let things ride. To say nothing."

"Did you tell her about the GPS route, the bloody hoodie he was wearing, the medallion?"

"Yeah, I told her. I told her I was in possession of the medallion and that I'd seen the GPS route north into the Rutherford drainage. I didn't mention I'd saved it to my computer, though. At first I thought she was in some kind of denial. But then she shocked me by saying I had a choice to make. I could keep quiet, go back to Edmonton, look after my career, stay clean and clear of all this. Or I could make a huge stink trying to take my own family down, my own mother, own brother, and that I had no evidence to go on. I went straight to look for the medallion, and it was gone from my drawer. I thought it was Luke who took it."

"It was her."

He nodded. "A single mother protecting her boys. And, I think, also protecting my father's legacy as a police hero. In turn my mother became a cop who didn't care that an innocent man went down for a crime he didn't do. And she made damn sure he went down for it. She buried him. She believed he was a bad person, expendable. My own goddamn mother."

"She planted the shirt?"

"I figure it was her who logged it into evidence, fudging the date. When this discrepancy in the log was questioned during the hearing to overturn Jeb's case, counsel claimed it was simply a police error, that someone forgot to log the hoodie in initially and the oversight had been redressed. By this time my mother's dementia had progressed too far to question her directly."

"The other DNA on the shirt?"

"My guess is it matches Luke's."

Worry flared sharply in Brandy's eyes. "Luke's gone, Adam. He can't be tested. Or punished."

"Familial profiling will work. The DNA profile from that shirt will come up as a brother of mine. The son of my mother." He paused. "The things we do for love. For our children."

"So where is Merilee's body, then? What happened to her?"

"My guess is we'll find her in that mine."

"What if no one looks in the mine?"

"Jeb will get to that point. Rachel will get there. It's just a matter of time."

Brandy looked away, pressing her hand to her stomach. "But if no one tells anyone to look in the mine . . ."

"Brandy, look at me." He cupped the side of her face, forcing her to look at him. "It's over."

Panic flared through her features. "What do you mean, over?"

"I need to do the right thing now. I need to make the choice I should have made nine years ago."

"Why are you telling me this? You didn't need to tell me this. You don't need to tell *anyone* this."

He got up, pulled on his clothes. He felt oddly at peace now. He hadn't realized how heavy the weight of suppressing a dark secret could really be, how much of a toll it had taken on him over the years. And what a catharsis confession was.

"I already have, Brandy. I wrote out a full confession. I included the medallion and a flash drive containing the GPS route."

She stared at him in silence for several beats.

"What's this going to do to *us*, to your boys?" She avoided mentioning Lily. Lily was like a blind spot to Brandy. "What will this mean for *our* future?" Her voice was going high, her eyes shining wildly.

"My boys will grow up knowing their father finally did the right thing, the honorable thing. It's better this way than me being prosecuted and put away, with them growing up while their father is behind bars. It's just a matter of time. Already I've been sidelined."

"What do you mean?"

He held his hand out to her, helped her up, and kissed her deeply. Her body was rigid in his arms. "Good-bye, Brandy," he whispered over her mouth, kissing her lightly one last time.

He made for the door.

"Where are you going?"

He stilled, hand on the doorknob. "I love you. You know that."

"You are going to leave her, right? We *will* be together one day, like you said, when the boys are a bit older. We'll have children of our own, like you said. We . . . we will get married one day . . ." Her voice strangled itself. Her eyes were manic.

"I love you. I will always love you."

"Adam, don't give that confession to anyone!"

But he was gone, door closing behind him.

Brandy raced to window. She watched him running lightly down the stairs in the beating rain. Panic struck like a hatchet. She flung open the window. "Adam! No!" But he was getting into his truck. The door slammed shut. And he was gone.

Fuck.

If Rachel and Jeb didn't go looking down the mine, Adam could stay safe. They could stay together. Have their future. Desperation clawed through Brandy's chest and panic rose in her throat. Everything she had ever wanted was crumbling in front of her.

She cursed viciously, dragging her hands through her hair. Her eyes burned. She started to shake.

She thought of the group of mothers at the base camp when she'd brought the kids down earlier today, how they'd told her

Quinn was Jeb's child. How Rachel's bringing Quinn to Snowy Creek had lured Jeb back, and now everyone's lives were tearing apart.

The things we do for love . . .

Suddenly Brandy made a decision. She knew what she had to do.

She spun round, grabbed her jeans, yanked them on with angry movements. She tied her hair back, pulled on a ball cap, and shrugged into her jacket. She laced her hiking boots on tightly, then crouched down and pulled out her kit bag from the bottom of her closet. She checked her ropes, cell battery, radio, flares. Hauling it over her shoulder, she locked her front door and ran down the wooden stairs, wind whipping branches, the smell of smoke thick. Choppers thudded somewhere behind the clouds in the darkening sky and sirens threaded down the valley. She got into her old beater of a truck.

She hit the gas and squealed into the street. Driving too fast, she dialed Adam's cell. It went to voice mail. She cursed viciously and tried again. This time she left a message. "Adam, don't do anything yet. Just don't—I've got it under control." She dropped the phone to swerve round a vehicle as she ran a red light. Her heart was pounding.

———

Adam felt incredibly calm. The manila envelope containing his confession sat on the passenger seat next to him. He drove first to his mother's condo to make certain Rubella was ready to evacuate her.

Then he drove down to the station. There was chaos outside, first responders rushing here and there. He caught site of Annie Pirello running past. Adam rolled down his window, called her over. He handed her the envelope. He had no intention of entering the station and possibly being detained. He had no desire to look Mackin in the eye, to be swayed from his purpose.

"Can you make sure Chief Mackin gets this."

"What is it?"

"It's something he needs. Urgent."

She held his eyes. "You okay, sir?"

"You're a good cop, Pirello. I saw the way you were watching me, second-guessing, taking nothing at face value." He paused. "Don't ever forget why you became a cop. Stay the good cop."

He rolled up the window, drove off, leaving her standing there. His phone rang again. He let it go to voice mail.

———

Pirello watched him go, a strange feeling curling inside her. She heard her name being called over her radio. Quickly she keyed the mike.

"Pirello."

"Phase one mandatory evac going into effect. They need you to work with emergency social services going door-to-door, south end. Start with the eight hundred block. Novak has the nine hundred block. Knock on every door. This station is closing down. Secondary command base is being set up further south."

She ran to her cruiser, threw the manila envelope onto the passenger seat, and pulled out of the parking lot, wipers whipping across the windshield. She flicked on her siren.

———

Clint Rudiger's cell phone rang. People were calling his name from all directions. He was busy talking into his radio, helping coordinate the multiagency response and the setting up of a mobile command base farther south. Already landlines were down. One of the radio towers was out. Cell communication was still available, for now. Mobile repeaters had been set up and amateur ham radio operators called to action. Communicating with agencies in the city farther south was going to be a problem.

Plus there was another wildfire that had broken out closer to a larger urban population than Snowy Creek. It was being driven by fierce winds and fueled by drought-ravaged forests, and it was threatening to turn into a massive interface fire. It had drawn down the forestry resources that would otherwise be available to Snowy Creek.

Heavy smoke, low cloud, and lightning had also shut down most air approaches. They now had to rely on whatever local emergency personnel and equipment they could find.

Participating agencies currently included the province's wildfire management branch, ambulance service, Rescue One, the SCPD, BC Hydro, the natural gas companies, plus the Snowy Creek Amateur Radio Society and emergency social services volunteers, who were currently going door-to-door with the help of police.

Clint had meanwhile orchestrated the positioning of a Type 1 Structural Protection Unit, or giant sprinkler, at the base of Bear Mountain. It was watering down the buildings there. The Mount Barren fire was approaching the Khyber drainage. It would likely jump the creek.

Three helicopters and air tankers were on standby at the municipal heliport to action the fires. Objectives included building control lines around the fire perimeter and tying them into natural rock features. The steep terrain in the Khyber drainage and other mountainous areas would be a problem.

Clint worked best under this kind of pressure. His military training helped. He kicked into a zone and was able to keep such a cool, collected head, be so devoid of the usual emotions, that his team had fondly dubbed him the sociopath. Inwardly he found this amusing; he'd never been big on empathy.

His cell rang again. He checked the incoming number. Beppie. He ignored it. She knew what to do. His wife was a capable farm and mountain woman. His girls would be safe.

Assistant Chief Kerrigan Kaye came rushing over to him with another report. As he took it from her, Beppie phoned yet again.

Clint turned his back, answered. "Bepp," he said curtly. "I'm busy—"

"Clint, she knows."

He stuck his finger in his other ear. "What did you say?"

"Rachel Salonen knows what happened."

"She knows . . . *what*? What are you talking about?"

No words came. Just a funny breathing sound, the noise of an engine, as if she were driving. A weird kind of foreboding struck like an ax. Clint stilled, everything around him—time, sound, scents—turned thick and black as molasses.

"Beppie, where are you? Are you driving? What's the matter with you?"

"Rachel said Amy remembered. The dragon tattoo . . ." A shaky breath came out. "Amy remembered you . . . hurting Merilee. You and the others . . . you raped her . . . with the others." His wife made a choking, gagging sound. "You killed her. Down the mine . . . she's down in the mine. All this time . . . she's been in the mine. The evidence is in the mine."

Silence.

Clint's mind galloped as he tried to process what his wife was saying, the implications.

"Chief Rudiger!" Clint held his up hand to the man calling him, his world narrowing, a tinnitus beginning in his ears, the taste of copper in his mouth. He went into the small storeroom, shut the door.

"She's lying. Whatever she said, she and Cullen are just pressing buttons. Trying to spook everyone. They're dangerous. They have no evidence of any of this. Cullen has gotten into Rachel's head and now she's messing with your mind."

"They'll get the evidence in the mine. After the fire and everything has died down. Merilee's down there, isn't she? Down a shaft, all this time. Is she there?"

Banging sounded on his door. Sweat broke out over his body. He wasn't so cool and collected now. Shit was hitting the fan. If there was one thing Clint was about, it was about self-preservation.

"It's a *lie*. All of it." His voice was brusque now. "We'll talk after—"

"God will protect my children. God will purge the Evil . . . God—"

"Beppie, listen to me—"

"We must do what we must in the name of God . . ."

His brain raced. The mine. Evidence. Without evidence they only had Jeb's accusations, his theories. Amy was dead. Her therapist had been silenced. Luke was MIA and no worry. Zink and Levi wouldn't breathe a word or they'd go down.

He could still control this.

"Where are you?"

"In the truck. Driving. Near the gravel pit turnoff."

"Calm down and listen carefully to me. Take that road to the gravel pit. Cross the rail bridge and drive up to the trailhead. Park there. Wait for me. Understand?"

"Why? What are you going to do?"

"I'm going to stop this. And you're going to help me."

"I can't, Clint, I can't."

"Yes you can. Think of the girls. Do it for the girls. Once this is done, it will all blow over. All the misunderstandings will be gone. Do you understand me?"

She made a muffled sound. He could hear the truck engine. Worry sparked through him.

"Beppie? Do you understand?"

"Yes." She sniffed. "Yes, I understand." Her voice was thick. She sounded strange. "I'm doing it for the girls. I must do it for the girls."

Clint killed the call and left the storeroom. He made for the exit.

"Where are you going?" Assistant Chief Kaye called after him. He didn't answer.

He ran for the Rescue One building.

———

Beppie turned off the highway and crossed the Green River rail bridge. She bumped up the logging track to the Mount Rogue trailhead, her wipers slapping as rain slashed at her windows. Mud was thick under her tires, she could feel the wheels slipping. It was hard to tell what was smoke and what was cloud, but it was dark, her headlights hardly helping at all.

She knew her husband. Deep, deep, deep down she'd known him all along but hadn't want to think about it. He was a fighter and a survivor. She'd known he'd come here if she called him and told him what she knew. She knew he'd try and get rid of her, too, now.

Repent. Repent in the name of the Lord . . . purge the Evil.

The shotgun lay on the backseat, next to the boxes of slugs. Next to his bag of trinkets and human trophies.

———

Trey pulled into the public safety building parking lot. There were personnel everywhere. Traffic was already thick on the highway, a stream of bumper-to-bumper cars heading south.

He ran up to the Rescue One building, yanked open the door. His goal was to dismantle the Rescue One ham radio and antenna on the roof, take it all south.

But as he entered the room, he heard someone inside.

"Who's there?"

A clatter. Locker door? Then a crack. Someone was in the bomb room, where they kept the avalanche explosives.

He flung open the door.

Clint Rudiger turned around. He had a heavy box of dynamite in his strong arms. The look in his eyes was strange.

"Rudiger?"

He set the box down on the table next to him.

"What are you doing?"

Rudiger reached for his boot, pulled out a knife. It glinted in his hand. He waved it, slowly, back and forth, his eyes boring into Trey. "Back off, Somerland. Just back off and let me out of here."

Trey took a step back. "What the fuck are you doing?"

Rudiger went into a crouch.

Trey reached for his radio, realizing too late it was in the truck.

Rudiger lunged. Trey spun away, hitting the table hard. The box toppled to the ground, dynamite sticks rolling all over the floor. Rudiger slipped on one and Trey ran at him in a head butt. He hit hard. Rudiger grunted but his abs were iron. An uppercut took Trey under the chin, flinging him backward. He landed on the floor among the dynamite, hard. Winded. For a few moments he couldn't breathe, couldn't move at all, pain sparking through his back and chest.

Rudiger loomed over him. His eyes were cold. He took his knife and plunged it straight into Trey's stomach, liver area. He extracted the blade, wiped it on his pants.

Trey was filled with disbelief. This couldn't be happening, yet it was. Real. He was stabbed, blood welling from his abdomen. He tried to breathe, moving his hands to staunch the flow, block the wound. Unbelievable pain, a dull, consuming pain, filled him from the inside.

Rudiger was working fast to gather the dynamite sticks, putting them back into the box.

"It . . . was you . . ." Trey's voice was hoarse. He was going weak. So weak. Lightheaded. "Stacey . . . told me what Rachel said . . . at the bike park. I . . . it was true. She's down in the mine." His eyes went to the box of explosives. "You're going to blow it up . . . copper mine."

"You shouldn't have let her bring that kid back here, Somerland." Rudiger picked up the box. "He might not have returned otherwise. You helped fuck this up."

Trey tried to speak, couldn't. His body went limp and he closed his eyes. In some distant part of his mind, he felt Rudiger nudge him with his boot. When Trey didn't respond, Rudiger made for the door and exited, kicking the door shut behind him with his steel-toed boot.

Trey heard the lock turn.

He was getting lightheaded, drifting. With Herculean effort he opened his eyes and tried dragging himself, inch by inch, over the floor, sliding in his own hot, thick blood. He grasped for the cell phone that had fallen from his pocket and slid under the table.

The tips of his fingers touched the phone. His world darkened. *No. No, not yet.* He tried to reach a little farther.

———

I always have emergency bags packed, but I'm packing a few extras. Quinn is still upstairs, dressing, getting some books and things together. I've already got Trixie's crate and food in the truck. I have the fire safe with personal documents on the table along with my laptop and some other essentials ready to go. I've called work and everything has been backed up to a remote server. Staff have cleared out what they can.

Jeb is battening down the house.

My phone rings. Startled, I check incoming.

Trey?

"Hello," I say, putting the phone to my ear.

I hear a sound, a rasp.

"Hello—Trey, is that you?"

"Rachel." It's more a breath than a word. Anxiety slices through me.

"What's happening, are you all right, where are you?"

Jeb comes quickly to my side.

There's no reply, just a wet breathing sound.

"Trey?" I say, hand over my other ear. "Are you still there?"

"Clint . . . knifed me . . . in bomb room. He's got dynamite . . . going . . ." Coughing and wheezing drown the rest of the words.

Oh God.

"Tell . . . Jeb. Jeb can stop. Clint is on way. Destroy proof. Merilee . . . in mine. Jeb needs that proof."

Another gasping cough.

I turn to Jeb. "It's Trey. He's been hurt. He says Clint is going to blow up the mine. He's taken the avalanche dynamite from the Rescue One bomb room. He's on his way to the copper mine now . . . he . . . I think he stabbed Trey."

"I . . . tried to stop him . . ."

"Have you got help? Is help coming?"

"Too . . . late . . . I'm . . . sorry. So sorry. Stacey . . . overheard us on phone, about Quinn being Jeb's. We had fight. My face . . . she hit me."

"Don't talk. I'm going to hang up and call for help."

"Can't. Circuits busy. Landlines down . . . no help."

"I'm coming!"

"No . . . look after her . . . Quinn. Yourself . . . I . . . I love you . . . always have . . ."

Silence.

I'm shaking. Jeb is staring.

"He's been stabbed. He needs help." I try to dial 9-1-1. He's right, I can't get through. The phone in the kitchen doesn't work either. I move to the front door, then stall. I'm suddenly ripped apart. "He's going to blow up the mine," I say again.

Jeb grabs my shoulders. "Listen to me. Focus. Take Quinn. Drive south, get out of here. You can try and call for help on the way, but you look after our child first."

He is fierce, resolute. A father. The man I love.

"I'm going to stop him," he says.

"No, you're coming with us. He'll kill you, Jeb."

"Listen to me. You and Quinn have given me everything to live for, but we need that proof—I can't let him destroy it. I can't have my child doubt me, ever. I promised Sophia I would not tell Quinn until I had that proof. She gave me everything, Rachel. I have to do this. And you have to keep Quinn safe."

"No, no you don't."

"Do you still have your father's hunting rifle?"

I feel sick. I am immobilized by indecision.

"Where is the rifle? Is it still in here?" He's gone into the study where the gun safe always was, and still is.

"Jeb!" I run after him.

"Keys, where are the keys for the safe?"

"I . . . top drawer, desk . . . I beg you . . ."

"Listen to me. I'm not going to do anything stupid. But I'm *not* going to stand by and do nothing, either. Clint has to drive all the way from the village. We're already ten miles closer to the mine than he is. If I move now, I can head him off." He finds the keys, unlocks the safe, grabs a rifle and ammunition. Rushing into the kitchen, he snags my dad's SUV keys from the counter. He stops, kisses me hard.

"Believe me, I have *everything* to come back for now. Everything to win by doing this. For so many reasons."

He's gone.

I'm shaking like a leaf. I can't believe this is happening. I try 9-1-1 again. I still can't get through, all circuits busy. I hear Trey's voice in my head. Nausea, desperation ride through me. Suddenly I get an idea and rummage in my purse. I find the card Constable Annie Pirello gave me. It has her direct cell number.

I dial it, mouth dry. I can smell smoke inside the house now. We need to leave. Soon.

"Quinn!" I yell upstairs while the phone rings. "We need to go—bring your stuff down. Now!"

"Pirello," comes a curt voice from my phone.

"Constable Pirello, Annie Pirello, it's Rachel Salonen." I talk fast, watching up the stairs for Quinn. "Clint Rudiger has stabbed Trey Somerland and left him for dead in the Rescue One bomb room. Clint has taken the avalanche dynamite. He's going to blow up part of the old copper mine near the Mount Rogue trailhead. Merilee's body, the evidence, is down one of those mine shafts. He's trying to get rid of it. He did it, raped Amy, killed Merilee. He and those other three."

"When did he leave?"

Relief gushes through me.

"A few minutes ago, I think. Trey needs help. He's been stabbed. He's in the bomb room."

"I'm on it." She hangs up.

"Quinn!" I yell. "I'm going to put the rest of the bags and Trixie in the truck. We've got to leave!"

I grab the bags off the table, open the front door, run out into the rain, and dump them in the truck. I go back for another load, then put Trixie in back, close the door. I dash back to the house. Pushing wet hair off my brow, I run up the stairs.

I knock on Quinn's door. No answer. Panic sparks through me. "Quinnie?"

Not a sound comes from inside her room. I open the door, heart hammering.

The room is empty.

"Quinn?" I run down the hall to the bathroom. Empty. I go frantically room to room. Nothing. Thunder crashes. Wind and rain lash at the windows and the panes rattle.

"*Quinn!*"

No reply. She's nowhere in sight.

I clatter down the stairs. "Quinn, goddammit where are you?"

There's no one downstairs. I can feel the emptiness of the house, like a big hollow in my chest. Nausea rides up through me. How can this be?

Calm, stay calm. Panic is your worst enemy. You know this from rescue missions.

But I can't stay calm. Tears burn into my eyes as I go room to room again, looking under beds, in cupboards. I catch sight of a wet patch on the carpet in front of the French doors in the spare room.

A chill shoots down my spine.

I drop to my haunches, feel it. Sodden. Water has come in. Rain. From the French doors—they've been opened. I lurch up, try the handle. It's unlocked. My heart pounds in my throat as I yank open the door and dash out onto the tiny balcony. Wind and rain lash at me. Lightning flickers over the lake. Smoke smells thick. I hear sirens. I can see a red-orange strip of fire burning along the crest of the mountains.

But there's nothing on the balcony. I clamp my hands over the balustrade and peer down into the blackness but can make out nothing out on the lawn below apart from the shadows of swaying trees. Horror floods my brain. I spin round, see the tree next to the balcony. My heart kicks. Once when I was a kid, I climbed down from this balcony using the branches of that tree. Could Quinn have climbed down?

Run away?

Why?

It hits me like a mallet. *Her adoption.* The questions she was asking about her real parents. We must have said something terribly wrong and scared her away. *Oh, God.* I start to shake violently. I've done this. I've chased her away. And there's no one I can turn to for help now, either. There's fire coming. I need to find her. Where would she go? Where would I go if I was eight and I wanted my mother?

"Quinn!" I yell into the blackness, water pouring down my face.

The sky responds with another clap of thunder, right overheard. Rain comes down harder.

CHAPTER 25

Annie called Assistant Fire Chief Kerrigan Kaye's cell, told her to check the Rescue One bomb room next door. Somerland was in there, hurt. Then she left the door knocking to Novak and the emergency social services volunteers. The evacuation alert was going smoothly in this subdivision. She'd take flak, she knew this. But this was her case. And more. It was personal. Her own sister, Claudette, had gone missing in the Cayoosh mountains near Pemberton, along with her new husband. Annie had a thing about missing people. About never knowing. She knew firsthand what lack of closure could do to people.

She got into her cruiser, tried to call it in, but there was radio interference. Dispatch was overloaded. Radio towers down. And she knew this would not be a priority—a cold case, an old copper mine, the vague possibility of old evidence—while the lives of hundreds and billions in real estate might be at stake from wildfire. She stepped on the gas, flicked her siren on. Traffic was virtually bumper-to-bumper heading south, but the road north wasn't that bad. And vehicles moved to the side to make way for her squad car.

———

Sweat breaks out under my wet clothes. I'm breathing hard but trying to control my panic as I stand under the balcony and scan the darkness with my flashlight in search of Quinn. Nothing. Not even a sign. I race down to the boathouse. I know she's been fixated with the place. The windows rattle in the wind. Waves chuckle against at the dock. The rope around the canoe tethered to the side slaps the siding. But there is no one here, the door still locked.

I spin round. Maybe she's in the carport, or the gardening shed. My fervent hope is that she's just hiding somewhere here on the property. I dash up to the carport, frantically shining my light into all the corners. I catch a raccoon's eyes and my heart jumps. But no Quinn. I sprint to the gardening shed and yank the old door open. It's dank inside, mossy. My dad used to pot his plants in here. But there is no sign of Quinn. I don't know where else to look. Maybe I missed something in my tunnel vision of panic. I need to call Jeb now, if I can get through. This is serious. Quinn comes first. But suddenly I glimpse headlights. A vehicle is coming down my driveway. I race up the lawn as a truck parks behind mine in the driveway.

I rush up to the driver's door as it opens.

"Oh, thank God, it's *you*," I say, lungs burning. "Quinn is missing. I need help to find—"

"It's okay, I found her out on the road," Brandy says, getting out of the driver's side. Something about her makes me stall.

"Where is she? What was she doing up on the road?"

"She was running away. She's in the truck. Relax, Rachel." Brandy holds both her palms out at me, as if to tell me to calm down. And she's coming toward me.

My gaze shoots to her truck. I can see a little shadow in the backseat. Tears of relief prick into my eyes. "Oh, thank God, Brandy. Thank you." I rush toward the passenger door, physically aching to hold Quinn in my arms. I want to bury my face in the scent of her hair. But Brandy grabs my arm.

Surprise flushes through me. I spin to face her. "What—"

"Where is Jebbediah Cullen?" Her grip tightens. I realize her eyes are shining, wild.

It strikes me suddenly as odd that she was even heading this way. "What are you doing here, Brandy? There's an evacuation order—"

"Where is he?" she demands. A dark, cold sinking feeling slides through my stomach. The image of Brandy huddled with those other mothers at the bike park slices into my mind. Had she just learned who Quinn was at that point? Suddenly I am both terrified of her and enraged.

"Let go of me!" I order. "I want to see my niece." I jerk my arm but she holds even tighter. A trickle of fear slides down my throat. "I'm warning you," I growl, adrenaline rising inside me. "Let. Me. Go."

But I register too late as she brings her other hand round in a sharp downward swing, and I feel a deep, piercing sensation in my thigh muscle. My gaze flies down to my jeans. In the headlights from her truck I see that she's plunged a syringe in to the hilt. Fear strikes like a hatchet.

"What have you done!"

"Tell me where Jeb is." Her voice is going shrill. She looks confused.

I feel dizzy. My vision is blurring. Tongues of panic lick through my stomach but my brain can't react. I'm slowing down, getting heavy. Brandy releases my arm, and I stumble sideways, bumping up against the front of her truck. I brace my hands on the hood and hold myself up. The world is spinning. I feel spacey, dissociated. Rain is streaming down my face and through my hair, yet I can't seem to feel the coldness or wetness of it anymore. Quinn. I must get to Quinn. I try and pull my way along the truck.

"Tell me where he is." Her voice seems to come from a long, dark tunnel.

"He's . . . gone . . ." My words are slurring. My hand slips off the wet hood. I slide down but manage to grab the wheel, pulling myself up again as I painstakingly shuffle my feet, one then the other, round to the passenger door. "Quinn . . . where are you . . ." But my tongue is thick. The words come out in a slurred mumble.

I moved my head slowly to look at Brandy. The whole world tilts sickeningly. "What . . . have you done?"

She comes over. She seems bigger. Everything is out of proportion. She pushes my body against the truck, holding me up with her knee as she takes my hands and ties them together behind my back. I can't even resist.

"Ketamine," she says as she opens the passenger door.

I force my brain to think. Brandy's sister is a large-animal vet in the ranching community up north where Beppie and Clint live. Brandy might have accessed the drug through her sister. It's an analgesic, tranquilizer, hallucinogenic. Brandy is a trained paramedic, knows how to administer meds. My legs suddenly give way fully, but she hooks her hands under my armpits and wrestles my feeble body into the passenger seat.

The interior light is on. I see Quinn slumped against the backseat. Like a wet rag doll. A strip of duct tape has been plastered over her mouth. I want to scream, lunge, tear at Brandy's hair. I want to kill her for drugging Quinn. But I cannot move or talk at all now. I'm a prisoner inside my own body and my brain is also fading.

She clamps the seat belt over my chest. My head lolls to the side. Drool comes out the side of my mouth. I remain conscious, though. I try to hold on.

She brings her face close to mine. "Tell me where Jeb is."

I want to laugh in her face and ask her how she thinks I can tell her now that I can't even talk. Her hands rummage through my jacket pockets. She finds my cell phone. I stare helplessly as she scrolls through my contact list and finds Jeb's number. I wish fervently that I'd put password protection on my phone. I've never felt a need to, until now.

She hits the dial button.

I struggle to lift my hand, to slap the phone from her grip. But I can barely move a finger.

It's ringing. I can hear it ringing . . . there's still a cell tower working. It strikes me that she wants Jeb more than us. She hasn't killed us because she wants to use us to bait him. I can't quite make sense of why Brandy would want this. I'm trying to find links, to think, but my brain is molasses. My vision starts to pinprick. I can't hear anything anymore, can't see . . . then my world goes dark.

———

Jeb parked the SUV and cut the lights. He positioned his headlamp on his head, opened the door. Rain came sideways at him. The smoke was thick here, and it burned acrid in his nasal passages.

He'd come the longer way round and up the north side of the gorge to avoid the trestle bridge, but he'd made good time. Carrying Rachel's father's rifle and spare ammunition, Jeb hiked the rest of the way up to the mine entrance, keeping his headlamp off. If Clint was already on the other side of the bridge, Jeb didn't want him to see light. There was a chance Clint might come up the same way, which was why he'd hidden the SUV about a quarter mile back in some trees.

The air was colder higher up the gorge. Rogue Falls thundered below, sending up mist. Jeb found the mine entrance. A black maw. The air coming from it was icy, as if the mountain itself was exhaling from its deep, frozen interior. He peered inside. Darkness was complete. Jeb felt a shiver as he thought of Merilee perhaps lying deep down in there somewhere, waiting for closure, justice. He crept farther along the narrow road above the gorge, keeping well away from the edge because the road barrier was long gone.

If he could get closer to the old trestle bridge, he might be able to stop Clint from coming across. And in case Clint came the other way, he needed a position from which he could see that, too.

But as Jeb rounded a rock, he pulled back, his pulse quickening. There was a light moving on the other side of the gorge. Slowly he peered back round the rock. There was another light moving in an irregular fashion behind the first. He realized it must be headlamps. Two people. Clint must have brought one of the others. *Shit.*

The person with the first headlamp turned round to face the second, and Jeb saw with a start that the second person was a woman. Fair hair. Plump.

Beppie?

His heart hammered and his brain raced. Why Beppie? Was she helping him? It didn't make sense.

A buzz in his pocket suddenly made him jump. His phone. Swearing inwardly, he thrust his hand into his pocket, felt for the sound button, and turned the buzzer to silent. Blood thudded in his ears. He held dead still. Had they heard it? Jeb peered slowly back round the side of the rock. They were not looking his way. The rain, wind, waterfall must have drowned the sound. He reached into his pocket, checked to see who'd called. Only a handful of people had this number—Sophia and Peter, the UBC lawyers, Rachel.

He saw Rachel's number.

Worry stabbed into him. But before Jeb could think further, he heard yelling. Quickly, he moved to peer back round the rock. The couple was arguing. The woman—Beppie—carried a gun, shotgun or rifle. Her headlamp lit clearly on Clint's face. It was unmistakably him, the big square features, correct height and build. He was carrying a heavy box. The dynamite? They seemed to be quarreling about who was going to walk over the trestle bridge first. The woman had a bag slung across her shoulder.

As he watched, Jeb saw that Clint was making Beppie go first, her headlamp darting through the blackness as she grasped the low railing with her right hand, gun in her left. Cautiously placing one foot in front of the other along the wide outer support beam of the bridge, she began to cross toward the middle of the plunging chasm. Something gave underfoot and she almost dropped to her knees, catching herself as one of the crosspieces went tumbling down into the white mist. She stalled, then slowly started to move again.

The bastard was using her as guinea pig to test the stability of what was left of the bridge. When she was halfway across, Clint started coming over himself. Carefully balancing along the same support beam Beppie had used as he carried the box.

Conflict twisted through Jeb. He hadn't counted on Clint's wife being present. Beppie was nearing the other side now. Clint was in the middle of the bridge. Jeb had to make a move, soon. His phone suddenly vibrated again in his pocket. But before he could fully register, Beppie suddenly spun round and lifted the gunstock to shoulder. She aimed directly at her husband.

Shock sliced through Jeb.

Clint stopped dead in his tracks.

Without a word, Beppie pulled the trigger. The sound boomed and echoed off the gorge walls. A scream, raw, rose above the water.

Jeb blinked.

Clint was still there. Standing on the bridge. She'd shot wide. But he'd dropped his box of dynamite. Some of the sticks were rolling along the trestles. Others had plunged down into the gorge.

"What the fuck, Beppie, put that thing down!" Clint screamed. "What in the hell do you think you're doing?"

"Thinking of my girls, Clint. In the name of the Lord God Almighty, in the name of retribution, I can't let you do this." She raised her gun to her shoulder again, peered down the barrel.

Clint clutched the railing. "You're not thinking straight, woman."

"Was Merilee the first? How many others after her, Clint? How many?"

"Put that thing down, goddammit."

"So you can blow me up with the evidence in the mine? I know you, Clint, I—"

He took a step toward her and she fired instantly over his head. He ducked, swore.

"Was it just you?" she yelled, reloading. "Or did the others rape her too? Tell me. I want to know everything that happened that night or I swear on my girls' lives I will kill you right now, right here."

"Beps, just listen to me—"

She fired again, blasting a chunk out of the trestle near his boots. Jeb saw her reloading.

"Jesus, fuck, okay, okay. I'll tell you. They wanted it, Beppie. They both wanted it."

"Louder! I can't hear you, tell me louder!" she yelled.

"We used the drugs. Date rape drugs in their booze so their memory would be fucked!" He screamed over the water. "Satisfied, woman? Is that loud enough for ya? The drugs made them limp, like jelly. Easy pickings. I started with Merilee, in the mine."

Beppie staggered backward. Water roared. Time stretched.

"All of you?" she finally yelled. "Levi, Luke, Zink?"

"Just put it down, okay?"

She fired again.

Clint ducked, swore.

"Okay, okay! It was me first, then Zink. We made Amy watch. We had a rope around Amy's neck and we made her watch. Levi was gung ho, ready to go, dick out of his pants."

Beppie reloaded. She had shells in the bib of her dungarees.

"But Levi chickened out when I used the gun to fuck Merilee. I used a gun, okay! I got off on it. But Amy started screaming hysterically and Levi, he freaked. He said, no man, this isn't cool. We got in a tussle. We bashed into Merilee and she cracked her head on a rock. Her neck went all funny. Limp. There was blood everywhere. She was choking on it. I yelled at Levi to bring something to stop the bleeding. He ran to the Jeep and brought Luke's sweatshirt. Luke, the asshole, was passed out in his T-shirt in back of the Jeep. But by the time Levi got back, Merilee was dead. I don't know what happened, she had no pulse. Maybe she drowned on her own blood, choked, or some shit. Or maybe it was injury to her brain, or her neck. Dead. You never saw guys sober up so fast. We panicked. She was full of our semen, our DNA. Mine and Zink's. We pushed her down the shaft. Okay, satisfied?"

Beppie was eerily still.

A sick coldness settled through Jeb. There was no fire of rage in him, but something else. The reality of what this man, those guys, had done, it steeled his muscles. It made his brain numb.

"Beppie," Clint yelled. "You satisfied? Will you put that gun down now?"

"Go on!" she screamed, edging closer. "I want all of it. Every detail. What did you do with Amy?"

"Amy saw it all. We didn't know what to do with her. I wanted to push her down the shaft with Merilee, but Levi said they'd come up here, looking. They'd find their bodies. They'd find our semen in Merilee. We'd all go down. So we took Amy and put her in the Jeep. I drove. We went north. I was amped from drugs and booze. Levi was freaking out. Luke didn't know what the fuck was happening, he was still passed out cold. We figured we'd dump Amy far enough away, and if they found her, there wouldn't be any of our semen on her. And then they'd look for Merilee in that area, too. No one would think to look way south in the mine. We made a pact to say we saw Cullen going north with them. That part was easy because they'd been in his car before they saw us at the rail crossing. Beppie?"

Another shot blasted chunks of the railing into the air beside Clint.

"All of it!" she yelled.

Jeb didn't dare move. His muscles were humming, tight. He wanted to hear. All of it. Like Beppie.

"We drove her up the Rutherford drainage, to the old trapper's cabin. The others waited in the Jeep while I took her in. She was blathering, stumbling, falling as I led her by the rope around her neck. Like an animal. It turned me on, okay? It made me feel powerful. I hurt her in the cabin. Knocked her about, raped her with my gun, front and back, and then I strangled her. I thought she was fucking dead. Her pulse must have been so low from the drugs that I didn't feel it, or I was too amped up to register it. And you know what, Beppie?" he screamed. "I fucking liked it, okay! It whet my appetite. I did more women after her, in Bosnia, while on deployment. And in Sierra Leone I did one of the military females. She dropped charges, but it got me kicked out. Now I go hunting for one or two each fall, along with the moose and the caribou, and I bring back my trophies."

Silence.

Just the thundering of the water far below, the sound of beating rain. Thunder in the hills.

"What about the hoodie? How did it get in Jeb's car?"

He laughed. Loud and guttural, like some kind of wild man on the bridge. "I only realized when we got back it was still in the Jeep. I took Luke home and put the damn thing on him, left him outside the door. He woke up as I was hauling him out of the Jeep. I figured he'd wash it or whatever. He wouldn't know what the hell happened anyway. But I got edgy at home. I remembered there was a GPS in the Jeep. So I came back before dawn to wash the Jeep down and erase the route recorded by the GPS."

"You tried to kill Jeb the other night, didn't you?" Beppie yelled. "You burned down his land, started the Wolf River fire. You used my truck."

"Me, Zink, and Levi did. I got rid of that therapist and Amy, too. Just need to finish off here now, Beppie. And it's all under control." Clint threw his arms out wide, put his head back, and laughed again. As if he was all-powerful, king of the wilderness. Jeb tensed. Things were coming to a head. He sighted Clint down the barrel of his rifle, aiming for just below the glow of the headlamp. But he had a bad line. Beppie was in his way. He didn't want to risk hitting her. And Clint was edging closer and closer toward his wife, who seemed rooted to the bridge.

Jeb tightened his finger softly around the trigger.

Move, Beppie, move, dammit.

Jeb knew in his gut that Clint was going to send her over that bridge. No way in hell would he be telling her this stuff if he had any intention of allowing her to live.

If Jeb yelled for Beppie to move, it would distract her, Clint would take the gap. Jeb cursed. It was a tough shot as it was. It had been almost a decade since he'd last hunted, fired, or even touched a rifle. He'd been an ace marksman once. He didn't know if he still had it.

Suddenly Jeb caught sight of another light approaching rapidly on the far side of the gorge—someone holding a flashlight, running. His gaze flashed back to the bridge. Clint had his back to the approaching person. He had no idea someone was coming.

"Your actions will not touch my girls, Clint!" Beppie screamed suddenly. "You must pay for this. The world must see what you did to Merilee and Amy. Justice must be done. A man must be set free—your family must be set free!"

"Police!" came a voice.

Everyone froze.

"Put that gun down, Beppie Rudiger. You don't want to do this." The voice was female. Strident.

Jeb stepped out from behind his rock, aiming his rifle at Clint as he approached the other end of the bridge. "Listen to the officer, Beppie. Let her take him in!" he called over the water. "Put the gun down. I've got him covered."

She hesitated. Confused suddenly.

Then she whipped the stock back to her shoulder and fired. The shot boomed. Clint whirled sideways and went over the barrier, a tumbling black shadow into white mist and roaring water. Beppie dropped her gun and lowered herself into a sitting position on the bridge. The shotgun spiraled down into the foaming gorge after her husband. Beppie held her knees, rocked, moaning.

Jeb got to her before the officer did.

He reached down for Beppie's hand, helped her up, and he guided the sobbing woman across to the cop, who was approaching from the other side. It was Pirello, the same cop who'd come to Rachel's door looking for him, the one who'd responded to the call at school when Quinn got in trouble.

Pirello took Beppie's hand, helping the woman back onto solid ground on the far side.

"I'm so sorry," Beppie said. She was soaked through, shaking like a leaf. "I'm so sorry, so sorry, sorry . . ." She slumped down onto a rock, taking off the bag she had strapped across her shoulder. She held it out to Pirello.

"What's this?" Pirello said.

"His trophies. His hunting trophies." Her voice was shaking. "He was going to put me in that mine and blow me up with all his trophies." She dug into the bib of the dungarees she was wearing and took out something small and dark, around the size of a cell phone. "And this." She held it out to Pirello with her trembling hands. "I got him. I got him on tape."

Pirello glanced at Jeb.

"I made him yell loud enough so he could be heard over the water." Beppie was shuddering hard now, the aftereffects of shock taking hold of her body. "I . . . I hope I got him." She looked up at Jeb. "I . . . I'm so sorry for what they did to you."

CHAPTER 26

I come round slowly.

My head feels as though it has exploded. My mouth tastes strange. I'm in a vehicle—I can feel the motion, hear the engine. I manage to open my eyes a little. Wipers are going. Rain. Thunder. I smell smoke. I move my head slightly to the side.

Brandy. Driving.

Quinn.

Shock slams through me as I remember. I struggle to look over my shoulder. I can see her. She's come round. She's staring at me—her eyes huge above her taped-up mouth. A force explodes through me—I can't let anything happen to Quinn. But I can't seem to move. My limbs are still paralyzed.

"What . . . what . . ." My mouth is thick, throat raw and dry. "Brandy . . ."

She glances at me and her face scares me. Her eyes are red-rimmed, puffy, wild.

"Where is he?" she barks.

My brain is slow. "Who?"

"Jebbediah Cullen. Why won't he answer his phone?" Her voice goes shrill. Her fists are tight on the wheel. Her neck is all corded muscle. I realize we're going up the mountain, up a switch-back road. I can see fire burning across the drainage. We must be on Bear Mountain because the last I heard, Mount Barren was aflame. She's taking us up Bear Mountain while the entire village below is being evacuated. Wipers are streaking rain and ash like mud across the windshield.

I try to move my legs, but can't. Things seem strangely distant. I swallow, forcing moisture into my mouth. My arms are squashed behind my back, a zip tie cutting into my wrists. She hasn't killed us. She could have. She might still. But she wants Jeb first. I must buy time, try to figure her out.

"Why . . . do you want him?" My voice comes out hoarse.

Her gaze shoots to me. "You shouldn't have meddled. You should have let him be. If I fix this, if you go away—" She beats the steering wheel with the palm of her hand.

"Let . . . who be?"

"If you all just go away, if I stop you all from digging into this. The evidence will never be found. It'll all die down. We can still be together. I need him. I *need* him." She slams her hand on the wheel again. "Where is he, Rachel?" The truck slides in mud as she almost misses a switchback.

"Who?" I croak. "Who could you be together with?" Suddenly I recall the night the fire broke out on Jeb's property. I phoned Brandy to look after Quinn. I remember thinking when she answered that someone was in her bed. She's not mentioned a man in her life.

"Shit! Shit, shit. You screwed it up. You were *all* supposed to be at home." She reaches onto the dash, grabs my cell. One hand on the wheel, she dials again.

I hear it ringing.

I struggle to move my arms but they're stuck fast behind me. With colossal effort I lurch my body sideways, knocking the phone out of her hand. She backhands me hard across the face, flinging me back into the seat. My head strikes the side window with a thud. My skull hums and I taste blood at the back of my nasal passage. Blood leaks over my mouth and down my chin.

Quinn suddenly rams the back of Brandy's seat with her feet. She's ram, ram, ramming. Brandy's body jerks from the impact as she redials Jeb's number. "Shit, you little runt. Stop it." She tries to reach into the back and strike Quinn. The truck almost goes over the side. She swears again, dropping the phone as she rights the vehicle with both hands. Desperately, I seek a way to distract her.

"What . . . would you have . . . done if we were all home?" I gag as blood goes down my throat.

She doesn't answer. I imagine she might have tried to drug us all, take us somewhere where the fire might consume us, and no one would think to do a tox screen on our bodies.

"How can you hurt Quinn?" I say her name, choking on the blood in my throat. I want Brandy to think, to snap back. She's cracked on some psychological level. This is not the same woman I trusted with my niece. "You love Quinn, Brandy. You've . . ." I cough again but can't clear the blood and spittle from my mouth and nostrils. "You've looked after her, you want your own kids. You don't have to do this."

"I do! I . . . I have to finish. It wasn't supposed to be like this." She reaches down for the phone, picks it up.

Quinn kicks harder, moaning under her duct tape. I turn my head slowly. I look into her big round eyes. "It's . . . going to be okay." I try to make the words come clearly, but I gag and cough again. Desperation swells in my chest.

Brandy redials. With a sick feeling I hear Jeb answer. Brandy looks panicked for a second.

"Jeb Cullen?" she says. "I . . . I have them. I have Rachel and Quinn." Her voice is shaky and weird now, her eyes frantic. "If . . . if you want to see them alive again, do what I say."

"Who is this? What are you talking about?"

I hear his voice, loud, strident. I try to move my legs but can only shuffle my feet slightly. I'm trapped inside my body. I can't help Quinn.

"I've got them on Bear Mountain. We'll be . . ." Her gaze jerks up as she yanks the wheel round another bend and hits the gas. Gravel and mud spit out from under the tires as we almost go into a spin. Fire is fully engaged on parts of Mount Barren. I can now see that the gondola terminal on Barren is ablaze. Smoke smells thick inside the car. Brandy looks panicked as she peers through the ash-streaked windshield. I realize she hasn't formed a concrete plan. Her first plan failed and she doesn't actually have a backup. I need to use this fear and insecurity I see in her.

Suddenly she's staring at the burning gondola station on the other mountain.

"We'll be at the Summit-to-Summit Gondola station. I'll wait exactly forty-five minutes for you to get here, or they die."

Quinn kicks the back of Brandy's seat with her heels again. Brandy jerks forward, curses.

"Wait—" I hear Jeb yell. "How do I know you have them?"

Brandy hits the brakes and the car slides sickeningly on mud. She lunges into the back, rips part of the duct tape from Quinn's mouth. Quinn screeches in pain. I lurch my body at Brandy again. She shoves me back into the seat.

"Say something to Jeb," Brandy orders Quinn, holding the phone to her face.

"J-J-Jeb, I want my m-m-mom. Brandy h-hurt Rachel . . ."

My stomach contracts. I need to throw up. My pain for Quinn is unbearable. I have to stop this.

Brandy yanks the phone away from Quinn. "Satisfied?"

"Why are you doing this? What do you want?"

But Brandy kills the call, retapes Quinn's mouth with a fresh strip. She rams the truck back into gear and spins the steering wheel as she hits the gas again. A scream of rage rises in my chest. I hold it in. I must not panic. Panic kills. I need to negotiate with Brandy. I know Brandy, don't I? Who could she be protecting?

. . . The evidence will never be found. It'll all die down. We can still be together. I need him. I need him . . .

Who is *him*? My world spins again and I fade in and out. I struggle to pull my mind back into focus. I force myself to think of the men who lied about Jeb. Clint, Levi, Luke, Harvey. I don't know that any of them are connected to Brandy. Then it strikes me. *Adam.* Luke's brother.

Adam with the Jeep and the ska music. Adam whose mother led the charge to convict Jeb. If Adam was involved in the rape or cover-up, he stands to lose everything if exposed now.

Brandy told me once a while back that she'd met Adam at a support group for people who had family members with Alzheimer's and dementia. Her mother is suffering from Alzheimer's. She told me that she and Adam bonded over this. I try to cast my mind back. I recall the look in her eyes as she spoke about him. I remember thinking she really liked this married man, and I wondered briefly at the time if there was more to it.

"Adam," I say. "It's Adam . . . you're doing it for him." I cough and I struggle for more energy, more words. "You were with him when I called you to look after Quinn, the night the wildfire started. What . . . did Adam do nine years ago?"

She returns her attention to the road.

"I love him," she says simply. "He loves me. We're going to be together. He . . . he balances me. I *need* him."

Balances me. Brandy is unbalanced. I know very little about mental illness, but I am aware that people can appear normal for years, then the next thing you know is they've killed themselves. People miss the signs. I've missed the signs in her.

I love him. He loves me. We're going to be together . . .

My world spirals, slides again. Jeb said he loves me. I know he loves his daughter unconditionally. He will come for us. He will die for us. I don't want him to die.

The things we do for love . . .

"This is not going to help Adam," I say. "You can stop. You don't have to hurt anyone."

She curses violently. "You fucked it up. I *can't* stop! I can't. I have to finish it!"

I lurch my body at her again. She swears violently as she elbows me back. I try again. She rummages in the kit at her waist, finds the syringe. She jabs the needle deep into my leg.

"Just shut the hell up, okay? Shut up."

My world goes black.

———

Annie drove through the stop-start southbound traffic with Beppie Rudiger in handcuffs in the backseat behind the barricade. She kept her siren off. There were real emergencies out there that needed the road, and she was using the time to see if Beppie would talk more.

Jeb Cullen had asked if the handcuffs were really necessary, but she was going by the book. This whole clusterfuck involved cops— LeFleur and his mother in particular—and she wanted everything squeaky clean. She was covering her ass, and she wasn't going to take the fall for anything, no matter what Novak said.

She'd listened to the first part of the recording Beppie made. Some of what Clint said was audible. A tech might tease the rest out. Beppie was a witness and would talk. Jeb would testify too. Backed up with the recording, they could have what they needed to nail Clint Rudiger for the murder of Merilee Zukanov and the sexual assault on Amy Findlay. The one thing Annie was super-edgy about was Clint himself. She was pretty damn sure she'd seen the shot hit him before he had wheeled over the railing. But it was dark. Even so, no one could survive a fall down that gorge. They'd find his body downriver, if at all.

"There's another one," Beppie Rudiger said suddenly in back.

"Another what?"

"Trophy." Beppie Rudiger rattled something against the barrier as she tried with her cuffed hands to pass it through to Annie. "I forgot about this one. This is the one that made me think about what else might be in that box of his. You must have them all. All of it. I don't want them near me. This one was in the back of his drawer. I found it when I was looking for cutters for my bee fence."

Annie glanced out the corner of her eye. Her heart stalled, then started to hammer hard. Keeping one hand on the wheel, she reached for the ring Beppie Rudiger was trying to poke through the grid.

A hexagonal turquoise stone set in silver.

Immediately she pulled over onto the verge, flicked on her emergency light bar, no siren. She put the interior light on. The ring was engraved inside with the letters *CL*.

Claudette Lepine.

Annie's blood turned cold.

It was the ring she'd given her sister.

———

Brandy was blind with adrenaline, terrified. On some level she knew she'd snapped again, like the time during the RCMP training course at Depot Division, which is why they'd kicked her ass out. It had been over a guy, too. She'd loved him. Unrequited love that put her over the edge, made her do stupid things. But that was long ago. She'd begun to think it was a one-time thing, that she was in control now. But losing Adam . . . she couldn't. She needed him like she needed air to breathe. He was going to be with her forever.

She glanced at Rachel in the seat beside her. She was out. Maybe she'd given her too much. It didn't matter. She didn't have time to think about Rachel now. Quinn was dead quiet.

Ash-mud smeared thick across the windshield. She bent forward, straining to see through the streaks. Smoke was obliterating everything. Suddenly she made out the lights of the Thunderbird Lodge.

With a shaking hand, she palmed her wet ball cap off her head, trying to think this through. It shouldn't have been like this. Her only weapons were bear spray, ice ax. Ropes. Her strength and endurance. The ketamine was gone now.

Shit.

She'd gotten this far. There was no going back now, surely? Perspiration dampened her body. She pulled in next to the gondola terminal entrance. The fire was still raging on the Mount Barren side. Wind was fierce, smoke swirling. The gondola would shut down in wind this strong. But she was one of the patrollers who'd received the emergency evac and ropes training. She knew how to override and jam the thing.

All she had to do was get them all into one gondola cabin and send them over into the furnace consuming the Mount Barren terminal. If they didn't burn when they docked, they'd never get down that mountain alive, not with the way the wildfire was engaged and the wind was going. But she was scared. She'd never killed anyone. She could do it. She could. Quinn suddenly rammed her seat from behind again and started moaning like some horrible animal. Brandy started to shake violently. She was doing it for Adam. She had to make sure he hadn't told anyone, wouldn't confess. She reached for Rachel's phone, dialed his number.

It rang. Again, he didn't pick up. Brandy started to panic. She left a message.

———

Jeb swore at the traffic clogging the highway southbound. Smoke was dense. Sirens everywhere. Forty-five minutes Brandy had said.

J-J-Jeb, I want my m-m-mom . . . Brandy h-hurt Rachel . . .

He'd never make it in forty-five. He flicked on his hazard lights and leaned on the horn as he swerved round the line of cars. He raced down the oncoming lane, blaring his horn, hazard lights flashing. Headlights came at him head-on. He ramped up onto the opposite curb and bombed along the sidewalk, clipping a lamp-post and a parked car, then he veered back into the oncoming lane once the vehicle had passed. A wailing siren approached behind him. Jeb glanced into his rearview mirror. The strobing lights of an ambulance were coming up behind him fast. It was also driving in the oncoming lane, cars were pulling over where they could. Jeb ramped back up onto the curb, and as soon as the ambulance passed, he tucked in right behind the ambulance's rear, following it almost into town, where he cut down a side street and wound round to the base of Bear Mountain.

The skiers' parking lot was deserted. The dark shapes of humans were silhouetted against pulsing emergency lights as they ran through the village, evacuating things. Someone was watering down the Shady Lady Saloon with a fire hose. A giant sprinkler was watering other buildings near the base. Jeb started up the dirt road that led up Bear Mountain.

Mud was slick under his tires. Rain came down hard, and it was gray and sludgy against his windshield. The deluge, however, was doing nothing to kill the fire raging on the Mount Barren side, where orange flames licked and leaped into the blackness. As he climbed, the lights of the village below disappeared into smoke. Higher up, he saw that the Barren fire was creeping down into the Khyber drainage. It looked like the whole town would burn if the wind didn't change in time. Everyone was fleeing the other way, and he was going up. Into the inferno. Because everything that meant anything to him was somewhere up there in that smoke.

His heart hammered. It was a trap. Brandy wanted him. He had no idea why, or how she was tied into this thing. But he'd do anything to save his child and his woman. Anything.

He had his proof.

He now wanted his life. His family. He'd tasted it. What it could be like. He'd been given everything to live for.

And die for.

———

Adam always thought if the time came when he was forced to take his own life, it would be by eating his weapon. Cop-style. The honorable way. That time had come. He had the balls to come clean, but not for being arrested, facing trial. Or for sitting in a prison cell. A cop in the slammer? It never ended well.

This was the honorable option. The only option.

His boys wouldn't have to grow up with the stigma of him on the inside. Lily would be free to move on, to hold up her head. But he couldn't eat his gun, not if he wanted to look after them. He had to make it look like an accident, or Lily and Tyler and Mikey wouldn't get the life insurance.

As Adam sped north along the twisting highway toward the narrow bridge that spanned the aptly named Suicide Gorge, he felt an incredible sense of relief. Almost elation. All the loose ends had been tied. He'd left instructions in an envelope on the table for Lily. He'd passed the confession to Pirello, who would have given it to Mackin by now. He'd said his good-bye to Brandy. She would get over him. She was young, beautiful, had her whole life ahead of her, and it was best that Lily never found out about her.

When he neared the bridge he began to accelerate, his wet tires screeching. He had to hit the barrier hard, and sideways, as though he were swerving in an effort to avoid the collision.

His phone rang. Something pinged through his determination. He clenched his jaw, trying to ignore it. It rang again. Heart thudding, perspiration breaking out over his body as he neared the barrier, he suddenly slowed, snatched the phone off his seat. He checked the incoming number. Rachel? His heart jumped up into his throat as panic hit him, and reality. He slowed right down and pulled over, scrubbed his hands over his face while the call went to voice mail.

Shit. He'd chickened. He was going to have to turn around and take another run. Unable to stop himself, Adam hit the number that would take him to his messages. One last listen.

There were several frantic messages from Brandy telling him not to give his confession to anyone. Yet. His pulse started to race. With each message she sounded progressively more hysterical. He hit the last one, which had come from Rachel's phone.

"Just don't do it, Adam. I have them. Up at the gondola. It's going to be okay." She started crying. "I'm making it right for you. Don't do anything, baby, okay? They'll be gone soon . . ."

The message cut off

Quickly, Adam tried to return the call. It rang twice, then cut out. He tried again, but there was no longer a signal.

He stared dazedly through the driving rain running down his windshield at the bridge over the canyon ahead. What in hell was Brandy doing? Why was she on Rachel's cell? The town was being evacuated, the mountain burning. Who did she have up at the gondola? He recalled the look on her face as he'd told her that Rachel and Jeb would get there, they'd find the evidence in the mine . . . and it struck him like an ice ax.

Adam rammed his vehicle into gear, spun a U-turn over the bridge, and floored the gas on his way back to Snowy Creek.

———

As Jeb neared the Thunderbird Lodge, he saw that a building on Mount Barren was engulfed by fire. His gaze flared back to Thunderbird Lodge and he realized it must be the new gondola terminal that was burning on the other side. He'd read about the construction of the Summit-to-Summit in the papers while in prison. He pulled up next to the dark-blue beater of a truck parked outside the brightly lit terminal. It was Brandy's. He recognized it from when she'd picked up Quinn.

A band of tension strapped tight across his chest as Jeb grabbed the rifle and flung open the door. Ash rain streaked him with gray paste as he ran toward the building. The sky glowed orange behind thick smoke. The door to the glassed-in terminal was unlocked.

He entered, coughing.

The place was starkly lit with neon. Empty. He blinked away the ash grit in his eyes. "Brandy?" he called.

No answer.

He moved toward the line of red gondola cabins. "Brandy?" he yelled again. His voice echoed. The place was deserted.

He spun round, heart thudding. What had Rachel told him about Brandy? Ski patroller. Mountain girl. Had worked on the mountain since she was a kid. Knew mountain operations. Great with children—wanted her own.

Jeb's throat constricted as he thought of Quinn. Of Rachel being hurt.

Holding his gun, he ran along the line of cabins, looking in each one. Thunder boomed overhead and wind whistled through architecture. Smoke was blowing in through the gaping hole at the end of the dock.

"Quinn! Rachel!"

From the corner of his eye he caught a sudden movement up in the glassed-in control room. He stilled, watching. Had someone just ducked down up there? As he stared up at the control room, he heard a sound. A soft thudding.

He waited, listening under the whistle of the wind. Jeb heard it again. It was coming from one of the gondola cabins closer to the opening at the end of the docking station. Jeb raced to the cabin. As he neared, he saw the dark curls of his daughter in a cabin three from the end. The doors were wide open. "Quinn!"

He entered the cabin. His daughter was tied to the railing with zip ties, her legs bound with climbing rope, her mouth duct-taped shut, her eyes wild. Rachel was also tied to the railing with straps, but she hung from her wrists, the rest of her body slumped on the floor, unmoving. She was covered in blood, ash, her face turned away from him.

His heart kicked into a fast jackhammer. *Triage. Focus.*

"Quinn, are you okay?"

She nodded, trembling like a leaf. She was in shock. He dropped to his knees beside Rachel, felt for a pulse at her bound wrists. *Alive.* Relief burned into his eyes. He set his weapon down, turned her head to the side. Her face was encrusted with blood. But she was breathing.

"Rachel?" He slapped her face lightly. No response. He needed to know what had happened to her.

Jeb lurched over to Quinn and began to peel the duct tape from her mouth. She squirmed in pain, tears streaming from her eyes. As he pulled the tape away, it tore off skin, fine hairs from her face, leaving her raw and bleeding. Adrenaline pounded through him.

"What happened to Rachel? How did she get hurt?"

"I . . . I'm sorry, Jeb. I was running away. I . . . wanted to go h-h-home, to my mommy and daddy. It . . . it's my fault. B-Brandy got me on the r-road. R-Rachel was looking for me in . . . in the rain."

"Quinn. It's all right. Focus. What happened to Rachel?"

"B-Brandy jabbed her with a needle."

She'd been drugged.

"Did she jab you too?"

"Yes, but I woke up. Rachel did too. Then when she started fighting with Brandy, Brandy wanted to make her shut up and jabbed her again."

This meant it might wear off again, it might not be fatal.

"Where is Brandy now?"

"She's gone. I don't know."

Jeb shot a glance over his shoulder. He needed a knife, something sharp to cut through the zip ties tying them both to the railing. There was a reason cops used these as emergency handcuffs—they were impossible to remove without a blade of some sort. He dropped to his haunches and fumbled to untie the ropes that bound Quinn's legs.

As he worked, he felt the gondola cabin move. His heart jumped and he looked up. They were sliding along the docking platform, the doors slowly beginning to close.

Christ. That was what Brandy was doing—she wanted to send them in an enclosed coffin into the fire on the other side. Even if they made it out of that burning terminal, they'd never get down that mountain alive. Jeb's mind raced. He wouldn't be able to free them both of these zip ties before this cabin launched out of the dock. Then they'd all be trapped, heading inexorably into an inferno.

He had to stop this thing. Even if the cabin launched, if he could stop the system, there had to be a way to winch them back, or get to them via the towers and cables.

Jeb dived out of the cabin, raced along the platform. He could see Brandy's red hair and blue jacket now, up in the control tower behind the glass.

"Brandy!" he screamed. "Stop the damn gondola!"

She turned to face him. Her face was white, streaked with ash. She looked inhuman. Jeb put the rifle stock to his shoulder, aimed up at her. "I'll shoot if you don't stop it," he yelled.

The line of cabins kept moving.

He fired a warning shot. She dived down. Fissures raced across the glass, then the whole pane shattered down to the platform. The line was still moving, Quinn and Rachel's cabin nearing the gaping smoke-filled maw. He sprinted toward the metal stairs that led up to the control tower, started clattering up them.

Brandy yanked open the door at the top of the stairs and threw an industrial-sized fire extinguisher at him. It bounded and clunked down the stairs. He ducked, then fired.

She screamed. "You won't be able to stop it—I've overridden the controls. I've broken them, jammed them."

Jeb could smell electrical smoke coming from the control room. Indecision flared through him.

"Jeb Cullen!" a male voice called from behind him.

He spun round in shock. *Adam.*

He had a gun. He was running at him.

Jeb raised his rifle. "Stay the hell back or I swear I will kill you."

"Go!" Adam yelled. "Go help them. I'll stop this thing. I can talk to her."

Confusion rushed through Jeb.

"Adam!" Brandy yelled from the top. "Oh God, Adam. What are you doing here?"

"Go, Jeb," Adam screamed. "Goddammit, go save them."

Jeb clattered down the stairs and sprinted for the cabin that contained Quinn and Rachel. It was nearing the very end of the dock.

"I'm doing it for you, Adam," Brandy shrieked behind him. "So we can be together."

Jeb reached the cabin as it began to tilt over the edge. The doors had already closed. He could see Quinn's panic-stricken face in the lighted window. He leaped for the ski rack attached to the back of the cabin just as it swayed into the air. His legs swung down into the blackness, his gun spinning into the void below. Wind blasted them instantly. His mouth was dry, his heart galloping. He craned his neck up, saw Quinn's face. She was screaming. And they were moving insidiously toward the raging inferno on the other side.

———

"Listen to me." Adam gripped Brandy's shoulders. "You will go down for murder. And then what? You still have your whole life ahead of you."

"You . . . you weren't going to leave Lily, were you? It was all a lie, wasn't it?"

"Brandy, you are young, you are beautiful. You are smart and engaging. You will find someone. Now show me how to stop this thing. We can go back down together, okay?"

"And then?" Her voice was shrill. "Then, what—you go back to her? You go down for being a crooked cop all those years ago? For sending Jeb Cullen to prison? No, *no*. This has to be finished. I can't get out of this now." She backed up against the controls. The minutes were ticking. The cabin was going to reach the blaze on the other side. Adam could no longer live with the guilt that he'd helped send an innocent man to prison. And if there was one thing more he could do with the time he had left, it was to save that man's life now, along with the lives of an innocent woman and a child. He could not let his mother's legacy come to this. It had to end.

He aimed his weapon at Brandy. She went white under the ash streaking her face.

"Stop it. Now," he said.

She glared at him, eyes wild as she reached for an extinguisher on the wall. She unclipped it, released the safety. "Back off, Adam." She aimed the extinguisher at him.

She'd gone mad. Stark raving mad. Why were all the women in his life mad?

"Where is the stop switch?" he demanded.

"You can't stop it. I jammed it."

He moved to the controls.

"No!" She squeezed the extinguisher trigger. A powerful jet stream struck Adam square in the face, forcing a burning powdery chemical into his mouth, nose, eyes. Blinded, pain searing, he staggered back, hands going to his face. She sprayed again. Screaming. "Just back off!"

Blindly, he lunged at her. She swung the canister. He raised his arm to deflect it. But she kicked at his leg, dropping him. And the heavy extinguisher smashed into his skull as he was going down. He was flung sideways, his head crashing against the console. Adam felt his skull crack. He hit the ground, couldn't move. Blood, thick, filled his mouth. He felt his world going gray.

"Oh, God, Adam, no, please, no. I'm so sorry." She dropped down to his side, gathered him up in her arms, crying, rocking him, kissing him. She seemed so distant. He was slipping away. And as he felt his life go, he saw his father. Standing large and proud against the mist in red serge with his Stetson and high boots. Or was it Sam Steele, up at the top of Chilkoot Pass, in the swirling snow, stopping the rabble-rousing whiskey traders and the prospectors unprepared for the harshness from crossing into Canada? He could have been a good cop. He would have been a good Mountie. But then those two women had gone missing . . . on a cold, fateful fall night . . . and everything had changed . . . all those years ago . . .

The things we do for love . . .

His world went dark.

———

Jeb's muscles burned. His eyes watered and his throat was raw from smoke. The cabin was moving slowly into the middle of the chasm, high above the forest canopy. High enough at midpoint, he'd read, to fit the whole Eiffel Tower underneath. Falling would bring certain death. Another gust of wind and rain slammed into the cabin. It swayed on the cable. His legs swung below him. He craned his neck to look up again. He had to try and pull himself up, reach for the bottom rung of the emergency ladder that ran up the side of the cabin to the roof. He doubted the windows could open much, if at all. It would be too dangerous to design windows that people could climb or fall out of. But there had to be a way into the cabin from the top for evacuation purposes. Quinn was looking down at him, her eyes terrified. It galvanized him. He could not let his daughter watch him fall to his death. He could not fail her. Or Rachel.

Jeb strained to pull himself up higher. He released his right hand, grasping for the bottom rung of the ladder. But the rung was slick with rain. His hand slipped. He almost lost his grip with his left hand, too, almost went down to his death. His heart stalled. He took a breath, gathering focus. He tried again. He caught the rung, held fast.

Jeb refocused again, taking another deep breath, then he let go with his left hand as he pulled himself up with his right. He clamped his left hand on the rung, his legs swaying below him. His muscles were shaking. He took another breath, pulled up, and slapped his right hand on the next rung. Then his left. He repeated the process for the next three rungs. Once he was higher, he managed to draw his legs up, and he found footing on the ladder. He paused, trying to gather his strength. But he was spent. He could not move another muscle. His whole body was shaking. His lungs were raw and his eyes burned from smoke.

Quinn was watching him intently from the window.

Jeb met her eyes. His flesh and blood. The future. He could see Rachel's limp shape on the floor behind Quinn. They were getting closer to the fire. He had to do this. He could not fail. And with every ounce of energy he had left, Jeb summoned the strength to pull himself up one more time, and he edged his body up onto the slick roof. The wind was blowing hard. He spread-eagled himself on the roof, inching slowly forward on his stomach as he felt along the wet surface for a door. His heart sank. He couldn't locate an opening. Then suddenly his fingers touched a ridge. He found a handle. Pressing himself flat against the wind, muscles juddering from strain, he managed to open the escape hatch.

He dropped down into the cabin with a hard thud.

"Jeb," Quinn cried. "You made it!"

Panting from exertion, he dug in his pocket, finding the truck keys. It was all he could think off. Using the jagged end of the keys, he struggled to saw at the zip ties. "Hang on, Quinn, I'll be with you next." Desperation swelled in him. They'd reach the fire before he could free them at this rate.

Quinn was staring, eyes still wide with shock. Suddenly, she said, "Rachel—she has a pocketknife on her key chain."

Quickly, he felt in her pockets, found her keys. Thank the almighty heavens—Quinn was right. He threw her a huge grin. "You rock, kiddo, you know that?"

He sliced easily through the straps on Rachel's wrists with the small pocketknife attached to her fob. Lowering her gently onto the floor, Jeb cradled her head. Smoke was beginning to fill the cabin. Quinn coughed.

"Rachel, can you hear me?" He lightly slapped her face.

Her eyes fluttered open. She moaned softly. Relief gushed through Jeb. But smoke was getting thicker inside. They were almost at the terminal. He could feel heat inside the cabin now. He could hear the fire.

"I'm going to free Quinn," he said, quickly untying the rope around her legs. He moved to Quinn, sliced her wrists free. She flung her arms tightly around his neck, burying her face into his wet clothes. He couldn't breathe. His heart hurt at the thought he might die right here, with the aching joy of having his child's arms wrapped around him like this. He held her back.

"Let me help Rachel, 'kay?" The roar of the approaching fire was growing louder.

Jeb glanced round the cabin in desperation. There was no way to stop this thing. No brakes. They were moving slowly, inexorably, into the inferno. They were doomed to dock.

He caught sight of a slim fire extinguisher mounted on the cabin wall in the corner between the windows. He unclipped the extinguisher.

Quinn was watching him. He forced a smile. "We're going to get out of this, kiddo, don't worry. But you need to listen to me and act fast. Do everything I say, okay?"

She nodded quickly. Her hands were fisted at her sides. His heart cracked.

"You better take off that fleece jacket," he said. Fleece was highly flammable. He shrugged out of his leather jacket. "Put this on, zip it up. It'll help protect you. When we go out there, you try and keep some of the jacket over your head, okay?"

She swallowed, took the jacket from him.

He dropped down beside Rachel again and lifted her head and shoulders up. "Rachel—you need to wake up, try."

She blinked. "Jeb?"

His heart punched.

"Can you sit?" He helped her into a sitting position, wiped some of the blood from under her nose and around her mouth away with his damp sleeve.

"Can you stand? Walk?"

"Quinn?" she said, suddenly looking panicked.

"I'm here, Aunt Rachel. I'm okay. You're going to be okay."

"Listen, we're in the gondola. We're going to dock. There's fire. We need to go through it. You *have* to try to stand." He pulled her up onto her feet. She looked dazed but she managed to reach out and hold on to the railing, wobbling on her feet. Almost instantly, she sank back down.

The heat was growing inside. He heard an explosion. They were almost there. She tried to stand again, but her knees gave out and she slumped back to the floor.

"I . . . I can't. Not yet . . . I . . ."

"I'll carry you. Don't worry."

Jeb got Rachel up onto the bench in a sitting position. He turned around, crouched down, and taking her arms around his neck, he maneuvered her onto his back in a piggyback position. But her legs hung limp. "Just try to hang on."

Jeb used the rope that had bound her legs to tie her wrists together under his neck. He strapped the rope from Quinn's legs around both himself and Rachel, securing her body to his as best he could. If she lost all ability to hold on, she'd be hooked on to him. He hoped she wouldn't choke him if that happened, but it was his only option. He gathered Quinn to his side and got the extinguisher ready.

Taking a deep, shaky breath, he said, "You hold on to my belt, okay? Whatever happens, do *not* let go. I won't find you in the smoke if you do. Got it?"

She nodded, eyes like saucers.

"Jacket over your head."

She shrugged into the oversize leather jacket so that it covered her hair.

Smoke grew thicker. It felt even hotter. They were all coughing now, eyes watering as they came in to dock. The lights in the car fizzled, then went out.

They were in blackness.

The gondola car bumped against its moorings. The doors started to open as it slid into the dock. Smoke flooded in. Jeb was disoriented. He wasn't familiar with the terminal. Sprinklers were spraying water everywhere, fire alarm blaring.

"To the right," Rachel said in his ear. She coughed. "Go . . . to the right."

They moved quickly through the thick smoke and blackness.

He shoved through the fire doors. Heat was intense. Once through the doors he could see a bit more because of the flames behind the windows. Everything inside was blackened, smoking. His eyes streamed. Quinn was choking inside the jacket, her hand gripping his like a little vise.

It looked as though the fire had raged quickly through this area, which was mostly concrete and glass.

"Straight!" Rachel coughed into his ear. "Go . . . straight."

As he negotiated a path, a beam crashed down. Quinn screamed and Jeb flung himself sideways, landing on Rachel. His extinguisher rolled across the floor. Quinn was screaming. She was on the other side of the beam, which was crackling with flames.

Jeb groped over the hot floor, hands burning, until he found the extinguisher. He managed to get onto his knees, then his feet, hauling Rachel up with him. His body was wet with perspiration. He was covered in soot.

He sprayed the extinguisher in bursts as he made his way to Quinn. "Give me your hand!"

Another beam crashed down near the exit.

She reached for him. He sprayed at another burst of flames, then yanked her over the beam fast. Quinn was shaking like a leaf, choking on the smoke. No time to waste. Had to get out of here before more of the roof came down.

"Hold my belt—stay low!"

He could feel Quinn's weight as she clutched on to his belt. He moved with purpose, hunched over, eyes burning, tears streaming down his face. Each breath felt as though he were drawing acid into his lungs, stripping them raw. Rachel slipped and her bound hands caught under his neck, gagging him. He jerked her back up, and she held on again. She was so quiet it frightened him. He hoped he hadn't injured her internally when he'd fallen onto her with his full weight. Sprinklers showered on them as they neared the doors.

They reached doors, pushed through into the night. It was hot. Ash rain slashed at them. Jeb stalled. To the right, the buildings were burning fiercely, the air blisteringly hot. Downdrafts and crosswinds blasted them, rain hissing into fire. Behind the buildings the entire forest was ablaze, flames leaping into the blackness.

To the left, down into the steep drainage, the forest was still untouched. Dark. Wet. He checked that Quinn was okay.

"Rachel? Can you hear me?"

"Yes," she whispered near his ear.

"Are you all right?"

"N . . . numb."

She could talk. She was lucid. He could only pray now that the drug would keep wearing off.

"Remember that waterfall?" he said. "The ice cave?"

"Yes, yes, I remember."

"I'm going to try to get down there. Can you hang on?"

"Try . . . trying."

They started down the steep hiking path, moving as fast as he dared through the darkness with Quinn and Rachel. His muscles ached. He was shaking. His throat was raw, his eyes burning. If he could get them all down to the waterfall and into the cave behind the water, they might be able to stay safe even if the fire burned down through this gulley and over them.

As they got lower into the gulley, he could hear the water rushing. Jeb moved faster—and for the first time in many years, he prayed. He prayed to the universe and all that was good, that they would make it. That he would save his daughter and the woman he loved. That he could buy them all a second chance. The fire was cresting the ridge above them. But the air was cooler down here, filled with mist from the falls. As Jeb caught sight of the glowing white water of Khyber Creek, he heard an explosion.

Up across the valley on Bear Mountain, part of the Thunderbird Lodge had erupted in flames. Jeb swallowed, thinking of Brandy and Adam. They resumed their rapid descent.

The fire was coming fast. He feared they wouldn't find the cave in time.

———

Harvey Zink was spraying water on the exterior of the Shady Lady Saloon. He'd turned on the fire sprinklers inside as a last resort. He had to leave, soon. He looked up, hose in hand, a wet bandana over his nose and mouth. Fire was coming down Bear Mountain now, eating its way toward the ski village. He could see the entire Khyber drainage ablaze on the other side. No way anyone could survive that. His cell rang. His provider still had coverage, although he didn't expect that to last, either. The cell tower for the other main service provider in town had already gone down.

"Zink," he said, moving his bandana aside. His eyes were watering.

"It's Levi. I'm on the highway, heading south. My wife and baby are already at the West Van condo—I'm going to join them. Listen, my PA, Vickie, told me that Rachel and Jeb believe Merilee is in the mine. I told Vickie it was a bunch of crock." Levi was speaking fast. Which meant the man was worried. This made Zink edgy. His buddy was the definition of calm and cool. "But I thought you should know. Because when this blows over, they're going to go looking down that fucking mine. I can't get hold of Clint." He paused. "What do you want to do?"

"We say nothing. Stick to the old story," Zink said. "Until there is proof, they've got zip on us. I'm going to head down to West Van as well now. I'll call you when I get there." As he spoke, Zink watched in horror as a line of condos up on the benchlands went up in flames. He had to move his ass. Now.

Zink left the hose running. He raced for his car in the lot. For the first time he was shit scared they would go down for that old crime. He cursed violently as he ran. They weren't going to be able to keep burying this. When this fire was over, they would find her body. Jeb would not stop looking. Neither would the damn media now. Zink wasn't certain he'd have a business and home to return to if this fire kept coming.

Maybe it was time to take the gap.

CHAPTER 27

Quinn sat quiet as a mouse, shivering as Rachel's head rested in her lap. Rachel was sleeping, Jeb had said. She was going to come round later. She was going to be all right. Quinn stroked Rachel's hair gently with her good arm. She'd fallen badly on the way down and hurt her other arm—Jeb had said he thought it was broken. Her aunt's hair was stiff with dried blood on one side. Her nose was crooked from where Brandy had smashed her. Quinn kept her mouth very tight because she did not want to cry. She just wouldn't. She'd be strong. For Rachel. But she was scared and her arm hurt and she wanted Jeb to come back and she was cold with no jacket.

They'd had to come through beating water to get into the cave. They'd gotten sopping wet. And it was like a fridge inside. The cave was very deep and it had an eerie glow, which helped them to see. At the very back there was ice. But up near the front, behind the curtain of water, there was no ice and it was dry and flat.

Jeb had told her to wait here with Rachel.

He had said he was going to fetch dry wood and branches and pine needles to make a fire inside to keep them warm and dry their clothes. Quinn thought it was weird how the whole mountain was burning and they were going to make a fire to stay warm and get dry in the icy cave behind water. That's why he'd taken his jacket, so he could bundle it over the wood and get it through the waterfall dry.

Rachel stirred and moaned in her lap. Quinn's heart slammed. She studied her aunt's face carefully, but she couldn't tell if she was okay. Gently, she touched the cut where she'd hit Rachel in the face with her backpack.

"I'm sorry," she whispered.

But her aunt didn't hear.

Quinn wanted Jeb to come back desperately now. He'd saved them. Maybe he was an angel after all. 'Cause only an angel could have gotten up into the gondola cabin like that and brought them out of the burning building. And found a cold cave with ice in the middle of a fire. Maybe he was gone now because his job was done.

Suddenly he ducked into the cave with a big bundle wrapped in his jacket. He grinned. His blue eyes twinkled. And she felt better.

He tumbled the wood out onto the ground. "First batch," he said as he glanced at Rachel. Quinn saw something change in his face. He was worried about Rachel. That made her worry, too.

"One more load."

"But isn't the fire coming?"

"Yup. Almost here. Be right back."

"Jeb!" she cried.

He stilled. "What is it?"

"Please come back."

"I will, Quinn. Believe me, I will." And he was gone.

She stroked Rachel's hair some more. She believed him. He had a way of making her believe.

A few minutes later, Jeb ducked back in through the wall of pummeling water and entered the cave with his second bundle.

"Is the fire here yet?" Quinn asked.

"Down to the river. We'll wait it out now."

He dumped the second bundle onto the floor. He'd brought twigs and thin sticks and moss with this load. And a smoldering piece of log. His hands were burned, but he didn't seem to notice as he started to lay a fire.

He piled the dry moss and twigs on the smoldering log, cupping his hands and blowing until flames came.

"Once this fire is going," he said, gently adding more small twigs and puffing on the flames, "I'll try to find a way to strap up your arm, okay?"

"What about Rachel?"

"We're going to keep her as comfortable as we can, make her toasty warm and dry until she comes round fully."

A deep roar reached them inside the cave.

"Is that the fire?" Quinn whispered.

Jeb glanced up. The curtain of water was shimmering orange and yellow and red with flame light. "Yes," he said softly. "It's here."

"It sounds like a train, or an airplane," Quinn said in awe. "Look at the waterfall. It's flickering. Jeb, I'm scared."

"It's going to be fine. It's going to blow right over us. And we can always move right to the back of the cave, into the ice, if we need to. But there's so much dry fuel out there, and so much wind, it's going to roar right over us like a freight train."

His own fire crackled, spreading warmth. He poked at it with a stick, settling it, then he added another branch. The smoke was going out the front, being sucked by cold air currents flowing from the back of the cave into the hot air outside, which made the flames burn stronger.

Jeb took off his belt, and he made a sling for Quinn's arm, strapping it to her body in a bent position. "There," he said. "It'll help you keep it still. When this is all over we will get X-rays and a fancy cast."

"Can I pick the color?"

"They have colors?"

"Benny John at school had a black cast on his leg once. And in my old school, Sally Higgenbottom had a green one."

He laughed. "When I was a kid I think they just had the old plaster kind. Come, let's all move here, closer to the fire."

"Rach," he whispered, lifting her aunt's head off her lap. "I'm going to move you where you can get dry, okay?"

Her eyes fluttered open. She gave him a weak smile. It made something wobble in Quinn's chest. She went to sit closer to the fire. It was nice and warm. Jeb sat right beside her with Rachel's head in his own lap. He covered Rachel with his leather jacket and he put his arm around Quinn, drawing her against his warm, strong body. They sat cuddled together like that, listening to the fire and the sound of the waterfall. She felt safe in Jeb's arms.

"How come there's ice in the cave when it's not winter?" Quinn said after a while.

"I'm not exactly sure how it all works," he said. "But it's due to something called geothermal activity. This whole mountain range was formed by volcanoes, and there are still shafts of hot air and volcanic activity that causes these things." He stroked her hair and she let her eyes close as she leaned against him.

"There was an ice cave further north, in Lillooet, too. Like this cave, it only produced ice in summer. That's how it works. Before the days of fridges, the farmer who found the Lillooet cave sold his ice to restaurants. He sent great blocks of it down by train to Vancouver city, where it was the very favorite ice to put in drinks in the bars."

"How did you know this cave was here?"

He moistened his lips as though he was thinking far back. "Rachel and I found it many years ago, when we were young."

Quinn frowned. "You knew Rachel when you were young?"

Rachel stirred suddenly, opening her eyes again. She looked brighter this time.

"How are you doing?" he said to her.

"The fire?"

"Passing over. It's going to be fine." He bent down, kissed her lips softly. "I love you," he whispered.

Rachel stared up at him. "I love you, too, Jeb. I . . . I always have."

"I know."

Quinn's gaze shot to Jeb's face. Her angel's eyes were glittering. "Why do you love Rachel?"

He sighed very deeply. "It's a long story, Quinn." He looked down at her as if he was deciding whether to tell the story.

"I want to hear it."

He nodded his head slowly. "I first met Rachel when I was just a little older than you. We grew up together, here in Snowy Creek. She was my very best friend and then my girlfriend. Then, when I was nineteen, something terrible happened and two girls went missing."

She stared. "What girls?"

"Two girls from school. Some bad people hurt them, and they blamed me. I got sent to prison."

Quinn's mouth dropped open. "You? Prison?"

He nodded and rubbed her arm, keeping her warm. "But I didn't do it—I didn't take those girls." He looked down at her, like he was thinking hard again. "You know how you thought your mom sent me to watch over you?"

She nodded, feeling scared suddenly about what he was going to say about her mom.

"Well, it's the truth, in a way. Your mother helped me prove to a judge that I was not the bad guy." He was silent for a long time. As though he was having trouble with what he was going to say. He put a log on the fire. "Do you want to know why she helped me?"

"Yes."

"Because, Quinn, I'm your father. I'm your birth father."

Her heart started to stutter and patter.

"And that's why I came back to Snowy Creek. For you. To find you, watch over you. To protect you. To prove that those bad people were liars, to find the truth of who really took those girls. I came back, Quinn, because I want to be a father and look after you. Forever."

She couldn't talk. She felt like a sock was in her throat again. "Why did you give me away?"

"I didn't. They took you away from me because they thought I was a bad guy."

Quinn stared at him. "Who is my birth mother?"

"She's one of the girls who went missing." Jeb was silent a moment. "She's dead now, Quinn. But you have me." He looked at Rachel. "And you have Rachel."

Quinn started to cry. He gathered her tightly in his arms. He rocked her gently. He smelled of smoke. He felt safe. She liked him. He made the best pancakes, like her other dad. He was her mom's friend. Her mom had sent him. Quinn cried harder. He kissed the top of her head. He was like an angel. Better than an angel. He was her real dad. She still had a dad. And she had Rachel.

"Jeb?" Rachel whispered.

Quinn's gaze shot to her aunt. Her eyes were closed and she had a sad smile on her face. "Have I told you I love you?" she said softly.

"You were listening?" he said.

She nodded, but her eyes stayed closed.

———

Rachel came round more fully during the night. After a while she was able to sit up next to Jeb. Quinn went round and sat beside Rachel on her other side. Rachel put her arm around Quinn.

"How're you doing, button? How's your arm?"

"It hurts."

THE SLOW BURN OF SILENCE

"Thing about broken arms, they're usually an easy fix."

"Not like your leg and the skiing accident?"

"That one took a while. But even that healed."

"Will you still teach me to ski this winter?"

Rachel smiled and her eyes went bright and liquidy. "Of course." She hugged Quinn closer. "If we have a mountain left to ski on."

"The fire can't burn away the mountain!" said Quinn.

"Ah, but the lifts might be damaged. I tell you what, if that's the case, we'll go to another resort. I promise. Whatever happens, I *will* teach you to ski this winter."

"Will Jeb come?"

Rachel looked at him.

"Of course I'll come," he said.

Quinn studied Jeb for a while, then said, "Do you want me to call you Dad?"

His mouth curved into a slow, sad kind of smile, and his eyes sparkled with moisture. "One day, if you want to. When you're ready."

Quinn nodded. This seemed right. And deep inside, she felt warm, even though everything was still scary.

———

When the sky was light and everything was quiet, they all came out of the cave.

They walked down the mountain through the burned trees. Everything was black and gray and wet. It was raining hard. A few logs were smoking, but not many.

As they caught sight of the valley below, Rachel gasped, her hand going to her mouth.

"It's still there," she whispered. "The village is still there. The wind turned in time."

Only the condos near the top had burned down. They heard sirens. Jeb took Quinn's and Rachel's hands, and they made their way down together.

He'd said they were a family now.

Quinn had a new family.

And down there was home.

CHAPTER 28

Late November. Six weeks later.

Irony was a bitch, thought Annie, as she read the feature article in the *Snowy Creek Leader* covering the fallout of the "Missing Girls" case. Adam LeFleur had been protecting his mother and brother, and his mother had been protecting her sons. But Luke LeFleur had been passed out in the Jeep the whole time. He'd had no idea what had gone down. He was completely innocent of the crime.

His only crime had been to say in court that he'd witnessed something he hadn't.

Now Adam was dead.

He'd acted to save the innocent man he'd helped put away, while his lover had acted in a bizarre attempt to save Adam from his own past.

His charred corpse had been found in the gutted gondola terminal on Bear Mountain, gruesomely entwined with the burned body of Brandy Jones. The autopsy on LeFleur had shown that he had died before the fire. Brandy Jones had likely been overcome by smoke before she had been burned.

Annie had finally handed Adam's envelope to Chief Mackin, which made Adam's role and interpretation of the past crime clear. Yet he'd managed to die a hero.

Annie got up, put on the kettle for some tea. It was snowing heavily outside. The kind of fat, heavy flakes that could smother the world in minutes. Two feet of snow had already fallen yesterday. Winter had finally come to Snowy Creek. From her window, she watched the flakes spiraling slowly down from the sky, thinking that if Adam had pushed for the truth all those years ago when he was a young Mountie, his mother might have learned Luke was innocent. Luke might have learned himself that he had nothing to do with the crime.

Jeb might never have been framed by Sheila Copeland LeFleur.

Crime, Annie had learned over the years, was never so clean-cut and simple as television or books might have one believe. Motivation, human motivation, was far slipperier, trickier. Messy. There were not many premeditating hunter-type killers like Clint Rudiger out there. Not in her repertoire, anyway. And what always interested Annie were the spider threads of connection between the crime and the families and friends of the criminal. The fallout. The insidious collateral damage done when everyday life, ordinary people, were suddenly thrust into the intersection of an investigation. Those women, their kids, this town. All had been affected by that one night.

Her kettle whistled. Annie jumped, took it off the stove. She poured water over a tea bag and took her mug with the bag still in it to the table.

She reseated herself and continued reading.

Lily, Adam's wife, had left town. It didn't say so in the paper, but it was obvious that she'd learned of her husband's affair with Brandy Jones. Adam might have died a hero in some people's eyes, but not in Lily LeFleur's. She'd packed up her bags and taken her sons.

Beppie Rudiger had given a full statement. The techs had been able to pull a lot from the recording she had made, and it jibed with her account, and with Jeb's.

The poor guy. Imprisoned like that all these years.

Beppie herself was not being charged for anything, especially because she was cooperating now. The river had been dragged below the gorge but no body had been found. Clint Rudiger was probably wedged under a rock, or being held down by the force of the waterfall. They might not find his remains until years down the road, although they would try dredging again in the spring, once the snows went and ice melted. It niggled Annie, this. She was all about closure.

She reached for her mug, sipped her tea, turned the page.

Levi had been taken into custody in West Vancouver. Zink had been picked up trying to cross into the States at the Peace Arch crossing. Banrock was lawyering his son up, but the old man Rock was being uncharacteristically quiet, keeping a low, low profile. He was a fighter, though. He'd come through this personally intact. As for Levi, Annie figured he'd go down hard, thanks to Beppie. Zink was going to have an even rougher time of it because Levi, at least, had tried to stop them at one point. They'd really hammer Zink, especially in the absence of Clint, and given the fact he had been trying to flee the country.

Annie reached up behind her neck and undid the chain she was wearing. Threaded onto the chain was Claudette's ring.

She turned the ring slowly over her fingers as she listened to the sound of sleigh bells outside. Apart from this ring—which they'd let her keep after logging and examining it—investigators had so far found no other evidence that Clint Rudiger had been involved in the disappearance of Claudette and her husband, Jean Lepine.

From the trinkets and other evidence in the bag that Beppie had given them, it looked as though Clint was responsible for at least nine other missing women. A massive joint forensics investigation on a par with the investigation into Robert Pickton, the notorious pig farmer and sexual predator from the Lower Mainland, had been launched by the Royal Canadian Mounted Police and several other agencies. The SCPD had been sidelined on this one, though, because of local police "corruption" involving the Merilee Zukanov case. Mackin was not a happy camper there.

Merilee Zukanov's body had been located down the mine shaft, and the investigation team was opening up other cold cases and looking into unsolved reports of missing women around BC, Alberta, and the Yukon, where Clint used to hunt. They'd begun excavating the Rudiger property, starting under Clint's shed. DNA analysis on the contents of his freezer was also under way. Already, the press was reporting that DNA from three different women had been found in his freezer. Only very small amounts, and it had been on other meat. So far no human parts had been found. The DNA could have come from cross-contamination with a knife.

Annie inhaled deeply. It would be Christmas soon. And when the snows melted in the spring, she was going to try and organize a search party of her own to go up into the mountains. She was not going to give up on Claudette.

Claudette had never given up on her.

Annie would find her sister yet. She was closer to learning the truth; she'd done okay so far. She'd applied for her detective exam, and she had hope a promotion would follow all this.

Feeling a little stab of loneliness, she turned to build a fire. Thinking of Christmas usually did that to her. Maybe she should go down to that shelter and adopt a cat or something.

Maybe she should take up that invite from Rachel and Jeb to dinner.

A knock sounded on her door. Startled, Annie stilled. No one knocked on her door. The rapping sounded again. She went to open it. Snow flurried inside.

"Hey," Novak said, stomping his boots in the snow. "I was just heading down to the village to meet with the guys and do a little tribute thing for LeFleur. Nonofficial like, since . . . you know." He shrugged. "Just thought you might want to come along. Rescue One guys will be there, too."

"Tribute?"

"Excuse to get shitfaced." He looked awkward. Then again, the asshole always looked awkward. "They're also going to talk about starting a fundraiser for Trey Somerland. For his medical shit and stuff. Maybe . . . I dunno, just getting together and putting some peace to all this."

"I was just going to light a fire."

"Sure, okay." He turned to go, but hesitated. "Brad Nicks, one of the Rescue One guys, asked if you might want to come along."

"Why couldn't he ask me himself?"

Novak shrugged. "Yeah, well, I thought you wouldn't want to go." He stomped away, down the path in the snow.

Annie wavered, then yelled, "Wait! I'll get my coat."

———

I push open the door.

Trey is propped up against white pillows, looking pale and gaunt.

"Hey," I say, placing a basket of fruit and cookies on the table near his bed. "You're doing better, I hear. Much better than expected." I take a seat next to his bed. "You'll be back at the helm of Rescue One in no time."

He snorted softly. "At least I'm out of the coma, huh? Baby steps."

I moisten my lips, compassion mushrooming through me. It's been a hellish and long road for him. After several surgeries he developed a severe infection and slipped into a coma, but Trey is a fighter. He's pulling through. This is the first time I've been able to actually speak to him.

I smile.

His face sobers.

"I want to thank you for calling me," I say. "For letting us know that Clint was going to blow up the evidence. I think you saved Beppie's life, too, by doing that. Because I wouldn't have called Constable Pirello, and Beppie would never have gotten that confession of Clint's on tape."

He's quiet for a long while, watching me. I feel a pang of affection for him still. We go back a long way. I hope he will find the right person in his life. I feel guilt about him, too.

"I was wrong about Jeb," he says finally as he reaches for a glass of water. He takes a sip, struggles to replace the glass. I restrain myself from jumping in and doing it for him. I know Trey. He'll be wanting to do these things himself now.

"I was wrong about a lot of things," he says. "It's tough to swallow something like this, to think about the mistakes we make and how deeply those mistakes can affect another person's life."

"We were all wrong about a lot of things." I cover his hand with mine.

"Is he here?"

"Jeb? Yeah. Outside."

"I want to speak to him."

"You sure?"

He nods.

I call Jeb. We enter together. Trey looks nervous, Jeb looks antsy. I feel guilt again. These two are nemeses, have been since school. And I've been an issue between them.

He looks at Jeb. "I'm sorry," he says simply.

Jeb clears his throat. "Yeah, well. Thank you for calling us, about Clint. Jesus, you paid big-time, confronting him like that."

Trey glances at me, a sadness entering his glacial eyes. "Yeah, we all paid in a way for Clint's shit."

When do things begin and end . . . has the last ripple finally lapped against the shore . . .

Trey inhales deeply. "Look, I know I'm not exactly in a fighting-fit position to say this, yet, but I have every intention of getting back to the helm of Rescue One. And I sure could use a member with the mad man-tracking skills you once had, if you're up for it, and some more training. It's pretty intense."

Jeb stiffens. I can see he's shocked. And leery. But he's covering it up well. He stares at Trey in silence for several beats. Trey holds his gaze steadily.

"The other guys?"

"They're on board."

"Fuck, yeah," Jeb says. "Thanks. I . . . um, I got to go move the truck, parked in a no-park zone. Talk later?"

"For sure."

"See you outside?" Jeb says, touching my arm. I nod.

Jeb leaves fast. I know it's because he can't hide his emotion much longer. Jeb is being accepted again, he's being welcomed into an inner circle that he's been excluded from most of his life. Snowy Creek is, for the first time, opening its arms wide to Jebbediah Cullen. After all these years.

I lean forward and kiss Trey lightly on the cheek. "You're a damn fine dude, you know that, Somerland?"

"You ain't too shabby yourself, Salonen. I hope we see you back on the team more too now."

"Yeah," I say. And I'm in the mood for skiing again, for getting my ski legs back. And even though I'll never have the same skill again, I yearn to feel that winter wind in my hair, the mountain falling away beneath my feet. And it strikes me that something inside me has been set free, too.

I go out to the truck. Jeb is waiting in the snow.

We drive in silence to fetch Quinn from school, where she is rehearsing for the upcoming Christmas play next month.

As we pull in to the elementary school parking lot, he stops the trucks and says, "I want to get married."

My jaw drops. I recover, laugh. "And this is your idea of romance? Proposing here, in the school lot like this?"

"Actually," he says, turning in the seat to face me, taking my gloved hands in his, "I meant to propose a long, long time ago. But I had a few obstacles in the way."

Something inside me sobers. I feel nervous. Thrilled. Unsure. Overwhelmed by what we've all come through.

He glances at the squat, square school. The snow. The Canadian flag. The kids like bright jelly beans in their snowsuits, rolling around the kindergarten playground.

"Besides," he says with a slow, sexy smile that darkens his eyes with promise and mystery, "this is where I first met you, this school. You were my first friend." He cups my face, his thumb brushing my lips. "My best friend." He leans forward, kisses me, and I melt into him. The truck windows mist as snow quickly covers the windshield. Tears fill my eyes.

First love.

It's powerful. It's impossible to forget. I feel we've come full circle, and I've never been happier, so happy my heart hurts.

———

December. Christmas Day.

I'm on the lakeshore, near the dock. My down jacket is warm. Snow is falling: those fat, perfect flakes you can catch on your mitt and see the shape of the crystals. The air is still. Icy cold.

I know it sounds odd, but I've come down here because this is where I feel them. Here, looking out over this water with the snow-draped mountains soaring up into the clouds on the other side, I feel the presence, or spirit, or whatever you want to call it—memories even—of my father and grandfather. And now Sophia, too.

In my heart I offer thanks. And Christmas blessings. I want them to know, to feel, how complete I am now. I want them to understand how I've come home, become myself, become whole, in a way that I never dreamed possible after that terrible, fateful night.

Jeb has his daughter now. And I have them both. We're a family. Jeb and I plan to marry early next summer. He's organizing his new business and will reopen the Wolf River rafting and guiding operation. He's going to hire a manager to live out at the new lodge once he's built it. Jeb has money saved. He's a natural entrepreneur, and his energy has been infectious. He had time enough in prison to get a degree in criminal justice, specializing in restorative justice. Already he's started volunteering with the First Nations group in the next valley. His goal is to be in a position to stop kids with backgrounds like his own from getting into trouble, from being forced to wear a negative label. He explained to me how restorative justice is not about punishment. It's about understanding the crime, the victims, the damage done. It's about the community coming together, and it's about restitution, forgiveness.

Forgiveness is what I needed for betraying his secret. He has given me that. And I have told him that he needs to forgive himself for what happened with his father. The town, in many individual ways, has also asked for forgiveness from Jeb. Sometimes with an anonymous gift left outside our door. Sometimes with a touch of a hand in the supermarket. Sometimes an invitation to join a group. Other times with a direct request: Can you ever forgive me?

Where do things end, and where do they begin . . .

I still don't know the answer to that, but because of that terrible event nine years ago, the three of us have come together as a family.

After the "Missing Girls" case, many more women lost their lives. I hope Annie finds her sister. I lift my face to the swirling flakes and almost smile. Annie Pirello—I disliked her on sight. Now we're almost friends.

"Hey."

He's behind me, wrapping his arms around me, kissing my neck. I laugh. He smells, feels, so good.

"The kitchen buzzer went," he says. "Turkey is done. Quinn has finished making the cranberry sauce and icing the cookies. We're kinda stuck without you now."

I smile.

"I thought I'd find you here," he whispers, then turns me around and he holds my face, kisses me on the mouth. My hands slide into his jacket, into his warmth.

"I love you, Jeb."

"I know," he murmurs over my lips. "And I have always loved you. It's written."

"Oh, really? And where is this written?"

He laughs, the sound deep and masculine. "My mother would say it's written in the rings of trees, in the patterns of leaves, and in the sound of water." He takes my hand. "But why should it matter where it's written? Come, we're hungry."

Wind gusts and the flakes swirl. We walk up to our home, the Christmas tree lights glowing inside. I still haven't bought blinds. Trixie comes waddling down through the snow toward us. I reach down, ruffle her fur, and I'm glad she was locked in my truck and couldn't run away with all the noise of helicopter and sirens scaring her. She was sitting there safely, if thirsty, when we came home after our night in the ice cave.

As we slide open the door, Quinn jumps off her stool. "I finished the icing, look!" She runs over, holds out the tray.

She's made Christmas angel cookies with silver beads for eyes.

"Our first Christmas," I whisper, staring at the angels.

"One of many," says Jeb.

And I know we've all finally come home.

ACKNOWLEDGMENTS

Bringing a book to life is rarely a solitary endeavor and more often the combined effort of a small community. A heartfelt thank-you to Deborah Nemeth for her early editorial insight and for the galvanizing encouragement. Thank you also to those readers who took precious time to post reviews during what I shall call a "soft launch." You guys make more of a difference than you can know. Much gratitude to my dear writing friend, Alison Kent, aka Mica Stone, for helping bring this story to the attention of Montlake Romance. To JoVon Sotak for reading the book and extending an offer of partnership. To Lindsay Guzzardo and Deb Taber for the editorial polishing. To the Amazon Publishing teams behind the scenes who made my book look wonderful and who helped put it into the hands of readers. Thank you Toni Anderson and Olivia Gates for kicking my butt on this project when I needed it most. To Roxy Beswetherick and Nell White for the beta reads—you are both my harshest and most valued critics, and you keep that bar raised. And as always, much love and gratitude to my husband, Paul Beswetherick, for his unquestioning and continued support. Of course, I'd be remiss not to mention my hairy muse—the Black Beast who never ceases to remind me how to live purely in the moment—aka Hudson. It wouldn't have happened without you all.

ABOUT THE AUTHOR

Loreth Anne White is a multipublished author of award-winning romantic suspense, thriller, and mystery. A double RITA finalist, she has won the Romantic Times Reviewers' Choice Award for Romantic Suspense, is a double Romantic Times Reviewers' Choice Award finalist, a double Daphne Du Maurier finalist, and a multiple CataRomance Reviewers' choice winner.

Loreth hails from South Africa but now lives with her family in a ski resort in the moody Coast mountain range of North America's Pacific Northwest. It's a place of vast, wild, and often dangerous mountains, larger-than-life characters, epic adventure, and romance—the perfect place to escape reality. It's no wonder it was here that she was inspired to abandon her sixteen-year newspaper career to escape into a world of romantic fiction filled with dangerous men and adventurous women.

When she's not writing, you will find her skiing, biking, hiking, or running the trails with her Black Dog, and generally trying to avoid the bears—albeit not successfully. In the summer she will often be on the road, searching out remote camping/fly fishing spots with her husband or participating in tracking and air scent courses with her dog. She calls this work, because it's when the best ideas come.

Loreth loves to hear from readers. You can contact her through her website at www.lorethannewhite.com, or you can find her on Facebook or Twitter.

Made in the USA
Monee, IL
07 March 2023

29387127R00246